WEAVE
THE
LIGHTNING

First published 2020 by Solaris
an imprint of Rebellion Publishing Ltd,
Riverside House, Osney Mead,
Oxford, OX2 0ES, UK

www.solarisbooks.com

ISBN: 978 1 78108 790 9

10 9 8 7 6 5 4 3 2 1

A CIP catalogue record for this book is available
from the British Library.

Designed & typeset by Rebellion Publishing

Printed in Denmark

WEAVE THE LIGHTNING

CORRY L. LEE

SOLARIS

To Josh—
For always believing.

Resist.

3/11/2020

CHAPTER ONE

CELKA PROCHAZKA'S BREATH came quick in the pre-dawn darkness, beading condensation on the window. She wiped it away with her sleeve, straining for the glint of a signal lantern. The circus train's steady *clack-clack* of tires on track slowed as they neared the railyard, and the swaying sleeper car threatened to lull her back to sleep. Brakes screeched, metal on metal. Celka forced her eyes wide.

Her family's waking murmur sounded wrong—their voices hushed, covers rustling furtively, coughs cut with tension. A match hissed, a golden flare that shattered Celka's night vision as her cousin Ela lit a dark lantern, slamming its shutter quickly into place, plunging them back into darkness.

In a pause between the cry of brakes, Aunt Benedikta asked, "Who are we expecting?"

"Two people," Grandfather said, and Celka filled in the rest. Two resistance fighters her family would smuggle into their sleeper car. Celka burned to know what they had done or knew to be hunted by the Tayemstvoy—the secret police.

Cupping her hands around her face, Celka blinked to recover her night vision, squinting to spot motion. Beneath her nightshirt, her storm pendant hung heavy about her throat, and Celka could almost imagine Pa keeping lookout beside her. *The bozhskyeh storms will return soon*, he'd told her years ago as he unfastened the brass pendant from around his neck. *Your imbuements will be key to our victory against the State.* He'd placed the pendant over her head, and she'd been so proud to have earned his trust. But the secret police had dragged Pa away and, strain as she might during thunderstorms, the lightning flashing through Bourshkanya's skies carried no magic.

The circus train rounded a bend and, ahead, light streamed from the railyard watch house. Fighting free of memory, Celka blocked the brightness with her palm, searching for the resistance signal.

"Now," Grandfather said, and light flashed in Celka's periphery as Ela unshuttered her lantern in code.

After a moment, lamplight cut the underbrush in response. "There!" Celka cried. "I think." She'd spotted only a flicker, the distance too great or angle oblique. "I couldn't read the code."

Beside her, Ela repeated her querying signal. Celka bit her lip, awaiting the response.

The train lurched to a stop, swaying. Steam swallowed the night.

Faint through the steam engine's fog, the underbrush lit in a frenzied *flash-flash-flash*. Celka's stomach lurched. She'd memorized the code but had never seen it used.

"Pursuit!" Her whisper sounded dangerously loud over the ping of cooling metal.

Aunt Benedikta cursed. "We have to abort."

"No." Celka squinted into the darkness where she'd spotted the signal, hoping the warning had been a mistake. Her throat tasted of bile, but surely their contacts would only risk the rendezvous if they carried important information. "We have to help them."

"Silence," Grandfather said.

Shouts filtered in from outside, and metal clanged as the roustabouts decoupled sections of the train. Celka's breath sounded harsh in her ears. Part of her wanted to take back her plea. If the secret police were already in the railyard, further signals could lead them straight to her family. The Tayemstvoy could arrest them all. Kill them all.

"Quickly, Ela," Grandfather said, "signal the welcome."

Metal creaked as Ela unshuttered the dark lantern in a new pattern. Celka closed her eyes, touched her storm pendant, and sent a prayer for safety to the Storm Gods.

"Andrik," Grandfather said, "take Celka's watch. Celka, can you *see* anything?"

Celka's bunk sagged as Uncle Andrik knelt beside her, pressing his face to the glass. Outside, gravel crunched beneath running feet. The train swayed into motion again. Stopped too suddenly.

Blotting out the outside world, Celka focused on sousednia—the neighboring reality. The railyard scents of creosote and coal smoke receded beneath sawdust and manure. Sousednia coalesced around her until Celka stood on a high wire beneath a darkened big top, her feet in a perfect line, arms outstretched to aid her balance.

All her life, her sousednia had taken this form. Dust motes danced in her spotlight, and the air hung humid and heavy, hot like a midsummer's day. A dozen meters below, shadowy spectators gaped up at her. In place of her patched nightgown, sousednia costumed Celka in glittering sequins, her gossamer green sleeves rippling with the tiny motions of her arms.

Beneath her illusory big top, figures like smoke blurred towards her, their approach matching the crunch of footsteps in true-life's railyard. Celka released a shaky breath, relieved they appeared so weakly in sousednia. It meant they were mundanes, at least, not bozhki—State-trained storm mages. One potential threat eliminated.

A sharp knock threatened to yank her from sousednia, but she clung to the neighboring reality as Grandfather swung open the door. Two people stumbled inside, Aunt Benedikta shutting the door behind them with barely a sound. Metal creaked as Celka's older cousin Demian lifted his dark lantern's shutter, releasing the barest sliver of light, enough to make out the newcomers' haggard faces.

Kicking up a breeze beneath sousednia's big top to draw the newcomers' scents toward her, Celka inhaled deeply through her nose. Sousednia was a space of needs and ideas, and Pa had taught her to use it to understand truths otherwise hidden. The newcomers carried the stink of unwashed bodies and a chill, earthy damp that made Celka want to curl in on herself. She managed not to react to their terror, instead leaving her true-life body behind and closing the distance between them in sousednia.

In the railcar, low voices spoke words that didn't matter, innocuous enough to be code. The real code lay in hand signals. The gaunt newcomer rubbed their knuckles while the stockier one just doubled over their knees, wheezing. Grandfather straightened the collar of his nightshirt.

Close to the newcomers' smoke-forms in sousednia, Celka inhaled the tang of turnips. The smell carried echoes of a dark cellar, jackboots stomping the floorboards overhead. Words could lie, appearances deceive, but mundanes didn't control their sousedni-cues. Celka doubted even Pa could have faked their desperation.

She crushed the thought before worries about whether Pa was still alive could send her spinning. Her family wasn't safe yet. The circus train should have moved again by now, its engineers breaking it into segments short enough to park in the railyard. The train remained motionless.

Gusting a sousedni-wind away from her, Celka drove

away the newcomers' terror. She gulped deep breaths tasting of sawdust and manure, grounding herself, then shifted her focus back to true-life. "It's cold in here," she said. The code would tell Grandfather that she believed these people resistance fighters—rezistyenti—same as them.

"They followed us!" the gaunt rezistyent said, voice reedy. "You have to hide us."

As though ignited by their terror, a flare shattered the darkness outside. Celka spun to the window as soldiers swarmed the railyard, figures dark in the actinic glare. Red epaulettes slashed every shoulder like open wounds—the secret police, the Tayemstvoy. Dozens spread out to search the train.

Celka ducked down so they wouldn't see her.

Her family spoke in frantic whispers, and steamer trunks scraped the floor. Wood clunked as her aunt and uncle removed the false wall panels beneath their bed, and Demian helped the gaunt rezistyent crawl inside.

Outside, gravel crunched close to their sleeper car. Too close.

Ela grabbed a broom and frantically swept away the newcomers' muddy footprints. But the panels were still open, the wheezing rezistyent struggling to fit in the tight space. They weren't going to make it.

They'd all be arrested. Interrogated. Tortured.

Clamping down on her panic, Celka plunged back into sousednia. She had to buy her family time.

Beneath her darkened big top, two smoke-forms approached. Celka twisted her illusory high wire towards them and ran, arms outstretched, feet landing in a perfect line. Manipulating sousednia, she placed the soldiers on her high wire platform, giving herself space to maneuver. With more time, she could catch one soldier's foot and tumble them into the other, make it appear simple clumsiness. But mundanes appeared so faintly in sousednia that she couldn't afford the long seconds of concentration to resolve their shapes.

In true-life, hobnailed boots clunked on the sleeper car's stairs. She had to act *now*.

Focused on the leading smoke-form, willing the substance of their chest to solidify, Celka shoved them—hard.

It shouldn't have done anything. Needs and ideas were not pushes and pulls. You couldn't affect true-life from sousednia. But you could make someone *believe* you had.

Outside the sleeper car, boots scuffed the stair, and the leading soldier grunted.

The delay gave Celka time to resolve more of their amorphous shape. They were maybe twenty—about her cousin Demian's age—but short and lean. She envisioned herself behind them, strength of will changing sousednia to match. She kicked them in the backs of their knees.

They dropped. "What in sleetstorms?" Their voice filtered into the sleeper car, angry and surprised.

"You all right?" a higher voice asked, confused, muffled by the wall—the other Tayemstvoy soldier.

A hand grabbed Celka's arm, and she flinched into true-life—Grandfather. "Get into bed."

Disoriented, Celka obeyed without thought, wriggling beneath her quilt. Grandfather climbed into his bunk across from hers, light from the dying flare outside silvering his white hair. Wood scraped as Aunt Benedikta and Uncle Andrik shoved steamer trunks back beneath their bed. Springs creaked above Celka as Ela scrambled into her bunk.

A fist hammered the door. "Tayemstvoy. Open up!"

"Freezing sleet," Aunt Benedikta cursed, sounding like she'd been startled awake even as she heaved the last steamer trunk into place. "What time is it?"

Grandfather opened the door with far less alacrity than he had moments before. "What's going on?" He sounded muzzy with sleep.

The Tayemstvoy soldier Celka had disrupted shined their dark-lantern in Grandfather's face. "All hail the Stormhawk!"

Grandfather squinted and turned aside.

"All hail the Stormhawk," Celka echoed with her family, mingling fervor with fear.

The second Tayemstvoy clomped inside. "Everyone up. Move!" Pistol in one hand, lantern held high in the other, they herded Celka's family into the sitting area where the scratched wooden table and two banged-up chairs left nowhere to hide.

Stomach tight, Celka shuffled obediently into place, eyes on the floorboards. She struggled not to look at her aunt and uncle's bed. Instead, she stole glances from beneath her lashes while the Tayemstvoy ripped through their sleeper car. When they dragged out the steamer trunks, Celka prayed they wouldn't realize that the space beneath Aunt Benedikta and Uncle Andrik's bed was too narrow. She thought frantically for some sousednia trick to help, but she doubted even Pa could have changed the outcome now. Sousednia had limits, and all of Pa's skills hadn't helped when it really mattered.

She crushed the thought as the Tayemstvoy flung clothes out of her trunk. At least if they were making a mess, they weren't pulling aside the false paneling beneath her bunk where her family stored illegal documents.

Minutes crawled past, feeling like hours. Then the soldiers stomped over and started asking questions.

Celka tried to calm her frantic pulse. *Stay quiet, look scared, let Grandfather do the talking.* They were safe. They would be safe. Grandfather had been outwitting the Tayemstvoy for years. Two young soldiers would never catch him in a lie. Celka imagined touching her storm pendant, praying that remained true.

CHAPTER TWO

THE TROOP TRANSPORT lurched through a pothole, leaf springs squeaking, and a chill wind gusted exhaust fumes into Gerrit Kladivo's face. Evergreen branches slapped the transport's sides, spraying him and the five other Storm Guard cadets with remnants of last night's rain.

Gerrit ignored the cold droplets. They could have ridden in comfort—as much as the term ever applied to wooden bench seats in the back of a transport truck—but they'd deliberately folded back the oil canvas tarpaulin to give them a view.

For half an hour he'd been straining for his first glimpse of a bozhskyeh storm. Written accounts from earlier storm-cycles described Gods' Breath as subtly different from electrical lightning—flashing coppery carmine rather than bluish-white, though supposedly only a bozhk with a strong storm-affinity could see the difference.

Evergreens still crowding the horizon, Gerrit swallowed a grimace, his mouth tasting strange—gritty, somehow, with a metallic tang like touching his tongue to both leads from a voltaic pile. He dismissed it at first, but as it grew stronger, he turned to Branislav and Hana, seated on the opposite bench.

They were storm-blessed like him, capable of seeing and using sousednia and—more important now that the bozhskyeh storms had returned—trained to draw Gods' Breath into themselves and use it to imbue magical objects. Nothing about their olive drab battledress uniforms gave them away; Storm Guard imbuement mages wore the same lightning bolts on their collars as every other Army bozhk. But Gerrit had trained with both Hana and Branislav ever since the Storm Guard detected hints that the bozhskyeh storms were returning early.

Staring at the sky, Hana focused mostly on true-life, her sousedni-shape—visible to other storm-blessed mages—bleeding through only weakly. To Gerrit's eyes, it left her with a ghostly overlay in true-life, festive in a red sarafan, brilliant with emerald and cobalt embroidery. In true-life, she wore her dozens of black braids pinned at the nape of her neck, but in sousednia, they cascaded over her shoulders, sparkling with glass beads, rainbow colors matching her luxuriant earrings and contrasting with her skin's rich umber brown.

Unlike Hana, Branislav looked much the same in both realities, dressed in uniform. True-life's cloudy sky left his beige skin a little darker than beneath what must have been a sunny day in his sousednia, and his sousedni-shape had discarded his olive jacket and didn't yet wear an earring. He'd chosen his pronoun later than most children, and his sousednia must have formed before he'd made it official with the single earring; in true-life, that earring was now a lightning bolt of beaten gold, a gift from his family after he'd passed his gold-level bozhk exams.

Feeling Gerrit's attention, Hana and Branislav turned from the sky. Gerrit pointed at his mouth and made a face.

Hana smirked and nodded, eyes bright with excitement beneath the brim of her uniform cap.

Branislav's laugh exploded with bottled tension. "I thought it was just me. I forgot to brush my teeth this morning."

"You can feel it?" Filip tore his gaze from the sky, scrutinizing Gerrit. Filip was merely storm-touched; he could use magic, but not see sousednia or create new imbuements—apart from the strazh weaves that he'd trained with over the last three years. Strazh weaves didn't form into imbuements per se, but rather soaked up uncontrolled storm energy if an imbuement mage made a mistake beneath a bozhskyeh storm. With a strazh at their back, an imbuement mage could survive mistakes that would otherwise kill them. Not that Gerrit planned to make mistakes.

"Not feel it, *taste* it." Hana pulled a face, but her smile ruined the effect.

Jolana, Branislav's strazh, nodded in a pleased sort of

way but said nothing, returning to her vigil of the sky. Only Darina, Hana's strazh, seemed unamused.

"Boots too tight?" Gerrit asked, annoyed that Darina would grim up the morning.

They weren't headed out on boring field exercises today. This bozhskyeh storm would change *everything*. After today, they'd be important—critical to the regime.

Darina gave him a sour look. Her short black hair barely jutted out beneath her uniform cap, and worry flickered a violet protection nuzhda through her wavery sousedni-shape.

"Hey." Hana elbowed her in the ribs. "No one's going storm-mad today."

Gerrit smirked and focused back on the sky. Storm-madness was the sniper over the ridge for an imbuement mage, the threat lurking in every flash of Gods' Breath. A storm-blessed bozhk pulled magical lightning down from a bozhskyeh storm, channeling the Gods' Breath through themselves and into the object they wanted to imbue. The storm energy would crystalize magic inside the object like a kiln firing a pot to hold its shape.

A mistake could dump that storm energy into the imbuement mage instead of the object, tearing them from true-life. Enough storm energy could permanently shatter a mage's true-life grounding, leaving them storm-mad.

But Gerrit refused to let anything go wrong. Not now. Not when he was so close to getting everything he wanted.

Tense with waiting, Gerrit focused on his friends.

"Any word on last night's bozhskyeh storm?" Captain Vrana had kept them late in practicum, and he hadn't been able to ask around.

"They had three mages in place." Filip's dark brown eyes danced between them, asking the question that Gerrit couldn't help but voice out loud.

"And?" Gerrit tried to sound only academically interested.

"They didn't imbue anything stable," Hana said. "We'll still be the first."

"*Gerrit* will be the first," Branislav said, serious beneath his excitement.

Gerrit allowed himself the luxury of a smile, glad his friends had his back. He didn't doubt that Captain Vrana did, too; she knew how much it meant to him, a chance to finally prove his worth.

His enthusiasm darkened. When he'd begun imbuement training, his father had been disgusted. Gerrit couldn't hold true-life without the strenuous exercises that taught him to control sousednia, and Supreme-General Kladivo, the great Stormhawk and all-powerful leader of Bourshkanya, viewed that as weakness. One of Gerrit's many.

Back then, no one had expected the bozhskyeh storms to return in their lifetime. The storms followed a regular pattern: fifty years on-cycle, when Gods' Breath arced through the clouds and storm-blessed bozhki could create new magic; one hundred and fifty years off-cycle, when lightning sparked only electricity. When Gerrit had first fallen into sousednia, the world had been only seventy years into the off-cycle. Off-cycle imbuement mages became academics, their only purpose to keep knowledge alive for future generations. For one of the Stormhawk's children to stay cloistered behind the Storm Guard Academy's walls, teaching techniques even his students would never use... Gerrit may as well never have been born.

Instead, the bozhskyeh storms had returned decades early and with little enough warning that Gerrit was amongst only a handful of trained imbuement mages. And so far, none had successfully imbued.

The Stormhawk valued strength—and Gerrit scored consistently in the middle of his class at the Storm Guard Academy. The Stormhawk valued obedience—and Gerrit couldn't help challenging stupid orders. The Stormhawk valued mastery—and Gerrit lacked the force of will that made a prisoner spill their secrets at the first twist of a knife.

But all of Gerrit's failings paled beneath one overriding truth: for Bourshkanya to rebuild its former glory, the Stormhawk needed imbuements.

Gerrit had memorized thousands of nuzhda weaves—the technical core of magic—and had practiced building them under the harshest conditions. All he needed was a flash of Gods' Breath to crystalize his magic inside an object.

He would start small, of course. He followed orders, usually, and Captain Vrana's most of all. Today, he'd start with a magically sharp blade—the best you could do with a Category One combat weave. But he wouldn't stop there. Soon he'd imbue snap-to weaves to return a knife to its mage when thrown. He'd imbue rifles with increased accuracy and range and, when he'd proven those weaves stable, he'd imbue howitzers—just like Major Doubek was said to have miraculously done at Zlin.

The Stormhawk valued strength. Gerrit would give his father strength. After today, even Gerrit's perfect, storm-touched sister would be no more than his pale shadow.

"There's something you should know." Darina startled Gerrit from his thoughts. "Today might not be..." Worry tightened her voice.

"Might not be what?" Filip asked.

"Did anyone else see who got into Captain Vrana's staff car?" The grim set to Darina's jaw ratcheted up Gerrit's nerves.

"Red shoulders," Filip said with a shrug. No one liked the secret police, but they all expected the Tayemstvoy to keep an eye on them.

Darina shook her head. "Colonel Tesarik." The Storm Guard Academy's Tayemstvoy overseer.

Hana drew a sharp breath, her expression shuttering. Branislav shifted uncomfortably.

Gerrit locked his own churning hatred behind an emotionless mask. Tesarik was hail-eating scum, powerful because he'd supported Gerrit's father from the beginning, before the war. Helpless rage twisted Gerrit's stomach, and he felt Filip's gaze without needing to see it. Filip, warning him not to do something stupid but measuring how likely Gerrit was to do it anyway—and get them both caned.

No. Gerrit wasn't helpless today. Beneath a bozhskyeh storm, he was powerful. More powerful than the sleet-licking colonel.

"We're imbuing," Gerrit said. "That makes this a Storm Guard operation." The Storm Guard trained predominantly Army officers, and though some cadets chose to take Tayemstvoy commissions when they graduated, as cadets they obeyed the Storm Guard General—and she was Army; Tesarik was Tayemstvoy. No matter how the red shoulders wanted to control the world, that distinction kept Tesarik out of their chain of command. "Captain Vrana will give our orders in the field."

"Tesarik just gives us a better audience to prove our storm-blessing." Branislav managed to sound calm about it.

Voice tight, Hana asked, "Has he attended other imbuement attempts?"

"No," Filip said.

"Tesarik just wants us scared so we'll lick his boots." Gerrit tried to believe his own dismissal.

"Maybe." Darina clearly didn't.

"We'll keep an eye out," Jolana said. "You three"—a solemn nod to Branislav, Hana, and Gerrit—"just focus on imbuing."

They nodded, though the engine's growl had grown more ominous, each pothole's jolt more spine-jarring. Then the transport rumbled out of the trees and, just a few kilometers south, lightning lashed the clouds.

Gerrit focused, breathless enthusiasm hardened into

determination as he searched for a flash unlike the others. When it came, lighting the clouds as though they'd been cut and bled, he clenched one hand into a fist. Soon, he would imbue. Soon, his father would see true power.

CHAPTER THREE

CELKA CLIMBED THE steps to the Prochazka sleeper car as sunlight chased the early morning chill. She flung the door casually open, hoping the rezistyenti knew to stay out of sight.

"Of course it's *my* fault," Celka said, keeping up her cover conversation with Ela in case anyone wondered why they were in the railyard when the other performers were all at the fairgrounds.

"It's always your fault," Ela said, half in laughter, half in sympathy as she followed Celka inside.

Celka puffed out her chest in her best Aunt Benedikta impression, "If you hadn't distracted Demian with your chattering, he would have remembered the laundry."

Ela rolled her eyes. "Like Dem can't take care of himself."

The gaunt rezistyent crouched on Celka's bunk,

watching warily; the wheezing one sat on Grandfather's. Celka nodded to them but responded to Ela. "But Dem's so *busy* during our performances." She spoke with a mocking whine and kicked the door shut behind her younger cousin.

Ela took up the grumbling while Celka swung a pack off her shoulders. "We brought breakfast and fresh clothes," she whispered, low enough that even someone in the next compartment wouldn't overhear. The train should be deserted this time of day, everyone offloaded, the roustabouts erecting tents while the performers started on the day's chores. But the Tayemstvoy had ears everywhere, and caution kept rezistyenti alive.

Intellectually, she understood letting these filthy, hunted people sleep in their bunks, but it took Celka a supreme effort not to shudder at the thought of delousing her bed. Again. She made the effort, keeping a performer's smile in place. Rezistyenti like them risked their lives for Bourshkanya's freedom, and maybe Celka's generosity could get her some answers Grandfather refused to share.

After the morning's Tayemstvoy raid, Celka'd had no chance to interact with the rezistyenti, and she burned with curiosity. In the daylight, she spotted a simple copper stud in each of the gaunt rezistyent's ears, signaling her gender. The wheezing rezistyent wore only a single earring, of beautiful blue enamel. Celka handed him a meal of bread and hard cheese wrapped in a napkin. When she handed a similar breakfast to the gaunt woman, the rezistyent caught Celka's wrist.

With a yelp, Celka jerked her arm back.

"You bang your finger in the trunk again?" Ela called to cover Celka's indiscretion.

"Sleetstorms," Celka cursed, even as she focused on the gaunt rezistyent's face. The woman couldn't have been more than a few years older than her, maybe twenty, though worry lines and the dark circles hollowing her eyes aged her up a decade.

"We need to speak to your grandfather," she said.

"He'll be back this evening. He sent me to talk to you." Not quite a lie. People conversed over food.

The rezistyent held her gaze, measuring her, and Celka tried to look confident. Finally, the rezistyent pulled folded pages from her coat.

Ela snatched them. "What is it?"

Celka peered over her cousin's shoulder. Double-underlined across the top of the page, *Woman Imbues to Save Dying Husband*.

The world seemed to stop. Celka's eyes flew like trapeze artists across the handwritten text. A healing imbuement. One week ago. Storm-blessed. Tayemstvoy arrest.

She wanted to read every detail, but the rezistyent had pulled out black-and-white photographs. One showed an elderly couple smiling and holding hands. The second showed a branching, fernlike pattern. Frowning, Celka flipped the photograph over, hoping for clues. Written on the back: *A Civilian Storm-scar*. Celka studied the photograph again, realizing it showed the old woman's neck and back. The fernlike pattern radiated from the base of her skull, reaching fractal tendrils down her spine and across her shoulder.

Gospel spoke of Gods' Breath scarring those who touched it, but she'd never seen pictures. 'Scar' had made her imagine something ropy and ugly—like the puckered, glossy burn scars Pa had from the war. But the photograph reminded her of the marks Gods' Breath left on stones and floorboards, proudly displayed inside storm temples. She'd never imagined such beautiful, complex patterns inscribed on flesh.

"Is this real?" Celka asked.

"Saw it myself," the gaunt rezistyent said.

Celka took the handwritten page from Ela. The old woman's husband had been dying of black lung, rattling his last breaths during a storm. Remembering her gospel, she'd sung the Song of Healing for hours before the Storm Gods answered her prayer. Gods' Breath had bleached the floor of her tenement, the storm-mark radiating out around her feet. The lightning had left no other mark on the building.

The leaflet's last lines said,

The Stormhawk claims the Storm Gods favor only the regime. He lies. The bozhskyeh storms have returned, and the Tayemstvoy do not control them. If Bourshkanyans stand for freedom, the storm-blessed will turn from the State.

A crude woodblock cutting of a running wolf signed the leaflet. Heat radiated down Celka's spine from the base of her skull. *She* was storm-blessed. Had Pa spoken to the Wolf about her before his arrest? "The Wolf wrote this?" she asked.

"One of his lieutenants," the wheezing rezistyent said.

"No one's seen the Wolf in months," said the other.

Celka couldn't worry about whether the Wolf was alive. She needed to learn everything she could from these rezistyenti. "Is this the first non-State imbuement?"

They both shrugged. "Haven't heard otherwise."

"This says the storm-blessed will turn from the State. Does the resistance have mages?"

"That old lady was just a regular Bourshkanyan," the woman said.

"Storm blood in all of us," said the wheezing man, biting into his sandwich as though the issue was settled.

Celka shook her head. "I'm talking about bozhki, *trained* mages."

The woman narrowed her eyes. "Why do you want to know?"

"Just curious," Celka said, too fast.

"Curious rezistyenti get the rest of us killed," the wheezing man said.

Celka clenched her jaw. This could be her call-to-arms—the Wolf asking her to imbue for them—but she needed to know what to do. She'd never imbued before. She didn't know *how* to imbue. Pa's lessons seemed like dreams. She'd been thirteen when the Tayemstvoy had beaten him and dragged him away. She wanted to help the resistance, wanted to imbue weapons that let them destroy the State—but she didn't know how.

"What happened to her?" Ela whispered. "The old woman?"

The gaunt rezistyent grimaced and started rummaging in her rucksack. The wheezing one said, "Red shoulders loaded her on a train."

The words felt like falling off a horse, all the air struck from Celka's lungs. Ela's hand found hers, fingers gripping tight, and Celka finally drew a breath. "Why didn't the resistance save her?"

Silence filled the compartment, big enough to march an elephant through.

The gaunt woman finally turned from her bag, falsely cheery as though a smile could free the old woman starving in a labor camp. "We have plates for printing the photographs. You need to make leaflets."

Celka wanted to throw them both out into the railyard and tell them to take their own sleeting chances if they didn't care that the Tayemstvoy had arrested that old woman. Instead, she folded the page and made herself say, "We'll handle it."

Grandfather would have contacts that could print the leaflet, and Celka would find a way to ensure that she met them. With proof the bozhskyeh storms had returned, Grandfather would *have* to answer her questions. She'd finally be able to use her storm-blessing to help the resistance.

CHAPTER FOUR

Wind pummeled Gerrit with rain as he crossed a field, sinking ankle-deep in mud. He and Filip had left the troop transport behind, crushing early spring shoots beneath their hobnailed boots, sudden gusts threatening to tear their caps from their heads. Lightning arced above them, cutting the thunderstorm's darkness. Out of every dozen flashes, a few were coppery bright—Gods' Breath—and those yanked at Gerrit's skull as if trying to lift him into the clouds. Along with that tug, sousednia pressed against his senses—noon-day sun searing from a cloudless alpine sky as icy wind sighed across snow-shrouded boulders.

As each flare of Gods' Breath faded, true-life startled him, the rain pelting his cheeks incongruous with sousednia's alpine sun. He fought to hold both realities equally, as he'd been taught, but excitement made him want to reach into sousednia, brushing fingers across the storm-thread that seemed to grow from the base of his spine.

With his back to the others, he let soldierly neutrality fall away. Filip mirrored his grin, teeth bright white against his brown skin.

As ordered, a dozen meters from the others, Gerrit stopped. Schooling his expression, he turned back to his audience. Alongside Captain Vrana and the other Storm Guard cadets, Colonel Tesarik watched with a haughty sneer. At Tesarik's side stood Gerrit's sister, Iveta, resplendent in her gold bozhk bolts, lieutenant's stars, and red Tayemstvoy shoulders. She was Tesarik's attaché, which meant Gerrit should have expected her here; but he'd thought this bozhskyeh storm would be *his*, not something he'd have to share with his perfect sister.

Filip stepped behind Gerrit, laying a hand on the back of his neck—right over his storm-thread. Then, in sousednia, Filip's touch vanished. Gerrit shifted his attention to the neighboring reality.

As merely storm-touched, Filip appeared as a humanoid ripple—a heat mirage better-defined than a mundane, but without a storm-blessed bozhk's lifelike presence. Normally, Filip's true-form and sousedni-shape moved in unison; now, however, Filip crouched in sousednia, wavery hands disappearing into what Gerrit saw as snow.

Gerrit wasn't sure what memory Filip used to create a protection nuzhda—one half of the desperate need he'd use to ensure Gerrit's safety during his imbuement—but it looked oddly like gardening. Within heartbeats, protection nuzhda's violet glow sluiced Filip's sousedni-shape. He briefly rejoined his true-form at Gerrit's back before his heat-shimmer dodged away, throwing punches. It took Filip bare seconds in whatever violent memory he used to draw upon a combat nuzhda, then he stood again at Gerrit's back, rippling crimson and violet.

Expertly, Filip built a strazh weave from the base of Gerrit's skull, threading together the two nuzhdi into a pulsing glow that wrapped Filip's arm and body to plunge into the ground like the roots of a tree. Filip's weaves were a sensible precaution. If Gerrit lost control of any storm energy, the weaves would dump it through Filip to dissipate harmlessly into the ground.

Not that Gerrit would lose control.

Finished, Filip clasped Gerrit's shoulder. Gerrit double-checked his best friend's weaves—flawless, of course. Of all the strazh cadets, Filip was the best. Shifting his attention back to true-life, Gerrit nodded.

Across the field, Colonel Tesarik's smirk practically screamed that he expected Gerrit to fail. At his side, a frown creased Iveta's brows like she was worried.

You should be worried, Gerrit wanted to tell her. *You won't be Father's favorite for long.*

Shutting his eyes, Gerrit put his hands behind his back, preparing to pull against a combat nuzhda. He imagined rope cutting into his wrists, pinioning his arms. Singularly focused on that sensation, true-life's muddy field tunneled away.

Fear and an animal desperation surged with the memory, and Gerrit became the boy he'd been four years ago.

Breath harsh in his throat, Gerrit struggles on his side. The dirt road beneath him is frozen stone-hard. Rope cuts into his wrists as he works his arms around his feet, fighting to get his bound hands out in front of him. His pistol fell to the ground mere meters away, and the resistance scum didn't notice—or didn't think a thirteen-year-old enough of a threat to care. If he can reach it, he might be able to save his mother.

Icy air burns his sinuses, and he shivers violently, his uniform no match for winter's hard freeze. The gritty stink of diesel smoke hangs in the air from the idling motorcar—though Gerrit's driver and the guard are dead. The rezistyent filth who shot them have turned their backs, surrounding Gerrit's mother, metal pipes flying as they beat her. Mother fights like a thunderstorm, but blood already blackens her olive uniform. She can't win against so many—not alone.

The memory's visceral reality warped Gerrit's sousednia. Lonesome wind no longer howled across diamond-white snow; instead, sousednia resounded with the sick *crack* of pipe on flesh. The pine and ice scents of his core sousednia morphed into diesel smoke and frozen earth, and combat nuzhda oozed like crimson oil from the pores of Gerrit's sousedni-shape.

Screaming with rage, Gerrit wrenched his focus back to true-life. His attention split: in that brutal memory, he finally twisted his hands around his ankles; in true-life, he noticed Tesarik beneath the bozhskyeh storm's bruised sky.

Twisted by his combat nuzhda, Gerrit's lips skinned back from his teeth. Tesarik had ordered Gerrit whipped dozens of times, had grinned while the lash fell and Gerrit bit back screams. Just see how the sleet-licker smiled once his blood drenched Gerrit's blade.

Drawing his belt knife, Gerrit lunged.

Someone caught his arm. "Stop!"

The combat nuzhda urged Gerrit to tear free, to drive his blade deep into the chest of the boy holding him. But training made him freeze.

"Your nuzhda's too strong." Dimly, Gerrit recognized Filip's voice. True-life had become blurry, dream-like, overlapping with sousednia until the neighboring reality nearly drowned out the muddy field. In sousednia, Gerrit crawled across the frozen dirt road and finally closed his bound hands around the revolver.

His weapons were different in true-life and sousednia—knife and revolver—but his intent was the same. He had to imbue; had to fight. Tesarik would order him whipped again; in memory, the resistance scum would beat his mother to death unless he saved her.

But years of training had conditioned Gerrit to listen to Filip. "You're safe," Filip said. "You're standing in a muddy field, cold rain drumming on your cap."

The words focused Gerrit on those sensations, and the warmth of Filip's hand on his neck anchored him. Filip kept speaking, and the rain's rush and hiss drowned some of the resistance scum's shouting. True-life sharpened, and Filip solidified, his olive drab uniform dark with rain.

The panicked need to save his mother blurred into the sunlit clearing of Gerrit's core sousednia. From that alpine safety, Gerrit built rough granite walls around his combat nuzhda's panicked desperation.

In training, Gerrit had built nuzhdi from the terrors of his past a million times; for years, he'd always retained enough control to build these mental walls on his own. He'd never stood beneath a bozhskyeh storm before, though.

Scripture warned about bozhskyeh storms amplifying the weakest need, sparking minor arguments into murderous rages. Gerrit had believed those warnings exaggerated. He'd been wrong.

Filip shifted around to grip his face in both hands, and Gerrit fought to focus on his best friend's touch. This close, Gerrit could feel the slow rhythm of Filip's inhale and exhale, and he struggled to mimic it. That calm gave Gerrit the strength to tighten the granite walls around his memory, diminishing his desperation until only a sliver of his self snarled and raged.

In true-life, he sheathed the knife at his side.

"There." Filip's nod confirmed Gerrit's own assessment of his nuzhda. "Category One."

Gerrit exhaled relief, but gave himself only a moment to rest in his sunlit alpine clearing before stepping his attention through sousednia's granite walls.

Desperation stole his breath, and Gerrit fell to his knees, gripping his revolver with bound hands. Teeth bared, he fired at a rezistyent kicking his mother. The pistol's report cracked the frozen air, and Gerrit shifted reality, echoing the sound off his mental walls, shaping the resonance that would magically sharpen his knife.

The fraction of his consciousness immersed in his combat-warped sousednia wanted to fire again and again, kill all the hail-eaters, smash their dog faces into the blood already frozen on the ground. But most of his focus remained in his core sousednia, surrounded by sun and snow—so he resisted.

Filip's hand pressed against the back of his neck again, and Gerrit let one thread of his attention follow that sensation back to the rainy field. This time, when Gerrit drew his belt knife, he felt only the calm clarity that settled over him sometimes in field exercises. He was deadly, he could kill, but he was in control.

Inside his mental walls, Gerrit twisted reality to better match true-life. Instead of a revolver, he gripped his combat knife. When he wrapped his pistol-report weaves around it, his combat nuzhda coalesced until the blade appeared drenched in blood.

Focusing on true-life, Gerrit ensured that he held all three realities distinctly so that pulling down Gods' Breath would not damage his mind. His core sousednia, true-life, and his combat-warped sousednia were each clear if he shifted his focus—as though concentrating near to far.

Back in his core sousednia, the thread reaching from the base of his skull into the clouds had thickened, now practically a rope connecting him to the bozhskyeh storm. Filip's crimson-violet strazh weaves grew from that same point, travelling down Filip's heat-shimmer arm to dive into the ground.

Satisfied that he'd prepared his imbuement correctly, Gerrit mentally gripped his storm-thread. This was it, the moment he'd dreamed of his entire life. The moment he imbued.

With a yank, he called Gods' Breath down into himself.

Darkness flickered in his periphery, then lightning struck. Agony sluiced through his body from the nape of his neck like his blood flash-boiling. Teeth gritted, he struggled to hold his focus. Before he could cry out, a wave of euphoria transformed the pain, and his vision burst into flames.

SNARLING, GERRIT FIRED his revolver at one of the resistance scum. The rezistyent jerked and clutched their chest, and Gerrit fired again, hitting another rezistyent kicking his mother. They stumbled, but drew their leg back for another kick. Gerrit fired again, screaming, his throat raw. The second rezistyent fell, and Gerrit shifted his aim, pulling the trigger again.

But somehow the first rezistyent he'd shot wasn't dead. Gerrit screamed. He fired again and again. His revolver should have been empty, the resistance dogs should have been dead, but they weren't. He kept screaming, kept firing. Again. Again.

Time seemed not to pass at all. Or maybe days had already passed when Gerrit spotted a red glow in his periphery. But he couldn't stop firing or his mother would die. He pulled the trigger again, shooting a hail-eater with a mangy beard, but the glow beside Gerrit strengthened, yanking his attention around to where a figure wavered the color of blood. Not dark frozen blood like around his mother, but the brilliant crimson of blood fresh from a vein.

Before he knew what he was doing, Gerrit stumbled toward the glowing figure—a youth around his own age, familiar in some way that slipped from Gerrit like water. He snarled again, *needing* to raise his revolver and protect his mother—but instead, he reached out, touching the youth's face. The figure's crimson glow flowed over his hand, echoing with pistol reports, though Gerrit had stopped firing.

As he struggled to understand, the glow shifted, crimson shading aubergine, rippling lavender and marigold. The sounds changed too, subtly at first, a moan rising from the screams of injured rezistyenti, howling into wind across ice and snow.

Gasping, Gerrit reached for that howl with all his strength, needing in a way he didn't understand to feel that wind on his face, needing sunlight to sear his eyes and chase away the grim half-light of brutal death. Yet something resisted.

The world in which his mother succumbed had become too real, the grunts and shouts and sick crack of metal on bone too clear in a way he didn't understand but knew, suddenly, was *wrong*.

Straining harder, Gerrit gripped the figure's rippling,

half-real face. They mirrored his gesture, touch like brittle air, bright with pine and glaciers.

With a crack like a rifle shot, a fissure cleaved the frozen road.

Gerrit strained for a glimpse of fresh snow through the tear, and the fissure widened like unsafe ice. Screaming, Gerrit drove all his focus into that weakness.

The world burst—the dirt road and motorcar and resistance fighters shattered. Icy wind pulverized the shards and powdered them into snow.

Blinded by noonday sun, Gerrit gasped for breath as though he'd been drowning. He stumbled forward, boots crunching in fresh snow, treeless peaks jutting into the sky beyond a deep valley. Icy wind tore tears from his eyes, and he'd never known anything so beautiful.

"Gerrit, you have to come back." A voice whispered in the wind. A figure—the same figure—stood half a pace back, arms still outstretched as though to touch Gerrit's face. "It's spring. You're in a field fresh with new growth, though it's churned into mud from the storm. Rain's sheeting into us, drumming your cap. Did you see the lightning? Hear the crack of thunder?"

Gerrit struggled to understand even as part of him rebelled, desperate to stay in this perfect alpine clearing. But he recognized Filip's voice now and heeded him automatically, seeking the sensations his strazh described.

As Gerrit clawed into that muddy field, Filip's heat mirage solidified, his cap shadowing dark eyes, rain soaking his battledress uniform. True-life bled through

Gerrit's sun-bright sousednia until the sky roiled with storm clouds, lightning flickering their depths.

Disoriented, Gerrit looked around. Tesarik and Iveta stood a dozen meters away, Captain Vrana, Branislav, Hana, Jolana, and Darina beside them, mud staining their knee-high boots.

"I imbued?" The words felt gritty on Gerrit's tongue, distorted as though cotton stuffed his ears. The imbuement should ripple crimson, visible in true-life to anyone with storm blood.

He found his knife, fallen point-first in a muddy furrow. But it didn't glow.

Gerrit frowned, not understanding. He'd *imbued*. The crimson fires of crystalized nuzhda should pulse over the knife in true-life just as they did in sousednia. He shifted his attention to his alpine clearing, but couldn't even *find* the knife there.

Understanding landed like a kick to the gut. The knife didn't glow because his imbuement had failed. *He*'d failed.

There had to be some mistake. He must have missed something. That wasn't his knife. It couldn't be.

Desperate, he met Filip's gaze. "What happened?"

Filip's intense concentration collapsed, and he pulled Gerrit into a rough embrace. "You came back," he whispered, the words choked.

Only then did fear twist Gerrit's stomach. Locked in memory, he'd fired his revolver again and again, caught in a combat nuzhda fugue. He hadn't known anything was wrong. Hadn't been able to think outside his rage and desperation. How long had he stayed like that before Filip caught his attention?

For however long, he'd been storm-mad. If Filip hadn't pulled him back, Gerrit might never have returned. Today was supposed to be his great triumph, instead—

"I assume he failed," Tesarik said, strident over the rain. His disgust held a cruel, satisfied edge.

Gerrit wanted to scream at the Tayemstvoy colonel, wanted to plunge into sousednia and try again.

Filip released him, but Captain Vrana caught his shoulder, warning in her grim expression. "You're done for the day, Kladivo. Cadet Ruzhishka," she called to Hana, "you're next."

CHAPTER FIVE

GRANDFATHER READ THE resistance leaflet while Celka watched Ela and Demian warm up on the practice wire. She did her best to pretend like everything was normal, but couldn't match Aunt Benedikta and Uncle Andrik's nonchalance.

"He's turning peoples' faith in the Storm Gods against the State," Grandfather said. "It's a dangerous game."

"Does he know about me?" Celka asked.

Grandfather placed his gnarled hand on her shoulder. "Some secrets are too dangerous to voice."

Celka kicked at the weeds, frustrated but traitorously relieved. Her family had built her entire life around hiding her identity. Out loud, she called Uncle Andrik 'Pa' and Aunt Benedikta 'Ma.' To the rest of the world, Ela and Demian were her sister and brother. Only that fiction had saved her when the Tayemstvoy arrested Pa.

"Silence won't protect me forever." She turned so the tumblers who'd sauntered over couldn't read her lips. "You read the Wolf's words. He needs me."

"Your family needs you more."

In sousednia, Celka drew a deep breath, trying to understand the tightness in his voice. But he just smelled like Grandfather—boiled cabbage and sweat from a good workout on the wire. Frustrated, she said, "The bozhskyeh storms have returned. You can't deny that anymore. I need to learn how to imbue." She dropped her voice to mouth the last word more than speak it.

Grandfather stepped close, his whisper harsh. "Forget the madness Leosh told you before his arrest. No amount of *care* will protect you if you follow that path."

At first she could only gape, the air driven from her lungs as though she'd fallen from the low wire. "He prepared me to help. *Taught* me to help." Grandfather would take her meaning. When Pa learned the bozhskyeh storms were returning, he'd taught her everything he could about imbuing. The details might be fuzzy, but what other storm-blessed mage would turn so fully against the State? The resistance *needed* her—even if the Wolf didn't know it yet.

"You saw the Tayemstvoy drag him away," Grandfather said. "You saw what his arrest did to your mother." Celka's ma—her real ma—had fallen from the high wire just days after Pa's arrest. She'd survived, but the impact had shattered her heels. Every step she took now was agony, and she couldn't walk the wire. Summers were bittersweet for Celka, the joy of performing beneath the big top soured by Ma's absence, and she could only imagine how painful it was for Ma, left behind at their winter quarters to take factory shifts and care for her ailing mother. "We were lucky then," Grandfather said. "They could have arrested us all. If you follow his path, they will."

Celka touched her storm pendant, two fingers pressing the rounded brass rectangle into her chest. Pa could still be alive, trapped in a cell or labor camp. The State would never release him, which meant she had to help the resistance destroy the State. Scripture described the Fighting Miracles—imbuements powerful and terrible. If Celka could make those, the resistance might finally be strong enough to crush the Stormhawk and Tayemstvoy.

"I know you adored him," Grandfather said, "but the war made him reckless. You are important here. If you promise to forget his mad notions... I will teach you to help further."

Celka's chest tightened. Having the key to the resistance dangled before her, she couldn't help but reach for it. Yet the Wolf said the storm-blessed would turn from the State—he must have a way for her to imbue safely. But maybe it wasn't ready yet. Even just the thought of risking herself was terrifying; she couldn't risk her family.

"But you must do something for me," Grandfather said. "Increase your study of scripture. Comb the holy words for clues on how to ignore the bozhskyeh storms' pull. And, to avoid drawing attention from the Gods, you will sing the Song of Calming until it resonates in your bones."

Celka hated singing almost as much as she hated sitting still with a book on her lap, but she nodded. She could be patient—for a month or a season or a year. If she learned everything Grandfather knew about the resistance, when the Wolf called, she would be ready.

CHAPTER SIX

GERRIT PACED THE cramped cellar beneath his Storm Guard Academy barracks, waiting for Hana and Darina to arrive. Filip stood with maddening calm near the door. Branislav balanced on a chair that had lost its fourth leg, Jolana kneading his shoulders in the flickering candlelight.

Exhaustion left Gerrit's muscles shivery, but his mind snapped and buzzed, on edge from his failure that morning. He'd hoped to sleep until the Tayemstvoy's midnight patrol passed their bunkroom and left the way clear, but he'd tossed and turned, sousednia pressing against his senses, raw like salt in a wound.

When Hana and Darina finally arrived, smelling of mud from their trek across the fortress yard, Gerrit barely waited for Filip to ease the door shut before asking, "What went wrong?"

Everyone glanced around, silent and strained.

"We should have imbued," Gerrit said, unable to control his frustration. After his failure, Hana and Branislav had attempted their own imbuements; their efforts hadn't driven them from true-life, but they'd still failed.

"Your weaves looked fine," Hana said cautiously. "I was watching from sousednia." She nodded to Branislav. "Yours, too. It doesn't make sense."

"They looked perfect to me, too." Frustration tightened Branislav's voice.

"Something obviously went wrong," Gerrit snapped, though his friends didn't deserve his anger.

"There was... something," Darina said.

Gerrit frowned, surprised that a strazh—who couldn't properly see sousednia—might have noticed something the storm-blessed had missed.

"A dissonance," she told Gerrit, "in your weaves. Just before you called Gods' Breath."

"What kind of dissonance?" Gerrit asked.

"Your weaves sounded wrong. Out of rhythm for a fraction of a second."

"There were two," Jolana said.

Everyone turned to her.

"Close together, almost overlapping—but the dissonance didn't come from the same point."

Gerrit ran his hand through his hair, trying to figure out what that meant.

"I only heard one when Hana attempted to imbue," Jolana said. "Fainter."

Filip's head snapped up at that. "Darina, are you storm-scarred?"

Darina pulled a face in the flickering candlelight. "Barely."

Filip turned to Jolana. "You?"

She nodded.

"I'm not," Filip said.

Gerrit rubbed the back of his neck where a fern-like scar the size of a silver striber still burned. Storm-scars came from handling Gods' Breath, and the strazh mages would only have been scarred if their imbuement mages had overflowed storm energy into them. Something about both Darina and Jolana carrying those scars felt wrong, but before Gerrit could sort it out, Filip spoke.

"If the dissonance you heard was our weaves breaking, then it makes sense that Jolana heard two for me and Gerrit. My weaves didn't protect him." Filip's voice was tight. "Whatever went wrong for you three"—he nodded to the other imbuement mages—"it must have gone wrong for me, too."

They mulled that over before Darina asked Filip, "Did you hear anything unusual during the imbuements?"

Jaw tight, Filip shook his head. "I was focused on Gerrit. He—" Filip broke off.

"It's all right," Gerrit said, though he hated admitting weakness, even to his closest friends. "They should know." He dragged in a steadying breath. "I lost true-life. Completely."

Darina caught his arm. "Are you all right?" The flickering candlelight made it hard to tell, but her gaze seemed to de-focus, like Filip's did when he was struggling to build a picture of sousednia out of synesthetic rumbles.

He shrugged off her touch. "I'll be fine."

She didn't back away, still staring through him.

Gerrit cleared his throat, looking to the others for some distraction.

"You core feels off," Darina said before he could turn the conversation away. "Filip, something's still wrong, isn't it?"

Startled, Gerrit turned to his strazh.

He wanted Filip to say it wasn't true, but Filip kicked the dirt. "I'd hoped I was imagining it."

"Imagining what?" Gerrit asked.

"You feel like you're not quite... here." Filip scrubbed a hand across his jaw, struggling to explain. "Your core nuzhda's stronger. Like when you're focused on sousednia."

Ice coiled around Gerrit's spine. "But I'm not." Shutting his eyes, he listened for sousednia's mournful wind—nothing. Drawing a deep breath, he smelled only the cellar's mold and rat droppings. "I'm fully holding true-life." All day, sousednia had pressed against his senses, the smallest slip in attention leaving alpine freshness brightening the air. But he'd persisted—and he'd succeeded. He thought.

"You should talk to Captain Vrana," Branislav said. "If you lost true-life—there could be consequences."

Gerrit wanted to lash out. There *couldn't* be consequences; he needed to imbue in the next storm.

Already he could imagine Iveta's mocking laughter at their next family dinner, his brother Artur's solemn disappointment. Their plates cleared, his father would dismiss Gerrit like he was no more than staff, gathering Iveta and Artur to him with murmurs of 'important business.' Gerrit wondered sometimes how often his siblings ate with their father. Back before she'd commissioned as a bozhk officer in the Tayemstvoy, Iveta had certainly mentioned dinners without Gerrit. *Study harder, little brother,* she'd tell him, impeccable in her dress uniform. *Effort can provide what nature withholds.*

"Gerrit." Filip's touch startled him back to the cellar.

He needed to imbue, but Branislav was right. "I'll talk to Captain Vrana."

Silence settled over the room, failure an iron collar around everyone's throat.

"Wait," Gerrit said, finally realizing why the strazh cadets' storm-scarring had bothered him. Hana's knife had shattered seconds after she'd imbued it, her weaves filled wrong, the knife's magic unstable. Since she had imbued, she *could* have overflowed storm energy into Darina. But... "Branislav, your imbuement didn't fully crystalize." When Branislav had called down Gods' Breath, barely a trickle had flowed into his blade—insufficient to crystalize his nuzhda before the magic sputtered out. "You didn't pull hard enough on the storm. How did storm energy overflow into Jolana?"

Everyone frowned at that.

Eventually, Branislav said, "Maybe I directed the

energy wrong? Dumped it into Jolana's weaves instead of my own?"

"This doesn't make any sense," Hana said. "Imbuing felt intuitive. It felt *right*. I didn't feel out of control."

"Me neither," Gerrit said. "Well, not after I got a hold of my nuzhda."

The others nodded.

"So how did we fail?" Branislav asked.

Darina crossed her arms. "It's not like you're the first to try. How many bozhskyeh storms since the cycle began? A dozen? You're not the first to make mistakes."

"But we're the best." Gerrit couldn't say it with as much conviction as before, and no one met his gaze.

"Maybe intuition and training aren't enough," Hana said. "What if we're missing something? Something special about holding weaves beneath a storm or pulling against Gods' Breath? Something Captain Vrana doesn't know because she trained off-cycle?"

Gerrit turned to Filip. "Anything in your reading?" Filip spent his leisure time—when he wasn't flirting with everyone—poring over arcane manuscripts in languages no sane cadet wasted time learning.

Filip thought for a moment. "Multiple mages imbuing simultaneously is dangerous. We were all concentrating on sousednia to see what was happening. That could have interfered."

A better theory than they'd had before. "So, next time, only the mage who's imbuing touches sousednia," Gerrit said. "The rest of us hold true-life completely. Even the strazhi." The idea made him uncomfortable, and Gerrit realized that during their conversation, sousednia had insinuated itself back around the edges of his senses.

If Gerrit had considered ignoring the press of sousednia before, he abandoned that hubris now. He'd talk to Captain Vrana in the morning.

The others agreed. As they started for the door, Darina said, "As we were leaving the field, did anyone else hear what Colonel Tesarik told Captain Vrana?"

Gerrit was certain he didn't want to know. But ignoring intelligence lost battles, and a lost battle could lose a war.

"He said her methods didn't deliver results." Shadows made Darina's expression impossible to read, but her voice was wooden. "He said that next time, we'll do this his way."

"What does that mean?" Hana asked.

Darina shook her head. "I'll see what I can learn."

"Maybe he's bluffing." Gerrit wished he could believe it. He shuddered to imagine what a sadist like Tesarik thought would help them imbue.

AFTER IMBUEMENT PRACTICUM, Gerrit hung back, letting the slate-floored practice room empty while he fiddled with his sparring gear. When the door slammed closed behind the last cadet, Gerrit found Captain Vrana standing at the window, hands clasped behind her back.

He crossed to her side, trying to look casual for the Tayemstvoy corporal watching from the door. Four stories below, cadets marched in formation across the practice yard. «Is there anything else, sir?» he asked in sousednia. His neighboring reality echoed true-life, leaving him at a cliff's edge, staring down into the tree-lined valley. In true-life, he asked a mundane question about nuzhda weaves that would merit a complex, technical answer—to satisfy the watching corporal.

Captain Vrana launched into the explanation but turned a sliver of attention to sousednia. She'd debriefed the six of them this morning, making each storm-blessed cadet explain what had gone wrong in their imbuement and discussing how to avoid the same failures in future storms. At their theory of avoiding sousednia unless they were imbuing, she'd looked thoughtful and suggested they try it.

But a Tayemstvoy lieutenant had scribbled notes in the back of the seminar room, and Captain Vrana hadn't dwelled on Gerrit losing true-life.

«I don't have magic words of advice, Kladivo,» she said. «Imbuing requires practice. Practice usually involves failure.»

He ground his teeth, wishing that didn't sound so reasonable. But failure wasn't the only reason he was here. «Sousednia's different for me now.»

Her sousedni-shape sharpened, her attention shifting fully to him, though she continued to expound upon imbuement theory aloud. «Different how?»

He explained its unrelenting pressure. «And it's harder to transition out of. During practice today—»

«I saw.»

Relief flooded him that he didn't have to describe

how he'd floundered, struggling to find true-life after a sousednia-control exercise he thought he'd mastered years ago. He did his best to keep the emotion off his face. «So what do I do? How do I fix it?»

«Sanity is a fragile gift for us.»

Gerrit waved that away. Bozhki in general, and storm-blessed mages especially, tended to crack—if not go completely storm-mad—near the end of their lives. But Gerrit wasn't nearing flare-out, he was on the edge of gaining his father's respect—if only he could avoid another mistake. «If I'd lost control of more storm energy, Filip might not have been able to pull me back. How do I make sure it doesn't happen again?»

Light and shadow snaked across Captain Vrana's face, bleeding through from her sousednia. «What do you care about in true-life?»

Gerrit frowned, wondering how that could be relevant. «Serving Bourshkanya.»

Captain Vrana raised an eyebrow and waited.

Gerrit sighed. «My friends, I guess. Filip. Hana and Branislav; their strazhi.» Captain Vrana kept waiting, and he tried to think of something else. «I enjoy imbuement training—your classes.»

Shadows rippled across her face like laughter, and Gerrit realized it sounded like boot-licking. He started to protest, to clarify that dissecting nuzhda weaves got him through miserable field exercises and the endless monotony of marching drills and target practice.

She held up a hand. «It's not enough.»

«What does that mean?»

«You have the potential to be one of this cycle's greatest imbuement mages, but you must find an anchor in true-life. Something or someone you cannot bear to leave behind.»

Usually Captain Vrana's advice was practical. This? He had no idea how to even start. «And if I don't?»

«Given the nuzhda burn-in you suffered yesterday, you shouldn't be in another storm until you've regained control of sousednia.» Frustration tightened her voice.

«But?» he asked, dread a pit in his stomach. Cadets often joked that a wolf could be chewing off Captain Vrana's leg and she wouldn't break her implacable calm. Given the stories of what she'd done during the war, he believed it.

«But a nearby bozhskyeh storm is predicted in two days. You'll be in it.»

Excitement at another chance to imbue warred with stomach-churning fear. «How am I supposed to find a true-life anchor in two days?» Or at all, but that was a different problem.

«I'll excuse you and Cizek from your other duties. Practice transitioning fully out of sousednia.»

«Will that be enough?»

Her sousedni-shape wavered as she focused back on true-life.

He caught her arm in sousednia, willing to risk her censure if it could save his life. «Talk to my father.» A telephone line had been installed in the Storm Guard fortress last year. «Tell him I can't be in that storm.»

Captain Vrana tensed beneath his hold—though the

sensation was slippery, since he touched her only in sousednia and she focused strongly on true-life. For a long moment, she said nothing—apart from their meaningless discussion aloud. Finally, her sousedni-shape sharpened. «The Stormhawk will not protect you.»

«But he—» Gerrit broke off when he realized what she'd said. *Will* not, not *can*not. «You spoke with him?»

«The Storm Guard General has convinced him that 'coddling' any of you will make you too weak to be useful. He gave me one storm.»

Tesarik's words as they left the field seemed all the more ominous. «What is Tesarik planning?»

Captain Vrana's lips thinned. «I'll try not to let it come to that.»

CHAPTER SEVEN

CELKA HAD KNOWN a few resistance hand signals. Grandfather taught her dozens more. Every spare moment, she closed her eyes, imagining twitching her fingers or adjusting her blouse just so—engraving those motions on her memory. Grandfather taught her addresses and names, described memories that would verify she had the right person, and she lay awake in her bunk every night—after singing the Song of Calming five times—repeating the details to herself.

When the rest of her family shoved aside the table and chairs in their tiny sitting area, cranked the phonograph player, and took turns dancing with the 'travelers' while the circus train clacked down the track, Celka scoured a book of scripture for clues on how to either avoid the bozhskyeh storms' pull or use them to imbue. She studied the Miracles, imbuements that ended famines and plagues and wars, but the text was dense and metaphorical.

Lack of sleep made her eyes gritty, but any time she considered relaxing her study, she felt the weight of Pa's storm pendant against her chest. She had to believe he was still alive. If she wanted to see him again, she had to destroy the regime.

Grandfather had practical lessons, too. When the circus train pulled into Usov, Grandfather shook her awake in the pre-dawn darkness and whispered instructions for the afternoon. She would carry the rezistyenti's leaflet and photo-engravings to a forger in town, an old friend of Grandfather's from before the war. Petr would forge identification folios that would allow the rezistyenti to build new lives, and would pass the photo engravings and leaflet text to a contact that even Grandfather didn't know. The prospect of performing such an important errand for the resistance exhilarated her.

Walking with Ela into Usov, however, Celka's excitement soured into fear.

She carried a picnic basket with a bottle of wine and a paper-wrapped salami for Petr, the rezistyenti's photo-engraved plates heavy in the basket's false bottom. She'd stashed the leaflet's text in her boot sole and stitched the rezistyenti's old identification folios into her jacket lining. In theory, it would hide those treasonous materials even if she was searched. But, as the dirt road from the fairgrounds became cobblestones and Usov's stone buildings crowded close, theory seemed terrifyingly different from practice.

Celka forced slow breaths. She needed to learn how to vanish into the resistance. Today's errand was far less dangerous than being hunted by the Tayemstvoy for imbuing.

At Celka's side, Ela practically skipped, her embroidered skirts cheery next to Celka's elephant-gray trousers and simple linen blouse. Ela must suspect that this errand was about more than window shopping, but she'd avoided learning details, instead chattering about ribbons.

No matter her cousin's cheer, Celka couldn't ignore the prickling in her shoulder blades as they neared a Tayemstvoy checkpoint.

Usov's townsfolk made her feel doubly conspicuous, everyone laughing and chatting, cheerful after the circus's matinee performance and hardly even lowering their voices as they approached the barbed wire and sandbag barricades. The sky's oppressive gray, at least, fit the danger of a checkpoint in an unfamiliar town.

Sooty green and aquamarine paint brightened the doors around her, and Celka tried to shake her unease as a Tayemstvoy private waved the man ahead of her through the kill zone. The man scuttled down the maze of sandbags, glancing furtively at a soldier perched behind a machine gun turret.

Celka handed the private her identification folio just a beat behind Ela.

"We're sisters," Ela said, as sleeting cheery as everyone else. "Beauty and brawn." The soldier didn't need Ela to point out which she was supposed to be.

The Tayemstvoy private smiled at Ela—actually smiled. It made Celka's skin crawl. "I can tell," he said, and Ela giggled.

The private started to hand back Ela's folio—at least some good would come out of Ela flirting like an idiot—but he paused, the smile dropping from his face. Celka struggled to keep her own expression bland. He'd just noticed their address. *Nothing's wrong. Stay calm.*

Frowning, the private flipped to the second page of Ela's folio, checking for a travel permit. He found it—their papers were perfectly in order, the circus's route cleared by the Tayemstvoy months before the train set wheels on track. But that never stopped the red shoulders from being suspicious.

The private shouted for a superior and scrutinized Ela and Celka carefully, comparing them to their photographs.

"We're with the circus," Ela said, though the travel permit would have made that obvious. Celka didn't understand how she still sounded so carefree. This happened at practically every checkpoint, but that made it more dangerous, not less. And if the Tayemstvoy decided to search them—which they sometimes did—Celka was terrified the picnic basket's false bottom wouldn't be enough to conceal the photographic plates.

"Our family does the high wire act," Ela said as the private handed their folios to a sergeant with deep lines at the corners of her eyes that Celka would never believe came from smiling. "Are you coming to our evening show? You should—we're thunderclap."

The private seemed to struggle between flirting back and looking serious for his sergeant. Flirting finally won. It made Celka sick. She focused on the sergeant's knees. At least if she drew her truncheon to beat them to the cobbles she wouldn't smile while she did it. Unless that was where the smile lines came from. She was Tayemstvoy, after all.

Minutes crawled past and Celka grew more and more certain that the sergeant would order them searched. Finally, the woman held Celka's folio back out and jerked her chin. Celka flinched, but the sergeant turned away.

Ela slipped her arm through Celka's and winked at the private. She pulled Celka along, and Celka fell into step without really believing their fortune. All the way through the kill zone, she kept expecting a bullet in the back.

"What's gotten into you?" Ela said once they were several blocks away, alone on a narrow street.

"Nothing," Celka snapped. "What's gotten into *you*?"

"Me?" Ela shook her head. "Were you *trying* to act suspicious?"

"Says the giraffe to the camel? No one *flirts* with the Tayemstvoy."

Ela waved a dismissive hand. "He was cute."

"Tayemstvoy aren't—" Celka started to object.

"Don't pretend to be so altruistic. I saw you adding extra flourishes during practice yesterday because Evzhan was watching."

"Evzhan?" Celka said, incredulous. "That's completely different!"

"Because you're so much older and wiser?" Ela asked, rolling her eyes. Seven months older—though they obviously claimed a larger gap.

"Because Evzhan doesn't have red shoulders! Besides, he sees me like a sister."

"You're sure about that?"

Celka scowled. Why were they talking about Evzhan, anyway?

"Have you even *talked* to him this season?" Ela asked.

"We played together as kids."

"Yeah, and he's not a kid anymore." Ela waggled her eyebrows. "You may not have noticed, but he's *built*. And he *wasn't* looking at you like a sister."

Celka scrubbed her hands over her face. "You're changing the subject. You were *flirting* with the *Tayemstvoy*."

"He was *cute*."

"He had red shoulders."

"So he can't be cute?" Ela asked.

"So glad you finally understand."

"You know what your problem is?" Ela said. "You judge people. Maybe the Tayemstvoy wouldn't be so bad if people weren't so afraid of them. That boy—"

"He's not a 'boy.' He's a Tayemstvoy private and if he'd been ordered to, he would have beaten you senseless, thrown you in a cell, and raped you."

Ela flinched. "You don't know that."

"They're *twisted*, Ela. Either they start twisted or the regime twists them, but the moment they put on that uniform they're no longer some cute boy—they're the *enemy*. If he suspected what we're doing today, he'd arrest us before you could wink. *Never* forget that."

PETR THE FORGER had deft, knobby hands and wispy hair that barely covered a liver-spotted pate. Simple brass earrings high in their ears signaled Petr's neutral pronoun. Filling out false addresses on the rezistyenti's new identification folios, Petr asked, "You said there was something else?"

"Grandfather said you'd know someone who could print leaflets."

Petr's pen stilled, then they bent back over the folio. "How big are we talking?"

"As big as possible. It's from the Wolf."

The forger lifted their head, one gray eyebrow raised.

"Well, one of his lieutenants."

Petr grunted, filling in the vital statistics for the wheezing rezistyent, whose name was now, apparently, Dalibor. "It might take us a few days."

"Better for us," Celka said. A flood of resistance leaflets too close on the circus's heels could draw attention.

"You have the text?"

Celka unlaced her boot and handed Petr the photographs and handwritten page. For the first time that day, she felt something approaching her cousin's cheer. Ela wouldn't see it, of course; she was upstairs having tea with Petr's wife.

While Petr read over the leaflet, Celka slipped the image plates from the basket's false bottom.

Finished reading, they said, "Stormy skies, it's really happening."

Celka's stomach gave a little flutter. Did Petr know more about the Wolf's plan? "What's really happening?"

"The Wolf always said the Storm Gods wouldn't abandon us to an unjust regime. I thought he was blowing smoke for the common folk."

Celka tried to bury her disappointment as Petr bent over the wheezing rezistyent's old folio, carefully cutting free the photograph.

"Now I'm not saying there's anything wrong with your grandfather sending me these people," Petr said, aligning the photograph in its new folio, "but we're starting to get too much call for false papers. Our source only slips me a few blanks a month. Unless we get another source, no one'll be happy. I've seen some of the forgeries that come through—sloppy, mimeographed sheets that wouldn't fool a blind private who'd slept through training." They looked up while holding the photograph in place for the glue to set. "You tell your grandfather that."

Celka wasn't sure how many people the resistance smuggled from town to town but, over the last two years, her family had had 'travelers' more days than not. If those people couldn't get false papers, they'd be shuffled from one hiding place to another forever.

What questions would Grandfather ask? "Is it just identification folios that are the problem?"

Petr shook their head. "Ration books, travel auths. If it's got a government seal, we don't have enough."

"Do you know if other forgers are having the same problems?"

"I'll pretend you didn't ask me that."

Celka grimaced. *Stupid.* Of course they wouldn't know about other resistance cells. And she'd just revealed that she did, which put her family in more danger if the Tayemstvoy caught Petr. She sighed. Clearly she had a lot to learn. "Anything else you need?"

"Bottle of top-shelf Severnizemyen brandy wouldn't go amiss." They grinned and winked, and Celka relaxed.

"You looking to bribe a colonel?" she teased. "You know even the cheap stuff's impossible to find without shoulders covered in stars."

"Ah, to be young, my dear. You don't know what you've missed."

CHAPTER EIGHT

THUNDER CRACKED OVERHEAD, rain sheeting down on another field. Gerrit struggled to hold true-life and listen to Tesarik's exhortations about how the bozhskyeh storms had returned early to rebuild Bourshkanyan strength. Combing the colonel's words, Gerrit tried to uncover his plan—and whether Captain Vrana had stopped it.

But despite his best efforts, Tesarik's speech snapped and blurred. With every flash of Gods' Breath overhead, sousednia's alpine sunlight strengthened, becoming a physical force pressing against his mind.

"Captain Vrana"—Tesarik sneered her name like she was manure on his shiny black knee boots—"ordered you to restrict your imbuements to Category One. But to unlock the power Bourshkanya needs, you must not *hesitate*, must not *flinch*." He accentuated the words with a clenched fist. "Because Vrana taught you to cower from strength, I've ordered Sergeant Jezh's squad to fuel your combat nuzhda."

At Gerrit's side, Filip tensed, though Gerrit doubted anyone else saw it. Then metal clanked behind them, and Gerrit turned. Two more troop transports stopped on the dirt lane, and a dozen soldiers piled out, double-timing it toward them, steel helmets buckled under their chins and rifles slung over their shoulders.

Their movements, however, seemed stiff. Body armor, Gerrit realized with a start. The overlapping steel plates wouldn't stop a bullet, but they'd protect the soldiers from knife wounds and blunt impacts.

Dread settled like a live grenade in Gerrit's stomach. A dozen armored soldiers to 'fuel a combat nuzhda'? Tesarik couldn't be saying what Gerrit thought he was saying.

"You will make Bourshkanya *great* again," Tesarik said, "but only if you open yourselves to the power of the Gods. Today's exercise will continue until one of you achieves a Category Three combat imbuement."

"Category Three is too high," Captain Vrana snapped. "They—"

Tesarik drew his pistol and shot her.

Gerrit lunged toward her, but Filip caught his arm, yanking him to a stop. "Don't."

Captain Vrana straightened with a snarl and bared teeth, combat nuzhda exploding from her in sousednia as though she'd been drenched in blood.

Breath harsh in his throat, Gerrit fought to keep the

horror off his face. Tesarik had *shot* the Hero of Zlin as casually as if she was resistance scum trying to blow up a railway.

Tesarik re-holstered his pistol. "You forget yourself, Captain."

Captain Vrana pressed a hand to her shoulder where the bullet had hit. She drew a slow breath, the combat nuzhda draining from her even as blood washed down her hand. "The facts remain, Colonel." The strain clipping her otherwise impassive voice only made her more intimidating. Gerrit could suddenly imagine her during the war, a concealment imbuement allowing her to silently kill dozens of soldiers behind enemy lines before ghosting away. "I will gladly explain the situation to the Supreme-General, if you wish."

The rainwater driving down Gerrit's neck grew icy. No one *volunteered* to explain failures to the Stormhawk. If Tesarik had shot her for disagreeing, how much worse would Gerrit's father do to her? But Captain Vrana was the Hero of Zlin. Without her and Major Doubek, they would have lost the Lesnikrayen war.

Gerrit's gaze slipped past Tesarik to where Iveta stood half a pace behind him. If his sister was surprised by any of this, it didn't show.

"Now that you've created such a perfect opportunity," Captain Vrana said, turning to Hana as though her jacket wasn't soaking through with blood, "Ruzhishka can perform a healing imbuement."

"Combat, Category Three." Tesarik's lips twisted in a cruel smile. "We're through wasting time."

Something vicious and feral rippled across Captain Vrana's face before she controlled it. Gerrit struggled to keep his own expression impassive. Category Three imbuements required a hundred times more storm energy than Category One. Gerrit doubted that any mage who lost control of a Category Three imbuement would return from sousednia. Feeling like a coward, he prayed Captain Vrana wouldn't choose him for the attempt.

Several terrifying heartbeats passed before Captain Vrana nodded to Branislav. "Cadet Ademik. Make me proud."

"The exercise continues until Ademik imbues," Tesarik said, waving the others—including Jolana—to fall back. Jolana protested, but Tesarik drew his pistol again and she shut her mouth. "Or until he is fully incapacitated. *No one* will interfere."

In a pounding of boots on mud, the infantry soldiers closed on Branislav. Sickened, Gerrit backed away with the others. Against a dozen armored soldiers, Branislav couldn't win. At best, he could imbue and end the fight quickly.

Branislav must have come to the same conclusion, for his sousedni-shape sharpened, bleeding through more clearly into true-life. His sousedni-shape tracked his true-form's motions, dodging and kicking until the soldiers slammed him to the ground and Gerrit glimpsed only a churning mass of legs. Filip caught his arm, and Gerrit realized he'd stepped forward to defend his friend.

"It won't help." Filip sounded like he was trying to convince himself.

Gerrit squeezed his eyes shut, but that made the storm yank harder on his skull, sousednia slamming against his senses. Even knowing that another imbuement could drive him storm-mad, part of him yearned for Gods' Breath.

Teeth gritted, he forced his eyes open and listened to every grunt and shout and insult. If their theory was right, Gerrit could damage Branislav's chances by slipping into sousednia. So while Branislav fought the infantry squad, Gerrit fought the alpine sunlight. He had to give his friend the best possible chance to end this.

Beaten into the mud, Branislav stopped fighting, arms shielding his head from kicks. Sergeant Jezh barked something, and two soldiers dragged Branislav to his knees. Another slapped him while his squadmates screamed insults. Branislav hung limp in their holds, true-life eyes closed. Gerrit prayed that playing unconscious would buy him a few minutes' reprieve.

It didn't.

They struck Branislav twice more before Jolana screamed and sprinted across the field. She caught a soldier's arm before they could land another blow, a fluid move twisting them to the side and shattering their elbow.

At that, Gerrit cheered.

Darina joined Jolana, and they beat back the soldiers. Branislav slumped to the mud in true-life, but his sousedni-shape surged to his feet, teeth bared, fierce with concentration.

"Come on, Branislav," Gerrit called, Filip's grip still locking them both in place.

A pistol report froze everyone for half a heartbeat. "Strazh cadets, stand down." Thunder punctuated Tesarik's order, his pistol pointed at the clouds.

Darina hesitated, but Jolana ignored him, using the infantry squad's hesitation to drop another soldier with a blow from the stock of a stolen rifle.

"Get up, Branyek." Desperation clipped Jolana's voice.

Half the squad had fallen, crippled or dazed, but Jolana's attack spurred the others to greater violence.

Tesarik screamed again for Jolana and Darina to stand down, but the remaining soldiers closed on them. The two strazh cadets fought desperately, back-to-back. But outnumbered three to one and unarmored, their superior training couldn't save them.

Filip's grip tightened, and Gerrit didn't know which of them his strazh meant to restrain. A violet protection nuzhda rippled his sousednia heat-shimmer. In true-life, his weight had shifted to the balls of his feet, dark eyes intent on the fight.

With a sharp cry, Jolana fell beneath the soldiers' blows.

Just like Gerrit's mother had fallen.

Rope bit into Gerrit's wrists in an echo of the memory he used to pull against combat. But he *wasn't* pulling against combat. He *couldn't* slip into sousednia.

Branislav, abandoned by the infantry squad, lay crumpled in true-life's mud while his sousedni-shape spread his arms, crimson combat nuzhda oozing over him.

Someone slammed a rifle stock across Darina's face, and she dropped. Hana stifled a cry and stumbled two steps forward before stopping herself, hands balled into fists.

Gerrit expected the soldiers to return to Branislav, but they ignored him, kicking Jolana and Darina where they lay. The air pressure seemed to change, and Gerrit smelled diesel smoke and frozen earth, incongruous with true-life's sheeting rain. His chest tightened in panic— his sousednia was combat-warped.

The soldiers in true-life no longer screamed insults. Instead, the sick crunch and thud of their boots carried across the field—across sousednia's frozen dirt road. The infantry solders blurred, becoming resistance scum kicking his mother. "No!" Gerrit screamed, struggling for control.

"The soldiers are sparking," Hana said. "We have to help!"

"You can't." Filip caught her arm. "You need to—"

"She's right." Gerrit held true-life just enough to twist free of Filip's grasp. Just as the last storm had flared his combat nuzhda, today's made the soldiers spark— amplifying their violence. "They'll kill Jolana and Darina." *They'll kill my mother.*

"You two stay back," Filip shouted as he sprinted into the fight.

Before Filip had gone three steps, Branislav roared and surged to his feet in true-life. The soldiers turned to him.

"Infantry squad, stand down!" Tesarik shouted, but they were too storm-warped to obey. He fired into the air. "Everyone, *stand down!*"

A soldier snapped a rifle to their shoulder, aiming at Branislav's chest.

Filip drew his belt knife as he ran; his throw buried the blade in the private's shoulder, just past their body armor. They fumbled their rifle before raising it again.

Filip barreled into them as they fired. The rifle report cracked the air, and Branislav fell.

"No!" Gerrit couldn't stand back any longer—storms take the risk. Hana beside him, he sprinted for his friend.

Time seemed to slow.

True-life's mud and lightning-strike ozone scent crumbled into his combat-warped sousednia's oppressive winter, the road to his family estate frozen solid beneath his boots as Gerrit ran toward his mother, toward Branislav.

In sousednia, Branislav swelled, growing twice as tall as his smoke-form attackers, skin crackling with combat nuzhda like flame. A worn donkey cart blocked the road behind him—the barrier from behind which the rezistyenti had attacked Gerrit's family motorcar.

Another step in true-life while, in sousednia, Gerrit gripped a revolver, firing at the resistance filth. The sounds formed a rhythm, brutal and cruel and... beautiful.

Gerrit stumbled, pace shifting to match the nuzhda's rhythm—the rhythm Branislav had created, which somehow echoed through Gerrit's sousednia, *changing* Gerrit's sousednia.

Gerrit refused to let the resistance hail-eaters kill his mother, refused to let them hurt his friends. Sousednia sang with combat, and he reached out, adjusting the rhythm of blows to complement his pistol fire. As his bullets struck the rezistyenti, they screamed, and Gerrit fed their voices into the weaves Branislav had begun.

Branislav raised a knife, wrapping their weaves around it.

Gerrit ran another step, but he could barely see true-life now. Oily, glowing red smoke thickened in sousednia, pulsing around Branislav as his sousedni-shape continued to warp, hot coals glowing through fissures in his skin. Their weaves were ready to be filled with storm energy. Ready to destroy—destroy a Bourshkanyan infantry squad.

Wrongness tugged at Gerrit. He'd missed something.

His chest constricted. True-life. He shouldn't be in sousednia. The sharp *phap-phap* of gunfire as he shot the resistance scum threatened to drag the thought from his mind. He struggled to concentrate. Branislav's sousedni-shape had warped—which meant he wasn't holding true-life at all. If Branislav called the storm now, it would drive him mad.

Stumbling, Gerrit landed on hands and knees in true-life's mud and fought to see his best friend. "Filip!"

Jolana should have been at Branislav's side, should have wrapped him in strazh weaves to ground out all the storm energy a mage who abandoned true-life would overflow. But the soldiers had beaten Jolana into the mud.

"Filip!"—Gerrit couldn't see him, sousednia's enraged resistance fighters snarling around him—"ground Branislav!" Filip couldn't do as much as Jolana—he hadn't practiced pulling against Branislav's core nuzhda as often—but he might still save Branislav's life.

"Cadets," Captain Vrana bellowed, "full retreat!"

Gerrit strengthened his hold on true-life enough to meet Filip's gaze. "Help Branislav!"

"*Retreat!*" Captain Vrana ordered.

Filip grabbed Gerrit's arm and hauled him to his feet.

"No!" Gerrit screamed. "Help him!"

Filip only tightened his grip, dragging Gerrit away from the fight as the ground flickered between deep mud and sousednia's frozen dirt road.

Desperate, Gerrit focused on Captain Vrana, forming his words in sousednia. «*Help* him!»

«It's too late. Get out of sousednia, Kladivo. *Now.*»

«But Branislav—»

«*Now!*»

Hana stumbled past, her sousedni-shape's red skirts a mere heat-shimmer as she gripped true-life.

"No!" Gerrit couldn't abandon his friend. There had to be some way to pull Branislav back to true-life before he called the storm.

Filip dragged Gerrit back another step, but Gerrit returned to sousednia and reached for his friend's massive hand. If he could touch Branislav, somehow anchor him in true-life...

Fear made Gerrit hesitate, and Filip dragged him further away. Joint imbuements were incredibly rare.

Touching another bozhk while they channeled Gods' Breath could destroy them both, even if they were fully in control.

But if Gerrit didn't try, Branislav would go storm-mad.

Gerrit met his friend's gaze. For an instant, terror widened Branislav's eyes, the whites stark against his glowing, oilslick flesh. He reached for Gerrit's hand.

Then his fear vanished beneath the combat nuzhda's brutality. He snarled, and Gerrit flinched back.

If Captain Vrana couldn't save Branislav, what chance did Gerrit have? If he took his friend's hand, they'd both go storm-mad.

Turning to Filip's heat-shimmer, Gerrit fought back to true-life. Filip solidified, and mud squelched beneath Gerrit's chestnut knee-boots as his friend pulled him into a run. Then Gods' Breath ignited the air.

The mundane soldiers flung themselves back and away, arms up to cover their faces. Filip stumbled but kept his grip on Gerrit, dragging them away as Gods' Breath burned the taste of blood and electric current through Gerrit's tongue.

Before the soldiers could recover from their lightning-blindness, Branislav stabbed a knife between one's ribs, straight into their heart. The steel-plated vest should have stopped it, but the imbuement parted the armor like water.

As the soldier crumpled, Branislav slit another's throat, moving with uncanny speed.

A flash of Gods' Breath yanked Gerrit into sousednia. There, Branislav loomed three times his natural height, combat nuzhda glowing through his skin as he took another life.

«Branislav, stop! It's over,» Gerrit said. «They won't hurt you anymore.»

But the monster that had been his friend didn't hear him—or didn't understand.

A soldier leveled their rifle on Branislav. Before they could fire, Branislav's knife pierced their eye, sinking to its hilt. It reappeared, blood drenched, back in Branislav's hand. Someone was screaming, not yet dead. The remaining soldiers threw down their weapons and fled.

Combat-warped, Branislav scythed them down. Then he noticed Gerrit.

Gripping the knife, Branislav sprinted toward him across sousednia's snowy clearing, gusting the stench of rotting corpses.

Gerrit flung himself back, futilely trying to block as Branislav plunged the knife towards his heart. But Gerrit had helped shape the blade's imbuement; the strength of his arms would never stop it. «Branyek, no! I'm your friend!»

The knife's deadly arc didn't falter, but the air shimmered, and Filip's heat-mirage slammed Branislav to the side.

In true-life, Gerrit's boot heel caught in one of the field's furrowed rows. Stumbling, clawing back to true-life, Gerrit landed on his ass in the mud.

Filip and Branislav hit the ground together, but Filip recovered first, punching Branislav hard in the jaw. A second punch, and Branislav slumped, unconscious. The imbued knife dropped from his hand.

Gerrit stumbled to his feet while Filip pinned Branislav, shouting for restraints. Iveta sprinted over and clapped Branislav in irons.

A few meters away, Gerrit heard screaming. More distant, a soldier moaned. Gerrit dragged his attention from the olive drab lumps of wounded or dying infantry. Before Branislav had imbued, he'd been shot. Branislav first. They'd help the others if they had time.

CHAPTER NINE

THE AUDIENCE FAR below the high wire gasped, and tingly anticipation bubbled through Celka as Uncle Andrik bicycled out from the platform to begin her family's four-person pyramid finale. Their act tonight had been a perfect synchronicity of motion, winding the audience tighter with each impossible feat. Celka imagined the upturned faces below, tiny and moonlike in the dimness, waiting breathless.

A meter out from the platform, Uncle Andrik stopped pedaling, balancing on his bicycle. The bicycle had no handles and no tires, its grooved metal wheels fitting over the high wire. Demian settled a pole over Uncle Andrik's shoulders while Grandfather climbed onto his matching bicycle. The pole hooked over Grandfather's shoulders, forcing them to cycle in lock-step.

"Set," Grandfather called, and Demian released the

pole, leaving Uncle Andrik and Grandfather to balance.

Tightness gripped Celka's stomach as Demian climbed onto the pole between Grandfather and Uncle Andrik. Nothing in the world compared to performing on the wire. The frisson of danger. The thrill of a perfect step. The audience's gasps and cheers. On the wire, her family became one beautiful, unified organism of muscle and sinew and sequins.

When the Wolf called, she would have to leave all this. The thought left a sour taste that she tried to ignore.

Demian settled—one knee on the pole, his other foot planted in front—and reached out a hand. Taking it, Celka climbed onto his shoulders—step, balance, step. She crouched low and spread her arms like a hawk catching an updraft.

"Ready," she said, and Demian flowed to his feet.

With Celka perched on his shoulders, Demian hefted his balance pole and walked to the center of the pole connecting Uncle Andrik and Grandfather. The audience *aaaahed*. A little burst of applause. Celka grinned, even as pressure built behind her eyes.

The audience thought they'd seen everything. She loved the moment when they realized that the Amazing Prochazkas still had tricks up their sequined sleeves.

Ela slid a wooden chair from an earlier trick onto the pole behind Demian. The chair had a half-moon cutout on the beam connecting its two front legs and a matching cutout between the back. Those cutouts fit over the pole, but keeping the chair balanced was up to Demian and Celka.

Demian braced one foot against the chair then, with Celka still balancing on his shoulders, climbed onto the chair's seat. The world narrowed to Demian's minute shifts beneath her, to the careful sweeps of her own arms, to a play of muscles tightening in her stomach and back.

In the week since the rezistyenti had brought news of the old woman, Celka's thoughts kept turning to imbuing. Pa had explained that imbuements required supreme focus. Celka imagined it as similar to working the wire. While Demian executed the delicate maneuver of climbing onto the chair, nothing else existed. Nothing could exist or they'd fall. So instead, the world tunneled away.

Most people thought time marched at an unwavering pace, each second as long as the next. Those people had never walked the wire.

Demian planted his feet firm on the chair. Celka stayed crouched, waiting for his wobbles to dampen out.

Demian straightened. "Set."

Once Grandfather and Uncle Andrik had steadied, Grandfather spoke Celka's name. She rose to her full height, triumphant, grinning, and raised her arms overhead.

The audience gasped. Some cheered. Others, afraid to break the spell, waited while Grandfather called them into motion.

With each turn of bicycle wheels, they inched further across the ten meter gap separating the two platforms. The triumph of standing upright on Demian's shoulders narrowed into supreme focus. The audience vanished, Celka's attention settling within her body.

A distant buzzing rose in her mind. She blocked it, but holding her balance grew increasingly difficult, something tugging on her focus, threatening to shatter her attention.

Suddenly, pain knifed her temples. Crying out, Celka pressed her hands to her head.

The motion rippled to Demian. He grunted, struggling to dampen their motion before it flung the chair from its pole or threw Grandfather and Uncle Andrik from their seats.

"Halt!" Grandfather called.

Celka shot her arms out to her sides, stomach flipping in panic. Pain burned behind her eyes, and she panted harsh breaths, horribly, viscerally aware of the yawning chasm below the wire. A twelve-meter fall.

Ma had described the helpless horror, knowing that nothing you could do would prevent impact.

Celka could break her neck. Her back. She could survive only to find Grandfather, Uncle Andrik, and Demian all paralyzed or dead.

"*Focusfocusfocus.*" She fought for the balance that had come so effortlessly before. Crackling sounded in her ears like static at the end of a phonograph record. Then thunder cracked, and the spotlights winked out.

In darkness, a terrified animal noise escaped Celka's throat. Fire arced down her spine, and something jerked against the base of her skull.

"Everyone calm." Grandfather spoke with unshakable

gravitas. "You don't need your eyes. Trust your bodies." Strain sounded in his voice. Strain but not fear. "Relax. Breathe."

The lights blinked back on and the audience cried out. Celka couldn't spare the attention to imagine how they must look, how close to disaster.

"Breathe," Grandfather said.

Breathe.

Celka managed to loosen her knees, to dampen some of her motion. Demian swore beneath the sudden hiss of rain on the big top's canvas. Pain still splintered her senses.

She'd gotten headaches before, but never like this. Recently, some afternoons she'd felt pressure behind her eyes and little shocks twinging down her spine—but never before this all-consuming fire.

The storm playing havoc with the circus's lights was bad enough, why...? The storm.

A flash lit the circus tent red-gold. Time seemed to stop. Gods' Breath. Panic gripped her. She'd never imagined a bozhskyeh storm's pull would be so powerful. How could she balance through this?

Touch sousednia. Pa's voice sounded so clearly that she gasped, expecting to find him on the platform ahead. But only Aunt Benedikta waited there, brow furrowed, hand extended as though she could bridge the remaining four meters and pull them all to safety.

Four meters. They wouldn't make it.

Touch sousednia.

Finally, Pa's words penetrated. Dragging in a shuddery

breath, Celka reached for that deep part of her mind.

True-life snapped like a bubble bursting.

Her stomach twisted—the tight, somersaulting feeling like slipping on the wire—and reality shifted, distorted as though through a funhouse mirror. In sousednia, Celka stood alone in the center of a different high wire, spotlights bright, wire stretching into darkness ahead and behind. No family, no balance pole, not even a paper fan to stabilize her. Placing one foot in front of the other, Celka walked alone.

If she moved like that in true-life, she would plummet to her death. She would kill Demian, Uncle Andrik, and Grandfather.

She couldn't do this.

You can. Pa's voice. *You're strong.*

Stretching her arms to the sides, Celka sought stillness, straining to feel the true-life solidity of Demian's shoulders beneath her feet.

As those sensations dripped into sousednia, her desperation took on a strange resonance, thickening the air as if she stood in choking summer humidity. She would fall. The certainty terrified her, but the terror flowed from her, building into a buzzing numbness that spread outward from her fingertips.

She refused to fall. If she held a balance pole, she would not fall.

The buzzing in her hands coalesced into the smooth wood of a five-meter-long balance pole. The scents around her warped into the comfort of a wood fire on a cold winter's day, and the storm yanked against her spine.

With sudden understanding, she realized she was shaping an imbuement.

«No!» Celka focused all her will on seeing her hands empty. She didn't *need* anything. She'd performed this pyramid hundreds of times safely.

She couldn't imbue. Not in front of hundreds of spectators. Not when she didn't know what she was doing. Her family barely balanced as it was; if lightning struck, they would surely fall. And if the magic protected them, the Tayemstvoy would arrest them all.

Celka refused to let the State pervert the magic in her blood.

With that conviction, Pa's lessons filtered through. To imbue required a nuzhda's desperate need. Thus, ignoring a storm must require the opposite.

She didn't need magic to complete this act. She needed her muscles, she needed her mind.

Pain still knifed her temples, and true-life overlapped sousednia like a moving picture double-exposed, but Celka refused to give in. Grandfather was right—she didn't need her eyes. She knew Demian's motions like her own. Eyes squeezed shut, breath scraping her throat raw, she blotted everything else out and clung to balance.

Then the motion of Demian's shoulders changed. A hand caught her arm, grip fierce, and Aunt Benedikta snapped at her to climb down. The platform's metal grating pressed against her slippered feet and Celka mimicked her family's flourishing bows.

In true-life, applause roared over the hiss of rain before drowning in thunder.

Grandfather gripped Celka's shoulder. "You will claim illness and fake a limp."

On the ground, Ms. Vesely, the circus manager, met them, heart-shaped face lined with concern. Lieutenant Svoboda, the circus's Tayemstvoy liaison, flanked her. Svoboda wore the haughty suspicion that came standard with the secret police.

"What happened?" Ms. Vesely asked.

Grandfather crossed his arms and tipped his head to Celka.

"It's my fault." Clinging to true-life, she put a hand to her abdomen. "I had really bad cramps. They came on so sudden..."

"Celka twisted her ankle during our dismount." Even admitting mistakes, Grandfather spoke with unshakable gravitas. "We will remove her from the act until she recovers."

Celka's throat tightened. Surely he only meant for a day or two while her supposed injury healed?

Ms. Vesely touched Celka's shoulder, sympathetic, then hurried off. Her retreating back blurred as lightning flashed.

"Hey, Celka, let me help, all right?" Demian startled her, putting his arm around her back. "You want to lean on me?"

Following Demian's significant glance, Celka found Lieutenant Svoboda watching her, lips puckered like she chewed a lemon.

Celka flung her arm over Demian's shoulders, breath stuttering. Did the woman suspect?

As Celka limped toward the performers' entrance, time stretched and blurred, twisting into the habitual motions of changing out of costumes and riding wagons back to the railyard. Celka's family surrounded her, Ela chattering, Aunt Benedikta complaining. Trusting her family to attend to true-life, Celka struggled to need nothing. Hours passed.

Like waking from a dream, the bozhskyeh storm's tug on her spine faded. She smelled soap and a thunderstorm's freshness, heard the *clack-clack*, *clack-clack* of wheels on track. She lay in her bunk, the railcar swaying the rhythm that had soothed her since childhood.

Celka's bunk sagged as someone sat on the edge. She jerked upright.

"Quiet, now." The train's clacking nearly swallowed Grandfather's voice. "You're safe." Moonlight glinted off his eyes and flashed silver in his hair.

"Welcome back," Demian said.

Ela slipped down off her bunk and crawled in next to Celka, shoulder-to-shoulder, fingers twining with hers. Shadows flickered as the circus train chuffed through forest.

Celka's disorientation crumbled into exhaustion. Tears pricked her eyes, her muscles shuddery like she'd been practicing on the wire for hours. When she could make her voice work, she said, "I'm fine." But the words came out small, and even Aunt Benedikta patted her knee.

Silence fell, and she imagined her family all thinking the same thing. Everyone fell during practice—you didn't improve or learn new tricks unless you fell. Almost falling during a performance was another animal entirely.

"I can skip performances on Storm Days," Celka whispered. "We can check the weather forecasts. It'll be safe."

"You think the Tayemstvoy won't notice the giraffe amongst the horses?" Aunt Benedikta said. "I won't have her up there risking our lives."

"Celka will not perform until she demonstrates control," Grandfather said, an edge to his voice. "Scripture shows that to be possible."

"Sleet-cursed storm blood," Aunt Benedikta said.

Uncle Andrik laid a quelling hand on her arm.

"Her storm blood saved us the other day," Demian said.

"And nearly killed you tonight." Aunt Benedikta caught Celka's shoulders. "Your father was mad, you hear me? When he learned the bozhskyeh storms were returning, he wanted to imbue. Your mother *never* should have let him teach you those things."

Celka shrunk away. "I don't know how to block the storms." She struggled to keep her voice quiet. Exhaustion made everything feel hopeless. "I almost imbued. I didn't mean to, but I couldn't control it!"

Grandfather took her hands. "Breathe, Celka."

She struggled to bring her mind and body to the state of calm focus she reached on the wire. Tonight, that control seemed impossible.

Grandfather waved the rest of the family away, gripping Celka's hands until they sat alone. "You haven't studied hard enough."

She yanked her hands free. "I have! Scripture isn't practical, it's—"

"We will study together. Did you sing the Song of Calming?"

Celka swallowed hard. It hadn't even occurred to her.

Grandfather's disappointment felt like a mule kicking her chest. "Every night, you will sing it fifty times."

"Fifty?" she said, incredulous, but Grandfather's face was stone. She squeezed her eyes shut, remembering the yawning void beneath the wire. She'd almost killed people she loved tonight. Biting her lip, she nodded. Whatever it took, she'd learn to control her storm-blessing.

CHAPTER TEN

IN TRUE-LIFE, BRANISLAV slumped against the rough stone wall of a cell beneath the Storm Guard fortress, iron collar dark against the pale skin of his throat. The collar's chain dangled slack, a few links pooling on the floor before snaking up to the anchor ring in the wall.

Four days had passed since Branislav had imbued. In the field afterwards, Hana had imbued a Category One healing bandage, repairing the gunshot wound in Branislav's thigh—for all it helped. None of the infantry soldiers had survived, and Branislav...

He'd lost true-life with his imbuement and, despite everyone's best efforts since, he was still lost to storm-madness. To Gerrit's eyes, Branislav's sousedni-shape was as sharp as his true-form, and still warped. His fissured, glowing skin and charred uniform were almost as disturbing as seeing him continually beaten by enemies that existed only in his mind.

Since returning to the Storm Guard fortress, Gerrit and the other cadets had worked in alternating shifts, strazh mages trying to pull Branislav back to himself, Gerrit and Hana speaking to him in sousednia, trying to convince Branislav that he was safe.

It had helped—a little. Branislav's sousedni-shape had shrunk down to his normal size, but he'd never acknowledged them, never stopped fighting his endless battle except for when a strazh held his attention with a combat nuzhda.

Fighting the fear that his friend was never coming back, Gerrit had decided to try something different today. He'd lifted a circus poster from their barracks, the color lithograph showing scantily clad acrobats balancing on a high wire while elephants trumpeted from the ground. The whole academy buzzed with excitement for the coming circus and its attendant leisure day. Gerrit hoped to lure Branislav back to true-life with it, and the others had agreed to play along.

"I bet there'll be giraffes and camels," Hana said, her good cheer almost believable.

"And monkeys," Darina said at Gerrit's side, tacking one corner of the poster into a chink of mortar. Fading bruises greened the ochre undertones to her light skin, but at least the swelling had mostly subsided. Bozhk doctors had healed her internal injuries, but they never wasted old imbuements on superficial damage. "Definitely monkeys."

Filip snorted. "Right, because we care about

monkeys." He nudged Branislav with his elbow. "We'll
be checking out the performers, right, Branyek?" Filip
winked at Jolana. "You think you or Jolana will find the
cutest girl?"

Jolana didn't play along. She clutched Branislav's
hand, her shoulder pressed against his, bruises still
livid against her light brown skin. She'd spent her every
waking minute with Branislav, but he'd never even
acknowledged her.

"Hey." Darina bumped Gerrit's shoulder with her
own.

He turned back to the poster, crouching to hold the
bottom corners.

"It's a good idea." She nodded to the poster. A split
lip made her mouth lopsided, and blood still stained the
white of one of her eyes.

"He probably won't even see it."

"Still," she said. "It's better."

Poster hung, Gerrit crouched at Filip's side, letting
sousednia's alpine freshness banish the cell's stink.
«Filip's right, you know,» he told Branislav. Normally,
the wind's mournful howl relaxed him, but Branislav
fell to the snow, grappling with invisible attackers, and
Gerrit's throat tightened.

Struggling to ignore the fight, Gerrit gestured over
his shoulder, trying to draw Branislav's attention to the
cell wall. «You should see the girls on the posters.» His
sousednia echoed the cell's true-life confines, boulders
rising out of his snowy clearing to form unnaturally
straight walls. But Gerrit hated feeling trapped, so he

eliminated the cell's ceiling and reduced the walls to knee-high. «If the girls dress like that in real life, it should be quite the show.» He winked, feeling awkward cajoling Branislav the way Filip would.

Branislav twisted, attention snapping past Gerrit.

«What—?» Sweeping aside the boulders, Gerrit cleared his view. Captain Vrana strode towards them, her sousedni-shape mostly transparent. Gerrit concentrated, trying to determine if she was alone. Faint, a mundane's smoke-form stirred the air at her side.

«It's all right.» Gerrit laid a hand on Branislav's arm.

Branislav surged to his feet, illusory foes momentarily forgotten.

Gerrit clawed back to true-life, hating how hard the transition had become. In the cell, Branislav still slumped against the wall. "We have company," Gerrit said just as the iron-banded door slammed open and Tesarik strode in.

Branislav snarled and lunged for the colonel, teeth bared, eyes wild. The chain around his throat stopped him short. Growling, he lunged again.

Jolana caught his arm with a wordless cry, trying to stop him from hurting himself.

Gerrit leapt between Branislav and Tesarik. "Weapons trigger him, sir. If you could remove your weapons belt outside?" He struggled to keep his tone deferential and failed.

Tesarik spared Gerrit a disdainful glance and approached just outside Branislav's reach, forcing Gerrit to jump out of his way. Branislav kept snarling and thrashing, the iron collar cutting into the healing sores on his throat. Jolana shifted her grip and Filip caught his other arm, trying to subdue him gently.

Gerrit plunged into sousednia. Branislav stood motionless, hand outstretched. A pistol coalesced in his grip, hot-coals glow snaking the dark gunmetal.

When Gerrit touched his friend's arm, Branislav's head snapped around, the sudden motion followed by complete stillness: animal, but more deadly than his motions in true-life. «There's nothing,» he said.

Hope tightened Gerrit's chest. «What do you mean?» He made his voice soft, keeping his stance unthreatening.

«Nothing!» Branislav shouted like a frustrated child. Scowling, he aimed the pistol at Tesarik's smoke-form, his head snapping up as though seeking a scent on the breeze. He shook his head and adjusted his aim. «*Nothing.*»

The details clicked. «There's no storm.»

Branislav focused back on Gerrit, jaw muscles bunching. The red beneath his broken skin flared like someone blew on embers.

«You don't need a storm.» Gerrit reached for the weapon. «You don't need a gun.» Branislav edged away, suspicious, grip on the pistol tightening. «No one's going to hurt you. Come with me back to true-life.»

Hana had slipped into sousednia while they spoke and she, too, reached out. «Come see Jolana.»

Branislav lifted his head again, sniffing the air, seeking a storm as though they hadn't spoken. «Nothing. There's nothing.»

Bile choked Gerrit's throat, and he tore himself out of sousednia before he could start screaming at his friend. Before he could grab Branislav by the shoulders and shake him. He'd done it before. It only made him worse.

In true-life's damp, cold cell, Jolana and Filip had dragged Branislav half a meter back. Fresh blood stained his skin around the collar.

Taking deep breaths that stunk of stale urine, Gerrit struggled to ground himself in true-life, fighting a shuddering hopelessness. *Branislav isn't permanently storm-mad. He'll come back.* If Gerrit told himself that enough times, maybe he'd believe it.

"He's improving, sir, as I said," Captain Vrana said, voice tight. "Though this *isn't* helping."

Twisting, Branislav sunk his teeth into Jolana's hand. She grimaced, and Branislav wrenched free.

For a fraction of a second, Gerrit thought Tesarik had moved too close. Branislav would reach him. Would take him down with teeth and nails. He imagined blood spurting, Tesarik screaming.

The chain wrenched Branislav to a stop a handsbreadth from the Tayemstvoy colonel. As Branislav snarled, Tesarik smiled. "Improving? How did this unfounded optimism serve you during the war, Captain?"

"With all due respect, sir, you can't see sousednia." Her voice was ice. Gerrit ground his teeth. Captain Vrana was one of only a handful of bozhki to survive the war, and she'd completed more field operations than anyone but Major Doubek. Tesarik had spent the war in command posts far from the front lines.

Amusement tugged at Tesarik's thin lips as Filip and Jolana got Branislav back under control. Tesarik snapped his teeth, taunting Branislav and enjoying it. "Three days, Captain. I look forward to seeing what he can do."

The cell door banged shut behind him, but Captain Vrana remained, working with Gerrit and Hana to calm Branislav from sousednia. As Tesarik strutted away, Branislav lost his grip on the colonel's sidearm. His intense seeking became desperation, then he launched into motion, dodging and punching, falling back under the assault from his combat-warped sousednia.

"Sir," Jolana said once Branislav no longer snarled in true-life, "what did the colonel mean?"

"A nearby storm is predicted in three days," Captain Vrana said.

They stared at her, no one daring to voice the question for fear of confirmation: Tesarik wanted Branislav to imbue again. While storm-mad.

"They're insane," Darina finally whispered.

No one argued.

The silence stretched to breaking before Filip said, "The infantry squad carried live rounds during Branislav's imbuement."

Gerrit frowned at his best friend, the other cadets' confusion matching his own. Captain Vrana just raised an eyebrow, inviting Filip to explain.

"Colonel Tesarik intended to escalate the violence," Filip said, hatred thickening his voice. "No matter the consequences."

Gerrit had assumed that Tesarik had made a catastrophic series of mistakes that led to Branislav's storm-madness. If it had been deliberate... He struggled for air.

Captain Vrana said, "Some historical precedents are... open to interpretation. The Stormhawk has chosen to *encourage* more powerful imbuements in the face of coming war."

Like the metallic clack of a fresh round chambering, the events beneath the bozhskyeh storm snapped into clarity. "Tesarik didn't care if one of us went storm-mad," Gerrit said. "He thought it an acceptable risk."

"I don't understand," Darina said. "Bourshkanya only has a few dozen storm-blessed bozhki. *Why* would they risk destroying one of you for a single imbuement?"

"Because they expect more." Filip clipped the words.

"The Tayemstvoy think they can manage a storm-mad imbuement mage?" Hana asked, sickened.

"The colonel is looking forward to the experiment." Captain Vrana rubbed the shoulder where Tesarik had shot her.

"The *experiment?*" Gerrit ran a hand through his hair as he realized what Captain Vrana wasn't saying. "Freezing sleet. This isn't over, is it? If half of us crack but can be managed, and half of us become more powerful..." Gerrit tasted bile. "As far as the Stormhawk's concerned, Tesarik will have strengthened Bourshkanya."

CHAPTER ELEVEN

With Grandfather's help, Celka dug deep into scripture's archaic text, combing every word for clues. A dominant theme emerged: control. Controlling needs and controlling emotions. Mundanes achieved control with Songs but, in scripture, the storm-blessed rarely sang. Grandfather argued it was so much a part of their lives that no one had recorded it, but Celka had felt a bozhskyeh storm yank on her spine. A Song, no matter how ingrained, would not have shielded her.

She'd managed some meager control by trying to need nothing, but either she wasn't doing that right or it wasn't enough.

So she combed back through Pa's teachings—even from before he'd known the bozhskyeh storms were returning. She struggled to distinguish lessons from play, but much of what he'd taught had focused on sousednia. Could the neighboring reality hold the key to control?

Scripture's passages that spoke of forming imbuements—pages Celka read secretly—described intricate sousedni-scapes and weaves of light. Before her near-fall, she had thought the language metaphorical, but the way the balance pole had coalesced from mist made her wonder whether the descriptions tried to capture something most people had no reference to understand.

Pa had taught that building an imbuement involved pulling a true-life object into sousednia and wrapping a desperate need around it. So if Celka separated her true-form and sousedni-shape, maybe it would be harder to bring anything into the neighboring reality. And sousedni-dislocations definitely required control.

But even if her theory was right, the technique wouldn't work perfectly the first time. Tricks never worked the first time. You had to practice. And practice some more. And maybe after a lot more practice you'd finally be ready to perform. Which meant Celka wouldn't be walking the high wire any time soon.

Her 'sprained ankle' bought her only a few days, so she concocted something better. Supposedly healed, she climbed the rope ladder to the high wire platform with her family. A few meters up, she froze. The near-fall had traumatized her. She couldn't perform.

The excuse had seemed brilliant, but after two days, Celka couldn't bear the pitying glances and whispers when people thought she couldn't hear. She hated how some performers watched with barely disguised glee, whispering bets as to whether she'd ruined her career.

She needed to do something. Prove she wasn't washed-up and moping.

The plan involved cherry lipstick and heavy eye makeup, a white, sleeveless blouse and wide-legged trousers drawn tight around her calves. Adding bronzing powder left her a stranger in her steamer trunk's mirror.

In the sideshow tent, the other performers eyed her when they thought she wasn't looking. Voices from the crowded midway and the sideshow's band formed a background roar, and Celka's palms sweated as she reached for Nina—a beautiful, three-meter-long python.

The sideshow's actual snake charmer had grown sick with consumption before the season began, so only her snakes were on tour, caged in the menagerie. Celka's new act would make them exotic and appealing—and all she had to do was stand with a python wrapped around her, smaller snakes at her feet. No risk of falling, no matter how a storm yanked on her.

Yet as Georgs led the first group of spectators out of the darkened illusion tent, Celka's stomach churned. Was the crowd really going to be standing close enough to touch?

Three dozen people approached, *oohing* and *aaahing* while Dobromil swallowed fire, then Georgs led them to Celka's platform. She didn't have any neat tricks, so she smiled and lifted Nina's head toward the audience while people stared at her.

Georgs launched into an invented tale of her childhood in a distant land, and Celka struggled to convince herself that the people were staring at Nina and not her. What happened when bozhki toured the sideshow? People crowded *so close*, how could another storm-blessed bozhk see her and not suspect? Almost worse than that, though, some of the spectators ogled her like she was a piece of fresh meat, already bought and paid for.

When that first group moved on, she squeezed her eyes shut in relief.

By the time Georgs led the last group out of the tent an hour later, Celka felt as drained as if she'd been practicing on the wire all afternoon. She slumped on her platform. "Sleetstorms," she said to Ivana, the sword swallower on the neighboring platform, "how do you do this every day?"

Ivana turned, eyes hard in her long face. "Not to your liking, Prochazka?"

"It's just..." Celka unwrapped Nina from around her shoulders. She hadn't expected the snake's massive weight, either. "On the high wire, everyone's so far away. They're watching, but it's different."

"Don't like being the *freak* on display?" Standing, Milan came barely to Celka's waist.

Celka winced. "No, it's just—"

"Does the attention offend your delicate sensibilities?" Ivana asked with a sneer.

Celka pulled Nina close again, like serpentine armor. She'd hardly spoken to these people before; why were they acting like her very existence insulted them?

Alesh, the 'World's Tallest Man' who stood next to Milan to accentuate their height difference, snorted.

"What is it?" Celka asked. Several illusionists had come out of their tent, and everyone stared like she was a new and disgusting specimen of bug. "What did I do?"

"Climb back on your high wire." Milan spit on the dirt at her feet.

"I can't!" Celka said. "You think I'd be here if I could just—?" She snapped her mouth shut as she realized what she was saying.

Ivana stormed past. "The sideshow isn't a fallback plan for the rest of us, Prochazka."

Celka swallowed hard. "That's not what I meant."

Ausra, an illusionist about Celka's age, glared at her, arms crossed over the bright sequins of her low-cut blouse. "Yes it is."

CHAPTER TWELVE

GERRIT CLENCHED HIS fists behind his back as a Tayemstvoy private cranked the troop transport's starter. The truck coughed black smoke and Gerrit retreated into sousednia, letting the icy air clear his lungs. Adapted to the pre-dawn gray, the sunlight blinded him, and the building storm tugged faintly against his spine.

Inside the transport—a boxy collection of boulders in Gerrit's sousednia—Hana caught his eye, Darina's wavery heat-shimmer at her side. Chained deeper in the transport, Branislav's sousedni-shape fought his eternal battle against invisible attackers.

Gerrit swallowed hard. Captain Vrana had kept Gerrit out of that transport, but he knew the reprieve wouldn't last. Gerrit's family name saved him from being a test subject, but if Branislav imbued today and Tesarik and the Storm Guard General thought this monstrous process tenable, the Stormhawk would give them leave to push as they wished. *They* had his respect.

What does your father value more, Captain Vrana had asked when they last spoke alone, *family or power?* The question could have been rhetorical.

To save his friends and himself, Gerrit needed to imbue and prove his power. But sousednia still pounded against his senses, and Gerrit couldn't risk handling enough storm energy to make something truly impressive—if he had any choice in the matter. The idea of being forced to imbue—or even being required to work with a high-Category nuzhda when he might lose control—terrified him. He didn't want to wind up like Branislav.

The transport truck's engine revved, and Gerrit snapped his attention back to his friends.

«See you soon.» Hana looked like she'd swallowed a fistful of bullets.

«Come back in one piece,» Gerrit said.

Grim, she nodded.

«You, too, Branislav.» Gerrit tried to sound like he believed it possible.

Branislav's head jerked around. «What?»

«Branyck?» Hana grabbed his hand in sousednia. Branislav flinched then searched her expression, panicked desperation replaced by confusion.

Gerrit's throat tightened. «Branislav?»

The transport lurched into motion, and Branislav twitched, lips skinning back from his teeth. Then he squeezed his eyes shut and focused back on Gerrit. «No.»

«Branislav!» Gerrit stepped towards him, turning the step into a run in sousednia as the truck accelerated toward the fortress' outer wall. Pain split his temples at the sousedni-dislocation, and he snapped back, sousedni-shape slapping into his true-form. It left him gasping like he'd been kicked in the chest.

In true-life, Gerrit tightened his fists until his knuckles ached, holding himself motionless. Captain Vrana stood nearby; she would have seen as well as he had. If she couldn't help, nothing Gerrit could do would get Branislav out of this storm.

Just before the transport passed out of the fortress, Branislav lifted a hand in solemn farewell.

Gerrit's throat closed off.

Behind him, Captain Vrana ordered Filip to escort Jolana back to barracks. Jolana should have been in that troop transport, too. But Tesarik didn't want anyone getting in the way.

If it weren't for Hana and Darina going out in the storm, Gerrit would have prayed for Branislav to trigger a madness cascade, pulling so much storm energy that it leapt even to the mundanes, destroying them all.

Tesarik was playing with fire. Gerrit prayed it immolated him—before it could burn Bourshkanya's every storm-blessed mage.

Captain Vrana's sousedni-shape solidified at his side, and Gerrit struggled to make his expression flat. «Does it get any easier, sir?»

«Does what get easier?» she asked.

«Losing your friends.»

She said nothing, but the set to her jaw gave answer enough.

«How did you keep going?» he asked.

«During the war we had a clear enemy. We fought to keep the Lesnikrayens from overrunning our homes.»

Gerrit kicked at sousednia's snow. None of that helped him.

«During the war,» she said, «our role as bozhki... changed. Many of us put on our uniforms voluntarily. We expected to take them back off.»

Gerrit turned from the empty switchbacks, surprised that the Hero of Zlin—someone the cadets joked didn't even *own* civilian clothes—might not be wearing her uniform by choice.

«But the Stormhawk needed to consolidate his power. We became a part of that.» Her gaze stayed distant for a moment, then she turned to Gerrit. «If you'd been born during the last storm-cycle, no one would force you to salute mundanes who have no concept of what you risk beneath a bozhskyeh storm.»

«Sir.» He made his tone warning and glanced over his shoulder. Only storm-blessed bozhki could see sousednia—or, in theory, overhear them—but the Tayemstvoy had ears where you'd swear they didn't.

Captain Vrana waited until he met her gaze. He expected her to dissemble, to say she was tired and didn't mean it. Freezing sleet, how could the Hero of Zlin criticize the regime?

Instead, Captain Vrana said, «If the Tayemstvoy force you to imbue—even if you hold true-life—it will leave you forever on the knife's edge of madness. They want this. Fragile imbuement mages, easily controlled, who build weapons for the regime.» She laid a hand on his shoulder. «You could be so much more, Gerrit.»

Her touch was as unexpected as his given name, and emotion thrashed beneath the dark water of his mind. «How?» His voice came out small.

«They may have trained you to salute instinctively, but you're more like your mother than you realize.»

The air went out of Gerrit's lungs, and he fought to keep his face emotionless.

«She and I were friends from childhood,» Captain Vrana said.

His eyes burned. Sousednia's fresh snow darkened into an icy dirt road stained with blood.

At the end of that fight, Gerrit had held his mother as she gasped for breath, her skin gray where it wasn't stained with blood. He'd screamed for help until his throat was raw, but it had arrived too late.

Don't become like them, his mother had whispered, so faint he had to press his ear to her lips. *Never become like them.*

Captain Vrana gripped Gerrit's shoulder, shaking him free of the memory, snapping sousednia back to alpine brightness. He flinched; he hadn't kept the grief off his face. Instead of smearing his face in that weakness, she said, «She would be proud of you.»

Anger tightened his jaw, and he gave it free reign to banish his fear. «The resistance *murdered* her. I'll make her proud when they're nothing but ash.»

«The resistance didn't kill her.» Captain Vrana's whisper was so at odds with her usual confident command.

«I was there. I held her as she died.»

«I know.» He strained to hear, leaning closer despite his revulsion. «But the attackers weren't resistance. They were Tayemstvoy.»

Gerrit stumbled back. «What in sleetstorms are you talking about? The *resistance* murdered her. They wanted to abduct me. They wanted to weaken my father and destroy the regime!»

Captain Vrana's expression remained impassive, but her eyes grew sad. «The bozhskyeh storms were returning early. The Tayemstvoy wanted to ensure you could imbue weapons.»

«That's a lie!»

«You were thirteen and the bozhskyeh storms still four years off. You would have been a liability to the resistance. But you were still young enough to be—»

«The hail-eaters wanted to strike at Bourshkanya! They couldn't get to my father so they attacked *us!*»

Pain lined the corners of Captain Vrana's mouth. «After an attack on his family, no one questioned the Stormhawk tightening his grip on the State. He sent the Tayemstvoy to hunt bozhk deserters and others who'd suffered during the war—people who remembered the old Bourshkanya and might be strong enough to see its return. They arrested—»

«They arrested *traitors*.» The memory of the sleet-lickers beating his mother overwhelmed his sousednia. Combat nuzhda drove Gerrit to the balls of his feet, desperate to fight. He struggled for control. This had to be a test. Captain Vrana could not believe what she was saying. She couldn't be a traitor. «The resistance *murdered* my mother. Don't you dare blame that on the Tayemstvoy.»

«Do you remember your sousednia before?» Captain Vrana asked.

«I was weak before.»

Captain Vrana inclined her head as though he'd made her point for her. He opened his mouth to protest, but she said, «And your step-mother? Have you never questioned the favorable munitions contracts her family's factories grant the regime?»

«My father rose from tragedy and strengthened Bourshkanya.»

Captain Vrana held his gaze beneath the shadows and skeins of light snaking her sousedni-shape, face solemn, like she was waiting for him to understand a complex nuzhda weave in practicum. She waited, as though he only had to study the problem and he would understand.

He refused to understand. She spoke madness. She spoke treason.

«I knew your mother well,» Captain Vrana said. «What would she think of the red shoulders watching from every corner? What would she think of them forcing you to imbue?»

His stomach curdled. He wanted to return to true-life and scream for the Tayemstvoy to arrest her. Instead, he said, «I'm not a traitor.» Dragging himself back to true-life, he turned on heel and left her behind.

CHAPTER THIRTEEN

HUNDREDS OF METERS above the Storm Guard fortress, Gerrit sat cross-legged on a rock outcrop, gold storm pendant heavy in his hand. Lightning flickered over the plains, and the hairs on the backs of Gerrit's hand prickled as he rubbed rabbit's fur over the pendant, charging it in prayer. The prayer, however, didn't come, his worries too nebulous and churning, so he touched his finger to the metal, wincing at the spark, and began charging it again.

Scattering pebbles warned him of Filip's approach.

Gaze locked on the horizon, Gerrit clasped the storm pendant back around his throat and tucked it beneath his shirt. He didn't like anyone, even Filip, to see him in prayer. His mother had given him the pendant shortly before her death, and holding it always shook his control.

"I didn't see you at breakfast," Filip said as he stretched out next to Gerrit, battledress uniform an olive bruise on the coppery pine litter.

Evergreens screened the Storm Guard fortress' clay roofs, but circus tents sprouted like dirty mushrooms from the valley floor. By now, the other cadets would have walked into town.

No one should have been able to find him here, not after he'd slipped through underbrush and scrabbled up boulders to this perch, and Gerrit wasn't sure if he regretted the strazh bond that allowed Filip to find him, or if he was profoundly grateful for it. The bond helped ground Gerrit and gave Filip a sense for his true-life location. None of the other imbuement-strazh pairs shared such a bond, and Captain Vrana had sworn them to secrecy—the process to create the bond too dangerous for weaker mages to attempt.

As Filip reached into his satchel, Gerrit wondered if Captain Vrana had known, when she'd helped create their bond, what the Tayemstvoy would do to Bourshkanya's storm-blessed. Knowing the Tayemstvoy had murdered his mother, she must have guessed how much further they'd go.

Filip extended a cloth-wrapped bundle. "I guess even the cooks were excited about the circus."

Hunger seemed as distant as the world of elephants and acrobats, but Gerrit took the bulging napkin.

"Captain Vrana said you needed to talk," Filip said.

Gerrit unwrapped the napkin to avoid looking at his best friend. Cinnamon and cardamom wafted from the slightly smashed crescent rolls, their tops black with poppyseeds. "The cooks made loupak?"

"Couldn't let you miss loupak. Sorry they're not hot."

Gerrit folded the napkin over the sweet rolls and handed them back. A flash of distant Gods' Breath made him wince. "I'm not hungry."

Filip leaned back on his hands, refusing the loupak. Waiting.

Gerrit dipped into sousednia first, the transition as easy as rolling downhill, and swept aside true-life obstacles. He searched his sun-bright clearing, seeking bozhk heat-shimmers or mundane smoke-forms. Finding no one, he dragged himself back to true-life, satisfied they were alone. Even still, he dared only a whisper. "The 'resistance' ambush that killed my mother... the attackers were Tayemstvoy." Saying it aloud made Gerrit's chest feel hollow.

Filip stared at him in shock, then looked reflexively over his shoulder, scanning the woods as though they might be watched. "How do you—?"

"Captain Vrana told me."

"But I thought... you were there for the interrogations. You said they confessed to being resistance."

Gerrit stared back out at the sky, struggling to recall exactly what the surviving attackers had said in his presence versus what his father had told him later. "They could have been lying." The Tayemstvoy going into that attack must have known they could be captured, must have planned what to say. Their interrogators, too, could have been in on the charade.

"But someone would have found out," Filip said. "Traced their families, questioned everyone at the train station."

"Not if the same Tayemstvoy arranged the attack and carried out the investigation."

"How could they guarantee that?" Filip scrubbed a hand across his jaw. "Maybe Captain Vrana's wrong."

Gerrit wished he could believe it. "Do you remember my core nuzhda from before?"

Filip frowned. "I hadn't trained to understand core nuzhdi yet."

Gerrit waited. Filip had always watched people, had always seen deeper than most.

He sighed. "It was strengthening and preserving, mostly. Not combat, not like now."

Gerrit's throat tightened at the confirmation. Captain Vrana had been right, too, that his sousednia had changed. Before, he'd seen the back courtyard of his family estate, fountain plashing, sun washing a notebook filled with designs for horseless carriages and aeroplanes. Before the attack, he'd struggled to pull against combat. He'd hated target practice and sparring. He'd been weak. That, combined with his storm-blessing, had made him an academic, useless to the regime.

Then the Storm Guard's most sensitive instruments had detected the returning bozhskyeh storms. Two months later, the 'resistance' had attacked Gerrit and murdered his mother. Raging, Gerrit had risen in his class, pulling against combat as easy as breathing. His imbuements would help crush the resistance.

How had he never equated the timing? "The resistance shouldn't even have known the bozhskyeh storms were returning. And if they had? They couldn't hope to hold *me* for four years—my father would have turned Bourshkanya upside down. If they'd wanted an imbuement mage, they would have picked an easier target."

"Unless the resistance isn't what we think," Filip said.

Gerrit frowned, not following.

Standing, Filip paced. "What if that confession was true, but so was Captain Vrana's intel?"

"They can't both be true," Gerrit said

"Unless there's a Tayemstvoy faction in league with the resistance, trying to overthrow the regime."

Gerrit straightened, the pieces sliding into place. "Tesarik could be leading that faction. If the Storm Guard General and some well-placed officers are working with him, they could have prevented Captain Vrana from warning my father. Tesarik and the Storm Guard General are clearly trying to undercut imbuement mages' power."

"Which makes sense if they're planning a coup," Filip said.

Cold spread down Gerrit's spine from his storm-thread. "My father trusts them. He's busy governing Bourshkanya; he might not even know what they're doing here. Captain Vrana said he wouldn't protect me from Tesarik's experiments, but maybe that's because he trusts Tesarik to oversee the Storm Guard."

"All the while, Tesarik's building his own empire."

Gerrit scrubbed his hands through his hair, trying to think. "But what can we do? If Captain Vrana can't get through..."

Filip stared out at the plains. "The storm's not that far away."

Fear jolted Gerrit, followed by hope. He stood, slipping his hand into Filip's. The contact seeped calm through his panic, the forest's copper and green deepening, a jackdaw's metallic *chyak-chyak* anchoring him in true-life. "You think we could steal a motorcar? Even if I successfully imbue, the Tayemstvoy won't like it."

"Horses," Filip suggested. "Bribe one of the grooms to look the other way. It'll be easier to travel cross-country."

Gerrit closed his eyes, inhaling snow and ice and feeling his storm-thread tug against his skull. "The storm's forty, maybe fifty klicks southeast. But it's fading." He gripped Filip's hand harder, using that contact to tear free of his mountaintop. He'd trained all his life to imbue, and now the thought terrified him. Self-loathing twisted a pit in his stomach. "Besides, my hold on true-life's too weak."

Filip's calm cracked, and he turned abruptly away.

A bolt of Gods' Breath pulled Gerrit's attention back to the storm. How could he possibly escape Tesarik's schemes and imbue enough to gain his father's respect? And even if he could slip past Tesarik's net? Gerrit had spent the last week practicing transitions out of true-life and following Filip back to his core nuzhda, for all the good it had done. Sousednia still pressed against Gerrit's senses, and he had no idea how to find something in true-life that he couldn't bear to leave. Maybe if his mother were still alive—

He crushed the thought. Faced with Tayemstvoy traitors, Gerrit could not afford weakness.

When Filip turned back, he'd regained his strazh calm. "Captain Vrana told me to make sure we went to the circus. She wanted you to pay attention to the high wire act."

"She what?"

"It has to be some sort of clue," Filip said. "She must think there's something we can do."

Gerrit straightened his shoulders and drew a steadying breath. "Let's go figure it out."

On the circus midway, a band's cheery march punctuated the crowd's babble. Over a loudspeaker, a man extolled the sideshow's virtues. "In just minutes, a fearless fire-eater will extinguish a burning torch by swallowing its dancing flames! Yes, brave Bourshkanyans, he will eat fire before your very eyes!"

The midway, however, already crawled with horrors. Civilians wore their Storm Day best, bright fabrics and embroidery distracting from the uniformed Tayemstvoy prowling their midst. Gerrit scrutinized the Tayemstvoy faces, as though he'd find clues about their plot so easily. How had he never noticed how many red shoulders watched him? For every Storm Guard cadet or officer, he counted two Tayemstvoy. How many more dressed as civilians to better overhear whispered conversations?

As though summoned by the thought, Tesarik stalked through the crowd. A four-meter-high canvas poster baked in the sun behind him, showing a woman's head on a spider's body. *"Alive!"* it promised in marigold above her web.

Tesarik spotted Gerrit, and his lips twisted into a cruel smile.

As he sauntered over, Filip placed a steadying hand on Gerrit's back. "Breathe," he whispered.

The sweet smell of frying ponchiki and the heavier greasiness of sausages wafted towards them. Jungle shrieks from the menagerie cut through the crowd, inhuman and ominous.

"Enjoying yourself, Cadet?" Despite the dense crowd, a bubble opened around them; no one dared jostle a Tayemstvoy colonel.

Gerrit tried to force out a bland 'yes sir,' but the words wouldn't come. "Is Ademik hurt?" He struggled not to imagine Branislav bruised and bleeding, chained in another cell.

"Nothing that won't heal." Tesarik gave Gerrit a slow once-over, as though inspecting a shipment of cartridges the wrong caliber to fit their guns. "I've ordered his neighboring cell cleaned out. I expect it will be... occupied soon."

Ice chilled Gerrit's veins. Branislav must have imbued, must have proved to Tesarik's satisfaction that storm-mad mages could be managed. "Did Ruzhishka imbue?" He fought to feign a cold detachment as he imagined Hana snarling at the end of a chain.

Tesarik brushed imaginary dust from his immaculate sleeve. "Ademik achieved a Category Seven combat imbuement. The Stormhawk is most pleased."

Gerrit had never even *seen* a Category Seven imbuement. How had they tortured Branislav to force that? What demon would he see if he touched sousednia near his friend? "And Ruzhishka?"

Tesarik stepped so their chests nearly touched. Lowering his voice so Gerrit had to strain to hear, he said, "Another storm is predicted in two days. I expect you're anxious to serve the State, little Kladivo."

The Tayemstvoy colonel turned away, taking two steps before pausing. People started to edge around Gerrit, but he waited, motionless. Tesarik was baiting him.

Tesarik turned back, and people skittered away like cockroaches. Tesarik met Gerrit's gaze and held it, waiting for Gerrit to break. Sweat slid down Gerrit's back, cold despite the glaring sun. He held Tesarik's stare, refusing to look away. Tesarik might cheer at driving him storm-mad, but Gerrit would uncover his plans, would find some way to stop him before he could destroy the regime.

"Your father sends his regards." Tesarik smiled. "He's looking forward to seeing what you can do when... motivated."

Hands fisting at his sides, Gerrit watched Tesarik disappear into the crowd.

"Step right up, brave Bourshkanyans!" A cheery voice called from kilometers away. "Don't miss a spectacle that will amaze and astonish!"

Heavy clouds bulked overhead, blocking the midway's sunshine, and the sound of blows drowned the band. As Gerrit's combat nuzhda swelled, the need to wrap his hands around Tesarik's throat overwhelmed his awareness of the crowd. He reached out with his thoughts, seeking the storm that had faded into vague, distant rumblings. Tesarik thought himself untouchable. See how smug he'd be with Gerrit's imbued blade in his back.

"Gerrit, the storm's gone." Filip's touch on his cheek startled him. The gold bozhk lightning bolts on Filip's collar glinted too bright for sousednia's heavy overcast. "They're talking about a snake charmer now, and a band is playing. It smells like sweat and dirty fry oil."

Gerrit concentrated on his best friend's words, teasing those sensations out from his memory of the icy road. As the crowd began to resolve, Gerrit regained control of his sousednia and shredded his combat nuzhda. His sinuses burned, his ears popping as sousednia changed and sunlight seared over his mountaintop once more.

Following Filip's touch back to true-life, Gerrit scrubbed his hands over his face, weak and shaky without the combat nuzhda. "Freezing sleet," he muttered.

"I take it that wasn't intentional." Filip's wry voice chased away the nuzhda's last echoes.

Gerrit shook his head, focusing past Filip to check whether Tesarik had seen. Watching Gerrit lose control would make the hail-eater's day.

"This is what he wants," Filip said. "He's baiting you."

"We need to find out if Hana imbued."

"Does it matter?" Filip asked.

Gerrit swept the crowd, the Tayemstvoy dark bruises backed by posters of slender acrobats hanging by their hair and precarious pyramids of tumblers. "It might." If Hana had imbued something powerful—not Category Seven, but at least Two or Three—then it shouldn't take many storms for him, either. If he could imbue with control, his father would respect him, listen to him when he explained Tesarik's plot.

He balled one hand in a fist, frustrated to come so close and still see no solution. How could he imbue on his own terms?

"Find out if Hana imbued." Gerrit gripped Filip's arm. "Make sure she's all right. I'm going to look for clues."

THE ROUND OF gawkers moved on, and Celka sat, adjusting Nina to relieve a cramp in her shoulder. She squeezed her eyes shut. The afternoon sideshow was almost over. She'd survived almost half the day in Solnitse with uniformed Storm Guard and Tayemstvoy peppering the crowd like mold on bread.

Her hands tightened into fists at the thought, and her breath quickened, ready to fight. She struggled to loosen her fingers, to stroke Nina's scales and match her breathing to the Song of Calming. The storm had finally passed, her tide of rage and violence diminishing.

She hadn't expected her technique to work perfectly today, but she'd expected *some* progress. Sousedni-dislocations required control, for sleet's sake—but apparently they didn't *give* her any. Normally she could crush down her hatred of the Tayemstvoy when she saw them, but the nearby bozhskyeh storm had flared it like wind on a grassfire. They'd taken Pa, tortured him and might be torturing him still, and she wanted to kill them all. When those thoughts slipped through her mind, her gaze locked on a pistol or a knife, and the object bled into sousednia. Her fingers itched to reach for Gods' Breath. Several times, she'd almost convinced herself to try, rage overriding reason.

If the storm had been directly overhead, she wasn't sure she could have resisted.

She was missing something. This puzzle had to have a solution.

"Hi." The voice, close by Celka's platform, made her jump.

She noticed the uniform first and forgot to breathe. They'd found her. They'd realized what she was.

No. Dragging in a slow breath, she pasted on a smile.

The uniform's polished brass buttons and gold braid gleamed despite the sideshow tent's weak light. Gold lightning bolts adorned the uniform's collar, marking a highly trained and skilled bozhk. Combined with the four open gold pips on each shoulder, she faced a senior Storm Guard cadet.

Celka forced her gaze to the mage's face even as her heart sped to a terrified patter. As if the uniform's buttery-soft wool and impeccable tailoring weren't enough of a clue, the bozhk wore a single lightning bolt earring of diamond and gold. The earring had to be worth more than most houses, though its wearer was around her own age—eighteen, tops. He was tall and pale, shimmering with sousednia bleed-through, and the intensity in his golden brown eyes seemed to pull her in.

She had to get out of here.

Instead, she made herself pick her way towards him around the smaller snakes. *Just an ordinary circus performer.* "Did you want to buy a postcard?" Celka struggled to keep her tone light.

"What?" he asked.

She pointed at the souvenir postcards she'd had printed: a sepia-toned photograph of her in costume, Nina wrapping her waist. "Only ten myedyen." She held a postcard out, innocent.

"Oh," he said. "Sure." He fished in a pocket and pulled out a silver striber, worth a hundred copper myedyen.

"I don't have change." Celka spoke the expected lie.

He shrugged and held out the striber. Celka took it, her fingers brushing his.

A jolt like an electric shock burst up her arm and, for an instant, the boy stood on her high wire platform in sousednia. Instead of his tailored dress uniform, he wore rugged olive trousers and a short-sleeved undershirt that showed off the lean, whipcord muscles of his arms.

Celka recoiled, tearing free of sousednia. She met his gaze with wide eyes. He straightened, surprised, but something in his expression suggested he'd expected her reaction.

"Who are you?" he asked, calm—too calm.

Celka swallowed, her throat dry. Nina lashed her head back and forth, reacting to her fear.

The boy wasn't just Storm Guard, he was an imbuement mage. And he'd seen her in sousednia.

"Gema Alatas." She tried to give her sideshow name like nothing had happened, but her voice shook. "Here's your postcard." She held it by the edge, careful not to touch him.

The boy took the card, still studying her. "What are—?"

"Gerrit," another Storm Guard cadet hurried up to him, "we need to talk." The new cadet's dress uniform looked rumpled, gold bozhk bolts and russet knee-boots not as shiny as the boy's. Instead of a regular bozhk heat-shimmer, the newcomer appeared double-exposed, and when Celka shifted her focus, she found them wearing fine embroidered skirts and a brilliant pair of earrings dangling with precious stones.

Another imbuement mage. Celka squeezed her eyes shut and sent a silent prayer to the Storm Gods. Maybe today they'd deign to listen.

"You're all right?" Gerrit looked the new imbuement mage over. He sounded relieved.

"I wouldn't go that far." She caught Gerrit's arm, ignoring Celka like she didn't exist. "You have to talk to your father."

Gerrit recoiled.

"Please, you have to do something."

Gerrit glanced up at Celka, but he looked distracted now, frustrated. She smiled wanly and turned away, crouching to pick up one of the smaller snakes. She held her breath, praying he would go away and decide that he'd imagined the flash of her in sousednia. She clung to true-life with every fiber of her being, weakening her sousedni-shape as much as possible. *Just a normal girl. Nothing to see here.*

"Did you imbue?" Gerrit asked the other Storm Guard cadet.

She sighed. "A stable Category Three healing bandage. I reattached an infantry soldier's leg."

"Storm Gods, Hana..." Taking the girl's arm, Gerrit led her away, saying something that Celka couldn't hear.

"They chained him to a field gun," Hana's voice faded as they moved away, "had a squad use him for target practice..."

"Wax bullets," Hana said, "but still."

"How is he?" Gerrit led Hana toward the crowd around a fire-eater, now holding a flaming torch over their open mouth. He didn't want her to notice the snake charmer's sousedni-shape, though the girl held true-life strongly now. If he needed further proof that she was trained, he had it. He'd never seen anyone but Captain Vrana retreat so quickly from sousednia.

"Your sister carried a sniper rifle loaded with tranquilizer darts," Hana said. "She shot him as soon as the Gods' Breath faded."

"Did it stop him from firing?" He didn't have much hope. Hana had reattached a leg, after all.

"He fired once, simultaneous with the imbuement."

Gerrit's stomach twisted. "Has anyone tried to activate it? *Can* anyone activate it?"

"I don't know," Hana said. The largest historical imbuement they'd worked with had been Category Five. Each category was ten times as strong as the one below. When Gerrit had activated the historic Category Five sword, he'd nearly run Filip through just because his best friend had approached too aggressively. Holding that nuzhda for five minutes had left him belligerent for days. Pulling against combat hard enough to activate a Category Seven imbuement, even long enough to fire once, would probably break most mages.

He forced the worry aside. Unless he came up with some way to outsmart Tesarik's Tayemstvoy faction, Branislav wouldn't be the only one imbuing objects as dangerous to bozhki as they were to the enemy.

"Has Branyek come to?" he asked.

"In the cell." Her voice was tight.

"And?"

Hana's lips pressed thin as she shook her head. "He's not coming back."

"Did they let Jolana—?"

"They're keeping her away. Tesarik rescinded all our access."

Gerrit locked down the urge to run screaming to the Storm Guard fortress' dungeon, to fight and bully his way through to see his friend. *He's not your friend anymore. Branislav's gone.*

Dark, slippery fear tunneled his vision. Unless he came

up with a plan, he could be next.

If the Tayemstvoy force you to imbue, it will leave you forever on the knife's edge of madness. Captain Vrana's words echoed through the churning darkness. *You could be so much more.*

"No," he said.

"No, what?" Hana asked.

Gerrit turned. He hadn't meant to speak out loud. "I won't let them do this."

He stole a glance back at the snake charmer. Their eyes met and she looked hurriedly away.

Captain Vrana had sent him to the circus, had wanted him to pay attention to the high wire act. He'd assumed she meant the literal act, but the snake girl's sousedni-shape had stood in a costume of glittering sequins, her feet in a perfect line, balancing like she stood on a wire. She was a trained storm-blessed bozhk who didn't wear bolts—and she was here, in the circus, not in imbuement training in the Storm Guard fortress.

When the bozhskyeh storms had been confirmed, the State had recalled all storm-blessed bozhki for intensive imbuement training. For the snake charmer to still be performing, it meant the State didn't know about her; meant she'd hidden her abilities. But all school children were tested for storm-affinities; she couldn't have escaped unless she had help. And who better to help than the Tayemstvoy?

"Captain Vrana asked me to give you this." Hana held out a sealed envelope.

Frowning, Gerrit tore it open.

Do what you have to. We'll buy you time.

The note was unsigned, written in stilted block letters that wouldn't give away the sender.

"There's something on the back, too," Hana said.

Gerrit flipped it over. Printed much smaller, *How did they know where to ambush you?* He frowned, not understanding. He'd figure it out later. What mattered now was that Captain Vrana would buy him time. *If* he could figure out a plan.

"What is it?" Hana asked.

Gerrit crumpled the page in his fist, mind racing. "I'm not sure yet." But one thing he knew: he was through clicking his bootheels and saluting traitorous red shoulders.

CHAPTER FOURTEEN

AFTER THE EVENING sideshow, Celka returned to the snake trailer, a cage of small snakes in each hand, Nina wrapped around her shoulders. Shadows sliced the back lot, and every time a bird flitted between trailers or a rabbit startled from beneath a bush, Celka flinched.

Exhaustion weighed her down, but the imbuement mages hadn't returned. No one had arrested her.

Maybe Gerrit hadn't realized what she was—he could have thought she was just a poorly trained bozhk who liked snakes and was willing to be ogled for a few myedyen, even though mere copper bolts could get her a well-paid job in one of the big cities. Or maybe he didn't know that the State had recently rounded up everyone with a storm-blessing. Or maybe he secretly supported the resistance and had decided not to turn her in. She wished she could believe it.

Her boots clunked on the snake trailer's wooden stairs, and Celka swung the door open, wrinkling her nose at the stink of mouse droppings and the earthy, musky smell that she couldn't scrub from some of the smaller snake cages. At least Nina didn't stink.

Over the big top band's bright trumpeting came shouts and laughter as roustabouts struck the sideshow tent and moved the menagerie animals back into their trailers. In an hour or two, one of the teamsters would hitch a pair of horses to the snake trailer and pull it to the railyard to be loaded onto a flatbed railcar for its jaunt to the next town. The circus was a major event, and businesses shut down for people to attend. But even in wealthy towns like Solnitse, the circus typically stayed only a day. After today's terror, Celka was profoundly grateful that she wouldn't face Solnitse's bozhki for another year.

Normally, after returning the snakes to their cages, Celka worked through sousedni-dislocations until she couldn't see straight for the pain. Once her headache ebbed, she returned to the dressing tent to study scripture and practice her resistance mnemonics until her family finished their performance.

Tonight, exhaustion made her want to cry. She wanted to curl up in bed.

She wanted to be safe.

Nauseous with fear, she hadn't eaten anything since arriving in Solnitse. Though she'd made it the whole day without anyone shouting for the Tayemstvoy, she couldn't shake a cold, crawling feeling on the back of her neck—like she was being watched.

As she latched the last snake cage, the *crump* of a boot in snow startled her. Heart hammering, she looked around. Snow? She must be imagining things. The fairground was mud and weeds.

Another crunch sounded, closer. Another. Like footsteps breaking a thin crust of ice.

Celka plunged into sousednia. Beneath her illusory big top, a breeze tickled Celka's cheeks, cold where the big top should be hot from the summer sun.

She swept aside true-life's echoes and inhaled deeply, searching for nuzhdi that didn't belong. The chill breeze carried a hint of pine resin and a smoky, chemical smell that made her think of soldiers. In the darkness beyond her spotlight, a bluish glow hinted at the shape of a person. If not for her sousednia's darkness, she would never have seen it. The figure was tall and thin—and headed straight for her. The imbuement mage, Gerrit.

Panic tightened Celka's chest, but she clung to balance. Think. He moved slowly, placing his feet carefully, sneaking.

Except for the strange glow, she could see little of him—as though he held himself strongly in true-life. Like he didn't want her to spot him in sousednia.

Inhaling deeply, she tried to determine whether he was alone. Not knowing his core nuzhda made it difficult to tell, but the pine and battlefield scents seemed to fit together, and she didn't spot other forms nearby.

So he was alone. Why didn't matter. The fact that he'd come at all meant she was in terrible danger.

Biting her lip, Celka forced herself to concentrate on

true-life, searching for a weapon. She had Pa's imbued knife strapped to her ankle, its magical signature hidden by the sheath's own imbuement, but the Storm Guard trained its bozhki for war. She wouldn't win a fair fight.

Someone had stashed lumber against one wall, and Celka hefted a sturdy board. A glance at sousednia showed the bozhk nearing the trailer.

Celka crept to the door and opened the latch, leaving the door shut but easy to kick open. To lure the bozhk into position, Celka shaped the trailer's stairs beneath her sousednia's big top then dislocated, descending with only her sousedni-shape. With luck, he would think she'd left the trailer in true-life, and would look for her around the side, never expecting an attack from behind.

In sousednia, she willed a mirror into existence, holding it so she could see over her shoulder while not appearing to watch him. A headache needled into her temples from interpreting the two realities, but she pushed it aside. When the bozhk passed the snake trailer's steps in true-life, Celka kicked the door open.

At first, she saw only the empty back lot. He must have used an imbuement to make himself invisible. But she knew his position from sousednia and, squinting, could just make out a ripple of sousednia bleed-through. If she hadn't known where to look, she never would have spotted him.

Board gripped in both hands, she swung for the heat-shimmer's head. The board connected hard, jolting up her arms. Gerrit blinked visible and crumpled to the ground.

She raised the board for a second strike. He didn't move.

Suddenly terrified that she'd killed him, she crouched to search for a pulse. Reaching for his throat, she froze. His sousednia left a shimmering suggestion of army green trousers and a tan undershirt over his true-form, no longer glowing the imbuement's blue. She snatched her hand away. If she could see his sousedni-shape, he couldn't be dead.

Celka dropped the board and grabbed the bozhk's arms, dragging him over her shoulders. She struggled to stand with his weight across her back, stumbling her first steps before getting him balanced. Crab-walking sideways to fit through the door, she staggered into the snake trailer.

When she slid him to the floor, he took up most of the trailer's open space. She pulled the door shut and lit an oil lamp. Unlikely anyone would walk by, but better to avoid questions she couldn't answer.

She flopped the bozhk onto his stomach and gingerly touched the back of his head. A lump was already forming but—she held her fingers to the lamplight—no blood.

You just attacked a Storm Guard cadet.

She forced the panicky thought aside. She couldn't stop and think. He could regain consciousness any second.

He wore a knife at his belt. She unbuckled the sheath, setting it on a crate behind her. Grabbing a coil of rope, she tied his hands behind his back. Then she bound his ankles together. There, she found another knife.

She strapped its sheath about her left calf. Pa's knife remained a comfortable weight against her right.

Even with him lying bound, face down, Celka's stomach twisted with fear. He was Storm Guard. Not only would he have family connections high up in the regime, but the Storm Guard Academy started its bozhki young, shaping them into elite Army officers trained to fight by day and silently assassinate in darkness—or concealed by imbuements.

Imbuements. She snapped her attention back to sousednia. He'd been using an imbuement before, one that rendered him invisible in true-life.

A glow like a bright summer sky lit one of his pockets, and Celka reached in, finding a small stone pulsing with light. She slipped it into her pocket and returned to true-life.

When she rolled Gerrit onto his back, one of his jacket pockets clunked against the plank floor, heavy and metallic. She reached in, nervous to be so close to him, fingers closing on smooth, warm metal. She pulled out... handcuffs.

She dropped them, scrambling back all the way to the door.

Calm down. He's still unconscious.

Balling her hands into fists, she kicked the handcuffs toward the door. She didn't know why Gerrit had come alone, but he wouldn't have brought handcuffs unless he planned to drag her away with him.

Snatching up another length of rope, Celka tied it through a mounting bracket on the wall then dragged

Gerrit along the floor and heaved him into a sitting position. She looped the rope through the coils binding his hands and pulled it taut. Adjusting his position, she minimized the rope's slack then pulled a little harder, wrenching his hands up behind his back.

She bit her lip, wondering whether she should loosen the bonds. No. He was Storm Guard. She needed to know what he was planning. A little discomfort might make him more willing to talk.

Squeezing her eyes shut, she tried to calm her panicky breath. She'd already attacked a Storm Guard cadet. The Tayemstvoy could execute her for less. If she was digging her own grave, might as well make it a good one.

With hands confident from rigging safety lines and guy wires, Celka tied off a solid knot then reached into Gerrit's other jacket pocket. There, she found two clear glass ampoules. Each had a glass-capped needle on one end and a plunger on the other. Fear coiled in her gut. He must have intended to drug her so she couldn't scream while he dragged her away.

She released a shaky breath that was half sob.

Get a hold of yourself.

Since learning of the old woman's imbuement, she'd been training for this day. She'd never expected it so soon, but she couldn't let her own fear harm her family. Grandfather had taught her enough—she hoped—that she could get away. She dropped the ampoules into her pocket. She'd warn her family, grab her false identification papers, and vanish into Solnitse.

The panicky sob threatened to well back up. She couldn't vanish into Solnitse. The place crawled with Tayemstvoy. She'd abducted a Storm Guard cadet; worse, an imbuement mage. The Tayemstvoy would come looking for him—if they weren't already waiting outside.

She focused back on Gerrit, anger crowding aside her fear.

She wouldn't let it end like this—not while she had any hope of fighting free. Gerrit had come to her alone and she had stopped him before he could attack her. Maybe she still had a chance to escape. But to do it, she needed answers.

CHAPTER FIFTEEN

GERRIT WOKE TO water splashing his face. His stomach heaved, and he lurched to the side—jerked to a stop by his bound hands. Head spinning and stomach protesting, he tried to get his legs beneath him, but his ankles were bound and all he succeeded at was twisting further to the side. He would have fallen on his face, but the rope about his wrists wrenched him to a stop, torqueing his arms hard behind his back.

His stomach wouldn't wait.

Vomit splashed off the floorboards, sticky and hot on his face. He struggled, shoulders screaming as he heaved again and again until he spit up only a thin stream of bile. Panting harsh breaths, his mouth sour, Gerrit struggled to right himself, struggled to relieve some of the pressure on his shoulders.

He couldn't. He could barely keep his face out of his

own vomit.

Someone dragged him upright. Agony burned through his shoulders, his hands numb from the restraints. Teeth gritted, Gerrit swallowed, trying to clear the taste of bile from his mouth. Where was he?

He struggled to remember what had happened. He'd been sneaking up on the snake charmer, concealment imbuement hiding him from view. He remembered pain in his head. He'd been attacked from behind. By whom?

Careful not to move his head, Gerrit panted short breaths. Slowly, his vision cleared.

They were holding him in a small space that stunk of rats. Someone stood before him, arms crossed. Light from an oil lamp behind them shadowed their face.

"Why are you here?" they asked.

Gerrit swallowed hard, deeply regretting that he and Filip had managed to steal only a single concealment imbuement. Then again, if Filip had been at his side, they might both be tied up right now. He needed to understand what was happening and, more importantly, he needed to make sure they didn't suspect what he knew.

"Where am I?" he asked.

"*I'm* asking the questions."

He expected them to hit him. They didn't. It confused him. The Tayemstvoy took any excuse for violence. But maybe his interrogator was playing kind so the inevitable brutality would be that much worse. "Who are you?" he asked.

They grabbed the lantern and thunked it onto a crate where it would illuminate their face. The snake charmer.

She wore a faded blouse tucked into plain trousers, her brown hair pulled back in a simple ponytail. Her complexion was lighter than in the sideshow, just a little darker than his own, and her green eyes held his unflinchingly.

Gerrit couldn't believe he'd been such a fool. He'd known the girl had Tayemstvoy allies, why hadn't he expected she could best him?

"Why were you sneaking up on me?" she asked.

He tried to think fast, scrambling for a story that would end with her untying him. But she was a trained imbuement mage plotting a coup. He'd discovered her. She would never let him go alive.

"What's your name?" she asked.

"Gerrit Skala." He used his mother's family name instead of his father's—just as he had before the Storm Guard predicted the returning bozhskyeh storms. The thought gave him pause. What if Father had suspected some of the plots against him? When Gerrit was younger, the Stormhawk had required him to use his mother's family name—not that Gerrit objected, he would have chosen her name had he been allowed. But what if that order had been intended to protect him from conspirators? Gerrit had always assumed it was because the Stormhawk didn't want his name associated with his disappointing youngest son—until the bozhskyeh storms' return made Gerrit valuable.

"That's a lie." The snake charmer's voice snapped his attention back to her.

"It's not." He wiped his mouth on the shoulder of

his battledress jacket, trying to clean off the vomit. His vision smeared, his stomach spasming. Even if she'd looked at his identification folio, she should believe it— *Gerrit Skala Kladivo* was printed plain and clear; it was irregular to change your primary name without reversing the order on official documentation, but paperwork was a pain, so people did it all the time.

"Fine." She started for the door. "I'm sure my brother will be happy to beat the truth out of you."

"Wait!" He struggled up onto his knees. It didn't matter whether she believed his name, he needed to learn more before this turned into a real interrogation. His head reeled and he almost threw up again, but kneeling took some of the pressure off his hands and shoulders— though his fingers stayed numb. "Wait, please."

She turned back, suspicious. "Why?"

The plan began to pull together even as he spoke. "You're a trained imbuement mage."

"I don't know what you're talking about."

In sousednia, Gerrit sprung to his feet, grabbing the girl's shoulders. Her edges sharpened as she focused on the neighboring reality. She recoiled, but he was stronger, and he didn't let her go. «Now who's lying?» Gerrit made his voice low, threatening.

He expected her to fight, but she froze like a startled fawn.

«Who trained you?» he asked.

The girl shook her head, breathless, scared. «Let me go.»

Crushing his confusion, he snapped, «Answer the question.»

«Let me go!» She tried to twist free, punching him uselessly in the chest before he spun her around, tripping her, intending to pin her to the floor. The discomfort of a shoulder lock—even just in sousednia—might encourage her to talk.

Instead, pain cut through the sousedni-dislocation ache in his temples. Nausea overwhelmed him, and his stomach heaved.

Before Gerrit realized what was happening, he was face down in true-life, vomiting again. His shoulders screamed, rope cutting his wrists. Gasping, he managed to right himself. The snake girl gripped a stout board, raised for another blow.

Weak and shaky, Gerrit touched sousednia. As in true-life, nearly two meters separated them. He climbed to his feet, the sousedni-dislocation worsening his headache.

«Take one step and I'll knock you out again.» Seeing the set of her jaw, he believed her.

Choking down his roiling stomach, Gerrit flexed his true-life hands, trying to determine whether he could break free. His struggles had only tightened the rope. And she'd taken his knives, so he couldn't cut free. In sousednia, he clenched his fists at his sides but sunk back to his knees, reducing the discomfort from the dislocation.

"Who knows you're here?" she asked.

He struggled to reach the knot on the rope binding his wrists. Why would she lie about her training? He'd clearly seen her in sousednia. And why hadn't she fought him there? Did she still think he'd believe her an innocent civilian? "No one," he said, though Filip knew.

She drew a deep breath through her nose. "You're lying."

"I'm not, I swear." He squeezed his eyes shut, rallying for a desperate gamble. "I came to talk to you." He did his best to strip any threat from his tone. "I thought maybe you could help me."

"Why would I help you?"

"This afternoon, the friend Hana and I were talking about—he's another storm-blessed cadet. Last week, we were sent into a bozhskyeh storm. The Tayemstvoy ordered a squad of soldiers to attack my friend to 'help' him imbue. They beat him to the ground, shot him in the leg."

The girl gripped the board again, the motion reflexive. "Did he imbue?"

Gerrit nodded. "And it drove him storm-mad. They forced him to imbue again today." He let the horror into his voice. "He imbued a Category Seven field gun."

Her expression didn't change. Sleetstorms, she was hard to read. Had she known about it? How much did her Tayemstvoy allies tell her?

"That makes it the most powerful weapon in all of Bourshkanya—probably in the entire world. The Storm Guard General will push more of us to imbue. They don't care if it drives us mad."

"So why come here?"

"I was hoping to run away—with you." He put desperate belief into the words. Actually, he'd planned to question her and, if he failed to find usable intel about the Tayemstvoy-resistance conspiracy, drug her and bring her to his father. That second option was, if you looked at it just right, basically like running away with her. "You know how to hide your storm-affinity from the State, right?"

She glanced away. "I was doing pretty well until today."

"What about your instructor? Are they here, too?"

She chewed her lip, studying him in silence. He twisted his wrists again, hoping to restore circulation. It didn't work.

Finally, the girl propped her board against the wall and sat on a crate within easy reach of his belt knife. "Not anymore."

Gerrit inclined his head, hoping she'd keep talking.

"The Storm Guard found him four years ago."

What did that mean, 'the Storm Guard found him?' Had some other faction—not loyal to Tesarik and the Storm Guard General—arrested her instructor?

"Do you know if..." Her voice came out small. "Had they done that to anyone else before? Driven someone storm-mad?"

He considered it, suspicious at the change in her demeanor. She wanted him to lower his defenses before more questioning. Two could play that game. "The way Colonel Tesarik reacted... no. I think this was new." He watched for a reaction to Tesarik's name, but if she knew the Tayemstvoy colonel, she didn't show it.

"My teacher, would they have killed him?"

Gerrit struggled not to let her apparent weakness make

him underestimate her. "A wild imbuement mage..." He pretended to think about it, hoping to learn more.

"He was Storm Guard," she whispered. "He left after the war."

A deserter. A picture started to fall together: Tayemstvoy traitors seeking out the disaffected, playing on their fears of the regime to build the 'resistance.' How many former Army bozhki had the traitors recruited? And how could Gerrit uncover details of their plot?

But if Tesarik controlled enough of the Storm Guard that Captain Vrana couldn't warn Gerrit's father, then surely they could have kept their pet traitors from being arrested. Unless... could Celka's instructor have realized who he was truly working for and tried to escape? "Did he have a family?"

"A wife," she said.

"Children?" Gerrit asked.

Her eyes flashed, angry for reasons he didn't understand. "No."

Gerrit sat back on his heels, wincing as the motion reminded him of his concussion. "Did anything happen to his wife?"

"They didn't arrest her."

"Then he's probably still alive," Gerrit said. "Trying to imbue for..." He wasn't sure who to implicate. How much did this girl know about who she supported?

"He hated the Storm Guard."

Gerrit studied her in the golden lamplight, wondering if she could be so naïve. "I suspect he hated torture more."

She flinched, shook her head.

"You don't think they tortured him?" Her willful ignorance made him angry. She was jumping at the end of a traitor's leash trying to overthrow his father's regime and she thought the world was sunshine and roses? "You think whoever arrested him brought him good food in a clean jail cell and asked him *nicely* to do their bidding?"

"He wouldn't imbue for them." She didn't sound so confident anymore.

"Not to save his wife? Look," Gerrit struggled to bring the conversation back around. What he'd learned so far had only left him with more questions. "We're both hiding from the State now. You have to know what that means."

He expected her to deny it again, but she straightened, meeting his gaze. "How quickly will they look for you?"

"I made arrangements." He dropped his gaze to the floor, trying for vulnerable. "I didn't want anyone coming after me tonight."

She squinted, as though trying to read whether he was lying.

"Untie me, please," he whispered. "If you'll agree to hide me, I'll stay here." He would, until she was out of sight.

She studied him for a long moment.

"Please," he said. "I need your help."

Standing, she dug through a pile until she came up with a filthy towel. When she turned back, her gaze raked him, cold and hard. She wrapped his knife in the towel then started for the door. "Nice try, Cadet."

*　　*　　*

As soon as Celka's feet hit the muddy field, she felt a tug from sousednia.

«I'm telling the truth.» The edge in his voice reassured her—his earlier pleading had almost made her forget what he was.

She folded her arms. In sousednia, Gerrit knelt on her high-wire platform just as he'd knelt inside the snake trailer. Despite his bonds, he looked dangerous, like a crouched tiger. Caged, but only until she made the slightest mistake.

The memory of him catching her shoulders in sousednia—of how easily he'd overpowered her—made her shudder. Pa had taught her to fight, but she'd never expected anyone could move so fast.

Celka met Gerrit's gaze, keeping her expression hard. Training tigers was a mind game; you could never show fear, never turn your back. «Then tell me your name.»

«It's Gerrit—I swear by the Storm Gods. Gerrit Skala.»

His alpine scent in sousednia remained but, when he spoke his family name, it picked up a sour note, like stale urine. The stink was subtle—not a full-blown lie, maybe, but like he was trying to hide something. She wished she'd thought to check his identification papers while he was unconscious. «Enjoy your night.» With a practiced twirl, she changed directions on the high wire and started away.

«Wait. Please.»

She should walk away, make him sweat. Curiosity stopped her.

A slow spin, balancing on one foot, turned her to face him. The snake trailer's walls presented no barrier in sousednia. She said, «I could slit your throat, dump you in a ditch out in the countryside. Might be safest.» She kept a performer's face as she said it, acting like she believed the words and blowing her sousedni-cues away from him—not that he seemed to know how to use them.

His eyes widened. Good, he believed her.

In a heartbeat, cold confidence and calculating hardness replaced his fear. She expected nothing less. The Storm Guard molded its cadets to obey the Tayemstvoy and the Stormhawk. They were monsters.

Pa couldn't have become like them, could he? She crushed that hope. She couldn't hobble herself with fantasies. The Storm Guard officer who'd arrested Pa had spoken his real name and had known Celka was his daughter. That the Tayemstvoy hadn't arrested her could mean only one thing: Pa had cut a deal to save her. He'd agreed to return to the Storm Guard, to lick Tayemstvoy boots. Why else would Celka still be free?

At least that meant he was alive. In true-life, Celka laid a hand on her storm pendant, warm beneath her shirt. Somehow, she would free him. Together, they'd destroy the regime.

«Don't tell anyone I'm here.» Gerrit said it like an order.

Focus. She could worry about Pa later.

She didn't have to feign the sneer. «Thank you for your suggestion.»

Maybe the resistance could use an imbuement mage. If the Tayemstvoy could force bozhki to imbue, why couldn't the resistance? And Gerrit might know important State secrets. He kissed the Stormhawk's boots like the rest of the Storm Guard, after all. She'd talk to Grandfather. At the very least, handing Gerrit to the resistance would get him out of her snake trailer—and leave her a little safer.

«As soon as the Storm Guard realizes I'm missing, they'll turn Bourshkanya upside-down looking for me,» Gerrit said. «Breathe a word to anyone, and they're more likely to find... *me*.» The way he twisted the word made the threat clear. If they found him, he'd be sure to take her—and anyone she told—with him.

He spoke as cold and threatening as when he'd pinned her in sousednia, but the smells around him changed, his alpine battlefield scent twisting into urine and damp stone. As she focused on him, her stomach clenched and she tensed, expecting a blow.

He was afraid, desperate. Of course he was. She'd ruined his plan to hand her to the Storm Guard. He probably would have gotten a big reward. Maybe, if he'd been telling the truth about his friend, he could have gotten out of a forced imbuement—by having the Tayemstvoy force *her* to imbue.

She owed this Storm Guard cadet *nothing*. If she let him seduce her into trusting him for one second, he'd throw her to his red-shouldered friends.

CHAPTER SIXTEEN

GERRIT SAWED HIS bound hands back and forth across the sharp wire mesh edge of a small snake cage. He'd untied his ankles during the night and, legs free, kicked the cage loose from its ties.

Metal clanged in the darkness. Voices filtered in from outside.

Gerrit froze, straining to hear. The voices were muffled, indistinct. Filip? His chest tightened with hope, but the intonations were wrong. Workers? A Tayemstvoy patrol?

He struggled to quash his rising panic. Filip hadn't found him during the night. He'd known where Gerrit was headed. He should have come searching when Gerrit missed their rendezvous. Had the Tayemstvoy conspirators captured Filip, too?

More clanging, then the trailer lurched.

Gerrit's stomach lurched as well, and he swallowed his gorge. His vision blurred as the snake trailer rocked side to side then rolled down a ramp off the railcar.

Workers then, just workers.

Think. Could it be morning already? The train had stopped maybe half an hour ago, but no light seeped under the door. He'd thought he still had time. The rope binding his hands to the wall had barely begun to fray.

He had to get free and find Filip. He had to get free before the snake girl returned with a Tayemstvoy escort to beat the sleet out of him. His ruse of running from the Storm Guard wouldn't last past them looking at his identification folio.

The trailer's motion stilled, and the snort of horses joined the murmur of voices. Once his head stopped spinning, Gerrit redoubled his efforts at freeing his hands.

THOUGH GERRIT'S SOUSEDNI-SHAPE knelt motionless against the snake trailer wall, Celka opened the door warily, gripping Pa's imbued knife. She didn't like to activate it; usually she had to remember the Tayemstvoy beating Pa and dragging him away before its buzzing energy *clicked* in her mind. Today, just thinking about Gerrit attacking her in sousednia had done it.

Holding the knife active left her nerves on edge, anticipating a fight. It made her want to bury the knife preemptively in Gerrit's chest.

She resisted, studying Gerrit as he squinted into the

sunlight slanting through the open door. He knelt in the same place in true-life as on Celka's high wire platform, his arms behind his back.

She waited for him to say something. He didn't.

"Decided not to scream for help?" She dropped the metal bucket she'd carried and shrugged out of her pack. The trailer stunk worse than usual today, Gerrit's day-old vomit adding to the bouquet.

"I don't want the Tayemstvoy to find me any more than you do." His alpine scent in sousednia suggested truth, but beyond that, she couldn't read him. How many lies did that truth hide?

When the teamsters had shown up last night and Gerrit hadn't shouted for help, Celka had started thinking. She didn't trust him—an innocent desire to run from the Storm Guard wouldn't have required handcuffs and drugs—but maybe the Storm Gods had delivered him as an opportunity, one she needed to use wisely.

She didn't know how to control the storms, but this boy had been trained to do exactly that. If she asked nicely he would never answer her questions, but he'd spent the whole night tied up after a blow to the head. Grandfather talked about what the Tayemstvoy did to their prisoners. She wasn't a monster, but to get answers from one, she might borrow a few tricks.

But no matter Gerrit's potential utility, Celka suspected Grandfather wouldn't like her harboring a Storm Guard cadet—so she'd decided not to mention him. Not yet. Not until she knew how much she might learn.

After lighting an oil lamp, Celka pulled the snake

trailer door closed. Gripping Pa's knife, she approached Gerrit. He shifted to face her, and she couldn't tell if he was still tied to the wall, couldn't see whether rope still bound his ankles.

Her stomach tightened and she stopped a meter from him. "Lean forward so I can see the rope."

Gerrit leaned a little to the side, and Celka craned to see. As she did, he leapt to his feet and lunged.

She stabbed for him, but he dodged, hooking her ankle with his foot. She fell hard, the impact slapping Pa's knife from her hand. Gerrit's hobnailed boot slammed into her shoulder, then he jammed a knee up under her ribs, driving the air from her lungs. Pinned beneath his weight, she shot her hand out, reaching for Pa's knife. Gerrit's shin smashed down on her forearm. She would have cried out, but her lungs weren't working right.

"Make any noise and I'll crush your throat," he said.

Celka froze. He looked murderous. His hands were still tied behind his back, but it hadn't even slowed him down.

He held her gaze as though waiting for her to acknowledge her helplessness. How had she been so stupid as to come alone? Why had she thought she could use him? The Storm Guard trained its tigers to kill.

"I'm going to release your hand." Threat simmered beneath his measured tone. "You're going to untie my wrists."

What then? She shuddered, unable to form words.

He shifted, lifting his knee off her forearm.

She bucked beneath him, trying to twist free. He

jammed his knee hard under her ribs again, and she failed to draw breath. "Untie. My. Wrists."

She had to untie him. She couldn't.

She had no choice. Teeth gritted, she reached for his hands. The angle was painful with his weight on her. She blinked tears angrily aside. *Think, Celka, think.*

When she fumbled at the knot, he eased up.

She had to stop him from dragging her to the Storm Guard. They'd force her to imbue. They'd turn her into a monster. They'd make her like him.

Like him.

The thought gave her an idea.

Diving into sousednia, she shifted reality so that she stood next to him rather than pinned beneath his weight. When Gerrit had attacked her last night, he'd done it purely in sousednia. Celka could do more. Making a fist like Pa had taught, she brought true-life and sousednia simultaneously into focus and punched Gerrit in the face.

A PUNCH OUT of nowhere snapped Gerrit's head to the side. His vision smeared, and sousednia shattered the snake trailer's darkness. In the long seconds it took to claw back to true-life, the snake girl squirmed out from under him. She snatched up her knife and scrambled toward the door. As Gerrit faced her, the knife's Category One combat imbuement flared.

She held the knife like she knew how to use it, and fear bubbled through Gerrit's control. He beat it down.

"You can't fight me." Gerrit made his tone a deadly threat. She'd seemed frightened of him before; secret Tayemstvoy training aside, she wasn't Storm Guard.

She swallowed hard but held his gaze, knife still active.

With two steps he could close the distance. A kick would shatter her knee. She'd scream, but he couldn't help that, not with his hands bound. Her Tayemstvoy co-conspirators would come running. They might hesitate at his uniform, but if they suspected he'd uncovered their plot, they'd kill him for sure.

There had to be another solution. Could he continue his earlier ruse, just a little longer? Learn more and escape when she lowered her guard?

Fighting his panic at spending one more second bound, Gerrit dragged in a slow breath. Releasing it, he drained the threat from his posture. "It doesn't have to be like this. I wanted your help. I came to talk."

"You brought handcuffs and drugs because you wanted to *talk*? You threatened to crush my throat."

"After you gave me a concussion and tied me up!" Maybe talking to her was stupid. "You tied the bonds to be *deliberately* painful. You left me to suffer all night while you decided whether to kill me."

"I didn't—"

"*Don't* lie to me."

Her grip on the knife tightened, her muscles locked in a way that would slow her reactions. Stormy skies, could this be an act? Her knots had tightened when he struggled; surely she'd intentionally wrapped the rope to cut off the circulation in his hands. As torture went, it was easy and demoralizing, plus it made him less likely to escape.

But despite her training, she didn't actually have red shoulders. Maybe she retained a scrap of humanity. Maybe he could use that. "You're going to claim *this* wasn't deliberate?" He made himself turn so she could see his hands. A sliver of attention on sousednia, he hoped he could react fast enough if she tried to stab him in the back.

CELKA INHALED SHARPLY when she saw his hands. Blood stained the rope and crusted his skin. His fingers were swollen and blue. Stormy skies, she'd done that to him. No wonder he'd tried to get free. No wonder he'd attacked.

Gerrit turned back, violence simmering like banked coals.

"I'm sorry," Celka whispered. "I didn't..." Except she'd known. She'd tied self-tightening knots. She'd wrenched his arms up behind his back. He was Storm Guard. He was a monster.

Suddenly, that justification made her sick. Her hold on the knife's magic slipped, and she couldn't get it back. Maybe Ela had been right all along.

No—Gerrit had come to drag her to the Storm Guard. But, un-warped by the knife's combat nuzhda, Celka knew that they only stood here talking because Gerrit had decided not to kill her. Maybe that meant he really did want to escape.

And if not... she had left him bound all night and planned to deprive him of water and food until he answered her questions. She was supposed to be fighting for Bourshkanya's freedom—for what was right. What would the Wolf think if he saw her justifying torture because Gerrit wore a Storm Guard uniform? If the resistance became as bad as the Tayemstvoy, it wouldn't be victory even if they won.

Before she could talk herself out of it, Celka said, "Let me cut you free."

Gerrit hesitated, his eyes sweeping her, lighting on her knife. His jaw tensed, but he nodded once and turned his back. Every muscle in Celka's body screamed at her to run, but she forced herself to approach.

His hands looked even worse up close, blood seeping from dozens of thin cuts above the rope. Her stomach twisted further, but she refused to blubber another apology.

When the last strand of rope parted, she unwound it from his wrists—careful not to touch his skin after what had happened in the sideshow—and edged back toward the door. He turned warily to face her, rolling his shoulders. She expected him to grimace, but his expression betrayed only solemn intensity.

She wanted him to say something, even if it was just to tell her that she'd made a horrible mistake.

GERRIT FISTED HIS hands and stretched his fingers, fighting to ignore the pain of returning circulation. He hadn't expected her to free him, not in a million years. Sometimes she seemed so... genuine. His belief in her Tayemstvoy connection began to waver.

Disconcerted, he focused on her face. He needed to learn more. "How did Captain Vrana know you were here?" He flinched at his stupidity. If she told her Tayemstvoy conspirators that Captain Vrana had known—

But the girl recoiled, eyes wide. Her sousedni-shape, which had balanced with arms extended, serene on her high-wire, stumbled, her ghostly arms waving wildly as she struggled for balance.

Gerrit scrabbled to understand. "How do you know her?"

The girl's fear sublimated into anger, and she activated her imbued knife as though it was nothing. "She must have promised him—to force him to work for the State—she must have *promised* to leave me alone. But if she sent *you*, she's not technically breaking her word."

"What are you talking about?" Gerrit said.

"My teacher. Vrana arrested my teacher."

"That can't be."

"What, you want me to describe it, you red-shouldered boot-licker? You like hearing people scream?"

Gerrit raised his hands, defensive. He didn't understand the girl's rage, didn't understand how Captain Vrana could have anything to do with her teacher's arrest. "I don't know what you're talking about."

"Then *what*? She wants you to drag me to the Storm Guard, let them torture me until I imbue?" She closed the distance, menacing. "I never should have cut you free. I never should have kept your secret!" With the last word she lunged, stabbing for his stomach.

Gerrit struck her knife hand aside, shifting to catch her wrist. His joint lock dropped the blade from her hand, but she snarled and tore free. She nearly elbowed him in the head. He dodged and shoved her away from him.

She crashed into a stack of crates and turned back, fists clenched, lips skinned back from her teeth. "I won't go with you!"

Head reeling from the sudden motion, Gerrit steadied himself on the wall, managing to kick the knife behind him. Swallowing nausea, he fought for focus. "I don't understand. When did she arrest him?"

"Four years ago." She still glared murder at him, eyes darting like she sized him up for attack. Normally, she'd be no match for him, but with the concussion, he wasn't so sure.

Four years would place her teacher's arrest around when the Storm Guard realized the bozhskyeh storms were returning. Gerrit struggled to put the pieces together. Captain Vrana had talked about the Tayemstvoy hunting Storm Guard deserters around that time, but if Captain Vrana had been *personally* involved in those arrests, Gerrit's theory about the snake charmer's teacher uncovering a Tayemstvoy conspiracy fell apart. "You're certain it was Captain Vrana?"

"He called her by name. They clearly knew each other."

Gerrit leaned harder against the trailer wall. "And she knew about *you?*"

"She's storm-blessed." The girl's nuzhda-fueled violence began draining away, though hatred still colored her voice.

"So she would have seen you in sousednia." And in no world would Captain Vrana have failed to notice the girl's sousedni-shape. So Captain Vrana had known this snake charmer's teacher, had arrested him at... the Stormhawk's orders? The Storm Guard General's? Yet Captain Vrana had kept the girl's storm-blessing a secret—even though hiding a storm-affinity was treason. None of this made sense. "Why didn't you tell anyone about me?" he asked.

She seemed to debate what to tell him. When she finally spoke, her voice was small. "I wanted to learn to imbue."

"You haven't succeeded." It was a relief, of sorts, to know he wasn't the only storm-blessed having trouble.

"I don't... know what to do," she said.

"As in, you're not trained?" But she'd mentioned an instructor... oh. Her instructor had been arrested four years ago—before even the Storm Guard knew the bozhskyeh storms were returning. But she must have had other training since—unless his theory of conspiracy was total slush.

At her denial, Gerrit balled one hand into a fist. He wasn't ready to abandon all his theories. She had attacked him and threatened to slit his throat. "What, the resistance only teaches you to torture and murder?"

"No!" She seemed genuinely offended. Then her expression hardened. "You were sneaking up on me. I had to protect myself."

"But you don't deny it, that you're *resistance*." He spat the word. Even if they weren't working with the Tayemstvoy, even if they hadn't murdered his mother, rezistyenti were cockroaches.

"I don't know what you're talking about." Her denial came too fast.

He snorted. "Who's supporting you from the Tayemstvoy?"

She scowled. "What?"

"*Who?*" Gerrit struggled to keep the desperation out of his tone. If he'd been wrong about the Tayemstvoy-resistance conspiracy, where did that leave him?

"The red shoulders drag innocent people from their homes and *beat* them in the street. They torture and murder and lie. I would *never* work with them."

Gerrit lowered himself down on a crate, struggling to think as the world spun. "Are they searching the fairgrounds for me?"

"No."

He glanced toward the door, not quite believing her. "Have you seen any bozhki?" If his theory about Tayemstvoy conspirators was wrong, no one should have stopped Filip from finding him.

"Not since yesterday."

Exhaling seemed to drain away all his strength. He put his throbbing head in his hands, his wrists aching. If no one was searching for him, Captain Vrana must have covered his disappearance. *Do what you have to, we'll buy you time*, she'd said. But Filip still should have found—Vrana's note had said 'we' not 'I.' If Filip had gone to Captain Vrana when Gerrit missed last night's rendezvous, she might have stopped him from coming after Gerrit—if her plan all along had been for Gerrit to escape with the snake girl.

Except the girl hated Captain Vrana. Nothing made sense.

He lifted his head, finding the girl watching him, wary. "Captain Vrana is my imbuement teacher," he said, not sure he should tell her, but not sure what else to do. "She didn't want the Tayemstvoy to drive me storm-mad. I don't know what happened with your teacher, but Captain Vrana sent me here—and she kept your secret. Even though doing so is treason."

CHAPTER SEVENTEEN

SLUMPED ON THE crate, looking like he was about to pass out, Gerrit didn't seem so terrible. He seemed confused, and that confusion smelled genuine in sousednia. Sleet, *she* was confused. Ever since Pa's arrest, Vrana had been a monster in her nightmares. Even thinking her name was enough for terror to twist Celka's stomach. While the red shoulders pummeled Pa with boots and truncheons—at Vrana's casual order—Vrana had struck Celka and threatened her. Except... had they been threats?

Celka flinched away from those memories, focusing back on Gerrit, who looked utterly miserable. "I brought you water." Edging past him, she pulled the water skin out of her rucksack and handed it to him.

Relief softened Gerrit's face as he drank, then he slipped outside to pee. Celka debated fleeing while he was distracted, but abandoned the thought. He'd no doubt stationed himself in front of the trailer door. If she tried to escape, he would stop her. Even concussed, he was more than a match for her.

She couldn't beat him with force, which meant she had to be cleverer.

When he returned, Celka tried to lean casually against the wall. "I don't know if you actually care about staying hidden"—she forced a lightness to her tone— "but if you do, you should take off your jacket before going outside."

His expression hardened, and she expected him to snap questions. Instead, he lowered himself onto a crate. "How about we talk. An answer for an answer."

She swallowed hard. Conversation was better than interrogation, though she doubted he intended a two-way exchange.

"What's your name?" he asked. He didn't look like he wanted to start shoving bamboo under her fingernails just to watch her scream, but Ela thought Tayemstvoy privates could be 'cute boys,' so what did looks tell you?

"Celka," she said.

"Celka what?"

She opened her mouth to answer, but snapped it closed again. An answer for an answer, he'd said. She'd see if the offer was genuine. "Show me your identification folio."

"No."

She crossed her arms but decided that felt aggressive. The last thing she wanted was him getting aggressive back. So she sat across from him on another crate, struggling to feign confidence. She had come up with a list of questions, but she'd expected him to be tied up, no chance of running to the Tayemstvoy when he realized her resistance sympathies. He already suspected, but she didn't dare confirm those suspicions.

Beyond questions about the regime, she wanted to ask how to block the storms. She swallowed the words. Who knew what a Tayemstvoy boot-licker would do once he realized how desperate she was for that information.

"How long have you been with the Storm Guard?" she finally asked.

"Since I was seven."

"Is it horrible?"

He frowned. Realizing she'd broken the answer-for-an-answer deal, Celka expected him to snap out his own question. Instead he said, "Sometimes."

In sousednia, the answer carried his pure alpine scent of honesty, and her stomach tightened, confused that he would admit it—that he would even be human enough to *think* it. Shouldn't a regime toad just click his heels and salute the Stormhawk?

"Have you imbued?" he asked.

"No. Have you?"

"No." A gust of urine and diesel fumes beneath her big top suggested the answer hid a deeper shame.

"Did you try?" she asked.

His jaw tightened. "Have you tried?" Right, his turn.

"No—but I almost imbued anyway." The words slipped out. Why was she giving him more than he'd asked for? He'd take everything she said back to the red shoulders. But he'd answered her question about the Storm Guard Academy being horrible, and the hollow in her chest from nearly throwing her family from the wire left her aching to tell someone who understood.

"Why didn't you?" Gerrit asked.

She bit her lip, wondering if she could tell him or if she was being stupid wanting to talk to some Tayemstvoy-kissing bozhk.

"I tried to imbue," he said into her silence, his voice wooden. "I failed. If I'd succeeded... maybe it would have saved my friend."

Celka drew a deep breath in sousednia, wondering if he was lying to convince her he wouldn't stab her in the back. But that urine stink boiled off him, the guilt and shame a stark contrast to true-life's emotionless, soldierly face.

"I thought I'd prepared my weaves perfectly," he said, "but they shattered, and the storm energy drove me from true-life—even though my strazh mage was with me." His jaw muscles stood out. "I was so *certain* I'd succeed—and maybe... but my friends failed their first attempts, too. And then the Tayemstvoy—the *sleet-lickers*." He spit the word, anger driving back some of the urine and damp stone stink of failure. "You've been in a storm, you *know* how hard it is to concentrate. They sent a dozen soldiers with rifles and body armor to beat Branislav so he could 'pull against a stronger nuzhda.' Like that's all it sleeting takes. Like we're prison workers, and the more they beat us the better we'll imbue. Like all our training is *worthless*. Like we're—" He cut himself off, breathing hard.

For a moment, the regime soldier vanished beneath a boy so helpless and scared and alone that Celka wanted to catch his hands and tell him she understood. But he still wore a Storm Guard uniform, and his terrified uncertainty lasted only a second before his face was all hard angles again. His eyes flashed to hers, his sousedni-cues becoming oiled leather and cold granite. His posture shifted subtly, and some animal instinct made her want to shrink away.

Instead, she forced herself to say, "I was on the high wire during our finale. I'm Celka Prochazka, of 'The Amazing Prochazkas.' I was at the top of our pyramid when a storm broke overhead." The threat drained from him and he leaned forward, listening. As if a dam broke inside her, the words tumbled out: the storm's sudden pull, the overwhelming conviction that she would fall unless she imbued, her struggle to need nothing so she didn't throw her family from the wire.

At some point, she closed her eyes, gripped by the memory. She wrapped her arms around herself as though that could ease the pain. She didn't dare look at Gerrit. Maybe he was staring at her like she was the most pathetic bozhk he'd ever seen or maybe he was readying a length of rope to tie her up now that she'd admitted she'd be able to imbue for the State. She'd made so many mistakes since spotting him sneaking toward her last night, but part of her wanted him to *understand*. However different their lives, when they stood beneath a storm, he was like her. It wasn't much, but maybe it could be enough.

Finding him still seated on the crate, expression inscrutable but somehow gentler, she said, "I never realized my storm-blessing might kill my family. I won't let it hurt them—no matter what I have to do."

"I can't believe you balanced on a high wire during a storm," he said.

"I almost fell."

"But you didn't. After I lost true-life, I kept slipping between true-life and sousednia. I fell on my ass just trying to run across a field."

"I thought the storms would be so wonderful." Her voice came out a whisper. "So... magical."

He snorted an awkward laugh. "When I first got orders to imbue, it was like I'd never handled a nuzhda before. I nearly attacked a Tayemstvoy colonel with my belt knife."

Celka shuddered, remembering the balance pole coalescing in her hands. Studying Gerrit across the gap between their crates, she wondered if—despite his lifetime in the Storm Guard Academy—if he could be a good person beneath the uniform. "There was something... beautiful in the storm, too," she said. "Despite all the risk and the pain, I *wanted* to pull down Gods' Breath. Not calling the storm felt like holding my breath... for hours."

"I *want* to imbue." Gerrit didn't say it like an elite soldier, but like a... person. Like someone Celka could understand and, maybe, come to like. "I've never wanted anything so badly. I just want to choose when I do it."

She studied him for a long time, breathing the alpine scent of him, trying to convince herself he was lying. Despite his uniform, she didn't think he was. "You really want to escape the Storm Guard?"

"Maybe not forever, but I don't want to imbue with a gun to my head."

"We could work together. Train together." She swallowed acid, wondering if she was a fool. She should learn what she could, warn her family, and flee. But Gerrit talked about imbuing like it was a science he understood. She kept telling Grandfather that the resistance needed to start taking risks. This would be one sleeting big risk, but maybe the payoff would be worth it.

Gerrit studied her solemnly, taking her measure. Finally, he sighed, exhaustion slipping past his soldierly mask. "How about you find me something to eat."

CHAPTER EIGHTEEN

W HEN C ELKA RETURNED to the snake trailer the next afternoon, costumed from the sideshow, Gerrit squinted up at her. He hadn't worn his uniform jacket since she'd warned him about it, which made him seem a little more human, but his khaki shirt, battledress trousers, and hobnailed boots kept her from complacency. Which was good. Tiger trainers who grew complacent got their throats torn out.

"Hey." She closed the door, plunging them into oil-lit dimness.

He stood and leaned against the wall. Pa's imbued knife pulsed a lazy red on the crate beside him. She wrenched her attention from it like it didn't matter that he'd taken it from her, unwrapping Nina from her shoulders and returning the python to her cage.

They'd hardly spoken since Celka had brought him

food yesterday morning, Gerrit woozy and exhausted, Celka afraid to ask questions that risked betrayal. But hiding him was dangerous; if she learned nothing, that risk was pointless.

"I've been trying to activate your concealment imbuement," she said. His gaze sharpened, though his posture remained deceptively relaxed. "I can't get it to work."

He raised his chin, face studiously impassive. Beneath his gaze, she felt shabby, painfully aware of her fraying cuffs and faded blouse. Recalling the ease with which he'd paid a silver striber as an excuse to talk to her and the gold thread that had draped his dress uniform, she wondered what he must think of her.

As monstrous as the Storm Guard Academy made its students, it was one of the State's most elite institutions. And from what Gerrit's friend Hana had said during the sideshow, his father was well-placed in the regime. He and Celka came from different worlds, and she suddenly understood some of what the sideshow performers must have felt around her. Facing Gerrit in his martial confidence, Celka felt small.

Voice neutral, he asked, "Have you used concealment before?"

"Not in years." She tried to sound unconcerned. Pa had had a necklace that made people's attention slip away. It had been weaker than Gerrit's imbuement and wouldn't stop someone from seeing her if they looked, but it made sneaking around on pranks easier. She crushed the memories down. Pa was gone. "But it was easy. It's not easy with yours."

He ran a hand through his hair then winced, aborting the gesture. "Maybe you're not pulling hard enough on the nuzhda."

Her next words felt like baring her throat to a tiger, but she forced them out. "I can't figure out *how* to pull on it." Pa had taught that she needed to want something with her whole heart, that concentrating on a memory could help. But she didn't remember ever *doing* that. And thinking about her childhood before Pa's arrest made her sick with longing for something gone and dead—destroyed by the sleeting regime.

"Can you pull on anything else?" he asked. "Besides combat?"

She shrugged. "I pulled on hunger a few times, I think, but we never had any imbuements to test it on. My teacher didn't seem too concerned."

"What *did* he teach you?"

Celka felt the chasm between them stretch wider. Even in his more rugged daily uniform, Gerrit wore privilege in his polished knee-boots, in the gold and diamond studding his ear. It dripped from his confident bearing and refined accent. She tried to keep her shoulders from hunching as she said, "Sousednia stuff mostly."

"Like what?"

Celka shook her head. She hadn't gotten anything out of him. A concealment imbuement could help her disappear into the resistance. It didn't matter if he thought himself above her; they were using each other, they weren't friends. "How do *you* pull on concealment?"

Gerrit's expression hardened.

Celka turned away in frustration. So much for learning from him. But her steadying breath in sousednia smelled off, and she inhaled more deeply. Around Gerrit, the air tasted salty like tears and sour like urine.

Carefully, she sat on a crate, searching his face for some hint of what he was hiding. He looked every bit the snarling tiger, but sousednia didn't match. "Tell me? Please."

"Standard bozhk methods." His voice was cold, dismissive, but the urine and tears scents strengthened. "I return to the cell where I was beaten until I could activate a nuzhda bell."

Celka recoiled. Instinctually, she gusted a wind through her big top, driving his morass of pain and terror away. After a moment, she forced the sousednia breeze to slacken. She needed to learn from Gerrit, no matter how unpleasant his truths. "What's a nuzhda bell?"

His cheek twitched, but he said, "An imbuement weak enough you can instinctually connect to it even with a faint nuzhda. They're used to test children for storm-affinities after fasts for the Feeding Miracles."

Celka remembered staying overnight at school during some of the holy fasts, strange Storm Speakers visiting to read them scripture. Thinking back, she remembered the bells they brought and hung around the gymnasium—bells they never rang.

Gerrit cocked his head. "How did you avoid ringing the bells?"

For weeks before every holy fast, Pa had drilled

Celka relentlessly. "I sang the Song of Calming in my head. When that wasn't enough, I made mischief from sousednia to ignore the hunger."

Gerrit's superiority leaked away. "I don't know anyone who can avoid ringing a hunger bell after a fast." A smile curved his lip, though it had an edge. "When I was younger, some of the older cadets used to hide the Academy's bells in awkward places on fast days. They made it glaringly obvious which instructors snuck food from the kitchens."

His smile tingled warmth through Celka, sousednia's scents of pine and snow wrapping him like a fine cloak. For a moment, she forgot his uniform, seeing just a boy, tall and whipcord strong—not like the tumblers who supported the base of a pyramid, but like the acrobats who leapt into impossible flips off the springboard.

She wanted, for a moment, to draw out another reminiscence and bask in his smile, but she forced herself to concentrate. She needed to learn how to conceal herself from the enemy—the enemy like him. And she wasn't making the leap from fasting for the Feeding Miracles to being locked in a cell. "Why would beating you make you pull on concealment?"

His smile vanished. "You have to be desperate to disappear. It's not like you can get that from a fast."

Celka bit her lip. It made no sense. "Pa never beat me."

Gerrit straightened.

Panic subsumed her as she realized what she'd said. *Think.* She couldn't let Gerrit realize the truth. "And... my teacher didn't either. *No one* beat me." She glared at Gerrit, embracing her hatred for the regime. "No one except your beloved *Vrana*." She spat the Storm Guard officer's name.

While the Tayemstvoy brutalized Pa, Vrana had dragged Celka to the side where they could hear and see every sick thud of boots and truncheon. Vrana had demanded whether Pa was Celka's father. Celka had denied it, even when Vrana's fist burst stars through her vision and the viper's hobnailed boot doubled Celka over in pain.

"Your father," Gerrit said, quiet and even, "was your teacher."

"No, you sleet-licker. My uncle was. Pa still performs with us."

Gerrit sat on a crate, gaze never leaving her face. "It makes sense. You're so strong, you must have storm blood from one of your parents."

"You know *nothing*."

"I know what it's like to lose a parent."

Her hatred choked, sputtered.

Before she could bluster past, he said, "My mother was Storm Guard. She was murdered. She wasn't my instructor, but... She was the one person who believed in me. My family name, Skala—it's her name."

Celka clutched the edge of her crate, throat too tight. In sousednia, every word smelled true. "How old were you?"

"Thirteen." Icy wind whipped around him beneath Celka's big top, carrying blood and diesel smoke, but also a crying emptiness. "She died in my arms."

Tears welled in Celka's eyes and, not thinking, she took Gerrit's hand.

An electric shock burst up her arm, dragging her into sousednia. Celka gasped and snatched her hand back. Scrambling to her feet, she asked, "What did you do?"

Gerrit's sousedni-shape stayed vivid, overlapping his true-form for a long minute before its edges wavered into translucence and he returned to true-life. "Nothing." He frowned up at her from his crate. "It felt like storm energy."

"There's no storm."

"It happened before," he said, "when you sold me that postcard."

Mute, Celka nodded.

Gerrit held his hand out. "I don't think it's dangerous." *Says the tiger.* But curiosity overwhelmed her caution. When their palms touched, the shock jolted up her arm again. Instead of pulling away, she clasped his hand. Sousednia exploded, vivid—yet true-life filtered through just as strongly. Normally she had to strain to understand both realities at once but, gripping Gerrit's hand, she heard the mice scrabbling in their cages as easily as she heard her illusory big top's band.

Gerrit stood from the crate, still gripping her hand, looking about in wonder. "I've never felt so in control."

Celka stepped towards him without quite realizing it. He smiled a genuine, gentle smile, and her stomach flip-flopped.

Dropping his hand, she retreated. The snake trailer grew drab, sun-bleached paint flaking off the crates.

Gerrit grimaced, steadying himself on the wall. It took him several long seconds to focus on her in true-life.

She eyed him warily. "Does that happen when you touch other imbuement mages?" She didn't remember it with Pa.

"No," he said once his sousedni-shape had faded.

Celka edged toward the door. Realizing she was retreating, she crossed her arms. "You still haven't taught me to use concealment."

He made a frustrated noise but, when she remained unmoved, said, "What if you listen to the stone? You need to remember the memory you immersed yourself in before. The imbuement's rhythm and your memory probably have similar elements."

She sat back on a crate, digging the concealment stone out of the empty dark-sheath where she normally kept Pa's knife—back before some sleeting Storm Guard cadet had stolen it. The imbuement pulsed lake-blue. Bringing it to her ear, she listened. "I don't hear anything."

"You're joking."

She returned a withering glare. "Yes, how hilarious." As she spoke, she caught a whiff of something out-of-place—musty yet cloyingly floral. She snapped her attention to sousednia, assuming she'd caught it from Gerrit.

But the smell didn't fit him and... it was too close.

Surprised, she brought the stone to her nose and inhaled. It made her choke. Coughing, fanning fresh air in her face, she returned to true-life. "Ugh."

But the smell triggered a memory of golden sunlight and flapping canvas, Pa at her side.

She flinched from it, hand automatically closing on her storm pendant. She couldn't think about Pa. She wouldn't.

"What is it?" Gerrit asked.

Celka's chest ached, her throat too tight for words. She wanted to run to the practice wire and work through difficult tricks that left no room for memory. But she wasn't a child. Learning to use concealment would get her closer to rescuing Pa.

Setting her jaw, she closed her eyes, remembering sneaking with Pa to Clown Alley—the tent where the clowns donned their makeup and switched out their props between acts. She struggled to tease out details while remaining apart from them. The concealment stone warmed from the heat of her skin, but nothing else happened.

Frustrated, she turned to Gerrit. "It's not working."

His eyes glinted in the lamplight. "You have to live it, not just remember." His voice was low, gentle. "You have to become the you from that memory, feel what she feels, do what she does."

Celka shook her head. The idea of feeling Pa beside her was a knife in the chest.

"It's the only way. I don't like concealment either."

With a shaky breath, she closed her eyes. To save Pa, she needed to master this. Imagining the perfume they'd dumped on the grumpy clown's wig in an earlier prank, Celka forced the world to re-form around her, Pa at her side.

With her back against tent canvas, Celka listens to the clown grouse about someone moving his props. Pa's

big hand warms hers. Sharing grins, they stifle laughter.
Then, stepping away from their true-forms, they ghost
through the canvas to make mischief.

The pebble vibrated, and a deep blue glow spread
from it, flowing over her hand and down her arm, slimy
and faintly buzzing. In true-life, her arm disappeared to
mid-forearm.

"Ha!" In triumph, her hold on the memory *slipped*,
and her hand reappeared. Celka wrinkled her nose.

Gerrit stared at her with the confused awe she saw
on people watching Ivana swallow swords. "You were
smiling."

She frowned. "Does the Storm Guard forbid smiling?"

"No, I just—to call up that nuzhda, where did you go?
What did you remember?"

"We tickled a clown from sousednia." She forced the
words past a tightness in her throat. "He kept blaming
the other clowns; they thought he was crazy."

Gerrit cocked his head like he didn't understand.

"Pranks," Celka said. "Pa loved pranks." The ache
in her chest remained, but somehow, speaking it aloud,
calling him *Pa* to someone else lessened the pain.

"Like stealing nuzhda bells?"

Celka laughed. "I bet he did worse when he was a
cadet."

Gerrit waited, rapt, and suddenly Celka wanted to
talk. "Sometimes we did simple, stupid things—like
sneaking salt into the sugar bowl. One summer we got
into a prank war with an elephant trainer. Pa bet money
that he could predict when the elephant would poop."

"You're joking."

Celka shook her head. "Elephants are trained to poop on command—you want them to go right before they enter the ring so they're less likely to make a mess inside the big top. Elephant poop is *huge*. Anyway, this trainer tickled her elephant under his chin to get him to stand on his hind legs—that way gravity helps the poop come out."

"And your father would do it when the trainer wasn't looking?"

Celka snorted. "We'd make sure she was nearby—preferably staring straight at the elephant."

"Then why didn't she see you?"

She couldn't believe Gerrit was this slow. "We'd do it in sousednia."

Gerrit frowned like he didn't get the joke. "You can't affect the real world from sousednia."

"We weren't trying to move a rock."

"Then how did you make the elephant poop?"

She cocked her head. "Don't you ever—?" From sousednia, she poked him in the ribs.

He jumped. "That felt real."

She shrugged again, awkward. If he'd never learned about sousedni-disruptions, it would explain why he hadn't used one when he'd attacked her in sousednia that first night.

"You can do that to mundanes?" His intense gaze set off flutters in her belly. "To *elephants*?"

Celka told her belly flutters to chew hail. Prowling grace and predatory strength made tigers beautiful.

When they roared, your heart thrilled with fear—fun only because they couldn't reach you through the cage. But bars didn't protect Celka. She had to protect herself. As nonchalant as she could, she said, "It takes practice."

He leaned closer. "Will you teach me?"

Staring into his honey-brown eyes, she wanted to say yes. But he'd beaten her to the ground and threatened to crush her throat. The thought of giving him more power quenched her remaining flutters. She opened her mouth to say no, but the calculating edge to his intensity stopped her. Gerrit wasn't asking out of idle curiosity, and he could still decide to hand her to the Tayemstvoy. If he really wanted this, she had currency to delay his betrayal. "Sure. If you teach me to keep that concealment stone active."

CHAPTER NINETEEN

Gerrit held himself in plank position on the snake trailer floor, practicing transitioning fully free of sousednia and wishing Filip was there to tell him if he'd succeeded. A quiet, triple tap on the door warned him of Celka's arrival, then she burst in on a gust of fresh air, silhouetted by sunlight.

He dropped to his knees and wiped sweat from his brow. At mid-morning, the snake trailer remained temperate, but with a sun like today's, the afternoon would be sweltering. At least the stench was better; he'd cleaned up his vomit and scrubbed the rodent cages with a vengeance.

Celka kicked the door closed and deposited his napkin-wrapped breakfast on a crate.

Gerrit stood. "I think you need to build walls."

"Uh-huh. Becoming a mason will certainly increase

my chances at holding a concealment nuzhda."

Gerrit wouldn't have smiled openly at the Academy, but here he didn't bother to hide his amusement. Her easy humor baffled him but, in her absence, he'd found himself trying out lines, imagining making her laugh. "Mental walls—to contain your nuzhda."

Celka crossed her arms and scowled.

Her unguarded emotions felt unnatural—but strangely refreshing. In the Academy, anything you revealed could become a weapon, and the Tayemstvoy were always watching. He didn't know how he'd believed her Tayemstvoy-trained before; she was nothing like the red shoulders. "Your father had some weird ideas about training an imbuement mage."

Her gaze slipped down him, her lip curling. "He probably thought he had more time."

Before her open hostility, his own expression hardened. *This isn't the Academy*, he told himself, trying to reclaim his light humor. Holes marred Celka's training like someone had taken a shotgun to her lessons, but she smiled while pulling against concealment and ran circles around him in sousednia. Last night, reviewing everything Captain Vrana had told him, he'd grown convinced that she'd wanted him to learn from Celka— not drag her to the Stormhawk.

And something about Celka made him want to shatter their wary silences. He was tired of holding his breath, waiting for her to make some critical mistake that left him with no choice but to hand her to his father. Sometimes, when her fear and anger fell away, her

CORRY L. LEE

vibrancy blindsided him. She carried a spark he'd only ever seen turned to destruction. Somehow, Celka made that flame beautiful.

But she'd tied him up and he'd attacked her, and he had no idea how to bridge that chasm. He could, however, patch some of the holes in her training. Maybe that would be a start.

"To think rationally while you hold a nuzhda," he said, "you have to wall off the desperate part of your mind. The more powerful the nuzhda, the harder it is. Any nuzhda that seeps through the walls affects your judgement—and you likely won't even know it."

"I couldn't even *hold* the nuzhda yesterday." She pulled out the tie in her hair and sat on a crate.

"Because you lost your grip on the memory. You concentrated on true-life, and that desperate need"—it felt strange to describe running around on pranks that way—"couldn't survive here." He gestured to the trailer. "While you're actively experiencing the memory, you have to seal it off—crawl outside it while still feeling it, and return to your core sousednia."

She looked pensive, so he continued. "It's one reason skilled bozhki are unstable. We break our minds apart, raging mindlessly inside the walls while thinking dispassionately outside them."

"How do you build them?" she asked.

"I imagine stone. Granite blocks reaching into the sky."

She nodded, but he wouldn't let this turn into a practice session just for her. He'd debated how much of his own

183

weaknesses to reveal, but he needed to imbue before the Tayemstvoy found him. The fastest way to results had to come from the truth. "And I need help figuring out how to ground myself in true-life."

Her head snapped up. "What?"

His shoulders tensed and his every instinct told him to lash out before she could use his weakness against him. He struggled to keep his voice level. "It's... hard for me to return from sousednia. I lost true-life completely when I failed to imbue. My strazh had to pull me back." Chills curled down Gerrit's spine and he tried not to think about future imbuements. If he screwed up here, Filip couldn't save him.

"Tomorrow it's Storm Day in the town where we're performing," Celka said.

Panic twisted Gerrit's stomach. What if attempting to imbue drove him permanently storm-mad? He squeezed his eyes shut, fighting panic. *Filip, where are you?* If Gerrit was really following Captain Vrana's plan, why hadn't she sent Filip after him?

"I've been trying to figure out how to block a storm's pull." Celka's voice was too soft, her expression taut with fear.

"Is that even possible?"

"It must be." She spoke too vehemently, like she was trying to convince herself. "I thought sousedni-dislocations would help." She explained her theory of control.

Gerrit didn't buy it. "How could a hand span of physical distance help?"

"I'm talking meters," she said. "A dozen meters."

"No one can dislocate that far."

Celka frowned.

"Why are you staring at me like I have a bayonet sticking out of my chest?" he asked.

She huffed a surprised laugh. "You're serious?"

He looked down at his chest. "Not about the bayonet."

A smile softened her lips. "Show me how far you can dislocate."

So much for light conversation. Gerrit crossed his arms and stared her down the way his father would. "I'm not here for your amusement."

Celka frowned, confused but not intimidated. "I'm not going to whip you if you don't go far enough. I have an idea about grounding. Show me?"

His glower crumbled. Freezing sleet, he was a hail-eater. Focusing too easily on sousednia, he stepped away from his true-form. Pain needled his temples. Gritting his teeth, he managed two more steps.

A knock on the trailer door shattered his focus, and he lost the dislocation, sousedni-shape snapping back to match his true-form. He clapped a hand to his mouth, trying not to vomit, and asked through gritted teeth, «You expecting someone?»

A finger to her lips, Celka nodded. "Just a sec!" she called. She pointed Gerrit to a corner then slipped outside.

If she'd called the Tayemstvoy—but she wouldn't; that would get her arrested, too. But if any circus performers spotted him, they might talk and—

Stop. He needed to focus. She hadn't returned his concealment stone, but her imbued knife was just across the trailer. Connecting easily to the combat imbuement, he walled off the nuzhda and crept toward the door, keeping his head as motionless as possible to clamp down on his nausea from the concussion. He couldn't make out words, so he sunk to a crouch, ready to fight.

The door opened a crack. "Thanks," Celka said, cheerful. Gerrit tensed while a voice murmured, then Celka stepped inside—alone.

She looked toward where she'd told him to hide, squinting in the dimness. She held a lumpy bundle under one arm. When she spotted him, she raised her eyebrows.

Gerrit straightened, crossing his arms, knife still in hand. "Who was that?"

"A friend. Here." She held the bundle out to him.

Warily, he took it. "A friend?"

She just nodded to the bundle.

He set the knife within easy reach, keeping the imbuement active. Unfolding the fabric, he found a pair of rugged work trousers and a faded shirt. Surprised, he met Celka's gaze.

She smiled. "You can't hide very well in uniform."

"So you found me new clothes? Just like that?" With so many new recruits needing uniforms, clothing—like pretty much everything else—was rationed. It made even used clothing hard to come by and, given the ragged state of Celka's wardrobe, he doubted she had the money for bribes. "How?"

She shrugged.

He stepped toward her. "Did you tell someone about me?" That came out sharp.

She glowered. "First, would a 'thanks' kill you? Second, no. I've kept your secret."

"So you just..."

"Stop asking questions and thank me."

"Thanks." It sounded wooden. The clothing would certainly make him less conspicuous, but he couldn't stop worrying the problem. He'd been here three days, and she'd gotten him worker's clothes with ease. As though he stared at a pile of scouting reports, the details snapped into place. He grabbed the knife. "The resistance."

Celka squeaked and stepped back. "What are you doing?"

He pressed his knuckles against the crate, struggling not to raise the knife. He'd spent so long hating the resistance that the loathing was instinct. Until now, he'd managed to mostly forget Celka's involvement. The Tayemstvoy may have murdered his mother, but the resistance still wanted to tear down the regime.

By hiding from the Storm Guard with Celka, he was as bad as Captain Vrana—helping the resistance just by failing to turn them in. But Captain Vrana was the Hero of Zlin. If Gerrit could trust anyone, he could trust her. So maybe it was a matter of degree. He could do more good for the State by learning to imbue and gaining his father's trust. Convincing the Stormhawk that the Tayemstvoy were plotting to control the Storm Guard had to be more important than stopping whatever Celka did for the resistance. Besides, by gaining Celka's trust, he might learn valuable intelligence to turn over to his father, striking a bigger blow to the resistance even as he secured the Storm Guard autonomy's and protected other cadets from being driven storm-mad.

Releasing the knife's imbuement, Gerrit shredded his combat nuzhda. Hands out, weaponless, he stepped back. "I'm sorry. Thank you for the clothes."

Celka's gaze darted to the knife, but she didn't move.

"I..." Gerrit forced himself to back away, seeking some explanation that would prevent her from seeing through him. "In the Academy, they taught that the resistance murders people, blows up trains, spreads foreign propaganda."

"We're not like that."

"You want to tear down the State." He couldn't keep disgust from his voice.

"No, we want to *save* Bourshkanya. *Free* Bourshkanya—so we don't have to watch what we say for fear the Tayemstvoy will drag us from our homes. So you and I don't have to worry about being driven storm-mad to build weapons!"

He told himself to act as though he accepted her warped view but, whether she admitted it or not, she worked with the people plotting to murder his father and destroy everything he'd built. Part of him still wanted to pick back up the knife.

"I've never blown up a train," she insisted, "or killed anyone or spread anything but the truth the Tayemstvoy try to bury." She edged toward him, like approaching a skittish horse. "I can only imagine what the Tayemstvoy must have taught you, but you *know* what they did to your friend. You told me you wanted to escape the Storm Guard. Was that a lie?"

Her intensity chilled him. Maybe he'd been wrong before, about her spark. She lacked the Tayemstvoy's gleeful violence, but she still wanted to destroy. Her emerald eyes held his, and he forced himself not to look away. "It wasn't a lie," he said. "I want to escape."

"You're hiding something," she said.

She'd done the same thing before, when she'd first abducted him. He'd dismissed that almost psychic confidence as his own muddled memory, but now he wondered. It was like she could read him as easily as Captain Vrana could. "I'm not."

She crossed her arms. "This won't work without trust."

Could she read him in sousednia? That would explain why Captain Vrana saw through him even when he kept his expression bland. He looked away, wondering what he could say that was fully true but hid his intentions. "Bozhki can't escape the State. Not forever." He turned back, remembering Branislav snarling at the end of his chain to draw his focus away from the lies of omission. "Your father would know."

CHAPTER TWENTY

THE OTHER SIDESHOW performers clustered near the heavy curtain that kept the illusion tent in semi-darkness. Celka tried to ignore them, setting Nina carefully on the ground, telling herself that she didn't care that they excluded her.

Today, she could almost believe it. She had bigger problems now. Like Gerrit almost slitting her throat.

She'd never expected that he might hate the resistance the way she hated the regime. And despite knowing that the Tayemstvoy had practically raised him, she still didn't understand how he could support the State so blindly. One look around showed people starving and casting frightened glances over their shoulders, worried the Tayemstvoy would construe something they said as treason.

But maybe that was his problem. Thinking about the

circus's audience in Solnitse, Celka didn't remember the same hungry faces and desperation she saw everywhere else. Solnitse was rich and pampered—like Gerrit himself. Which gave her an idea.

"Hi." A baritone voice made Celka jump. She jerked around to find a tall, broad-shouldered youth with rich brown skin and an easy smile that made her stomach somersault. A simple enameled star glinted from one ear. He looked about her own age, maybe a couple of years older. "I'm Ctibor." His deep mahogany eyes drew her in, and her stomach fluttered as she reached to shake his hand.

"Celka." She realized she was staring at his full lips, and forced herself to step back, looking him over, wondering how he'd gotten into the sideshow tent early and why creepy Georgs hadn't chased him out. He wore a khaki shirt and olive trousers, and Celka's stomach clenched—he was Army, with an enlisted soldier's short brown boots and puttees wrapping his muscular calves. Several combat knives hung off his belt. Even without a rifle or uniform jacket, there was no mistaking it. She tried to hide her disgust, turning quickly away, irritated that she'd missed the obvious signs and swooned over a handsome face.

"See you around," Ctibor said.

She focused on Nina, hoping Ctibor would leave, but his boots clunked onto the neighboring platform, hobnails scraping the wood. She risked a glance and found him talking to a vaguely familiar girl wearing a scant costume of ultramarine sequins.

Then Celka noticed the platform's wooden rack, holding a dozen more knives. Ctibor caught her eye before she could turn away. "I'm a knife thrower," he said. "Just joined up."

She tried to read some secret in his strong jaw and profuse dark lashes. Circuses never picked up new acts a month into the season—and certainly not from random, nowhere farming towns. Celka focused back on Ctibor's assistant, suddenly realizing why the girl looked familiar: she was the showgirl who'd sprained her ankle a couple days back. Word was that she wouldn't be performing for weeks. But presumably you didn't need good ankles to stand in front of a board while a handsome stranger threw knives at you.

Celka's mind spun. Not only had Ctibor arrived weeks into the season, he'd joined without an assistant?

"I wouldn't expect the Army to loan out soldiers for entertainment." She tried to keep her voice light. Was he Army—or Tayemstvoy? The uniform was wrong: the Tayemstvoy, even the enlisted ones, wore tall black boots and black leather belts. And Ctibor didn't carry a truncheon or a pistol. As disguises went, the choice seemed strange.

But red shoulders would explain Ms. Vesely adding him to the roster no questions asked. And the timing... she'd been hiding Gerrit for three days now. Could Ctibor be looking for him? She pushed the panicky thought aside. If the Tayemstvoy suspected Gerrit of hiding in the circus, they'd march a squad through, line everyone up at gunpoint and search trailer to trailer until they found him. They wouldn't send someone undercover.

But they might if they suspected resistance connections.

Ctibor's snort dragged her attention back to him. "I'm not really Army. Your Lieutenant Svoboda decided I'd make a nice poster boy." He snatched a paper from the edge of his platform. Celka expected a mug of him smiling that disarming smile, knives in hand. Instead, he held an Army recruitment flier. "No postcards for me—but every one of these that shows up at the circus's recruiting station..." Ctibor rubbed fingers and thumb together in the universal sign for money.

Celka raised skeptical brows.

"Bourshkanya needs *you!*" Cocky grin a mockery of every recruitment poster, Ctibor pointed at her and winked.

Despite herself, Celka laughed. Sleet, he was handsome.

"Places, people!" creepy Georgs called, and the other performers streamed past as though Ctibor wasn't there. He attempted a few greetings, but got the brush-off Celka knew so well. His smile slipped and he turned to his knife rack, studiously adjusting the blades.

Celka felt a twinge of sympathy, then her gaze dropped to his uniform and she turned away. She didn't need more trouble.

CHAPTER TWENTY-ONE

THE NEXT AFTERNOON, Celka clomped into the snake trailer and, before Gerrit could get a word out, tossed him his concealment stone and pulled both his combat knives from a pack. "I need to show you something," she said. "Turn invisible."

He pocketed the concealment stone and buckled his knives in place, hiding his relief at their return. "Where are we going?"

"Out."

"Out? It's Storm Day. What if it's a bozhskyeh storm?"

Grim, she said, "Then we practice blocking it. Let's go."

He caught her arm, refusing to let her whirlwind make him stupid. "We have no idea how to block a storm. And I doubt I can keep a concealment imbuement active with Gods' Breath yanking on me. *Where* are we going?"

"You'll see." Determination lit her emerald eyes, and he could so easily imagine her imbuing one of the Fighting Miracles, fierce and unyielding, channeling Gods' Breath to win a battle singlehanded. Part of him wanted to follow her blindly.

But he refused to risk his freedom. "If we're somewhere public, I could be spotted."

"We'll sense the storm building. You'll have time to hide. You *need* to see this."

Given he'd almost knifed her yesterday, he should be glad she was even talking to him, but this was too sudden, too dangerous. "Are you turning me in?"

"Would you just trust me for one sleeting second?" she said, exasperated.

So far, she'd earned that trust—despite being resistance scum. "Wait for me outside."

She crossed her arms, but Gerrit wouldn't back down. If she wanted to be mysterious about their destination, fine; he wasn't going to be her afternoon entertainment.

"Fine," she said. "Meet us on the road to town."

Ten minutes later, invisible and burning with curiosity, Gerrit caught up to her walking alongside a donkey cart. Two men walked ahead, holding hands while one led the donkey. They wore worker's clothes, not unlike Gerrit's. Celka looked overdressed in gray, wide-legged trousers and an embroidered blouse.

When Gerrit's efforts to uncover their destination proved futile, he said, «I had an idea about blocking the storms.»

Her sousedni-shape sharpened, her footprints in his

snowy clearing forming a perfect line as wind rippled her costume's emerald sleeves.

Certain he had her attention, he said, «What if you concentrate on a happy memory—something totally innocuous—while you do your dislocation?»

She cocked her head, pensive, but said nothing more.

Nearing town, the road crossed a bridge in a factory's shadow, and Gerrit pulled his shirt collar over his nose. Slimy brown goo coated the river banks, and waterwheels spun upstream.

«They dye your uniforms here,» Celka said. «That's why it smells so bad.»

He'd mostly gotten used to the stench by the time the cart clattered across cobblestones to halt in the town's central square. Celka and the circus folk unloaded the cart into the temple, and Gerrit stared at the storm tower, seeking clues.

Cumulus clouds bulked overhead but had not yet darkened, and his storm-thread felt weak as spider silk. The storm tower itself jutted up two stories, aged wooden beams supporting its lightning rod. The rod was as simple as the tower, an iron spear a few meters tall. Grounding cables radiated from it into sand-filled anchor points. Simple, ugly, and functional. Like the town.

Solnitse's storm towers vied for attention, each more elaborate than the last. Gerrit's favorite depicted scenes from the Fighting Miracles, wrought in iron and brass. Its metals weren't as precious as some, but the lack of gilt fit the Miracles' ferocity.

He turned, hoping the storm temple would make up for

the tower's lack. The structure could have been a barn, though it had the customary asymmetric roof, highest point facing the village square. The floor-to-ceiling doors swung wide so the townsfolk could watch lightning strike the tower during services. Solnitsan temples had glass-paned windows to protect the congregation from the elements; they sparkled with gilt and murals, their arches and onion domes celebrating the Storm Gods and Bourshkanyan might.

Shaking his head, Gerrit went to find Celka. Except for the circus workers setting up trestle tables in the back, the temple echoed empty, his boots loud on the plank floor.

The workers looked up. "Hello?" one called.

Gerrit froze.

"We're from the circus," the man called, nervous. "Just setting up. Won't be no trouble." He must have assumed the hobnail scrape meant Tayemstvoy.

Invisibility did Gerrit no sleeting good if everyone heard his bootfalls. Crouching, he slipped off his boots. Knotting the laces together, he looped the boots around his neck. The two men returned to their work, casting furtive glances. On silent feet, Gerrit padded past.

In the temple's kitchen, Celka stirred a pot of soup that dwarfed the wood-fire stove.

«Why are we here?» he asked.

«I want you to see the resistance at work.»

He gripped his knife's hilt. «What are you planning?»

She didn't flinch. «You'll see.»

Soon, villagers lined up, bowls in hand. Only when

Celka started handing out bread, a circus worker ladling soup at her side, did Gerrit understand. They weren't collecting money or ration coupons. This was charity.

«Look at their faces,» Celka said as the man beside her sloshed a gruel of barley and potato skins into a young mother's bowl. «Tell me what you see.»

Everyone was thin—no, gaunt. They looked tired and frightened. Bowls filled, they ate alone or in small groups, speaking in whispers. Their faces were clean, their clothes patched and worn. With a start, he realized that, this being Storm Day, they probably dressed in their finest.

«Of course they're hungry,» Gerrit said, turning away. «They wouldn't accept your charity if they weren't.»

In sousednia, Celka stepped toward him. Her high wire walk should have seemed awkward in his snowy clearing; instead, it made her graceful and otherworldly. The three-meter dislocation seemed completely unremarkable to her, though Gerrit could never achieve so much. «Across Bourshkanya, everyone's hungry.»

He scoffed, though the gravity of her expression made her hard to ignore.

«Walk through town,» she said. «See the rest of Hlavechnik.»

He would, if only to prove her wrong. «Where do you get the food?»

«We pool our ration books, and the circus quartermaster trades and scrimps so we have enough each week for an extra meal.»

«You deliberately eat worse so you can feed people you don't even know?»

She lifted her chin, holding his gaze. «Now you've seen the resistance.»

AFTER GERRIT LEFT, Celka searched the crowd while handing out bread. Educating Gerrit was only a side benefit of this outing. Grandfather expected her to be contacted by the local resistance cell, but knew only the signal: their contact would set their bowl on their bench before it was empty, adjust the shoulders of their shirt, and stare up at the storm tower. Celka hoped she didn't miss it. Grandfather seemed nervous about this hand-off, and nothing made Grandfather nervous.

She chopped more stale bread to refill her basket, and when she looked out across the temple, a form caught her eye, barely visible in one of the great doors' shadows, yet indefinably out of place.

A moment's study, and she dismissed them as another Tayemstvoy, watching from a distance while their two friends strutted around, making people nervous. The Tayemstvoy always loomed when the circus served food, hoping for a reason to arrest them. As if feeding people was a crime.

Drawing a steadying breath, she searched her basket for a less-stale hunk of bread for a toothless old man. He nodded his thanks and she tried to smile back, all the while feeling the new Tayemstvoy's gaze.

They knew. They'd been sent to watch for today's hand-off.

Another minute, and the new Tayemstvoy stepped

away from the wall and headed straight for her.

Halfway across the temple, she recognized Ctibor and almost collapsed with relief. He rounded the trestle table, smiling. With effort, she reminded herself to stay cautious. He could still have red shoulders. "What are you doing here?" she asked.

"I followed when you left the circus, but I got turned around. Can I help?"

She inhaled deeply in sousednia, wishing she had a better baseline for him so she'd be able to read his lies. He smelled like oiled steel and something a little musty but not altogether unpleasant. Over that coiled a faint, acrid smell like burning hair—the lie. "You must get lost easy," she said. "Hlavechnik isn't exactly a teeming metropolis."

Guilty, he looked down. "I didn't want to follow too close. I wasn't sure I'd be welcome."

She almost told him he wasn't, but swallowed the words. The stink of his lie had vanished. She searched the strong cut of his jaw, the fullness of his lips. "Why follow us?"

He lowered his voice. "Because I'd have so much fun in the back lot with the other sideshow performers?"

Sousednia smelled musty and steely. His mahogany eyes trapped her and, when he leaned forward, she imagined him reaching to stroke her cheek.

Instead, he grabbed a hunk of bread, handing it to the next person in line.

Heat rushed to her cheeks and she turned back to her task—what was she *thinking?* She didn't even know him.

"Let me help?" Ctibor said.

She felt him watching her—or maybe she just wished he was watching her—waiting, guardedly hopeful. She tried to imagine how he felt, a circus outsider, conversations hushing when he approached, glances as guarded as if he was Tayemstvoy. And maybe he was. But maybe he wasn't.

"You can cut more bread." She pointed behind her.

His grinned the grin that made spectators swoon, and Celka turned to the hungry villagers. She'd save her swooning for people smart enough to hate the State.

Ctibor went to work with one of his own knives, sousednia gaining a brightness around him like stepping outside at dawn, the air fresh and clean. Despite herself, she inhaled deeply and smiled.

For a time, they worked in a silence Celka would have called companionable if he hadn't been a complete stranger.

Depositing bread in her basket, Ctibor asked, "Do you miss Storm Day services?"

She shrugged. "Not really. During the season, I'm too busy to worry about much but the circus. Though Grandfather always makes us get up early on Storm Days and say prayers before the family altar." Since the bozhskyeh storms' return, she'd been glad Grandfather was so devout. The Storm Gods had ignored all her pleas to help Pa, but if prayer could encourage them to send her even the smallest aid now, she'd take it.

"You're lucky to be with your family."

The comment should have been meaningless, but it

goose-bumped warnings across Celka's skin—though sousednia still smelled like truth. "Missing them already?" She couldn't hide her wariness. "You're what, less than a week from your family farm?" Or at least, that was his story.

Ctibor paused a heartbeat too long, sousednia a tangled swirl before he said, "I haven't been away from home much."

The smells in sousednia settled down, but the answer was so vague as to cover a dozen lies. She should let it go, give him the cold shoulder like the rest of the performers. Instead, she asked, "Did you go to Storm Services often?"

He smiled, relieved. "Every Storm Day."

She wanted to read something trustworthy in that, but the Tayemstvoy attended Storm Services, too. "I miss watching lightning strike the tower," she said, figuring the statement for safe.

"Definitely the best part. Do you have a favorite Song?"

"The Song of Fighting." She said it to surprise him, though it happened to be true.

He smiled at his loaf of hard rye. "I kind of figured."

"What's that supposed to mean?"

He shrugged. "It fits you."

Celka expected his tone to carry judgement, but he spoke it like fact. Celka felt like she wavered on the wire. "You don't even know me."

He scooped a handful of bread into her basket. "Your snake act's on the neighboring platform, Celka, and people talk." His dark eyes caught hers again, only a hand-span separating them. "There's fire in you—and steel." The low rumble of his voice purred through her, and Celka's focus slipped to his lips. She imagined him closing the distance, his strong hand slipping around the small of her back and—

Focusing back on the crowd, Celka sought the resistance signal. The next person in line shuffled up to her and, cheeks burning, she handed out another chunk of bread.

Ctibor retreated to the back table to cut more bread. Celka wished she knew some way to keep him close—but she was being a fool. He could be the enemy. Trying to sound casual, she asked, "So, you grew up on a farm?"

"And learned to throw knives in the barn." His lie came easy but wafted acrid smoke. "Farming's boring."

She didn't even need his sousedni-cues. "You're too well-fed for a farmer." The State took a heavy tithe from every crop, leaving most farmers struggling to feed themselves. They did a little better than factory workers, since they could grow their own vegetables, but Ctibor was broad-shouldered and muscular. She'd bet he'd never missed a meal.

"It's a big farm. We have workers; we do all right."

Sousednia still stunk. "So why leave your posh 'farm'?" Three benches from her, an elderly woman in a red sarafan set her bowl aside, adjusted her shoulders' fraying embroidery, and leaned back to stare at the storm tower. Sighing, she picked back up her bowl.

Distracted by the resistance signal, Celka almost missed the welling of urine and antiseptic around Ctibor. She snapped around to look at him, but the scents vanished as quickly as they'd appeared. Ctibor focused a little too intently on cutting bread. "I wanted to see the world."

"And I'm a zebra." She'd given him a chance, and he'd given her lies. She focused on the townsfolk, waiting for the old woman to finish her soup and go outside.

The woman ate painfully slow, stopping a second time to repeat the signal before taking mouse-sized bites of soup-softened bread. Impatient and needing a distraction, Celka focused on what Gerrit had said on their way here—happy memories to distract from the storm.

Happy memories? Something from her summers in the circus, definitely, not her grim winters spent studying in their family's freezing apartment after school, trying to ignore the emptiness of Pa's absence. Not her weekend hours picking up factory shifts either, sewing buttons on olive wool jackets, head down as the Tayemstvoy overseers paced back and forth, fingers flexing over truncheons.

Happy memories.

Frustrated, Celka stepped away from her true-form, away from Ctibor and his lies, away from the hungry villagers counting on the Wolf to free them. She drew deep breaths of hay and sawdust overlaid with coiling blood and gun oil that reminded her of Pa's knife. She walked further along her high wire until the dislocation needled pain into her temples, then she ran her fingers along the base of her skull, seeking the buzz of a building storm. Fear settled like a rock in her stomach at the thought of Gods' Breath flickering overhead but, at the same time, she craved its power.

Her storm-thread lay inert. Had the temple meteorologists made a mistake? It happened sometimes, and she should feel relieved. Instead, she felt like she was holding her breath, waiting.

Before she could examine the feeling further, the old woman shuffled outside.

Celka returned to true-life. "Hey, Ctibor, can you take over? I have to pee." At least some good came from him having followed her to the storm temple.

The old woman waited in the back alley. After exchanging hand signals and inane comments about the weather, she handed Celka a thick envelope and patted her hand. "Storm Gods bless you, child." She shuffled away without a backward glance.

A MONTH AGO, Celka would have handed the envelope to Grandfather; tonight, she opened it herself.

Celka's heart raced as she skimmed the page. Grandfather, reading over her shoulder, grew agitated. The Wolf wanted her family to pick up a mimeograph machine in Vrbitse and use it to print two hundred copies of the enclosed pages. She flipped through them, eyes widening at diagrams of disassembled rifles and drills for learning to shoot.

"What is the Wolf planning?" Celka breathed.

"He can plan it without us," Grandfather snapped.

Celka stared at him, aghast. "The Wolf's counting on us."

Aunt Benedikta took the letter from Celka's hands. "He's never asked anything like this before."

"You think it's a trap?" Uncle Andrik asked.

"A mimeograph machine is too dangerous, even if this is real." Grandfather held his hand out for the letter, grim as though he wished no one else had seen this. "The Wolf can find someone else to print his filth." He yanked the remaining pages from Celka's hands. "Andrik, hand me a match."

"No!" Celka caught his hands. "You can't. The Wolf trusted this to us. He knows the risk; he'd only ask if it was important."

"You presume to know the Wolf?" Grandfather's low voice lost its gravitas, and Celka caught a hint of rot in sousednia. "He grows reckless. He risks our lives in foolhardy heroics that will kill thousands even if we succeed."

Aunt Benedikta clasped Grandfather's shoulder, leading him to their sitting area. "And if this is key to his plans? You trusted him before."

Having Aunt Benedikta take her side made Celka reel, but she seized the opening. "We could keep the mimeograph machine in the snake trailer. No one goes in there anymore and there are plenty of crates to hide it." Belatedly, she thought of Gerrit. What would he think of her dragging in a mimeograph machine? Printing rifle drills was a far cry from feeding starving villagers.

"We cannot get such a thing safely." Fatigue strained Grandfather's voice. "The machine would be heavy and large. To bring it through checkpoints would be suicide."

"Not if no one could see it," Celka said.

"You cannot disguise a machine the size of a sheep," Grandfather said. "One mistake, and the Tayemstvoy arrest us all. We *will not* take this risk."

Celka met his gravitas with a smile, unable to help herself. "I wasn't talking about a disguise."

"Magic?" Demian asked.

She nodded, stomach fluttering as all eyes turned to her. Could she really pull this off? She'd had no luck building walls yet. But Vrbitse was three days off. This gave her motivation to learn.

"What do you propose?" Grandfather asked.

Celka opened her mouth to explain, then snapped it closed. "Better if you don't know." She straightened her shoulders and blew her doubts away from him in sousednia. "I'll work out the details and let you know what I need."

CHAPTER TWENTY-TWO

"CELKA!"

She recognized Ctibor's voice and kept walking like she hadn't heard, looking forward to getting Nina off her shoulders and back into her cage.

Not taking the hint, Ctibor jogged up beside her. "We need to talk."

"Go talk to Ludvik." According to rumor, Ctibor and one of the tumblers shared a bed. Ludvik's attention had been endorsement enough for some, and Ctibor's disarming smile and easy laughter had evaporated everyone else's wariness.

"You've been avoiding me," he said.

"We see each other every day in the sideshow." The others could have him. She was busy. She needed to ghost the mimeograph machine out of Vrbitse tomorrow night, but she still couldn't hold a concealment nuzhda for long.

She'd hardly slept last night, lying in her bunk, activating that stupid rock. Over and over she'd watched her hand disappear from true-life and then—*pop*—reappear as soon as she stopped concentrating on the memory.

If she didn't figure this out soon, she'd have to abort the pickup. She hated the thought of admitting failure to Grandfather, but it would be better than getting arrested with an illegal printing machine.

She squeezed shut eyes gritty with fatigue. Maybe Grandfather could help her come up with an alternate strategy. She dismissed the thought. Grandfather would leap to abort the pickup.

"Celka, would you just stop?" Ctibor's frustration shook her, and she turned with a glare.

Plenty of people had secrets, and his might be no worse than theirs. She was too tired to care. "You come up with some new lies to try out?"

"That's not..." He scrubbed a hand over his jaw. "Fine. You're right. I didn't grow up on a farm."

When he didn't volunteer anything else, she turned to go. "This snake is really heavy."

Ctibor caught her arm. "Celka, wait."

She wrenched her arm free. "Don't."

He raised his hands apologetically and stepped back. "I just want to talk."

She sighed. Maybe listening would get rid of him faster. "Fine."

He looked surreptitiously around then motioned her into the shadow of a horse trailer. "It's about the soup kitchen."

Fear tightened her stomach, but she told herself to relax, kicking up a sousednia breeze to blow his cues to her and keep her own from reaching him. Mundanes couldn't use sousedni-cues the way she could, but Pa had warned that intuitive people subconsciously picked up on them. "What about it?"

"What did that old woman give you?"

Celka's chest tightened, but she made herself frown. "What old woman?"

"In the red sarafan with the tasseled belt. You followed her outside. She gave you an envelope." He stepped closer and she edged away, back bumping the trailer's brightly painted side. He touched her arm, just below Nina's coils. "Whatever you're doing, it's not safe. If anyone else had seen—"

"Stop inventing lies, Ctibor." She twisted away. "I don't know what you're talking about." She stomped toward the snake trailer, barely managing not to run.

He called after her, but she didn't turn. She kept expecting him to give chase, to grab her again and threaten to report her. Stormy skies, how much had he seen? She'd been certain she and the old woman had been alone. Ctibor shouldn't have known to follow her unless the handoff had been a setup or the Tayemstvoy already suspected her. Did the old woman work for the red shoulders?

Several trailers between them, Celka pressed a fist to her mouth, squeezing her eyes shut and struggling to think. By stomping away, had she made Ctibor more likely to report her? Worse, if he was Tayemstvoy and already watching her, could she truly risk this pickup, even if she learned to wall off her concealment nuzhda?

Just this morning, Gerrit had admitted that the concealment stone would barely stretch to cover two people, and that holding it so extended could shatter its weaves. Which meant she needed an innocent excuse to go into town, and would have to conceal just the crate. But she'd have to be unflappable about it, hiding the crate even if the Tayemstvoy questioned her.

Stomach twisting with dread, she climbed the snake trailer steps. She couldn't do this.

But the thought of failing the Wolf—of ruining whatever plans depended on these rifle instructions—made her want to scream. She returned Nina to her cage, the snake trailer strangely empty with Gerrit off, taking his invisible daily exercise. She hoped he would see more hungry townsfolk and start learning to think for himself.

Gerrit. She swallowed hard, an idea like a stone caught in her throat. She could avoid failing the Wolf. She just had to trust a tiger to do it.

AN ELABORATELY FOLDED piece of paper lay on the floorboards when Gerrit entered the snake trailer. Invisible, he stooped to pick it up. Had Celka written him a note? He'd left the trailer as soon as Celka had slipped him the concealment stone and spent the morning alone beside a stream, practicing sousedni-dislocations until he nearly passed out from the pain.

The practice was paying off, though. He could hold a two-meter dislocation now for almost five minutes. Maybe he was imagining it, but it seemed like his transitions out of sousednia were getting easier, too.

Trailer door pulled shut, he dropped his connection to the concealment stone. With a deep breath, he shattered the mental walls surrounding the sliver of his mind that had spent the morning crazed with fear. As the walls crumbled, concealment's panicky terror overwhelmed him, and his muscles clenched. He fought the need to draw into a protective ball, steadying himself against the wall while, in sousednia, he tore apart the cell where he'd been bound and beaten.

With deep, slow breaths, he relaxed his mind, reintegrating the part of himself he'd locked behind granite walls. He took the time to do it properly, focusing on the snake trailer's stink and the press of summer humidity bleeding into his alpine sousednia. His instructors had impressed enough times that this was where many bozhki went wrong. You could half-ass reintegration occasionally and not notice, but the more you left your mind fractured, the deeper the cracks grew.

Several minutes after he no longer felt any urge to cringe or hide, Gerrit opened his eyes. He still held Celka's note. Carefully, he unfolded it.

Instead of scrawled handwriting, he found blotchy type and black and white photographs. One showed a Tayemstvoy soldier with arm raised, lash's flails a blur; past them, an elderly person knelt, stripped to the waist and bound to a post. Hunger cut the victim's ribs against their skin, and they'd thrown back their head in a scream Gerrit could imagine too easily. The second photograph showed a youth who could have been Celka in the grainy print, face swollen from a beating.

His eyes skipped over the text despite his revulsion. Factory quotas increased as the Stormhawk prepared for an aggressive war, unleashing the Tayemstvoy to terrorize Bourshkanya's own citizens. A woodcut stamp of a running wolf signed the page.

Gerrit dropped it like it had burned him. Stormy skies, had Celka put this here? He'd heard that the resistance printed leaflets—mouthpieces for foreign propaganda, malicious lies to undermine State authority. Treason.

"Did you read it?"

Gerrit spun at Celka's voice. He hadn't noticed her slip inside. "Freezing sleet, Celka, don't *do* that."

She studied him, waiting.

"So the Tayemstvoy beat some workers." He crushed his horror to make his voice flat. *He*'d been beaten often enough during training. It's not like the photographs were shocking. "They were probably lazy."

"You're a piece of work."

"You might be feeding the starving masses, Celka, but the resistance isn't all sunshine." She'd been right, though, civilians everywhere were as rail-thin as the villagers at her soup kitchen. "I've heard confessions from resistance sleet-lickers. I talked to a man who'd been paid by a Lesnikrayen agent to betray Bourshkanya." He picked the leaflet up and crushed it in his fist like he should have done the instant he saw what it was. "That rezistyent was scum." The resistance may not have murdered his mother; that didn't make them heroes. "Who gave you this leaflet?"

She held his gaze, and he fought the urge to look away. He was in the right here, not her. When she spoke, her voice was low, chilling. "You want a name so your red-shouldered friends can pull them from their house in the middle of the night? You think that 'confession' you heard was real? Did it look like the 'scum' was talking of his own volition?"

"Of course not. Filth never talk unless they're motivated."

"*Motivated?*" She twisted the word. "The Tayemstvoy *torture* people. The man you saw was repeating what the red shoulders forced him to say."

"He'd broken. Finally admitted the truth."

"Yeah, he'd broken all right. He'd say anything to make them stop."

"You don't know that."

She held his gaze for a long time and he was so focused on her that he didn't realize she'd taken the leaflet and flattened it out. She pressed it against his chest, startling him into looking down and breaking their staring contest. "You're right," she whispered. "I don't. But you saw him. *You* do."

Gerrit opened his mouth to deny it, but the words caught in his throat. He remembered the man's desperation. His whimpers.

He crushed the memory back down.

"How do you do it?" His voice was supposed to be

hard, but the memory of the brutalized resistance fighter lingered. Freezing sleet, if Celka was right, he didn't even know what the man had done. Maybe he'd tripped and bumped into a Tayemstvoy officer on his way to work or complained about his factory overseer where the wrong person could hear. "How do you live every day knowing that could happen to you? How can you risk treason?"

"What made you run away?" she asked.

"Branislav. I told you."

"He's not the whole story. You could have arrested me and handed me over as collateral. You could have bought yourself time to imbue on your own."

She said it matter-of-factly. He'd assumed she'd never considered the possibility or she wouldn't have been willing to trust him. But Celka was never quite what he expected. "That *was* my plan."

She shook her head. "That wouldn't require you to come alone. You wanted to talk to me. You were thinking about running away even before I ambushed you."

Before he could deny it, she took his hand. Storm energy burst up his arm and sousednia brightened the trailer. After a moment, the energy dampened to a background buzz that left the world overly vivid.

"Gerrit." Her grip tightened, green eyes fierce in the alpine sun. "What *really* happened? Why did you leave the Storm Guard?"

Struggling to ignore the strange clarity, he studied her. She worked for the resistance. She was dangerous—to him and to the State. She also used sousednia in ways he'd never dreamed possible and smiled when she pulled against concealment. She was clever and beautiful and he loved the way her smile lit up her whole face.

Captain Vrana had sent him here. Captain Vrana, who knew his mother and who had told him the truth.

"My mother..." He focused intently on true-life where he couldn't hear her labored breath on the wind. His eyes burned, but he struggled to show no emotion.

"What happened?" she asked.

His grief flash-boiled into anger. How could he look at those photographs and pretend not to care? The Tayemstvoy wouldn't care. They would *enjoy* torturing the poor sleet-lickers who worked fourteen-hour shifts making rifles or uniforms or whatever the Army needed.

"The Academy grants two weeks' leave for Darknight festivities. I used to go home. My mother's family has an estate; it's where I grew up, before the Academy." An ache in his chest made it hard to breathe. "The last time... I was so excited. We'd just learned the bozhskyeh storms were returning early. I was finally going to *be* someone." Saying it now, he realized the dichotomy he'd forgotten over the years: his father had been disgusted with his storm-blessing, but his mother had always been proud.

"Mother met me at the train station in our new motorcar. We... detoured on the way home." How many times had he regretted that choice? "We drove to the edge of a ravine that had the most amazing mountain views." Anger twisted his chest as much as grief, and he pulled off his storm pendant, gripping the filigreed gold as he remembered his mother's smile when she handed him the wrapped box. *You're not our family's first storm-blessed, Gerrit, but you will be our greatest.*

"On the way back, there was a cart overturned in the road. I don't know if Mother saw something or if it was just instinct—but she threw herself down over me. Three gunshots shattered the wind-shield glass, killing our driver and our guard.

"Mother drew her sidearm and ordered me to stay in the car. I got the driver's pistol..." He kept talking, but wasn't sure what he said, the memory consuming him, fragmented. More gunshots. Shouting, bootsteps. The low thud of blows. The motorcar's door swung open and someone dragged him out, tearing the revolver from his grasp before he could fire. A fist drove the air from his lungs. He tried to fight, but he was thirteen and small for his age. Rope bit into his wrists, his hands wrenched behind his back.

His attacker dropped him like he was nothing and closed on his mother. She fought like a thunderstorm, but by the time Gerrit wrapped his bound hands around the revolver, they'd beaten her to the ground, her blood darkening the road. Only four of her attackers were still standing, but Gerrit was too late. Too slow. Too weak.

«I shot the one closest to her first, but they stabbed her in the chest as they fell. I don't really remember what happened next. I shot the others, I think, and ran to her. There was so much blood. I used my jacket to try and stop her bleeding, but I couldn't pull the knife out or

I might make it worse.» Gerrit wasn't sure when he'd transitioned into sousednia, but he couldn't speak these truths out loud. «She died in my arms.»

«Oh, Gerrit.» Celka knelt at his side in the alpine sun, hugging him. His tears ran hot down his cheeks before freezing.

After a long time Celka asked, «How did they know where to find you? You said you detoured. How did someone ambush you?»

With a start, he remembered the back of Captain Vrana's note. *How did they know where to ambush you?* How *had* they known?

«I didn't tell anyone,» he said, «and Mother wouldn't have.» When he'd been younger, his parents had fought about her taking him sightseeing. Father had insisted it made him weak. «Except... my sister guessed.» He felt as though someone had struck him across the face with a rifle. «I asked her not to tell Father, but she loves pointing out my failings.»

«You think your father had something to do with it?» Celka asked, sickened.

Something within him quailed. «No.» Gerrit put strength of conviction behind the word. «He couldn't have. He wouldn't.» He plunged ahead, unable to dwell on that sniper in the bush. «The Tayemstvoy took the survivors in for questioning. I read their reports. I stood in a cell while a woman confessed to trying to kidnap me for the resistance—so I would imbue for them. They wanted my mother, too, to force the State to release their filth friends.»

Celka recoiled.

He caught her hands before she retreated too far. «It was a lie. Our attackers were Tayemstvoy, not resistance.» He remembered his father's determination to exterminate the resistance that dared strike at the regime's heart. «The attack warped my core nuzhda toward combat, and I raged at my father's side, embracing the violence Mother wouldn't have wanted.»

Don't become like them, she'd whispered. Had she known she was fighting Tayemstvoy?

«Now the Tayemstvoy want to drive us storm-mad so they can control us.» He gripped Celka's hands, and she returned his grip just as fiercely. He felt stronger having told her. Determined and cleansed. «I won't let them. We're storm-blessed. I won't let mundanes order me to imbue.»

«Then help me,» she said.

He swallowed hard, sick with fear at what she would ask.

«I need to pick up something for the resistance. I thought I'd be able to use your concealment imbuement, but...» She stood in sousednia, spinning away, arms outstretched as she paced along the high wire he couldn't see. «I don't know why I can't get the walls to work.»

«It takes practice,» Gerrit said woodenly. «It took me years to get this good at it.»

She spun back to face him, dancer-graceful despite the frustration locking her jaw. «I don't have years.»

«So let someone else go.»

«There's no one else. It's too dangerous.» She returned

to where he knelt in the snow and extended her hand. «Unless you help me.»

He felt like he'd walked into an ambush. He needed her help to learn grounding and stay hidden. But hating the Tayemstvoy was worlds away from helping the resistance. «What are you picking up?»

«You don't want to know.»

«Foreign propaganda? Weapons?»

She shook her head. «A mimeograph machine.»

He scrambled to his feet. «Are you crazy? You plan to print propaganda *here?*»

«It's not propaganda. It's... instructions. On how to use tools. We're trying to help people, Gerrit.»

«You're trying to get *killed*.»

«I'm trying *not* to. That's why I need your help.»

He turned away, running his hand through his hair, managing to avoid the still-healing lump from where she'd knocked him unconscious. How could he condone actively aiding the resistance? But if Celka got herself killed or arrested, all his plans to ensure the Storm Guard's autonomy would fail.

Once he proved his strength, he could report what they'd done. He could hand the Stormhawk an entire resistance cell.

A little voice in the back of his mind insisted that Celka would never willingly betray her resistance contacts. He crushed it down. He'd find a way to persuade her.

CHAPTER TWENTY-THREE

DEMIAN STARED AT the pile of elephant dung, shovel in hand. "This *cannot* be worth the money."

"Money is money," Celka said, no matter how much she agreed. Five copper myedyen for a handcart full of elephant manure would never have gotten her out in the sweltering afternoon sun, shoveling at her cousin's side. As a cover for the mimeograph pickup, however... breathing resolutely through her mouth, she drove her shovel into the steaming pile.

"I should really practice for tonight's show," Demian said.

Celka rolled her eyes and flung the shovel-full into the cart. "This'll take a lot longer if you keep whining."

"I know, what about—hey! Hey, Ctibor!" Demian shouted. Celka froze, shovel of shit in the air, as Demian waved Ctibor over.

"What are you doing?" she snapped to her cousin. "Dem, leave him alone."

"Hey, farm boy," Demian said, undeterred. "I'll give you two myedyen to take over for me."

"He has better things to do," Celka said in her best Aunt Benedikta voice.

"I don't really." Ctibor took Demian's shovel. "You pay in advance?"

Demian fished two myedyen from his pocket and smirked at Celka. "Later, sis."

She glared at his retreating back.

"So, we're selling elephant dung now?" Ctibor asked, driving his shovel into the pile.

"Yeah." Celka went to work at his side. At least he didn't dawdle and whinge like Demian. She heaved more dung into the cart, shoulders crawling beneath Ctibor's gaze. "Some rich con wants it for her garden. Makes the best fertilizer, apparently. All I care is it's money."

"I thought your family earned top silver," Ctibor said. "Isn't that why the other sideshow performers hate you?"

"*They* earn top salaries. *I* don't. Not anymore."

He fell silent, accepting it. Celka kept her attention on the mound of shit. Whatever else she could say about Ctibor, he worked hard. Soon, they had to roll the cart forward to find more dung.

As they started shoveling again, Ctibor said, "I'm sorry I frightened you before."

"Don't. Just don't. You want to earn a few myedyen, fine. But I'm tired of your lies."

"I'm not going to report you."

"Report me? For talking to a villager?" She tried to sound incredulous, but his expression was so serious that she couldn't hold his gaze. She forced herself to move, to drive her shovel into the dung, but her muscles weren't working right and the shovel got stuck.

He took it from her hands, easily tossing the load into the cart before handing the shovel back, empty. "I've been thinking about the soup kitchen. It's too much food to be coming from your ration books."

"We pool them together and—"

"Now who's lying?"

She snapped her mouth shut, but resolutely heaved another shovelful. She wasn't stupid enough to admit illegal activity.

He sighed. "Celka, I know something's going on. False ration books or bribes or something."

Crossing her arms, she glowered at him. "If you're fishing for dirt, you can go somewhere else. I just serve soup. I help people. That's all."

He leaned his shovel against the hand cart. "I just... I want to help, too." He looked entirely serious, and she didn't smell any deception from him in sousednia. She drew a slow breath, inhaling oiled steel and the mustiness of—she recognized it now—old books, like a dusty library.

She met his gaze and held it, blowing a breeze through sousednia so his cues couldn't escape her. "Are you Tayemstvoy?"

"What? No." His surprise matched his sousednia.

"Do you work for them? Are you reporting to them?"

"No. And no." He held her gaze, unflinching. From his pure steel and library scent, she believed him.

"Then tell me who you are."

He looked away, jaw muscles bunching. She thought he was about to go back to shoveling, but he said, "What I left behind..." He shook his head, a damp, rotting mélange rolling off him, cut through with a cardamom sweetness and the scent of pine boughs. He crushed down the memories, the scents fading. When he faced her, his dark eyes were guarded but somehow beseeching. "Please don't ask me about it. I promise I won't hurt you. Can't that be enough?"

"Enough for what?"

"Enough for..." He spread his hands helplessly. "I don't belong here. I'm trying, but... I'm not a farm boy. I didn't grow up in the circus like the rest of you. I don't know how to always wear a smile, out to flirt with the world."

Her stomach did a little flip, but she told it to settle down. "You like flirting."

A bitter smile tugged at his lips. "I like eating candy, too. But it's not real food."

"I thought Ludvik was giving you something real."

He snorted and picked back up his shovel. "That's not what I meant."

His shovel made a wet slicing sound as it cut into the manure, then his arms and shoulders flexed as he heaved the load into the cart. He wore civilian trousers around the back lot, his suspenders taut lines down the strong triangle of his back. She stood, mesmerized by his strong, sure motions.

What was she doing? Cheeks flushing, she grabbed her own shovel and got back to work. "So, what? You need someone you're not interested in flirting with?"

She braced to throw her manure in the cart, but Ctibor's hand over hers froze her in place. He stepped close enough that she could smell his sweat over the manure stench. He smelled good, like dry grass and honest work. His fingertips brushed her cheek and she shivered despite the heat. "I need someone who sees *me*. Who doesn't fit in here either."

Celka's heart seemed to skip a beat but she forced a nervous laugh. "I grew up in the circus my entire life."

His dark eyes didn't release her. "Yet you barely fit in better than I do."

She swallowed, her mouth suddenly dry. "What's that supposed to mean?"

His fingers stroked her cheek before he returned to his shovel. "I'm still trying to figure that out."

Celka watched him get back to work, her stomach a tangled knot. She wanted to shout at him for his presumption, except that she also wanted him to touch her again. But how could he know she didn't belong? And if he saw through her comfort here, how much else did he see? How much else did he suspect?

Shoving aside those concerns, she focused on the squelch of manure beneath her shovel. Whoever Ctibor was or wasn't, she needed this cart loaded and ready before the dinner bell. Even leaving immediately after the sideshow, it'd be a close thing to get it emptied in time for tonight's real mission.

CELKA HAULED AGAINST the handcart's handles in the evening's long shadows, dragging the stinking manure across the weedy lot. She half expected Ctibor to appear out of nowhere and offer to help, but maybe he'd had his fill of manure.

She'd gotten the cart almost to the road when the load suddenly lightened. She glanced back to find Gerrit's wavery sousedni-shape pushing, wrapped in the concealment imbuement's lake-blue glow. «Thanks,» she said.

«Could you have chosen a less fragrant cover story?»

«Would you want to search my cart if you were Tayemstvoy?»

He snorted then pulled a face visible even in his sousedni-shape. Celka's nervous energy escaped in a laugh, glad she'd trusted him, glad she wouldn't face this mission alone.

They said little on the road to town, but her gamble paid off, and the Tayemstvoy passed her through Vrbitse's checkpoint with disgust.

As Celka dragged the cart uphill toward the estate expecting her, Gerrit said, «While you unload, I should do reconnaissance.»

Her stomach clenched. «Why?» Letting him keep the crate invisible was one thing; trusting that he wouldn't send word to the Tayemstvoy to have her contacts arrested was something entirely else.

«You're certain this isn't a trap?» he asked.

The cyanide capsule Grandfather had given her this evening dug into her chest where she'd stashed it in her brassiere. "You don't have to go through with this," Grandfather had said, the cork-stoppered capsule deadly on his open palm. "But if you do, take this and swear to me you'll use it."

Her hand had hesitated, bile souring her throat. "If I'm captured, can't the resistance get me out? I'm storm-blessed. I—"

"Which is why the State *must not* have you. They will torture you and learn what you are. They will force you to imbue. This is the only rescue we can provide." Grandfather closed his hand over the capsule. "Unless you choose a safer course. Do not risk yourself for the Wolf's caprice."

She'd taken the capsule from him, but his fear had shaken her.

«Celka?» Gerrit asked. «*Do* you think it's a trap?»

She shook herself. «No.»

«That wasn't exactly reassuring.»

«We stay together.»

«I thought we trusted each other,» he said.

«I trusted you to come here.»

«And I'm wasted watching you shovel manure.» The snap in his voice made her turn to find his sousedni-shape at her side, though his true-form kept invisibly pushing the cart uphill. «Let me verify the place isn't being watched. Let me find escape routes in case we have to run. You wanted my help—*let me help*. Tell me where we're going so we don't get shot by the Tayemstvoy when we arrive.»

She met his gaze, shivering at his predatory intensity. But he was right. If she wanted the tiger's help, she needed to release him from his cage.

CHAPTER TWENTY-FOUR

CELKA DESCENDED TOWARD the river, a rotten cabbage stench overwhelming her handcart's lingering stink of manure. She hurried through the twilit streets, squinting for landmarks, cart clattering behind her.

Unloading had taken longer than she'd planned, the gardener ordering her to shovel manure onto his flower beds instead of dumping it in a pile. She hadn't dared complain. The two-headed Tayemstvoy hawk hung from the mansion's balustrades, black with gold talons on a field of blood. She wanted to kick the roustabout who'd set up this delivery for not warning her she was fertilizing a Tayemstvoy officer's garden.

The roustabout's directions to the rendezvous had also seemed easy to follow when she'd sketched them with a stick in the dirt. *Mill Street, down by the river. You'll know it by the stench.* But Vrbitse was no tiny village, and the streets snaked and dead-ended.

«Celka.»

She jumped. Spotting Gerrit's sousedni-shape, she breathed relief.

«This way.» He gestured in sousednia, and she followed him down a narrow alley and up a small rise, winding between warehouses and ramshackle tenements. His steps were silent—he must be barefoot again.

Just as she started to worry he was as lost as she was, they rounded a corner onto an open lot piled with logs.

«There are guards.» He pointed to distant figures. «But they have a standard circuit. We'll wait here a minute then head behind those logs.»

Celka's cyanide capsule pressed a tumor of fear against her chest. «Did you see anyone else?»

«I thought I saw light inside the west building, but it went out before I got there. And all the doors are locked.»

«You can't pick locks?»

«I'm not a *thief*,» he said, offended.

«I just would have thought...»

«We use guns, Celka. The State doesn't skulk through the shadows.» The edge in his voice felt like a slap.

«Thanks for the reassurance.» He was probably just nervous, same as her. «How did you find me?»

«I looked around then climbed onto a roof to watch for surprises. A girl in glittering sequins stands out on a snowfield.»

The hint about his sousednia tantalized her. She resolved to ask later, when they were safe. «Did you see any? Surprises, I mean.»

He went silent, radiating worry as he watched the darkness. «Come on.» He waved her forward.

They stopped in deep shadow against a machine of glittering blades that looked like a nightmare's open mouth. The logs piled on one side loomed dark in the moonlight; on the other side, they gleamed white and barkless. She focused on the west building, visible from their hideout. The third door from the river was closed, the windows dark. «*All* the doors were locked?»

«Yeah.» Tension cracked his voice. «And there's no cover between here and the third door.»

«You didn't answer my question,» Celka said. «About surprises.»

«If I asked you to abort this mission, would you?»

She wanted to say *no*, but forced herself to ask, «Why?»

«I don't know. Something feels off. The guards are too regular, too alert. The area's too quiet. I don't like it.»

«That's it?» she asked. «You 'don't like it'?»

«Have you ever done something like this before? Was the communication standard?»

Her fingers brushed the cyanide capsule. Grandfather had been nervous, even before that first pickup, and the Wolf had never asked something like this of them. She drew a slow breath, trying to rein in her fear. «Bozhskyeh storms have returned. That changes everything.» If she aborted now, she could ruin the Wolf's plan. She kept telling Grandfather the resistance needed to act; printing rifle instructions had to presage action.

Unless this was a trap.

Gerrit held her gaze for a long minute in sousednia. «All right, we're already late. I'll go knock on the door. That way, if it's a trap, they won't see you.»

Celka caught his arm before he could move, surprised he didn't push harder to abort. «If anyone has experience with bozhki, a phantom knock might make them suspicious. Where are the guards in their rotation?»

The concealment imbuement peeled away, revealing an ornate gold pocket watch in his hand. He tilted it to catch the moonlight. «Freezing sleet. We lost our window. All right, I'll go distract them. Run to the door when you hear a rock owl.»

«You do bird impressions?»

«I have hidden depths.»

She swallowed a laugh.

Gerrit caught her hands. «Be safe.»

She squeezed back, hard. «You too.»

Then he was off, sprinting like a ghost across the lot and vanishing around a mountain of wood chips. She waited, shoulders crawling, for an owl's hoot. When it came, she leapt to her feet, the cart rattling terrifyingly loud behind her. A clang sounded in the distance, then shouts and running feet.

She knocked on the third door.

Trying to ignore the mill's rotting cabbage stink, she strained to hear voices or approaching footsteps. When a deadbolt clanked open before her, she jumped. The door flung wide, and she hoped Gerrit would make it back soon. If he didn't, he wouldn't be able to get in unobserved.

Celka pulled her handcart into the darkness, unable to see who had opened the door, unable to tell if they wore red shoulders. A meter inside, she stopped, letting her handcart block the door. A second passed, and she glanced over her shoulder in sousednia, searching her spotlit big top for Gerrit.

"Move inside," a rough voice said from the darkness. "You want a guard to see the open door?"

Celka squinted to identify the speaker, but the paper mill was pitch black. Someone caught her arm and dragged her forward. The cart was yanked in after her. Gerrit sprinted inside just as the door swung shut.

Fast as they'd closed the door, it made barely a sound as it latched, though the scrape of the locking bolt tore at Celka's ears. She was trapped, surrounded. She crushed the thought. These were her contacts. She hoped.

A match hissed, then a bulls-eye lantern shined in her face. She raised a hand and turned away from the brightness.

"You're late," said the voice, grinding like stones. "Were you followed?"

"No. I just got lost." She plucked at her collar in the agreed-upon signal, squinting at the shadow behind the lantern, unable to tell if they made the appropriate reply.

«There are five of them,» Gerrit said. «Mundanes. I can't tell any more from sousednia.»

"One girl and an empty handcart?" Another voice said, young and probably male. "This is either a setup or incompetence."

"I'm stronger than I look." Celka kept her attention on their leader.

"How do you expect to get your cargo through checkpoints?" The gravel-voiced person asked.

"That's my business." A wind through sousednia ensured she conveyed only confidence. "I'm not asking how you got the machine."

"No backup?" sneered the youth. "How do you even plan to drag it out of here?" They stepped from the shadows, kerchief hiding their mouth and nose, a hat shadowing their eyes. "Who'd you squeal to, traitor?" They advanced, but she refused to retreat. "Where are the red shoulders?" They caught a handful of her hair, wrenching her head back. She clenched her hands into fists. Gerrit circled behind them, but Celka managed to raise one hand in sousednia to tell him to wait.

She met the youth's shadowed eyes, a hard sousednia wind blowing her fear away. "The more time you waste, the more likely the guards will spot your lantern. Their rounds will bring them back in—"

«Five minutes,» Gerrit said.

She echoed him. "I can get the machine out of here. I can do as the Wolf asked, but not if you get us all captured with your paranoid bluster."

The grip on her hair tightened to the point that tears pricked her eyes, but she refused to flinch. "I could snap your neck right now."

Celka bared her teeth. "Who do you work for, the Wolf or the Tayemstvoy?"

"Enough," the gravel-voiced leader snapped. "Marcel, help her load the cart."

Marcel released Celka with a shove. "This is a

mistake," they said as they strode away. Celka glared after them, shaky with the fear she'd refused to feel before. They turned back with an impatient gesture. "Follow me."

Together with several other rezistyenti, Celka heaved a massive crate into the handcart. The cart's bicycle tires squashed flat beneath the load.

"You know how to use it?" their leader asked, shining the dark-lantern on the crate.

"No," Celka said at the same moment a squawk came from the rafters. The leader slammed closed the lantern's shutter, plunging them into darkness.

In the tense silence, Celka gripped the handcart, struggling to hear anything over the pounding of her pulse. Gerrit's sousedni-shape ghosted away around the hulking machinery.

«Where are you going?» she asked, panicky.

«To see what we're facing.»

She forced a deep breath. Of course. More reconnaissance. He was smart. She needed to be smart. Gerrit was checking the factory floor; she should check outside. Focusing more deeply on sousednia, she moved to step through the wall. But darkness disoriented her, and a dislocation that should have reached outside the building left her in open factory space, breathing the rezistyenti's fear.

A shout broke the held-breath silence, followed by the stone-grinding crunch of hobnailed boots.

"She turned us in." Marcel grabbed her upper arm, fingers digging bruises.

"Everyone run," the leader snarled.

"No!" Celka caught their jacket. "Leave me your lantern. Run, draw them away. I can still get out."

"They'll search the building."

"Please." She wafted all her terrified sincerity toward the gravel-voiced rezistyent, unable to see their face to know if they believed her. Marcel still gripped her arm and Gerrit was too far away to help if they decided to knife her in the ribs. "Don't make this for nothing."

The leader snarled wordlessly, but thrust the lantern into her hands. Celka scrambled not to burn herself on the hot metal as Marcel released her. Boots pattered as the rezistyenti ran.

Celka lifted the lantern's shutter, scanning for a hiding place. Barrels stacked against one wall offered no succor but, on the other side, a mixing machine hulked over a vat swimming with woodchips. Celka left the lantern open on the floor next to the handcart and sprinted to the mixing vat, barking her shins in the shadows.

«Gerrit!» she called. «Hide the crate.» If the Tayemstvoy found the mimeograph machine, her mission would fail even if she avoided capture.

She rounded the mixing machinery until it blocked the lamplight and climbed blind, feeling for foot- and hand-holds. Grease stained her hands and smeared her clothes, making purchase precarious, but she kept climbing.

A gunshot rang out, followed by shouting. Celka flattened herself along the top of the mixer, hoping the Tayemstvoy didn't look up.

Gerrit sprinted out around machinery, a streak of blue

diving for the handcart. The concealment imbuement would barely stretch to cover both him and the crate, so he flung himself on top of it.

Please, Celka prayed, wishing she dared move enough to touch her storm pendant, *let this work*.

Heartbeats after the crate vanished, four Tayemstvoy jogged into the light cast by Celka's abandoned lantern, rifles drawn. They spread out, and Celka held her breath, prone and vulnerable, legs stretched out along the mixing paddle's support beam. She turned her face away, unwilling to risk a reflection off her eyes.

A sousedni-dislocation put her on ground-level with the soldiers, and she struggled to resolve their wispy smoke-forms. But at best, she could destroy the aim of one shot. If they spotted her, no dislocation would save her from capture. She'd have to hope she could tear the cork from the cyanide capsule before they pulled her down.

One Tayemstvoy cursed and called another over. Celka missed their words, but they'd found the impression the crate had left on the floor.

"They must have gotten it out," one said. They pointed at another soldier. "Keep watch in case they return. The rest of you, with me." The three sprinted off, leaving a lone Tayemstvoy staring into the darkness, rifle in hand. Celka's abandoned lantern glinted off their polished black knee-boots. Another dark-lantern hung on the private's belt.

Celka waited until the others' footsteps had receded. «Gerrit, can you take this one out?»

«Tell me when.» Strain tightened his voice. She wondered suddenly what happened to *him* if the imbuement shattered.

Pushing with her hands, Celka belly-crawled backward along the mixer's spine. She tried to move silently, but they had to hurry—get out while most of the Tayemstvoy were distracted by the fleeing rezistyenti. As she clambered down, her grip slipped along a greasy drive-shaft, and she slipped, bashing her chin and crying out.

"What—" The private broke off with a grunt, followed by the dull thud of their body hitting the ground.

«Some warning would have been nice.» Gerrit dragged the private away by their feet.

Fear left Celka's throat too tight to speak. She heaved on the cart's handles, straining to get it moving. Gerrit blew out the private's lantern but left the other on the ground so they could find the door.

The cart lurched when he joined her, pushing invisibly from behind. They got the cart outside, then Gerrit ran back, blowing out the lantern to buy them more time. Together, they dragged the heavy cart toward the railyard.

CHAPTER TWENTY-FIVE

A HEADACHE NEEDLED Gerrit's temples from driving the concealment nuzhda hard enough to keep both himself and the crate invisible as they wound through Vrbitse. Fortunately, the circus workers made enough noise that the handcart's crunching progress through railyard gravel didn't give them away.

Inside the snake trailer, Celka began rearranging crates and cages to make space for her illegal printing press. Gerrit, still cloaked by the concealment imbuement, struggled to maintain the focus that had kept him moving while Celka's plan fell to pieces. He needed to drop the imbuement and reintegrate his mind, but he wanted desperately to avoid the crushing terror locked behind sousednia's walls.

What he wanted didn't matter. He couldn't risk his sanity.

Back pressed against the trailer door, he squeezed his eyes shut and shattered his mental walls. Concealment's panicky terror crashed like an advancing wave of enemy infantry over his sun-bright mountainscape. But instead of dissipating, that terror hit a resonance with his fear from the raid, and the pristine mountain clearing twisted into a granite cell. Restraints closed around his wrists, yanking his arms overhead. A panicky, animal noise escaped his throat.

«Gerrit.» Luminous in sequins, Celka took his face in her hands. Storm energy brightened the cell, sharpening true-life and sousednia. "We're safe," she said. "We made it out. We did it."

At first, Gerrit couldn't move his bound arms, but true-life strengthened until he drew a gasping breath, catching her face in an aching mirror of how he'd stood so often with Filip.

"You're safe," she said again, her confidence buoying him.

The Tayemstvoy hadn't found them, hadn't shot Celka. The concealment imbuement hadn't shattered and torn him from true-life. Snow and glaciers fractured the cold granite cell, and Gerrit drew a shuddery breath of pine-bright air. They were safe. Safe. And he was a traitor.

Flinching from the thought, Gerrit focused on Celka's fierce intensity, on her skin warm and soft beneath his hands. "Thank you," he said.

She grinned, giddy. "We did it."

The memory of her crying out as she slipped, of the Tayemstvoy private snapping her rifle toward the sound, tightened his chest. He stroked Celka's cheek with his thumb, struggling to believe they were truly safe. "You could have been killed."

That sobered her—a little. "I know. Thanks for your help." Her eyes dropped to his mouth and she stepped closer. "For everything."

Traitor, his mind screamed. *Traitor. Traitor.*

To escape, Gerrit pulled Celka to him and kissed her. She stiffened.

He released her. "I'm sorr—"

Her lips smothered his words, her hand wrapping the back of his neck to pull his head down to her. The contact sparked storm energy through him—fire and ecstasy, and a need as desperate as any nuzhda.

Then she stepped back, eyes too wide, breath too quick.

He wanted to ignore her fear and pull her to him again, lose himself in the taste of her mouth as he ran his hands down her strong thighs, so tantalizingly visible in sousednia. But the rest of the evening flooded back in, and he couldn't beat the knowledge back any longer.

He let her go. "I shouldn't have."

She pulled away, expression twisting with an echo of the disgust she'd worn when they first met. "You're Storm Guard."

Gerrit looked down. "I betrayed the State."

"You did what was *right*."

The words battled inside his chest. Part of him was glad he'd helped Celka, thrilled they'd outsmarted the Tayemstvoy. He wanted to laugh and spin her around the illegal press; the Tayemstvoy thought themselves so powerful, but tonight he'd proved they weren't.

But he'd betrayed his father and the State. He should feel like sleet. He didn't—and the thought terrified him.

"You know the regime is wrong," she said.

"No," he said. "I don't."

Eyes burning with belief, she caught his hands. "I'll show you. I'll prove it."

He yanked free. Her fervent belief reminded him too much of his Tayemstvoy instructors. "We need to hide the mimeograph." He shouldered past her, crouching to grab one side of the crate.

When Celka didn't immediately join him, he turned back and found her touching her lips.

Jaw clenched, he faced the crate. "Come on. It's late. Your family will be worried."

They heaved the crate into place without speaking. Innocent crates and cages piled around it, Celka started for the door. Gerrit wanted to call her back, wanted to explain that she shouldn't trust him.

Before he could summon the nerve, she said, "There's a storm predicted tomorrow."

"I know." She'd started bringing the daily newspaper with breakfast, and they read the weather section together, trying to disentangle the bozhskyeh storms from the regular ones.

She smiled a little. "I'll try your idea. Happy thoughts to block the storm."

The reminder of why he was here and everything he had to return to made it hard to breathe. He couldn't let

Celka's gleeful treason sweep him away. No matter how he hated the Tayemstvoy, most were surely loyal to the State. *He* had to remain loyal.

Her smile fell. "See you tomorrow."

He watched her go without saying good night.

CHAPTER TWENTY-SIX

THE FIRST BOLT of Gods' Breath the next day flared Gerrit's vision white. Alpine wind rose up, drowning the rain drumming the snake trailer roof. Sousednia's sunlight seared his eyes, and panic boiled through him. What if, in attempting to imbue without Filip, he drove himself storm-mad?

The bozhskyeh storm tugged harder, and sousednia's snow and ice blotted out true-life. Where normally his mountaintop calmed him, today it made him cold.

He'd committed treason last night, and he wasn't even sure he regretted it. He had to get out of here before Celka's burning belief and the wretched gaze of hungry villagers bruised his loyalty. He had to imbue and return home, gain his father's trust and save his friends.

Imagining Filip waiting for him beside Hana and Darina and all the junior imbuement and strazh cadets,

Gerrit fought his way back to true-life, struggling to leave sousednia completely behind. They needed his help. He had to imbue for them.

The next bolt of Gods' Breath lanced fire down his spine, but his hold on true-life barely shook.

Unfolding the napkin wrapping his uneaten lunch, Gerrit knelt. He would start with a hunger imbuement— further from his core nuzhda and therefore harder to pull against, less likely to consume him the way combat had. Holding half his sandwich, he embraced the hollow ache in his belly from the skipped meal.

When he'd started Storm Guard training at age seven, they'd locked him in a cell of cold granite, the Song of Feeding engraved on one wall, a nuzhda bell hanging beside it. He'd thought the test would last only a few hours. He'd rung a nuzhda bell after fasting for Feeding Miracles before. But they'd pricked his finger and dripped his blood onto this bell, claiming it would help him see the weaves and understand what he needed to do.

Four days later, his fists ached from pounding on the door. Screaming had left his throat raw. They'd given him water and a bucket for waste, and the cell stunk of his own excrement. He hardly noticed over the hunger scraping his ribs.

"Please." Gerrit's voice echoed weirdly in the snake trailer as he let the ache in his stomach consume true-life.

Slumped against the stone wall, Gerrit chews on his scratchy wool blanket, reading the Song of Feeding until his eyes blur with tears.

A spinach-green glow pulses through the blur. He

squints, wipes his eyes. Weak, certain he's delirious, he crawls beneath the nuzhda bell, hearing the hitching rhythm of his own exhausted breath echoing from it. Parts of the bell glow brighter, and he strains to touch them. A smell like grilling meat makes him salivate. He whimpers, wanting to cry for the guards to feed him. Instead, he levers himself to his feet, leaning on the wall.

Closer to the bell, he hears nuance in its rhythm. Matching the sound with his breath, he discovers intricate glowing swirls. Unable to reach the bell with his hands, he strains with his thoughts, imagining the distance vanished, imagining touching the four brightly glowing points to his eyes, his nose, his mouth.

The taste of grilling meat floods his tongue. Strength jolts him, and he straightens with a gasp.

Distantly, he hears the bell ringing, hears a bolt slamming back and boots clomping into the cell, but he can't turn away from the glow, can't think around the ache in his stomach and the taste filling his mouth.

In the snake trailer, Gerrit locked his sousednia in that moment.

Salivating, he strengthened the cell walls in his hunger-warped sousednia then stepped outside them, icy wind stealing his breath. In his core sousednia, the bozhskyeh storm tugged against his spine. His focus shuddered.

Teeth clenched, he split his attention, reaching a third thread of his thoughts into true-life. Staring at the half sandwich in his hands, he pulled it into his snowy sousednia then returned to that hunger-warped part of himself.

There, he struggled to keep from shoving the sandwich into his mouth. But it would do so little for his hunger; he needed it to become more. The green glow of hunger nuzhda seeped from his hands into the bread, and he wove the hiccupping sound of his exhausted breath around it.

The storm yanked at his skull.

Panting, Gerrit forced himself to ignore its pull. This time, he would make no mistakes.

Shifting his focus outside his mental walls, he breathed deep of sousednia's alpine freshness. Through the cell's observation slot, he peered into his hunger-warped sousednia, meticulously inspecting his weaves, checking for frayed edges that could shatter beneath the flow of storm energy. A regular, simple rhythm filled the cell, befitting a Category One imbuement. It would increase the sandwich's nutrition and hunger satisfaction by a factor of three. Such a modest increase on a small object would require hardly any storm energy to crystalize. Even if something went wrong, he'd hold true-life.

True-life. He flailed for it, at a loss without Filip's grounding touch. But he refused to give up, seeking faint sounds out of place. Swooshing rain anchored him. Then the snake trailer door banged open, spraying him with cold droplets.

Fear of discovery nearly distracted him, but he crushed it. Imbuing was all that mattered.

Tracing his fingertips along the base of his skull, Gerrit closed his hand around his storm-thread and *pulled*.

∗   ∗   ∗

WAITING FOR THE bozhskyeh storm to break stretched Celka's nerves, worsened by the sideshow spectators' staring eyes. Her mouth soured by the taste of hot horseshoes, she sought a distraction.

Ctibor had been his flirty, charming self during the matinee sideshow, and she'd expected him at the soup kitchen. He hadn't showed. Tonight, he pulled his knives from the board with ragged force, jaw locked. When he turned from the board, replacing his knives on their rack, Celka tried to catch his eye. He didn't notice.

Georgs brought another round of gawkers through the tent, and Celka pasted back on her smile. Then the lights flickered, and thunder rattled the tent poles.

Pain knifed Celka's temples, but she managed not to lose her smile, shifting her attention to sousednia and stepping away from her true-form. She imagined herself three summers younger, running wild across the back lot with Evzhan. They'd competed in everything, seeing who could juggle the most balls or walk on their hands the furthest. She remembered permanent grass stains on her palms and falling over with laughter.

Despite those memories, the first bolt of Gods' Breath overhead twisted Celka's vision, and she stumbled, shooting her true-life arms out to the sides as she nearly slipped off sousednia's high-wire. She realized her mistake too late and tried to cover it, gasping and flinching from the little snakes as though they'd frightened her.

She'd barely recovered when another bolt sparked her vision. Dragging her attention to the precipice between true-life and sousednia, she stretched her high wire into the distance until the dislocation stole her breath.

Reliving Evzhan daring her to climb higher in a tree didn't help. The Song of Calming didn't help. So she told herself she needed nothing, silently repeating the words over and over while she fought to keep a smile on her true-life lips.

Yet the world continued to dissolve.

Nina hissed, scales rippling as she shifted in agitation.

"Storm Gods above!" Georgs cried as he brought the crowd past her platform. "I guess that python doesn't like thunderstorms! Miss Alatas, are you sure it's safe to hold her?"

As if Nina could hear him, her coils tightened. At Celka's feet, one of the smaller snakes reared up and hissed.

Struggling to see both true-life and sousednia, struggling not to need anything since happy thoughts were so utterly useless, Celka touched Nina's head, fluttering her eyelids in frightened innocence. "They do seem terribly agitated, don't they?" Gods' Breath tore fire down her spine, and Nina's mottled chestnut and black patterns smeared.

"Here, let me help." Ctibor leapt to her platform. An earnest performance drove away whatever had been eating at him. "Those snakes are deadly."

Nina's head lashed towards him. The audience gasped, edging back.

Ctibor held up his hands. "Miss Alatas, let me save you from that beast!" He edged closer, stepping carefully to avoid the smaller snakes.

Celka didn't know whether he thought she was actually in danger, but the audience loved it.

"The heroic Army corporal!" Georgs cried.

Celka wanted to roll her eyes, but Gods' Breath made Ctibor waver. If only he'd left her alone, the audience would have moved on and she could have concentrated on her dislocations.

Instead, Ctibor reached for Nina. "Let me take her before she strangles you."

The audience cheered agreement.

"She is squeezing tighter than usual." A lie, but the audience tittered. "Careful. She's just afraid." Celka's voice shook. She wished she could blame that on good acting.

"I'll be gentle." He unwrapped the big snake from her waist. Nina accepted the transfer placidly, and the audience sighed relief.

"Best get Miss Alatas out of there, Corporal," Georgs said, "before another snake decides to bite."

Celka glanced down at the harmless snakes coiling around her feet, letting her eyes widen. "Oh, they're agitated, too! We'd best go quickly." She'd intended it as a lie, but several snakes lashed their heads, distressed. Were they reacting to the storm or to her own tenuous control?

Hail hammered the tent roof like bullets, and wind tore at the canvas. The lights blinked out for a long breath before flickering back on. Ctibor took Celka's hand, his heroics overblown considering they only needed to step over a low wire mesh to the stairs.

Given Celka's tenuous control, she appreciated his solidity. Ctibor's exaggerated assistance made it easy to play along, bantering about the terrors of thunderstorms in the tropics. The performance helped her ignore the storm's pull, and she eased up a little on her sousedni-dislocation.

Finally, the audience moved on and, over the wind and hail, the band's march urged people to their seats. Celka sighed relief.

"They loved it." Ctibor's voice rumbled over the hailstorm.

Only then did Celka realize she was still holding his hand. He squeezed gently and released her with a smile, gracious enough to dissolve her embarrassment.

"You want a hand moving the snakes?" Ctibor abandoned his bravado.

The storm yanked against her skull, and it took her a second to focus on him. "What? Oh, no. Thanks for the 'rescue,' though." This time she did roll her eyes.

He smirked, but his eyes were serious. "I'm happy to help."

"Then why weren't you at the soup kitchen? Get lost again?"

His expression hardened, then he smiled and she might have imagined it. "I'm not that hopeless."

She relieved him of Nina, wrapping the snake around her own shoulders. "Just had better things to do?" She hated the hurt edge to her tone. *You don't fit in here any better than I do.* Maybe he said that to everyone he flirted with. Maybe he'd said that to Ludvik.

Ctibor took her hand. "I wanted to come with you." Honesty swirled around him in sousednia, for all that she wanted to call him a liar. "Celka..." He seemed to struggle with something. "Let me help. I can carry—"

"Nina's not really that agitated." Celka pulled free and started for the performers' entrance. Gerrit would be in the snake trailer; she couldn't risk Ctibor seeing him.

"Sure, but... it's raining really hard." At least the hail had let up; otherwise she'd be stuck waiting it out.

"I don't melt," she said.

At the tent flap, the wind sided with Ctibor, driving rain at them in stinging sheets. Celka froze at the threshold, not relishing a drenching.

"Do you want my coat?" Ctibor tossed a thumb over his shoulder to where an Army jacket hung on his knife rack.

Lightning sparked down Celka's spine. "You always this gallant?"

He shrugged. "For a pretty girl in distress."

Celka managed a snort that she hoped sounded dismissive. "I'm not a wilting lily."

"Can't blame a guy for trying."

"Go pack up your knives."

He clicked his heels and saluted. "Yes, sir."

The gesture seemed too natural, and a chill iced Celka's spine. Terror exploded with the scents of blood and gun oil, and combat nuzhda shattered her tenuous control. Sousednia warped, her high wire lashing away to leave her near the cook tent. Blows echoed through sousednia as the Tayemstvoy beat Pa and Vrana dragged Celka to the side.

The knife hanging from Ctibor's belt caught Celka's gaze. She started to reach for it, but something deep within her screamed *stop!*

She made a fist at her side. Before the nuzhda could make her stupid, she ran.

Cold rain drenched her and she gasped, stumbling over weedy hummocks and crashing through bushes on her way to the snake trailer. She had no idea what Ctibor would make of her sudden flight, but she couldn't spare the attention to worry.

Nina coiled crushingly about her shoulders and waist as Celka flung wide the snake trailer door. Rain plastered her hair to her face. Gerrit knelt amongst the snake cages, a half sandwich cradled on open palms.

Celka fumbled open Nina's cage as the mouth-watering scent of seared meat rippled sousednia, competing with the stench of blood and gun oil that had thickened while the Tayemstvoy beat Pa. She reeled. She had no idea how she'd managed a coherent conversation with Ctibor. Now, her every muscle strained against itself, desperate to grab a weapon and call the storm.

She'd barely tumbled Nina into her cage when Gods' Breath lashed down. In sousednia, the brilliant, red-gold bolt threw the Tayemstvoy's snarling faces into stark relief. In the snake trailer, every shadow vanished, and Gerrit lit like a flare.

For one delirious breath, energy infused Celka—like she could scythe down all the red shoulders with a wave of her hand.

Then Gerrit's glow shifted, becoming the green of

boiled spinach, draining down his arms and bursting into the sandwich. The light vanished, and Celka's giddy high popped like a dream upon waking.

She dropped to her knees, shuddering, hearing the blows she hadn't been able to stop falling on Pa. Vrana's fist smashed into her jaw. Her storm-thread seared the back of her skull like a red-hot iron.

Gerrit flung the sandwich aside and snapped something.

Vrana's hobnailed boot drove into Celka's stomach while truncheons cracked the air with the stench of blood. Vrana was Storm Guard. She'd sent Gerrit to drag Celka back to them.

Gerrit leapt to his feet, moving to attack.

They'd taken Pa. Celka wouldn't let them take her.

GERRIT HAD FAILED. Again. A Category One hunger imbuement—he couldn't go any sleeting simpler. And yet the weaves hadn't crystalized. He hadn't pulled hard enough on the storm.

His frustration flared into anger as Celka bared her teeth, snarling at his weakness. Gerrit opened his mouth to fling back some cruel remark, but—something was wrong.

Celka's sousedni-shape doubled over, no longer clad in emerald sequins, but wearing a child's simple shirt and short pants. Gerrit snapped his mouth shut, slipping too easily into sousednia where oily red combat nuzhda slicked Celka's skin.

«What are you doing?» Fear cracked his voice. «Celka, that's a Category Four combat nuzhda!»

She snarled and lurched to her feet. «Give me your knife.»

«What? No!» He stumbled back, hands up. «Celka, listen to me. You have to release the nuzhda. You're sparking—pulling too strongly. It's not safe...» But she clearly couldn't hear him. Behind her, his snowfield bled into a barren, icy road, a donkey cart blocking the way. One of the disguised Tayemstvoy cursed as Gerrit's mother fought.

Rage gripped Gerrit, and his bound hands closed around his revolver.

No! Fighting his every instinct, he flung the pistol behind him. «Celka, drop the nuzhda!» His combat-warped sousednia put a harsh edge to his plea. His second storm, and someone else was going storm-mad.

No, no, no. He had to stop her. He had to help.

Clawing into true-life, he dropped to his knees—though her aggressive posture screamed at him to fight back. "You're not in danger, Celka." When she snarled, he dropped to his belly, hands on the back of his head. "I'm not going to hurt you."

Her reply was Gods' Breath igniting the air. A nimbus of copper and carmine engulfed her and, where in true-life her outstretched hand had been empty, a knife coalesced out of fire.

Horrified, Gerrit shoved to his hands and knees as Gods' Breath tried to drag him into sousednia. Crimson combat sludge dripped from Celka's blade, perfectly crystalized by the storm energy she'd wielded so casually. "Focus on true-life, Celka, please. You're safe, drop the—"

She snarled and lunged at him.

Gerrit scrambled to his feet, retreating, parrying and dodging to give himself space. He felt too light, his knife no longer sheathed at his side but gripped in her hand.

The blade passed centimeters from his ribs, and Celka let her momentum carry her past him then twisted to plunge the knife into his kidney. Gerrit blocked, tried to catch her wrist, but she darted back.

"Celka, it's me." His breath came hard as he struggled to defend. She'd clearly been trained to fight. Or was that the imbuement? "It's Gerrit. We trust each other. You're safe." His helplessness from Branislav's cell threatened to well back up.

She lunged again, and he risked edging into sousednia. Understanding both realities took too much focus, however, and her knife sliced across his ribs. He hissed and leapt back, fighting to see true-life. He had to make her to drop the blade.

Watching for an opening, he closed, catching her knife hand and twisting. The joint-lock should have forced her hand open, but she kept the knife and elbowed him in the head.

Gerrit reeled, exhausted from holding out against the bozhskyeh storm, still recovering from his concussion. She pressed his weakness, attacking. He brought an arm up to block, too late, catching the knife across his forearm. Adrenaline quenched the pain, though blood slicked his skin.

In an echo of sousednia, pistol reports shattered the snake trailer's near-silence, and Gerrit suddenly gripped an ice-cold revolver between his bound hands.

Dodging a thrust, he grabbed her wrist, twisting the blade to plunge into her stomach.

At the last second he realized what he was doing and shifted his aim, barely missing her. The fight was sparking a combat nuzhda, and he fought to dispel it. He had to end this before he lost control.

Catching Celka's next punch, Gerrit twisted her arm behind her, using her own momentum to spin her and put her back to him. He whipped his own arm around her throat. If he couldn't break her grip on the knife, he had to sever her hold on the imbuement.

She was shorter than him, their height difference perfect for a choke hold. But he had only one chance, a margin of less than a second. Her knife hand was free; all she had to do was shift her grip and she could bury the blade in his side.

But Gerrit had trained in hand-to-hand combat his entire childhood.

Celka hesitated, and Gerrit cranked down on the choke. Instead of driving her knife into his gut, Celka scrabbled at his forearm. Her nails dug in, drew blood. Then she went limp.

The knife dropped to the trailer floor, flaring red in true-life as unconsciousness broke her connection to it.

Gerrit eased her to the floor.

He had only seconds before she regained consciousness. He could take the knife, activate it so she couldn't, but he wouldn't have time to wall off the nuzhda. He'd face her while holding a raw Category Four combat nuzhda in a storm. It would drive him to attack her like she'd attacked him. She didn't have his defensive training. He'd kill her.

If he didn't take the knife, she could activate it again and attack. Thunder crashed overhead, and Gods' Breath arced fire down his spine. If she attacked again, he might lose control. Like Branislav imbuing to stop the infantry squad, Gerrit might imbue and lose true-life.

Risk killing Celka, or risk storm-madness.

Celka gasped, body arching as she flailed back to consciousness.

Decide now.

Gerrit kicked her knife away then retreated toward the door. If she attacked again, he'd run. Maybe someone would see him, but at least he wouldn't go mad.

CHAPTER TWENTY-SEVEN

A ROARING FILLED Celka's ears. A chaotic tumble of images, voices. She gasped, flailing, trying to grasp something solid. What had happened? Where was she?

Pain burned from the base of her skull down her back. As the colors and shapes straightened into crates and snake cages, silence settled like after a heavy snowfall. She heard only the quick, panicky rhythm of her breath.

Then a voice, wary. "I'm not going to hurt you, Celka."

She shoved up on trembly arms and found Gerrit kneeling near the door, hands up, palms out and empty.

Fear jolted her. What had happened? Why was she on the floor?

Something pulled her attention: a knife, glowing red, smelling sweet like gun oil and blood.

She remembered now. Gerrit wanted to drag her to the

Storm Guard so they could force her to build weapons. She scrambled for the knife.

"'Raise not a hand to strike beneath a storm.'" Gerrit's voice echoed weirdly in the trailer's silence. "'A palm becomes a fist, a fist a knife, and the blade strikes a killing blow.'" The quote from scripture made Celka hesitate. "'Harsh words can be undone, but beneath a storm, words carry knives. Death is eternal.'"

Gerrit still held his hands up, weaponless. But he'd attacked her with his hands bound behind his back and it hadn't mattered. "Please, Celka, you're not in danger."

The trailer shook, as though rocked by wind. Celka looked around, confused. Wind that strong, she should hear it. And hadn't a storm been raging overhead? Had she been unconscious so long it had ended? "What happened?" she asked.

Gerrit released a shaky breath. She could hear him just fine. Why couldn't she hear the circus band or the roustabouts loading trailers?

"You imbued." He nodded to the knife glowing like hot coals deeper in the trailer. "The imbuement's Category One, I think, but you used too large a nuzhda."

She had no idea what that meant. The statement's core percolated into her brain. "I imbued?" She licked dry lips and rubbed the back of her neck. "Sleetstorms, I attacked you, didn't I?"

He nodded, hands dropping to his sides.

Only then did she notice the dark stain on his chest, the ragged, bloody tear in his right sleeve. "Are you all right?" At his jerked nod, she said, "I'm sorry." Rain drumming the trailer roof seeped into her awareness, and she looked up, surprised. "The storm?"

"It's still going," he said.

"I couldn't hear it."

"The strike affects your senses," he said. "Overwhelms them and shuts them down."

"I heard you just fine."

He shrugged, but the gesture seemed forced, his wary gaze never leaving her.

"I'm not going to attack you." She rubbed the back of her neck again. Stormy skies, it burned. "The storm isn't even pulling on me anymore." Closing her eyes, she slipped into sousednia. The silken cord connecting her to the storms remained, but it didn't tug on her like before she'd imbued.

She focused back on true life. "You imbued, too, didn't you?"

Gerrit launched to his feet.

Celka tensed, blood and gun oil rippling her big top.

Gerrit froze, motionless as she got herself back under control. Stormy skies, how was she supposed to go about her normal life if a storm made her want to kill anyone even remotely threatening? She'd sleeting kissed Gerrit only yesterday, but beneath the storm he so easily became the enemy.

"My imbuement failed." Anger tightened Gerrit's voice.

"Failed? But I saw the strike. I saw the storm energy change into..." She struggled to describe what she understood at a visceral level. "Hunger energy?"

He shook his head, tense with frustration. "It failed to crystalize my weaves."

"What does that mean?"

Gerrit coiled motionless like Nina preparing to strike. "What do you know about imbuements?"

"Enough to make one, I guess."

"Though it's useless."

She stood to face him. "Useless?" He was unbelievable. "You're standing there bleeding because my imbuement's *useless*?"

"I'm standing here bleeding because you don't know how to wall off your nuzhdi. Because you made a sleeting Category One knife out of a Category Four nuzhda and holding it *warped* you. I'm standing here bleeding because *you* lost control during a storm!"

She felt like he'd slapped her. "I don't know what Categories are." Her gaze dropped to the blood soaking his shirt.

"Then maybe you should learn before you fling storm energy around again and get one of us killed."

"Then teach me," Celka said.

"Just like that? You crystalize Category Four combat and you're *fine*? You want lessons in the middle of a storm? Crystalizing Category Five combat *destroyed* Branislav and he'd trained for years. You're a *civilian*. You don't deserve to succeed where I failed. You don't deserve to survive where—" His mouth snapped closed.

"Where your friend didn't." She crossed her arms over her chest, struggling not to show how badly his words had cut.

"I didn't mean..." He dropped to a crate and ran both hands through his hair. "Stormy skies, I'm sorry. Celka, I'm..." He pressed fingers into his temples. "I didn't mean that."

She sat slowly across from him. Her muscles felt shuddery and weak like after a long day practicing on the wire, and her mind felt stuffed with cotton. She could barely hear the rain, and the world seemed grayed out. She squeezed her eyes shut against tears that rose from nowhere, and felt burning lines radiating down her neck and back. "I feel like sleet, too."

He choked a surprised laugh. "Right? Ugh." He scrubbed his hands over his face. "I thought that creating magic would be amazing. I never thought it'd leave me feeling..."

"Like you've been hit by a train?"

"Yeah." He waited until she met his gaze then said, "I *am* sorry. I just... Branislav was one of my closest friends. He was incredibly skilled. I could pull against combat easier than him, but he ran circles around me with other nuzhdi. I can't believe he's gone."

Celka fiddled with her storm pendant, keeping it beneath her shirt, trying not to think about Pa. She stared at the floor where she'd stood during her imbuement, and it took her muddled brain long moments to realize what she was seeing. "Blizzard's teeth," she swore. "I storm-marked the floor."

A branching, fernlike pattern burst outward from where she'd stood, bleaching the wood in a filigreed starburst. In sudden understanding, she pressed her hand against the back of her neck.

"You're storm-scarred," Gerrit said.

Panic took flight in Celka's chest. She hadn't meant to imbue. Now the Tayemstvoy would follow the lightning strikes and find her just like they'd found that old woman.

"Can I see?" he asked.

Dozens of pins held her hair up in an elaborate twist, despite the storm's drenching. Ela had done her hair this afternoon, and Celka had tolerated it as an excuse to get her cousin's advice about romance—sidestepping details of her kiss last night with Gerrit. In the snake trailer, Celka put her back to the lantern and looked down so Gerrit could see her neck. At least he could tell her how bad the scar was, how easily the Tayemstvoy would know what she'd done.

His fingers brushed her spine, tracing her burning skin. The caress crackled with storm energy, lifting some of the fog from her mind.

"It's beautiful," he whispered.

She turned, afraid to see his face but needing to know if he meant it. Wonder softened his expression. When he took his hand from her neck, the absence choked her throat.

"Do you have one?" she asked.

"Barely. I didn't pull enough storm energy."

She didn't understand how that was possible. Calling the storm just sort of... happened. "You said my imbuement was useless?"

A muscle in his jaw tightened. "It's... no, Category One imbuements are fine. You just built yours out of such a big nuzhda that not many bozhki will be able to safely activate it."

Celka's throat tightened. Why hadn't Pa taught her any of this? "I don't understand."

He sat across from her, their knees knocking. "Imbuing is like creating pottery. To make a pot you need quality clay, the skill to shape it, and a kiln to fire the clay so it holds its shape. The potter's studio is sousednia. Your nuzhda is the lump of clay, the weaves you build out of that nuzhda are the pot's shape. Storm energy is the kiln.

"With more clay—a stronger nuzhda—you can build more complex objects, but you need more storm energy to crystalize that nuzhda and realize the magic.

"The more skilled you are, the more intricate the weaves you can form using a given amount of nuzhda; but no matter your skill, a lump of clay only stretches so far without breaking."

Celka nodded towards the knife she'd imbued. "So the Category One imbuement you were talking about, that's the complexity of my pot—simple. But I made it out of a big giant lump of clay—the Category Four nuzhda?"

He nodded. "For another mage to activate the object, they have to pull against the same size and type of nuzhda as you used to create the imbuement. So to activate your simple knife, they have to become as combat-warped as you were when you tried to kill me."

Understanding filled Celka like hopelessness. "And because I still can't build walls, I attacked you." How was she supposed to learn all this fast enough to help the resistance? How was she even supposed to *survive* long enough to escape *into* the resistance?

"Category Four is hard to wall off completely, even once you know how. A lot of bozhki fail gold bolt tests because of it."

"So my knife—" Celka finally understood. "Its imbuement isn't useful enough to risk almost killing your friends."

He nodded, staring at the storm-marked floor. Gerrit's haunted expression reminded her that, for him, the risk wasn't hypothetical.

"I could have gone storm-mad," she whispered, chilled by more than her wet clothes.

"You didn't, though." His voice was tight, and she was too exhausted to read his sousedni-cues. "You controlled the storm."

"And now we'll be arrested for it." She needed to face the facts. If she stayed here, the Tayemstvoy would find her just like they'd found that old woman. She needed to talk to Grandfather and come up with a plan to disappear. She hugged her arms around herself. She'd never imagined fleeing into the resistance so soon. Grandfather's nightly lessons had barely scratched the surface of what she had to learn.

With a start, she remembered the mimeograph machine. They'd have to find somewhere else to hide it. When the Tayemstvoy followed the lightning strikes and found the storm-marked floor, they would search the trailer.

And what about Gerrit? She couldn't take him with her, but the thought of leaving him made her want to scream. She'd finally found someone who could teach her to imbue, and she'd recklessly destroyed that chance.

"We can rearrange the crates," Gerrit said. "And if you wear your hair down, no one will notice your storm-scar." He sounded serious, like he believed the charade would work.

"*Two* lightning strikes, Gerrit."

"Could have been a coincidence. Maybe no one saw."

She shook her head. "They saw."

"Can't your family come up with an alibi? Or your resistance contacts? Say you were playing dice or something."

She made a face. "Prochazkas don't dice." But his ideas shook loose one of her own. "We're thinking about this wrong. No one expects me to be storm-blessed, so as long as I don't act suspicious... *I'll* tell everyone, make a big deal out of the first strike. If I'm excited about having seen lightning hit the ground, no one will think I have anything to hide." She clapped a hand to her mouth. "Sleetstorms. The little snakes."

"You're not making any sense."

"I ran in here with Nina, but I left the little snakes behind. Ack." She started pulling pins out of her hair, wishing Ela hadn't taken such care. "Gerrit, help please?"

Awkwardly, he picked pins and flowers out of her hair. Despite the danger and horror of what she'd done, his touch quickened her breath.

A pin snagged, and Celka winced as he tugged it free.

"Sorry." His low voice was barely audible over the rain.

A lock of hair slipped free, and Gerrit ran his fingers along it before brushing her storm-scar ever so gently. She shivered, turning to him.

He stared at her mouth, his lips parted, eyes glinting gold in the lamplight. He brushed fingers along her temple, tracing her hairline. "Celka."

She swallowed hard, shiveringly aware of every moment of contact. But he was Storm Guard. And the Tayemstvoy would follow their lightning strikes.

Jerking away, she finger-combed her wet tresses down her back. "Does the scar show?"

Gerrit cleared his throat. "Um." He made a show of checking. "Your shirt hides most of it. If you wear something with a collar—"

"Good." She tripped toward the door. "Don't move any crates until I come back. If anyone notices the trailer shaking while I'm not in it, they might get curious."

"Celka—"

Before he could tempt her into kissing him again, she dove into the darkness.

CHAPTER TWENTY-EIGHT

Two steps from the snake trailer, Celka collided with someone coming the other way.

In the dark, the impact flung her off-balance. She tripped over a shrub and would have fallen, but the person caught her, both of them stumbling, spinning in an impossible dance that somehow kept them on their feet. When they came to a stop, Celka laughed, dizzy and relieved she hadn't face-planted in mud.

Lightning cut the sky, shattering the darkness like a flash-bulb. Ctibor held her, hands warm on her rain-chilled arms. "You startled me," he said.

"Feeling's mutual." Realizing how close they stood, she stepped back. "Thanks for the, uh, rescue."

"Heroics on-stage and off." A tightness in his voice belied the wry response.

She frowned. "Why are you here?" She'd fled after he'd

saluted, so he could have followed for an explanation... but that must have been twenty minutes ago. She glanced up at the night sky, getting rain in her eyes, wondering how much time had passed.

"You forgot your little snakes. I thought I'd save you the trip."

In the darkness and rain, she had a hard time reading his expression, so she edged into sousednia. He smelled like Ctibor, oiled steel and old books, except... She wafted a breeze across him, stirring his almost imperceptible smoke-form. The difference was subtle, but he smelled too of lilacs and turned earth. She tried to understand what it meant, but she didn't know him well enough. It didn't feel like a lie.

"Celka?" he asked, concerned.

She started. "Yeah, the little snakes. I was just going back for them."

"I brought them." He grabbed a wire mesh cage in each hand and held them up. "Want me to bring them inside?"

"No! I mean, no thanks." She interposed herself between him and the door. "Nina's really scared... I guess the storm... I only started the snake act a few weeks ago, and I think the change upset her."

Ctibor set the cages down and took her hands. Concerned and serious, he held her gaze. "Are you all right?"

A laugh caught in her throat. Her snake had been scared; she'd crashed into Ctibor and they'd nearly fallen. Of course she was fine. But the springtime garden scent of him strengthened, and Celka could almost feel moist black earth beneath her hands and sun warming her face. Whatever this meant, it made her want to answer his question honestly.

Because no, she wasn't all right. These last few weeks had been terrifying, and the future seemed even more perilous.

Hands clasped in his, Celka opened her mouth. But she couldn't find words.

What was she *doing?* Shaking off his touch, she backed up, bumping into the trailer steps. "Of course I'm fine." She forced out that laugh. "But what took you so long? The sideshow must have ended"—she cocked an ear; she could gauge time by what the circus band was playing—"half an hour ago." Strange timing to bring her snakes and—she realized with a start—he hadn't been holding them when they'd collided. What had he been doing?

"You seemed... upset. I wanted to make sure you were all right."

Sousednia didn't so much as ripple around him; but he hadn't really answered the question. "And you like standing in the rain?"

He looked past her, toward the trailer, then quickly away. "I wasn't sure you'd want to see me." His voice barely carried over the rain and wind. Lightning flashed, brightening his profile. The strain in his expression made her want to take his hands again.

But the thought that he might have been out here, lurking while she'd imbued and attacked Gerrit—it sent a chill down her spine. She swallowed hard and said, "Nina was crazy. It's good you didn't come inside. I... when I was on my way back here, lightning struck the ground, maybe four trailers ahead of me." She shook her head, struggling to immerse herself in the story and convince herself that the hurt in Ctibor's expression was just shadows. "Talk about terrifying Nina. I thought she was going to crush my ribs."

Ctibor opened his mouth to say something, but nothing came out.

"I'm sure you heard the thunder," she said.

"Yeah." Ctibor held her gaze a moment longer then bent to pick up a snake cage. He stayed turned away longer than the cage warranted, but when he straightened, a smile curved his lips, the serious, hurting boy gone. He pressed the cage into her hands. "There was another strike, too. Somewhere around here. I saw it when I was bringing your little snakes."

"I'd believe it." Warmth filled Celka's chest, relieved that he'd corroborate her story, relived that he didn't push. "I ran inside the trailer after that first one but, thunderclap, what a storm!"

CELKA RECOUNTED HER story of the lightning strike over breakfast the next morning. "I was almost to safety, rain sheeting down, when three, maybe four trailers ahead of me—boom! Lightning struck the sleeting ground. So of course I scrambled inside as fast as humanly possible— I'm not cizii." The word meant imprudent, someone who didn't respect the Storm Gods' might. "And Nina was crazy. I thought she'd strangle me for sure, and I could hardly see for blinking spots from my eyes."

"Wasn't the only strike to hit," said Ludvik, the lithe, handsome tumbler that Ctibor had been sleeping with, abandoning any pretense of ignoring the conversation.

"I'd believe it," Celka said. "I'd left the little snakes on my platform, but I wasn't going back out there. No way."

"Storm season," an older equestrian said with a shrug.

Another tumbler shook her head. "Not normal storm season. Bozhskyeh storms, come early. Vilem got in a fight with one of the roustabouts last night—should have been just words. We had to drag them apart, and it nearly turned into a brawl."

Ludvik nodded. "Josefa started singing the Song of Calming. Otherwise, none of us might have—"

A cry and the sound of shattering plates interrupted him. The crash of overturned chairs and the stomp of boots made everyone turn toward the tent's south entrance.

A dozen Tayemstvoy flooded the dining tent, ordering them outside. "Move. Lazy scum." They dragged people out of their seats and shoved them toward the back exit.

Celka stumbled to her feet with the rest of her family, heart hammering. *Run,* her instincts screamed. *They know. They're here for you.*

Grandfather caught her hand as they crowded in with the equestrian troupe, edging toward the exit. He squeezed her fingers briefly then let go. More Tayemstvoy loomed outside, rifles unslung, ensuring no one escaped.

The faint burning of Celka's storm-scar made her want to press a hand to the back of her neck. She resisted, squinting in the sunlight. More Tayemstvoy stomped around, red shoulders like fresh blood. The morning chorus of sledgehammers on tent stakes had ceased, the roustabouts presumably rounded up by more Tayemstvoy. Half-erected tents slouched like elders in the sun, and the other performers spoke in frightened whispers.

Celka felt like she was going to throw up. She had to warn Gerrit.

Fear sunk thorns into her skin. Since Celka and Gerrit had managed to cover the storm-marked floor, Celka had decided the snake trailer remained the best place for the mimeograph machine—but now she wondered if she'd been a fool. If the Tayemstvoy found it, they'd link it to her.

Shouting and waving their rifles, the secret police lined them up.

"Papers out," snapped a sergeant with a trio of silver pips on each red shoulder.

Two Tayemstvoy stomped down the line, checking identification folios. Celka held hers out, eyes on the weeds, glancing up only briefly as they snapped the blue pasteboard folio from her hand.

"We're looking for a boy," the sergeant said, fingers drumming her holstered pistol. "Seventeen years old. Sandy blond hair, pale skin, 185 centimeters." She held a hand above her head to indicate Gerrit's height. "He attended the circus last week in Solnitse, and may be hiding amongst you. The State is offering a reward for information leading to his arrest." She swept them with a flinty gaze. "Anyone found withholding information will be tried for crimes against the State."

Murmuring amongst the performers. 'Crimes against the State' meant life internment in a labor camp. They wanted Gerrit bad.

A soldier shoved a photograph in Celka's face. She jerked away, startled, then made herself study the image as if looking for a resemblance. In it, Gerrit wore a high-collared Army uniform without insignia. His expression was solemn, his gaze level. Celka flicked her eyes up to the soldier and shook her head before staring at her feet. The soldier moved on.

Closing her eyes and trying not to look relieved that he hadn't questioned her further, Celka let her darkened big top blot out the sun. Drawing a deep breath of hay and sawdust—and trying to ignore the blood and gun oil coiling around her—Celka shifted her high wire, arrowing toward the snake trailer.

She stepped quickly, struggling to keep some attention on true-life. Pain nestled in her temples. The snake trailer was at least thirty meters away. She'd never managed a dislocation that far.

Clasping her true-life hands behind her back so she wouldn't accidentally echo her sousedni-shape, Celka placed one sousedni-foot in front of the other. Twenty meters from her true-form, she struggled to keep the grimace off her face.

«Gerrit?» she cried, but she was too far to see him.

Another step. Another.

She had to warn him, no matter the risk of passing out in front of the Tayemstvoy. If they found Gerrit, they found her.

«Gerrit!»

Finally, olive green flickered in her spotlight as he focused on sousednia. «Celka?»

«They're searching the circus. You have to—»

A hand on her arm yanked her attention to true-life. Her dislocation shattered, her sousedni-shape snapping back into line with her true-form. It felt like a fall from the low wire, the ground striking the air from her lungs.

Vision blurry, chest tight as she struggled to draw breath, Celka made herself look up.

The Tayemstvoy sergeant gripped her arm. "You'll come with me."

CHAPTER TWENTY-NINE

THE TAYEMSTVOY SERGEANT sat Celka on a rickety wooden chair inside a trailer smelling of straw and oiled leather. Saddles hung next to bridles and tack, and a weak breeze stirred the dusty air through unshuttered windows. The sergeant crossed her arms and listened to Celka's story about the lightning strikes. Though Celka had worked out the details in her bunk last night, spinning the tale for the red shoulders made her break into a cold sweat.

The sergeant peppered Celka with questions then stabbed a finger at her. "Don't move." Not waiting for a response, she flung the door wide and jumped down. The door slammed shut behind her.

Shouted orders filtered in, and Celka strained to catch words. This trailer was only five or six down from the snake trailer. She wanted to look out the window, make sure Gerrit was safe. Instead, she combed her fingers through her hair, making sure it covered her storm-scar.

She clenched her hands on her knees. Where had the sergeant gone? What were they waiting for?

Celka's burning storm-scar filled her awareness like an itch she couldn't scratch. They knew about her. They knew she'd lied about the lightning. Or maybe they knew about the mimeograph machine. They could have captured one of the rezistyenti in Vrbitse, forced them to talk. They could have her description already, could be tearing the circus apart searching for the printing press, Gerrit's disappearance just a misdirection.

Minutes crawled past. Celka wiped sweaty palms on her trousers.

Think. She had to think. Grandfather had coached her on interrogation, and the most important thing was to keep her head. They wanted her to panic. They wanted her afraid so she'd make mistakes. If part of her story was false, she'd be more likely to change the details when scared. Or in pain.

A terrified noise escaped her throat, but she clamped her jaw shut. She could do this. She had to believe that the Tayemstvoy didn't know she'd done anything wrong. They'd be fishing, checking if her story fit with other reports. They'd yell at her and threaten her, but if she stuck to her story, they'd let her go.

Someone banged the door open and sunlight flooded the trailer. Celka squinted and raised a hand to shade her eyes.

Three people entered. The sergeant from before and two others.

"All hail the Stormhawk," one said.

"All hail the Stormhawk." Celka's voice sounded small.

The flesh down one side of the leading Tayemstvoy's face puckered and bunched, burn scars covering their jaw and running beneath their uniform's high collar. They reminded her of Pa, though Pa's scars had covered his back and arms. The Tayemstvoy had probably gotten theirs in the war, too—they looked old enough, maybe fifty, their red shoulders decorated with a gold star and bar. A major.

Her throat tasted of bile. In all of Grandfather's coaching, he'd told her to expect enlisted Tayemstvoy or low-ranked officers. They lacked the authority to escalate the violence without orders from their superiors. But a major... could do whatever they wanted.

Sunlight glinted bloody off a ruby in the major's ear. "Tell me what happened last night," he said.

She repeated her tale, wrapping a sousednia wind around herself so only terror and fervent belief reached him.

"Who else saw this?" he asked.

"Why does it matter?" She forced the words out, doing her best to act confused. "It was just lightning."

"Who can verify your story?" Threat clipped his words.

"Ctibor," Celka said, feeling sick. "The sideshow knife thrower." She told herself that the same rules applied to Ctibor; they'd question him and when his story matched hers, they'd both go free. But Celka knew not to fight back, knew to obey and stare at the floor and not do anything that might give the red shoulders an excuse to beat her. Ctibor... the way he'd saluted so easily, his comfort with combat knives... What if his big secret was that he'd deserted the Army? He might panic. If he tried to fight back or run, the Tayemstvoy would leave him bloodied and broken.

"The lightning struck a person," the major said.

"What? No."

The blow came from nowhere and flung Celka from the chair. She cried out and landed on her hands and knees, the side of her face hot with pain.

"Don't lie to me."

The sergeant dragged Celka up and shoved her back into the chair.

Celka cringed. "It hit the ground, I swear."

The major struck her again. The sergeant caught her shoulders, forcing her back upright.

Celka hid her throbbing cheeks beneath her palms. "Please, I'm not—"

"Where is he?" the major asked. "The lightning struck a boy. You saw it. You spoke to him."

Celka panted terrified breaths. How had they figured it out? Had they captured Gerrit?

No. This was exactly what Grandfather told her to expect. The major was guessing. Gerrit was safe. *She* was safe—if she could make them believe her. The sergeant jerked Celka's arms behind her and clapped her wrists in handcuffs. A terrified squeak escaped Celka's throat. "I didn't see anyone!"

The major raised a hand to strike her again, and she flinched.

"Major Rychtr," said the other newcomer. They'd stood back by the door, and Celka had forgotten them. "May I?"

The major inspected Celka like she was a cockroach crawling across his dinner plate. Finally he turned, gesturing for the sergeant to join him as he strode out. At the door, he said, "You have five minutes, Lieutenant."

The door banged shut, and Celka dug her fingernails into her palms as the lieutenant approached. Silver lightning bolts gleamed from their collar and Celka shrunk back, abandoning her sousednia wind to cling to true-life.

The bozhk lieutenant crouched before her, putting them at the same height. His single earring was a silver, garnet-studded lightning bolt—so he'd probably passed his silver-level bozhk tests with a combat nuzhda. He was mid-thirties with light brown skin and a beaky nose. Despite the Tayemstvoy uniform, his closed expression reminded her of Gerrit, its cold confidence a far cry from the major's open contempt. "Whatever he promised you, it's not worth it."

"What?" Celka asked, confused.

"This boy you're hiding. Whatever it was—money, power. Maybe he told you a sob story and you believed him." The lieutenant shook his head. "It's not worth what Major Rychtr will do to you. Because you *will* tell him everything you know. You can't hold out under that kind of pain. No one can." He laid a hand on Celka's shoulder and she flinched. "Just tell me."

"This boy you're looking for, he's a bozhk?"

The lieutenant nodded.

"Could he have... made that lightning happen from somewhere else? Because I didn't see anyone. I swear it. By the Storm Gods, I swear I didn't see anyone out by the trailers last night—except for Ctibor, and he was just bringing me my snakes. The lightning didn't *hit* anyone. It hit the ground." She searched his face, hoping her eyes were big and desperate and trustworthy.

"But you spoke to him," the lieutenant said calmly, patiently. He pulled out a photograph of Gerrit. "Take a good look."

Biting her lip, Celka studied the photograph. She shook her head. "I think, *maybe*, I saw him a couple of days ago? He might have bought one of my postcards during the sideshow. I..." She grimaced and looked away. "If it's the boy I'm thinking of, his uniform looked really rich so I... I overcharged him."

"You're sure you haven't seen him since?"

"I'm sure," she whispered. "I wouldn't lie." Her voice dropped so even she could barely hear it. "Not to the Tayemstvoy."

"What about the second lightning strike?"

"What?" She wished the desperate edge to her voice was from good acting.

"The second strike. Just minutes after the first. You said you saw it."

Her heart lodged in her throat. Had she slipped and mentioned a second strike? She racked her memory. They'd asked so many questions so fast. "I only saw one strike. Ctibor said he saw another, but I went into my trailer with my snake after the first one. I heard thunder. There could have been more. I don't..." She fought down tears and hoped her panicky voice sounded normal for an innocent girl. "I don't know."

"You told the major you saw a second strike."

"No, I—"

"I can't help you if you lie to me." He stood suddenly, and Celka cringed. He glared down at her then blew a frustrated breath. "Help us find him, and they'll let you go." He spread his hands wide. "Easy as that."

"I don't know where he is. All I did was sell him a postcard—*days* ago."

"The lightning, did it look unusual?"

"It struck the ground. I haven't seen that much."

He made a cutting gesture with one hand. "Did it look like normal cloud lightning? Was its color the same? The thunder the same?"

"The thunder was instant." She twisted her wrists against the restraints' unyielding metal, shoulders protesting having her arms wrenched behind her. "I don't know what you want. It was just lightning."

He studied her, cold. Celka held his gaze for a second, then stared at his black knee-boots. She wanted to touch sousednia, to read whether he believed her or if she should insist further. Instead, she clung to true-life as hard as she had since Pa's arrest. Storm-touched bozhki couldn't see sousednia, but they could catch hints of an imbuement mage's sousedni-shape if they concentrated hard enough. She couldn't give him any reason to suspect.

CHAPTER THIRTY

MAJOR RYCHTR CAME back. He screamed question after question. He hit her again. Threw her to the floor. He grabbed her by the hair and growled threats into her ear. She answered again and again, the words blurring. Finally, he left.

Curled against a stack of saddles, hands still bound behind her back, she shuddered. Waiting for him to return.

Time stretched, and she started remembering Tayemstvoy soldiers surrounding Pa in an olive drab bruise. Their grunts and shouts and the sick *smack* and *crack* of their truncheons had faded beneath her own terror as Vrana demanded whether Pa was her father. Celka had lied despite the blows. And it hadn't mattered. In the end, Vrana had spoken Celka's name. Her real name. Celka Doubek.

Then Vrana had walked away. The Tayemstvoy had dragged Pa behind them—the Hero of Zlin, Major Doubek—limp and bleeding. Vrana had known, yet she'd left Celka behind.

In the horse trailer, Celka whimpered.

Celka had never understood why Vrana had let her go— until Gerrit had shown up at Vrana's orders, handcuffs and drugs in his pockets. But maybe Celka still hadn't understood. Maybe this was all part of Vrana's plan. Maybe Vrana had wanted Celka to think she was free so she'd learn to imbue outside State control. Maybe all of Celka's lies in this trailer would do nothing because Vrana had already told Major Rychtr about her. The longer she denied her storm-blessing, the more he'd hurt her.

She curled tighter, trembling, shoulders and bound wrists aching. *Be strong*, she tried to tell herself. Major Rychtr might not know. She couldn't risk revealing herself if he didn't. Terror sparked connections that didn't exist. *They're just trying to scare you.*

It was working.

The bozhk lieutenant returned. Asked questions. Left. Then Major Rychtr again.

She had to pee, but they wouldn't let her leave the trailer. The morning's shadows shortened then stretched as afternoon wore on. She tried to tell herself that if they were still asking questions, they hadn't found Gerrit or the mimeograph machine. They didn't suspect her storm-blessing. But half the time she didn't know what words were coming out of her mouth. She couldn't think. She was thirsty. Hungry. And so very, very scared.

"I don't know," she told them. "I don't know. Please let me go."

Blood stained the shoulder of her blouse and crusted on her face.

The door slammed open again and Celka flinched. The sergeant stood silhouetted against the late afternoon sky. "Get up," she said, and Celka obeyed. The sergeant caught Celka's arms, wrenching her around. A click of metal, and the handcuffs fell away. "Get out."

Celka didn't move. It was a trick. She'd walk out that door and they'd beat her like they'd beaten Pa.

"Did you hear me?" the sergeant snapped. "Go."

Celka went. She had to squeeze past the sergeant, and kept expecting the woman to grab her and fling her to the floor.

She didn't.

Celka's boots touched the fairground's dusty weeds, and she wrapped her arms around her stomach, awaiting more orders. The sergeant was speaking again, but not to her. The woman gestured to two red shoulders, and they strode off. Suddenly, Celka stood alone. Shouts and orders sounded in the distance. The big top's band fluted tinny and distant.

Hugging herself more tightly, Celka stared at the familiar back lot as though she'd never seen it before.

"Celka!"

She flinched at the sound of her name.

Ctibor ran over and flung his arms around her. "You're all right. Thank the Storm Gods you're all right."

Her breath hitched, and she returned his embrace even

though she'd smear blood on his shirt. She'd thought she didn't have any tears left. She was wrong.

"It's over," he said, cheek pressed to her hair. "They let me go a few minutes ago. They're leaving. It's over."

She pulled back enough to look at him, found his lip split and bruises darkening his cheekbones. Fear tightened her stomach as it had so many times that day. "Did they... did they find what they wanted?"

"That boy?" He frowned. "I don't think so."

"They kept asking me about him."

"And the lightning—he must be a bozhk," Ctibor said.

Celka's shoulders hunched, expecting Tayemstvoy to leap from the shadows and drag her back inside.

Ctibor held her, stroking her hair. "It's all right." His touch and quiet voice helped calm her ragged breathing. "It's over."

CELKA APPROACHED THE snake trailer as the band played tense, tremulous music for the chair balancing act's finale. Evening sun cast long shadows across the fairgrounds. The last Tayemstvoy had left half an hour ago.

Shifting her focus to sousednia, Celka found Gerrit on her high wire platform, knees hugged to his chest. The concealment imbuement left him shimmering blue, barely bleeding through into true-life where he curled against one of the snake trailer's wheels. Beneath her illusory big-top, his knife that she'd imbued glowed like hot coals against his hip, though she couldn't see its magic in true-life.

«They're gone,» she said.

His head jerked up. «You're sure?»

She flinched at the edge to his voice. «I'm sure.»

A frozen, salty smell like blood gusted off him, and the knife's glow flared in true-life. Gerrit sprang to his feet. «Let's go inside.» He clipped it like an order, and Celka gritted her teeth as she pulled open the trailer door, reminding herself he'd had a hail-bitten day, too.

The trailer looked strange, backwards, the cages in all the wrong places. Last night's rearranging made entering the trailer awkward, though it left more floor space deeper inside.

Once she'd pulled the door shut, Gerrit blinked into view and slumped down the far wall to the floor. Seeing him in uniform twisted her stomach, but she forced herself to look past it.

"You look like you've been trampled by elephants," she said. Talking reminded her of her bruises, and she reached up to touch her cheek. She snatched her hand away before she could.

Gerrit squeezed his eyes shut, expression taking on a strained intensity. Celka wondered what he was doing. Unable to relax, she shuffled near the exit.

Several minutes later, he tossed his cap on the floor and dragged his fingers through his hair. "We need to trade knives."

"What? Why?"

"Your imbuement." He pressed thumb and forefinger to the bridge of his nose. "I had to hold it active all day."

She didn't follow.

"Did you see any bozhki?" he asked.

She nodded. Oh. "That lieutenant would have seen it?"

"Your sheath is a darkbag—an imbuement that hides magical signatures. They're made so you can hold them active just by having a weak desire to hide something. Even mundanes can unconsciously use a good one like yours." He shook his head, getting back to the point. "Without it, I had to keep your knife active all day— otherwise its crystalized nuzhda would have been a beacon." He tipped his head against the wall, eyes bruised with fatigue.

"You were able to wall off a Category Four nuzhda all day?" The violence in his voice must have been spillover.

"Mostly."

"You held two imbuements active for *six* hours?" She could hardly keep Pa's knife going for ten minutes, and it was Category One.

A jerky nod.

Celka made herself sit on a crate, trying to figure Gerrit out. "Why didn't you run? You could have left the fairgrounds. You could have dropped the knife's imbuement kilometers from here and just kept going." She didn't want to say the next words, but they'd been eating at her. "You could have left for good."

He studied her, face an inscrutable mask. "I still haven't imbued."

"But I can't help with that. I obviously don't know what I'm doing. And you know about sousedni-dislocations and -disruptions now."

"I can't do them like you can."

"They just take practice," she said.

"Do you *want* me to go?"

"No! That's not..." Her hand drifted up again, fingers brushing the bruises on her cheek. She sat on her hands.

"I'm sorry," he said. "If I hadn't come here—"

"I probably still would have imbued."

"They wouldn't have sent Major Rychtr after *you*."

She shrunk into herself. "You know him?"

His jaw muscles worked, gaze going distant before he focused on her. "Thank you for protecting me. It couldn't have been easy."

She looked away. "If they'd somehow found you..." She bit her lip, not wanting to ask but certain the not-knowing would haunt her. "Would you have told them about me?"

His expression hardened, and Celka wrapped her arms around her belly, squeezing her eyes shut as though it could erase the memory of Major Rychtr snarling threats in her ear.

"Celka." Gerrit touched her elbow and she flinched. "If I didn't tell them and they found you later, they would force us both to imbue. They'd chain us." He caught her hands and squeezed hard enough that she had to return his grip. Sousednia brightened. "If they'd caught me, I would have told them that I'd threatened your family, forced you to hide me. And I would have told them that you didn't know about your storm-blessing, didn't know how to use it, but that the imbued knife was yours. The State would train you, watch your family but not hurt them. We could work together."

She tried to pull away, but he didn't release her.

"Staying here increased the risk of them finding me," he said, "but I couldn't run. If you'd broken and told them about me... I had to be nearby."

"Why?" Celka asked.

"They would have hurt you—and others—to draw me out."

She searched his face, trying to disentangle her emotions. In the same breath, he admitted he'd betray her and offered to give up his freedom and maybe his sanity to protect her. Finally, she said, "I won't imbue for the State."

He dropped her hands, and Celka's sousednia/true-life clarity shattered. "Not to save my life?"

"How can you possibly think it would help? You're a *deserter*. You've proven you won't click your heels to their orders. They'll drive you storm-mad no matter what you do now—unless you stay free."

"You're wrong. When we return with imbued weapons, we'll be powerful. We'll have to prove our loyalty, but then we'll be safe."

"How are we supposed to prove our loyalty? You deserted the Storm Guard Academy. I lied to the Tayemstvoy to hide you. The only path left is the resistance."

He stood abruptly. "No."

"Yes, Gerrit." She stood to face him. "*Think* about it. The Tayemstvoy murdered your mother to twist you into their tool and you *ran away* instead. Major Rychtr doesn't want a bozhk sub-officer who thinks for himself."

"Major Rychtr doesn't control the regime."

"You think the *Stormhawk* wants you clever and thinking? He wants *pawns*. That's why the Tayemstvoy pull people from their homes and beat them on the street. They want us terrified so we don't dare question them."

"You're twisting everything."

"No, I'm trying to make you see their lies. Imbuing won't give you power, it will make you their slave. They will order your every imbuement and you will live in fear of them destroying you like they did your friend."

"The Tayemstvoy are abusing their power," Gerrit said, "I won't dispute that. But our enemies—"

"The *State's* enemies are people like *us*. People tired of living in fear."

"So instead you betray Bourshkanya? Weaken us for foreign invasion? You want to murder the Tayemstvoy so they can't arrest you for treason?"

"No." She held out her hands, hoping he'd take them. Major Rychtr's brutality should have made her cower. Instead, seeing Gerrit willing to slink back to the Storm Guard kindled a burning rage. Maybe someday the regime would find her; until then, she'd do everything she could to destroy them. "We'll save Bourshkanya."

He kept his hands at his sides. "The Tayemstvoy aren't the State. I owe the Stormhawk my loyalty."

"The Tayemstvoy are the Stormhawk's *hands*. You think he doesn't know what they do? You owe him *nothing*."

Gerrit choked a half laugh and put his back to her, pressing his palms against the wall. "You're wrong."

Celka watched his back rise and fall, waiting for more. She was about to give up when he spoke—so softly she barely heard him. "Today, while I was hiding, I started thinking. After my mother's death, everyone talked about her like she was a hero, tragically murdered by the resistance." His voice took on a bitter edge. "But before then, she and my father used to fight constantly. Father called her weak and cowardly. She hated how he—how the State kept giving the Tayemstvoy more power. She said we needed to build Bourshkanya up, not crush it down. But my father was convinced that the threats to Bourshkanya didn't stop when the war ended. Bourshkanyans needed strength, not coddling."

"Beating innocent people isn't strength," Celka said.

He turned to her, eyes haunted. "Before Mother's death, I'd started avoiding her when the rest of my family could see, worried the association would weaken me. But she fought off a dozen Tayemstvoy when they ambushed us. She was so strong."

Celka touched his arm. "You're not weak."

He looked away. "I am until I imbue."

"That's not true. There's so much you can do. So many ways you could help people."

He tensed beneath her hold, as though anticipating her next words.

"And I... I need your help. Again."

"I'm not a traitor."

"The mimeograph machine's instructions, did you read them?" Printed instructions and reams of paper had nestled in the crate next to the machine.

Jaw tight, he nodded.

"Then you know we need a typewriter." The beauty of mimeograph machines was that the printing stencil could be made with an ordinary typewriter, any drawings scratched by hand on the special waxed paper. "The circus has one."

He finally turned face her. "But?"

"It's Lieutenant Svoboda's."

"You're insane," he said.

"I need you to follow her, find out her schedule and what they do with the typewriter. I've seen it in the trailer she uses as an office, so if it stays there overnight, we could sneak in once it's loaded on the train."

"Unless they move it into her sleeper car," Gerrit said. "The Tayemstvoy love their reports."

"That's why I need your help."

He shook his head but asked, "How much time do you need?"

"I'm not sure. Cleaning the typewriter to print the stencil didn't sound too complicated, but I've never taken a typewriter apart before. Have you?"

"No."

"And I have a lot of pages to print. We probably need ten different stencils."

"This is madness. If she catches you, you're dead. Can't the resistance get you a typewriter?"

"Because they're so easy to come by?"

"They got you a mimeograph machine."

"Because this is important. Gerrit, please. Even once I figure out how to wall off a nuzhda, I can't disappear from the back lot to follow her around. I *need* your help."

"I *can't*. Don't you understand? I *have* to go back. Every time I help you, it makes that harder."

"Because you see how the State is wrong."

"No! Because—"

"Think about your mother," Celka said. "The Tayemstvoy have gotten so much worse since her death. What would she want you to do?"

"My mother was Storm Guard. She supported the State."

"And they *murdered* her. How can you still click your heels and salute? I *won't* let the Tayemstvoy win. If I have to do this without you, I will."

He paced away, shrugging out of his uniform jacket. He hung it on a nail, straightening the sleeves. Celka made herself hold true-life, leaving him to his decision even though she wanted to shake him.

Finally, he sighed. "I won't make you do it alone."

CHAPTER THIRTY-ONE

THE NEXT MORNING, Celka worked alongside Grandfather, hammering stakes and setting posts for the practice wire. Far across the field, workers shouted as they raised the big top, and sledgehammers rang on tent stakes. Normally, Grandfather would have rigged the low wire closer in, but the way he watched her sidelong made clear he wanted to talk.

As she worked, Celka tried out openings to discuss the storm, but kept losing her nerve. No matter how she dressed up what had happened, she'd endangered all their lives.

Rigging complete, Grandfather handed Celka a paper fan. She climbed onto the wire, but even holding her favorite balance tool, she felt awkward, unsteady.

Grandfather watched Celka warm up like everything was normal. Silence stretched into a gulf between them, the steel cable pressing too sharply into Celka's feet. She'd been skipping practices since the bozhskyeh storms' return, and the wire snapped and jolted beneath her.

Eventually, Grandfather joined her on the wire, empty-handed. "Act as though I'm giving you advice." He adjusted her arms as she wobbled. "You always wear your hair down now."

"I like it better." *Tell him*.

"Your story was very good. You did well to work through it before the Tayemstvoy arrived."

She nearly lost her balance thinking of Major Rychtr. Last night, after studying scripture together, Grandfather had asked if she wanted to talk. But the bruises along her jaw had throbbed at the memory, and she'd shaken her head.

"Face me, Celka."

She turned.

Grandfather's arms rested at his sides. He stood on the wire as comfortably as on solid ground. "Were those strikes you? Or this boy the Tayemstvoy seek?"

"I didn't mean to call the storm," she whispered.

"Did you imbue?" His stern expression tightened her chest.

Mute, she nodded.

"What did you make?"

"The... first try didn't work." She hated dodging the truth with Grandfather, but Gerrit was right. The more people who knew about him, the easier it would be to slip. Yesterday's interrogation had taught her the value of secrecy more vividly than any lecture.

"And the second strike?"

She darted a glance around the empty field. "A knife."

He frowned. "Where did you get a knife?"

"I..." She thought frantically. "Ctibor loaned it to me. I asked him to teach me to throw." She prayed he'd back her alibi and imagined touching her storm pendant to send that prayer to the Gods.

Grandfather studied her, shifting backwards and forwards on the wire. "Did he help you three nights ago?"

It took Celka a moment to realize he meant the mimeograph pickup. She opened her mount to say no, but hesitated.

"Demian said you went without him. That Ctibor helped load the manure."

She nodded.

"That machine is too heavy for one person to lift."

Drawing a deep breath through her nose and ensuring that a sousednia wind blew him only confidence, she said, "I understand the value of secrecy now."

"Not with your family." The snap to his words made Celka recoil, wavering for balance.

Grandfather closed the distance, fierce. "Did Ctibor see you imbue?"

"No."

"Yet he still supported your story?"

"He... saw the strikes at a distance. We ran into each other after."

Grandfather's blue eyes searched her face. "Secrets are important, but not from me. If you do not tell me, I cannot help you."

"I'm being careful," she said.

"Not careful enough. What does this knife do?"

"You know the one Pa gave me?"

Grandfather's expression darkened. "Yes."

"I made something similar." Or that's what she'd intended. "Similar, but not as useful. I think good imbuements take practice."

"Practice? Do not be a fool. You survived this storm through luck. And only luck saved you three nights ago. Luck runs out, and quickly. Imbue again and the Tayemstvoy *will* return. They will not believe your story a second time."

Celka wobbled, waving the fan for balance, remembering Major Rychtr pinning her to the ground and spitting threats in her ear. "I didn't plan on imbuing. The technique I tried for blocking the storm didn't work."

"And this boy, does he have ideas?"

"Ctibor doesn't know I imbued."

Grandfather folded his arms, immutable on the wire. "I will not tolerate lies, Celka."

"What do you want me to say? I haven't told him what I am."

"You are certain he does not know?"

She searched her memories. Grandfather didn't throw accusations blindly. "I don't think so. He's not a bozhk. His sousedni-shape's no more magical than yours."

Disapproving, Grandfather studied her. As the silence stretched, Celka paced forwards and back on the wire, feeling trapped. But each breath strengthened her resolve to say nothing about Gerrit. Grandfather would never abide her hiding him.

Finally, Grandfather said, "This machine, it requires a typewriter, does it not?"

It took her a moment to shift back to the mimeograph. "I have an idea, but it's risky."

"We will spend four days in Ratmyeritse beginning with our next rest-day. Do you know whom to contact?"

Celka wracked her memory. "Storm Speaker Stastny."

"She may be able to find you one."

"I'll try that." If Speaker Stastny could get her a typewriter, she wouldn't have to risk using Lieutenant Svoboda's—and wouldn't have to push so hard on Gerrit's loyalties. She shuddered, barely keeping her balance. He'd had it all planned out, exactly how he'd betray her. Yet she persisted in trusting him.

Maybe Grandfather was right. How long could her luck truly hold?

As she dipped to begin a dismount, Grandfather caught her hands. She wobbled, but he steadied her. "Be careful, child. Young people will say many things to win the heart of a beautiful girl. If Ctibor is truly ordinary, you cannot risk trusting him."

"I have to trust someone."

His hands tightened on hers. "Trust your family and the names I give you—no more. We have not survived so long through luck."

CHAPTER THIRTY-TWO

"Lieutenant Svoboda sleeps with the typewriter in her railcar," Gerrit said after he'd helped Celka take care of the snakes. He'd spent four days invisibly trailing the Tayemstvoy lieutenant and had a plan—but it would be risky.

Celka pulled a face. "Of course she does. Tell me she watches the evening performance, or something?"

"Not regularly. She's consistently out of her office for only an hour each afternoon—at the end of the matinee sideshow."

"An hour? That's all?"

"You don't have to do this. There must be another way to get a typewriter."

She wrinkled her nose. "I'm working on it. But we need a back-up plan."

With a sigh, he unfolded a map he'd sketched of the

back lot, setting it between them. The cuts across his ribs and arm from Celka's knife still hurt, but at least the symptoms from his concussion and the lump on his head had healed. He hadn't understood the quick recovery at first, but then he'd remembered: channeling Gods' Breath supposedly accelerated healing, a slight recompense, he supposed, for the risk of it driving you mad.

He pointed to the map. "Svoboda's office is always in the center, here." The position was classic Tayemstvoy—the better for everyone to know who she was questioning. You couldn't even be sure who went into that trailer voluntarily, spreading recriminations for extra ration coupons. "The door is usually aligned with the dressing tent. I can slip inside when Svoboda leaves and watch for an opening."

"The back lot's busy that time of day," Celka said. "It won't be easy for me to get in or out unobserved."

"I staked it out yesterday. It should be possible."

"I don't like trusting to luck. What about using the concealment imbuement to cover us both?"

"I could barely keep it over myself and the crate, and the crate wasn't moving. Maybe if we were both stationary—but getting the door open and getting through it?" He shook his head. "It's too dangerous. Unless—" He snapped his mouth shut.

"Unless what?"

"Nothing."

"Gerrit, what? If you have another idea, we should consider it."

"It won't work."

She crossed her arms and waited.

"If we were physically close, touching..." His ears went hot. "I think it's better that we wait for an opening. I can fling the trailer door open just as you get to it. It'll be—"

Celka touched his hand and his words crumbled. She crouched close enough that a deep breath would bring them together. She searched his expression, and he couldn't pull away. But neither could he close the distance.

"Gerrit," she whispered. The remembered feel of her body pressed against his made his breath quicken.

He snatched his hand free. "We can't."

She frowned. "Right. Fine. You'll help with the typewriter, but clearly what happened in Vrbitse was a mistake."

Back in the Academy, he would have left it at that, but Celka deserved an explanation. "It's not..." He abandoned the map to slump on a crate. "You asked how the Tayemstvoy knew to ambush me and my mother."

Her gaze sharpened, and Gerrit drew a steadying breath. Was he really about to say this? His certainty had grown with each passing day, but speaking his suspicion aloud would make it impossible to ignore.

"My father's... well-placed in the regime." It was as close as he dared get to the truth. He watched for her flinch, but she seemed to have expected it. "Before the attack, my core nuzhda was preserving and strengthening—I couldn't have tested more than a copper bolt with a combat nuzhda, despite Storm Guard training. Mother didn't care. She always said Bourshkanya needed builders more than it needed fighters. But my father... disagreed." Remembering his father's disgust made him feel so helpless. "Just weeks before the attack, the Storm Guard registered the returning bozhskyeh storms. I could finally be useful to my father—but only if I could imbue weapons."

Celka straightened, but he didn't give her time to speak.

"Mother was only a captain, but she was Storm Guard. That gave her a voice. Her connection to my father meant people would listen to her. I hadn't seen her at family dinners for a while before I went home. I don't think she and my father got along very well by then."

Celka snorted. "Your father sounds like a hail-eater."

"While we stood, looking at the view across the mountains... Some of what she said then..." His gaze slipped to Celka then away. "I think she was moving against him. I think she realized he wouldn't listen to her. That if she wanted changes, she had to make them herself."

Celka sat next to him, their shoulders touching. "Had she joined the resistance?"

Gerrit swallowed hard. He'd been trying to answer that question for days. "I don't know. Everything happened so fast after we spoke that I forgot about what she'd said. Until..." All the clues Captain Vrana had dropped in his lap, why hadn't she told him? He knew the answer. Gerrit wouldn't have believed her.

Part of him still didn't, desperately grasping for another interpretation.

He made himself look Celka in the eye. "Only one thing makes sense. There's no Tayemstvoy conspiracy. Tesarik's not plotting a coup; he's following orders. My father's orders." His throat choked, but he forced out the final, sleet-bitten words. "That attack four years ago, my father ordered it. He ordered my mother's murder."

Horror twisted her expression, but when she reached for his hand, he stood. She still didn't understand, and he needed her to understand.

"It's why we can't—" He gestured between them. "I still have to go back. My father will hunt me. The State will find me, even if it takes months. If you... if we keep..." He shook his head, struggling to explain. "There was a girl in my squad, back at the Academy. We snuck out past curfew a few times." He stared at his bare feet, remembering moonlight slivering Byeta's hair. "I kissed her once." He grimaced at the memory, awkward and wonderful. They'd sat in the weeds behind the stables, holding hands in the darkness. "Two days later she disappeared."

"Disappeared?" Celka asked.

"I disobeyed orders." A Tayemstvoy private had brought him before his father. *I take it we understand each other*, the Stormhawk had said after ignoring Gerrit's pleas to punish him instead. "I never saw her again. I don't even know if she's still alive."

Celka shook her head. "I can't... that's horrible."

Staring into Celka's beautiful emerald eyes, he could

all too easily imagine the Tayemstvoy dragging her away. "I won't let that happen to you."

"So let's not get caught."

Her unreasonable optimism left him wanting to scream. He struggled to keep his voice level, but a cutting edge found his tone. "My father sent *Major Rychtr* out hunting for me. They'll find me."

She closed the distance. "Is that what you want?"

"Of course not." The words were out before he could think. He struggled to breathe, to bury his panic. He hadn't even believed he could escape a rogue Tayemstvoy faction. He had no hope of escaping the State's full force.

To silence a potential adversary and warp Gerrit into his tool, the Stormhawk had ordered his own wife's murder. Even Captain Vrana couldn't fight the Stormhawk. What could Gerrit possibly do except obey? "My father will never stop looking for me. The longer I hide, the worse... the *harder* it will be to go back. To make him trust me."

"It doesn't sound like he's ever trusted you—or anyone."

"He trusts my sister and brother. Once we imbue weapons..."

Celka caught his hand and the crackle of storm energy shattered his justifications. "You could be free, Gerrit."

He wanted to believe her. He wanted to pull her against him, run his fingers through her hair, press his lips to hers and let storm energy tear him from the truth. She was power and beauty, and she made him want to be reckless. But his recklessness had destroyed Byeta's future. He couldn't risk Celka's.

CHAPTER THIRTY-THREE

RATMYERITSE'S STORM TOWER sliced a thin shadow across Speaker Stastny's kitchen table. Celka dropped the last box of cabbage on top of it. Ctibor deposited two sacks of potatoes on the stone floor. Hooking a chair out with his foot, Ctibor set about chopping as though preparing soup was the best way he could imagine spending a rest day.

Despite Grandfather's warning, Celka couldn't help but return his smile, though she watched Ctibor longer than she might have, wondering why Grandfather suspected he was a bozhk. Sure, Ctibor had secrets, but secrets was a long way from a storm-affinity.

Shaking the thought, she started chopping—and planning. Grandfather's suggestion that Celka talk to Speaker Stastny about a typewriter gave her the perfect excuse to ask even more.

Because Celka refused to believe Gerrit's fatalistic

conviction that the State would find them. The State had found Pa because he'd stayed in one place, kept one name, built a family he had to protect. Celka would disappear into the resistance and, when the State came looking, she would make them regret it.

"It'll be quite the soup today," Ctibor said as Celka scraped chopped cabbage into one of the massive tureens. They still had the usual carrot peels and potato skins, but whole beets and turnips, cabbage and potatoes were a rare addition.

"The circus quartermaster must have made a mistake again." Celka spoke the lie she'd heard a thousand times.

"I'm surprised Ms. Vesely keeps him on."

Celka shrugged. "He's her cousin, or something."

A smile tugged at the corners of Ctibor's mouth as he chopped another potato, clearly seeing through the excuse. "That explains it."

"Do you have family?" Celka asked.

He nodded. "Three sisters and my ma."

"Nice big farm family." Celka couldn't banish the sarcasm.

Ctibor met her gaze, then his eyes slipped sideways to where a couple of roustabouts sloshed pots inside from their trip to the pump. "Yeah." His jaw tightened and his gaze dropped to the potatoes.

Celka's stomach wrenched at having destroyed his smile. "Do you miss them?"

Around the back lot, he was always ready with a joke and easy laughter, but here he met her gaze, guarded and wary. The bruise ringing his left eye still purpled his brown skin, and a red line slashed his lip—though the swelling had faded.

Celka focused on another cabbage. "You don't have to talk about them. If you don't want."

They worked in silence for a time before he said, "My middle sister, I miss her the most. She's... fragile. I don't like being away."

"Fragile how?"

His silence weighted the air, and Celka glanced up through her lashes, hoping he'd let her past the lies.

Her last cabbage went in the pot before he said, "It's not something we talk about."

Celka sliced into a beet, juices staining her hands red. "You mean..." Looking around, she found the other workers in the kitchen, clustered around the coal stove—far enough away that they probably couldn't hear. Probably wasn't good enough. "Is that why you... help out here?" She didn't know how to ask why the Tayemstvoy had hurt his sister. No one talked about the red shoulders' brutality, not where anyone might hear.

When he met her gaze this time, fierce intensity lit his expression. "It's nice to do something good. To help people."

LEAVING CTIBOR AND the roustabouts serving soup, Celka followed Speaker Stastny into a gloomy office that smelled of dust and ink. Charts covered the walls, mapping Bourshkanya's weather patterns, and piles of reference books sagged the shelves. A slide rule and an ancient barometer teetered atop notebooks. Ratmyeritse was big enough to have dozens of Storm Speakers working on the region's weather forecast, maintaining their instruments and reporting back to the central church's scholars.

"I need your advice," Celka said. "There's a boy."

"The one outside?"

"No, it's—" She'd meant this to be a simple alibi while they exchanged hand signals, but remembering Ctibor's intensity as he talked about helping people, the denial stuck in her throat. Talking about Ctibor seemed worlds safer than discussing Gerrit. "Yeah."

Speaker Stastny waited.

"He seems nice, but he's new to the circus, so I barely know him." She rubbed the knuckles of her left hand while she took a seat across from the old woman. "How do you decide who to trust?" Grandfather's insistence that it took years didn't help. Celka was starting to suspect that trust was something, like faith, you just had to give.

Gerrit had admitted he'd betray her, but she needed his help, so she had to trust him. Ctibor suspected that they got their soup rations illegally, but still gave up his rest day to hand out stale bread. Trusting either of them could give the Tayemstvoy reason to tear apart the circus and destroy her family. But was she any better off standing alone?

"Come, pray with me." Speaker Stastny waved her before a tin altar with a red-enameled lightning bolt. She straightened her collar as they crossed the room, giving her side of the resistance signal.

Kneeling at the speaker's side, Celka pulled her storm pendant from beneath her shirt. The bronze oval felt hot in her palm as she pulled the charging cloth out of its gray wool pouch. Wrapping the top of the pendant in the woolen pouch to insulate her fingers, she rubbed her gray rabbit fur over the brass. The meditative motion often helped clear her head, but today, Speaker Stastny distracted her.

"What do your parents think of this boy?" Speaker Stastny asked, rubbing rust-colored rabbit fur over her own pendant.

"Ma wouldn't trust him to lift a box of onions. Grandfather..." She focused on the pendant, its enameled lightning bolt a faint ridge beneath her fingers. "He doesn't trust anyone."

"You spend much time with this boy?"

Celka nodded.

"What has he asked of you?"

She swallowed hard, wishing she'd chosen a different topic for 'advice.' Ctibor hadn't asked anything, except that she let him help at the soup kitchen, but if they were talking about boys, she was hiding Gerrit from the Tayemstvoy—and, apparently, from his high-ranked, hail-eating father. Favors didn't get much bigger.

"Do you have reason to mistrust him?" the speaker asked.

"Are secrets and lies enough? He's keeping things from me."

"Many of us have secrets."

Celka set the charging cloth on her lap. She wouldn't get more advice without sharing dangerous details. "Storm Gods hear my prayer." She focused on the prayer, holding it clearly in her thoughts—*please don't let them betray me*—and touched her pendant to the altar. A spark leapt between them. She sighed; trusting to prayer seemed about as smart as trusting to luck. The cover conversation had served its purpose. "Can you get me access to a typewriter?"

Speaker Stastny pressed her lips together and touched her own pendant to the altar, silent as she offered her own prayer. "You need to be unobserved?"

Celka nodded.

The speaker frowned at her altar. "My flock is factory workers and laborers. I'm sorry, but you'll not find what you need amongst them."

Celka tried not to let her disappointment show. "Then maybe you can help me with something else." At the speaker's encouraging silence, Celka leaned close and whispered, "I need a gun." Before Speaker Stastny could refuse, Celka caught her hand. "It's important."

"You have a mission?"

"Yes." Celka had practiced this lie and blew conviction toward the speaker.

"Getting such a thing would be dangerous. Carrying it—"

"—is my problem," Celka said.

"Do you know how to use one?"

"I know enough." Pa had taught Celka about guns,

though she'd never held one. If she couldn't figure it out, she could ask Gerrit—though the thought made her shudder. He'd been prepared to betray her to the Tayemstvoy. Fighting down her fear, she held the speaker's walnut eyes.

Speaker Stastny studied her in silence. "The Wolf would not ask this of you."

"He did."

"Youth think to act heroically, but assassinations fail, and the Tayemstvoy always find the attacker. Don't throw away your life. The Wolf needs us safe and ready for his call."

Frustration tightened Celka's throat, but she kept her voice steady. "I have no intention of throwing away my life. And I'm not planning an assassination. This is important. I can't explain why, but I *need* a pistol."

Celka would not waste the storm cycle hiding like Grandfather wanted. Gerrit planned to practice imbuing; she would find some way to practice at his side without alerting the Tayemstvoy. When she disappeared into the resistance, imbuements would ensure her freedom.

Speaker Stastny said nothing for a long time, and Celka waited, letting silence pressure her. Finally, the speaker looked down at her hands. "I will make enquiries and send word to the circus."

"We'll be here three more days," Celka said. "That's all."

"That may be enough."

After effusive thanks, Celka left the speaker alone. She would talk to Gerrit about combat imbuements;

surely he would have ideas for how to make a pistol more powerful. If Major Rychtr came for her again, she wouldn't cower.

The thought perfumed sousednia with blood and gun oil and, over a ghostly sound of blows, Celka smiled. Half focused on sousednia, she nearly collided with someone rounding the corner.

"Celka." Ctibor sidestepped neatly despite the enormous soup tureens he held in each hand.

She blinked back to true-life. "We run out already?"

"I was heading to get more. Lend me a hand?"

She shrugged and took an empty pot, still distracted by combat weaves. How did one deliberately shape scents into magic? What could you do to a gun? Make it shoot further and faster? Pa had quizzed her on diagrams of weapons, but she didn't know what to expect from a real gun.

Ctibor opened a door and she followed, expecting to step into the alley separating the temple from the speaker's cottage. Instead, they entered a room dimly lit by two north-facing windows. Battered wooden blocks and animals with faded paint littered a colorful rag rug. "Wrong turn?" Celka asked, but Ctibor slipped behind her and shut the door.

He set his tureen on the floor. "We need to talk."

"About what?" Focusing on sousednia, she drew a deep breath, trying to read him. But she smelled only blood and gun oil, the Tayemstvoy still beating Pa on sousedina's illusory back lot.

"I heard what you asked the Storm Speaker," Ctibor said.

Panic took flight in her chest, the crack of truncheons twisting it to rage that she struggled to control. Maybe he'd only heard the cover conversation. "So you're trying to show how trustworthy you are?"

"About the gun." He spoke so softly she barely heard him.

Her fingers tightened on the soup pot. Could she knock him down if she hit him over the head with it? She doubted it. With Gerrit, she'd had the advantage of surprise.

Teeth gritted, Celka struggled to feel the high wire beneath her feet. She needed to be smart, not warped by combat. "I don't know what you're talking about," she made herself say. She'd whispered the question behind closed doors; how had Ctibor even heard it? "I asked her for advice. About *you*." Behind her, the nursery's windows had glass panes. Maybe she could break through them—but fast enough to escape? Unlikely. Ctibor was stronger and bigger.

Finally, the high wire pressed into her feet, and she dragged in deep, slow breaths, struggling to read him. The smells didn't make sense, and fear made her core sousednia's hay and sawdust slippery.

Ctibor stalked closer and she retreated two paces before holding her ground. Only the soup tureen separated them. "I understand feeling scared after the Tayemstvoy questioned us." Despite the heavy door and the stone walls blocking them from the main temple hall, Celka had to strain to hear him. "But this isn't the solution. What if the speaker is a Tayemstvoy mole? Did you consider that? What if the person she sends to you goes to the red shoulders first?"

"Are you planning on reporting me?"

"No." That came out frustrated, as though she'd missed his point. "Go back in there and tell her you changed your mind. You were scared and didn't mean it."

"And if I don't?" Celka asked.

"You'll get everyone who helps you killed."

"Because you'll turn me in?"

"I'm *trying* to keep you safe," he snapped.

"I never asked for your help." She shouldered past him and started for the door.

As she grabbed the knob, Ctibor slapped his palm flat on the door, pinning it shut. He wore an iron ring on his thumb, his hands so much bigger than hers. He loomed, broad-shouldered and dangerous. "Please, Celka. I'll teach you how to fight. Bare-handed and with a knife. But if they catch you with a gun, it won't matter what you can do, they'll *make* you tell them everyone who helped you get it."

Her stomach curled against her spine. "What do you mean 'what I can do'?" Was Grandfather right? Had Ctibor realized her storm-blessing?

He hesitated, as though waiting for her to put it together. But she just glowered at him, struggling not to show her fear. Finally, he said, "On the high wire. Your family's fame won't matter if you cross the Tayemstvoy."

Celka exhaled shaky relief, but Ctibor still held the door shut, still stood too close, a strange scent of lilacs tangling about him in sousednia. The low, hard edge to his voice chilled her, but his springtime garden scent didn't match the menace. She studied him, finally recognizing desperation in his dark eyes. The pieces clattered into place, and her fear sublimated. "Is that what happened to your sister? She helped the resistance?"

His nostrils flared, and he shifted, subtly recoiling. She felt certain he would finally tell her what had driven him to the circus, but his hand on the door clenched into a fist, and he paced away. His back to her, he stood stiff as a soldier at attention.

Celka dropped her soup tureen on his, the steel clattering and wafting cooked cabbage. "I'll be careful."

"It won't be enough," he said.

"If you think they're so strong, why are you helping us?" She crossed to his side, needing to see his face. "You know this food isn't from pooling our rations."

"It's different. This helps people."

"I'm going to help people, too."

An antiseptic, chemical scent swirled around him in sousednia, sterile and cold. "Please," he whispered, "think about that Tayemstvoy major. Everything he threatened—"

She snapped her attention to true-life. "I'm doing this."

He shook his head as though denying it could change her mind. She wished she could reassure him that an imbued gun would keep her safe from the Tayemstvoy. But she couldn't risk him realizing her storm-blessing.

Finally, Ctibor scrubbed a hand along his jaw and looked away.

When he said nothing, she touched his elbow. "Let's go get some soup. Those people out there need our help." When he didn't respond, she started for the door.

"Celka, wait."

She stopped.

"I'll help you get the gun."

The offer startled a laugh from her. "Not a chance." She didn't need his puppy dog eyes pressuring her to change her mind.

"I can make it a little safer." His jaw muscles worked as though he fought against himself, but he took her hand. "If you'll trust me."

"How?"

"I was an Army cadet." His voice dropped so she had to lean in to hear. "I still have my papers."

She breathed a startled breath in sousednia, but he smelled honest—old books and oiled steel, with that lingering springtime perfume. "You deserted?"

"It's... more complicated than that. But we can get through checkpoints with fewer questions. They won't search us."

"Won't your name be on a... list, or something?"

He shook his head, and sousednia still smelled like truth. "It should be safe."

"I thought you didn't want to take risks."

"I don't."

She frowned, not following.

"You're not changing your mind." Tension cut his voice, but lilacs and the honest, earthy smell still wrapped him.

Breathing deep in sousednia near him made her feel warm and protected. She shook back to true-life. "Why risk yourself? Whatever brought you here, you're running from something. This is dangerous for you, too."

His expression took on a haunted distance, and he twisted the ring on his thumb. "I know what happens if you make a mistake."

CHAPTER THIRTY-FOUR

LIEUTENANT SVOBODA'S TRAILER smelled of citrus and ink, the tin of lemon candies on her desk a lure that Celka fought to ignore as she worked to free the typewriter's ribbon. Ink covered her hands by the time she got it out, rolled tight around its bobbins. She wiped her hands on a handkerchief, and set about cleaning the metal flanges that flipped up to type each letter.

«Is that your toothbrush?» Gerrit asked from where he stood invisible, peering out the window.

«The instructions said the typefaces have to be clean.»

«Don't worry, you'll still look lovely with ink-stained teeth.» An edge undercut his humor.

She rolled her eyes. Finished, she asked, «You brought the stencil paper?» He handed it over and she fought to thread the thick, waxed page between the machine's tight rollers.

«Here.» Gerrit flipped a lever that let her slip the page in easily.

«Let's hope the band covers the noise,» Celka said grimly, pulling her sheaf of folded originals from the back waistband of her trousers.

When she tried to type, however, she found the letters all in weird places. She had to hunt for each one, and typing just the first word took forever. At this rate, working for an hour a day would take weeks to finish the stencils.

«Have you ever used a typewriter before?» Gerrit asked once she'd managed half of the first line.

«No.» She sounded petulant as she hunted for the J. «Have you?»

She got through another word before he sighed. «Let me do it, or you'll never finish.»

She slid aside with profound relief, then remembered what she'd been typing and bit her lip.

«I'll transcribe your treason faithfully,» he said. But when he read the page, his whole demeanor stiffened. He flipped to the next page and the next before spinning toward Celka. «You said you didn't murder people.»

«We don't.» She realized how naïve that sounded. The pages explained how to clean and care for Uhersky rifles, gave instructions for bayonet attacks and shooting drills.

«If you want to lie to my face, you might choose something more convincing.» His voice was low, dangerous. «What is the Wolf planning?»

«I don't know.»

«You can guess.»

She raised her chin and held his gaze. «The regime is crushing Bourshkanya.»

«So you'll start a civil war?»

«We're already fighting a war—but only one side is armed.»

On her high wire platform, his jaw muscles tensed, and he looked away.

«Your father ordered your mother's murder, Gerrit. Why aren't you jumping at the chance to fight the regime?»

He glared at her, violence simmering in his posture. Celka didn't flinch away. The violence wasn't for her.

Finally, his sousedni-shape faded, snapping back in line with his true-form as he bent to the typewriter. The clatter of keys filled the trailer, and Celka released a shaky breath. «Keep a lookout,» Gerrit said, tense. «I don't want to get shot over this.»

Still not quite believing he'd gone along with her, Celka pressed herself into the shadows next to the window, scanning the sunlit back lot for Svoboda's Tayemstvoy swagger. Gerrit clacked across the keys, the typewriter dinging every few breaths as he neared the end of each line. The sound buoyed her, and she started to breathe more easily. Whatever Grandfather said, she'd been right to trust Gerrit.

Lulled by the clatter of keys, Celka nearly missed Svoboda's olive uniform striding out of the shadows. "Gerrit!" she called, belatedly realizing she should have spoken in sousednia. «Svoboda's almost to the trailer.»

He cursed and tore the stencil from the typewriter. Celka stuffed the originals into her waistband as Gerrit snatched up her toothbrush to scrub the wax from the typefaces.

«We don't have time,» Celka said, shoving him aside to cram the typewriter's ribbon back in place.

Hobnailed boots clumped on the trailer steps, and Gerrit caught Celka's waist, shoving her back against the wall, pressing the whole line of his body against hers.

In sousednia, his expression twisted in terror and pain. Celka snapped her sousedni-shape outside the trailer, intending to distract Svoboda, but Gerrit's fingers twined in her hair and he whispered, "I need your sousedni-shape here." His lips brushed her ear, voice tight with desperation.

She snapped back into line with her true-form and felt the concealment imbuement's oily electric power sluice over her just as the trailer door swung open.

Arms around Gerrit, Celka held her breath. His sousedni-shape rippled lake-blue, and she craned to see over his shoulder as Svoboda sat at her desk. The Tayemstvoy lieutenant popped a lemon candy from her tin, reclining in her desk chair with a satisfied smile.

Svoboda stared toward the window for a time before pulling out a notebook and leaning over it. Celka tried to breathe quietly, feeling Gerrit's breath in her hair. Time passed with only the scritch of Svoboda's pen. When the lieutenant failed to spot them, Celka's mind began to wander.

One of Gerrit's hands had settled against the small of

her back, holding the half-finished stencil against the pages tucked into her waistband. His other hand cupped the back of her head where she rested her cheek against his shoulder. With each breath, she smelled the pine resin scent of his sousednia, and the strong, lean muscles of his chest pressed against her breasts. She tried to dismiss the tingling in her skin as storm energy, but knew it for a lie.

Eyes closed, she imagined his hand sliding around her cheek to her throat, thumb caressing the neckline of her blouse as gently as he'd stroked her storm-scar in the snake trailer. Her breath quickened despite—or perhaps because of—the danger. They couldn't risk noise or inattention, but as she told herself to put the ideas out of her mind, the imagining grew until she could almost feel his lips against hers.

Since they'd first kissed outside Vrbitse, she'd tried to distance herself—he was Storm Guard. But he didn't have to be. He wanted to escape his twisted, power-hungry father. If Speaker Stastny could get her a pistol, she'd imbue it, and the power Gerrit talked about could be their power—together, supporting the resistance.

Mind whispering danger, Celka's hands slipped up Gerrit's back to his strong shoulders. She traced her fingers up his neck and through his short hair in a mirror to how he held her. He wasn't Storm Guard, not fully. He was an ally, and he could be so much more.

Tilting her chin up, she touched his cheek, not wanting to risk missing her invisible kiss.

His cheek was wet. She froze, frowning, and brought her other hand to his face. «Gerrit, are you crying?» She finally thought to focus on sousednia and found his face twisted in silent agony, tears streaking his cheeks.

Terrified the concealment imbuement was shattering, she tightened her grip on his face. «What's happened? What can I do?» Now that she was paying attention, she found his breath tight with stifled sobs.

Gerrit clenched his teeth. In sousednia, he caught her face in both hands, though his true-form still pressed her, motionless, against the trailer wall. «My mother, as she was dying...»

She shook her romantic notions. «What happened?»

«I held her as she died. I heard her say, "Don't become like them." I thought she meant the resistance scum who attacked us.» He shook his head, lost and alone, clutching her face like she was a lifeline. «But I think she actually said, "Don't become like *him*." Like my father. She knew. She knew he'd arranged her murder. She was trying to warn me.»

«Oh, Gerrit.»

«And now this? This is going to get us killed. You have no idea how strong the State is.»

«No, we'll hide in the resistance. We'll escape.» Somehow. But his words chilled her. Grandfather didn't believe the resistance was strong enough to hide even her. Could it possibly hide them both from Gerrit's murderous, power-hungry father and whatever forces he commanded? Was she trusting in luck like a fool?

«My father's too strong,» Gerrit said. «He'll find me. He'll drag me back there, and the Tayemstvoy will tear me apart and destroy all my friends. He's too strong, and I'm too weak. Just like I was too weak to save my mother.»

Memory of the Tayemstvoy beating Pa returned to Celka. Blood and gun oil saturated the air, and her high wire platform twisted into the springtime back lot. She'd been too weak to save Pa, too. The thought threatened to crush her but, as she focused on true-life, watching Lieutenant Svoboda cap her pen on notes she would use to destroy other people's lives, instead it made her furious. Svoboda stretched and sauntered to the door.

As the Tayemstvoy lieutenant disappeared across the back lot, Celka released Gerrit's face to grip his hands. «We're not children anymore,» she said as he peeled the concealment imbuement off her. «We'll find a way to fight. And we will *win*.»

CHAPTER THIRTY-FIVE

As CELKA AND Ctibor neared the first checkpoint into Ratmyeritse, Celka struggled to act like they were about some innocent errand. But the hand-drawn map in her pocket seemed to weigh as much as Nina, and Celka's heartbeat sounded loud in her ears. Today, if everything went well, she would get a gun.

If anything went wrong, she'd end up in prison—or worse.

She'd left Gerrit a note in the snake trailer, since he'd been gone when she'd dropped Nina off after the matinee sideshow. *If I'm not back tonight, run.*

Her boots felt stiff and awkward, the three illegal ration books she'd convinced Grandfather to part with as payment stuffed into her socks. "I talked with Speaker Stastny," she'd told Grandfather. "She can get me what I need, but it'll cost." Lying to Grandfather had made her feel dirty, but she couldn't tell him the real reason for this outing. At least he knew enough to warn their family if Celka didn't return to play snake girl in the evening sideshow.

Ahead, armed Tayemstvoy clustered around a sandbag barricade, checking papers. They'd chosen the checkpoint well—stone buildings, soot-darkened to the color of wet steel, caged both sides, leaving nowhere to run that wouldn't give a soldier plenty of time to gun her down.

Celka drew a breath to steady herself but ended up coughing as a motorcar spewed exhaust in her face. Vile things. A soldier lifted the barrier to allow a mule and cart through the roadblock, and Celka and Ctibor queued.

Staring at the backs of people's heads, Celka struggled to control her racing heart.

Ctibor squeezed her hand, and she tried to reassure herself that his Army papers would keep them safe. Since he'd confronted her in the storm temple, she'd expected him to continue pressuring her to tell Speaker Stastny that she'd made a mistake, but he'd reverted to his charming self. Around the sideshow, he included her in his grins and laughter, and the others reserved their glares for when they caught her alone.

A Tayemstvoy private tore Celka from her musings by demanding papers. Ctibor handed over a military-issue identification folio, crisp and blood-red. The blue paperboard of Celka's civilian folio was creased and dog-eared. Celka prayed Ctibor had been right, that his papers wouldn't earn them immediate suspicion and a full search.

The private flipped open Ctibor's folio with the bored air of someone who'd looked at a thousand already today. She read the page and stiffened, her gaze flashing to Ctibor's face. Celka's stomach tensed.

The private glanced back down at the papers. Swallowing nervously, she handed the folio back. "Sir."

Ctibor put a hand on Celka's back as the soldier opened her folio. The gesture was a little too pointed to be casual.

The private flipped Celka's folio open and closed so fast she could hardly have seen her picture. She handed it back with curt efficiency and nodded them through.

A red-shouldered corporal stopped them, and Celka expected them to order her and Ctibor aside for a search. Instead, they held out a black and white photograph of Gerrit. "Have you—" They broke off when the private whispered in their ear.

"Sorry to trouble you, sir." They stepped aside.

Celka kept expecting a trap. The Tayemstvoy were never this courteous unless they were about to hurt you. But Ctibor took Celka's arm and strode through the kill-zone as though he owned it. They left the checkpoint behind, one block then another, and still no one stopped them.

"Are you all right?" Ctibor asked.

Celka felt like she was about to throw up. His name *hadn't* triggered alarms. The Tayemstvoy hadn't been courteous because they were setting up a trap, but because of what they'd seen in Ctibor's papers.

She jerked them to a stop. Had she been completely wrong about him? Attention half on sousednia, she whispered, "I thought you were Army."

Ctibor frowned, sousednia the usual studious, military mélange around him. "Pardon?"

"They practically saluted."

He shrugged. "I was an officer cadet. Enlisted soldiers—even red-shouldered ones—know not to annoy someone who could cause them trouble." He took her hand and only then did Celka realize she'd backed away. "I'm not Tayemstvoy, Celka. I came along to keep you safe." Lilacs and turned earth perfumed sousednia, but beneath that coiled something colder, smelling of hospitals and loss. His expression was so earnest, so concerned that Celka felt like scum. No mundane could fake those sousedni-cues.

His thumb brushed her cheek. "What did they do to make you so scared?"

She considered ignoring the question, but she was tired of lies. "They arrested my uncle when I was thirteen. They beat him in front of me and dragged him away."

"Why?"

She wished suddenly that she could tell him everything and make him understand. "He was an officer during the war. It... broke him. He deserted."

Sympathy tightened his eyes. "My father fought, too." She barely heard him over the clop of hooves a couple of streets away. "For years I wished he'd deserted."

Surprised, she asked, "Why?"

"I might have known him."

Celka squeezed her eyes shut and nodded, the pain of loss as sharp as it had been four years ago. Ctibor wrapped her in his arms, and she clung to him, tears stinging her eyes though she refused to let them fall.

Ctibor's hold tightened as though he, too, needed the support. As the pain in her chest eased, she wondered at his loss. She wished he'd trust her enough to tell her what had driven him to the circus.

When she finally pulled away, she searched his handsome face, hoping for the beginnings of trust. He read her question, and his jaw tightened. "I can't."

To hide her disappointment, she pulled out the map. It led them deep into Ratmyeritse, to a green grocer in the same district as Speaker Stastny's temple. Holding hands, they walked in silence.

Inside the grocer, Celka browsed until the only other customer purchased a ration of flour and shuffled out. Celka left Ctibor amidst the shelves and, as instructed, approached the counter and asked for washing powder. "My sister stained her best dress and we can't get it out for all our scrubbing," Celka said.

The middle-aged woman behind the counter sized her up for a nerve-racking minute while Celka tried not to fidget, then shrugged. "I saved a sack for my wife, but I suppose I could sell it."

Celka sighed in relief that the rezistyent's response matched the code scribbled on the back of the map. That the code was words and not gestures made her skin crawl, wondering if she'd walked into a trap—but Grandfather trusted Speaker Stastny. "Thanks."

The burlap bag of washing powder weighed too much, and Celka smiled as she pulled the ration books out of her socks.

The green grocer made them vanish, then said, "That'll be three stribers."

Celka gaped at the price.

The woman shrugged. "It's my last washing powder."

Shaking her head, Celka fished out the silver, chest tightening to lose her entire savings. For washing powder, it was extortion. For an illegal pistol—assuming the sack actually contained one—the price was a steal.

Ctibor wandered up, paying a few myedyen for a new toothbrush. Outside, he offered to take the sack from her. Handing it over made Celka queasy, but he was right. If they got separated, his Army papers would help him avoid a search.

Nearing the circus, Ctibor said, "Let me make sure your purchase won't blow up in your face the first time you use it."

Celka squeezed his arm. "Thank you."

She followed him between the midway's canvas posters and down the row of trailers, the washing powder still tucked beneath his arm. He winked and waved to the performers they saw, and Celka was so busy concentrating on not looking suspicious that she didn't register where they were headed until Ctibor pulled open a trailer door. "Good," he said, "it's empty."

The trailer wafted leather and warm straw, and Celka froze.

"What is it?" Ctibor asked.

Barely able to breathe, Celka shook her head. Her jaw throbbed with remembered pain, and she wrapped her arms around herself, feeling Major Rychtr's breath hot on her face as he spit questions.

"Celka." Ctibor touched her elbow, and she flinched. "Stormy skies, is this where the Tayemstvoy held you?"

She managed a nod, unable to look away from the straw bales and piled saddles.

"I know it's hard," he said, "but it's just a place. It can't hurt you anymore." He touched her chin, gentle pressure turning her towards him. "Let's give it our own memories. Better memories. You have to learn to push past what they do, or it haunts you forever."

"You sound like you know." Her voice sounded small, unfamiliar.

"Red shoulders taught some of my classes. They like... discipline." His jaw muscles bunched, and he took her hand. "Come on. Let me teach you how to use this thing."

That shook her, and she forced herself to move. The longer they stood out here, the more likely someone would get curious. Legs wooden, she climbed into the trailer.

Ctibor set the washing powder on a workbench then grabbed a length of rope and tied it between the door handle and a hook on the wall. "To keep out surprise visitors."

"You've done this before," she said.

"It's the only place I've found to be alone."

The chair the Tayemstvoy had sat her in was gone, but she kept expecting the door to burst open on red shoulders. Rubbing her wrists, she forced her attention to Ctibor, who rooted around behind some straw bales. He pulled out a small, cloth-wrapped bundle then sat on the floor with the washing powder, patting a spot beside him.

"What's in the bag?" Celka asked as she sat.

"Supplies. You'll see."

Celka pulled open the sack of washing powder. Beneath a layer of white crystals, Celka found another bag, cinched tight. From it, she drew a dark steel gun. Her breath caught. Pa's drawings hadn't prepared her for its heft, and she felt suddenly, intensely glad to have Ctibor there to teach her to use it safely. When she looked up at him, however, his expression had gone flinty—the way Gerrit used to get when he didn't want her asking questions.

"What is it?" she asked.

"Nothing." He seemed to shake himself, and his smile returned. "May I?" He held out a hand.

"That wasn't nothing."

He sighed. "It's just... I was expecting something old. A revolver from the war, maybe. This... it's a Stanek pistol. The sidearm Army officers and Tayemstvoy carry."

"And that's a problem?"

"Yes. I mean, no, it's a good gun. But it's more dangerous... if you get caught."

She wasn't sure if she'd imagined his hesitation, but she placed the gun in his palm anyway. Modern or not, she didn't want it blowing up because someone had let it rust.

Ctibor took the gun and, barrel pointed away from them, pulled back the slide. "It's loaded." He spoke low so his words wouldn't carry outside, and got to work, pulling out the chambered bullet and dropping the magazine, talking as he went. "The magazine holds seven shots, though you can have eight if you start with a round chambered—which I don't recommend unless you're in the middle of an engagement. I'm going to field strip it and clean the barrel. I'll walk you through the steps later so you can do it yourself."

Fascinated, she watched him manipulate the gun, the ring on his thumb shinier than the pistol but still simple steel. Celka wondered about the ring, what it meant to him. With rationing tight and prices on everyday goods so high, most people sold what jewelry they could part with—though steel probably wasn't worth much.

His hands kept moving, twisting here, flipping a lever there, shifting the pistol's slide forward and back as he removed parts, talking as he went: plunger and recoil spring, bushing and barrel. Pa's diagrams had taught her the names of the pieces, but seeing the pistol come apart in Ctibor's strong hands was like watching a butterfly crawl out of its chrysalis.

"This gun's a mess," Ctibor said.

"It's beautiful," Celka whispered.

He grinned at her, eyes bright with amusement. "Wait until you see it clean." From his parcel, he pulled a few rags and a toothbrush. "See all this black gunk? Carbon from firing. We're going to scrub it."

"With your toothbrush?"

He shrugged. "I bought a new one."

Celka laughed, taking the slide and the rag he handed her, loving that he'd donated his toothbrush to the resistance as easily as she had. Ctibor got to work pushing a rag through the barrel. As she scrubbed, Celka watched his profile, welling with happiness that he'd prepared all these things that she hadn't even realized she needed. "Thank you."

He smiled. "It feels good. Like maybe I haven't lost everything."

"You miss the Army stuff?"

He nodded, focused on the blackened metal in his hands. "There was a clarity to following orders, to knowing I was part of something bigger. A small cog, maybe, but important."

"It sounds so alien."

"Does it?" His hands kept scrubbing, but his gaze fixed on her. "On the high wire you must have followed orders, known your part."

"I wasn't training to kill people."

A muscle in his jaw tensed. He picked up a small pin that attached the slide to the gun's frame, rubbing it down with singular attention. Had she offended him? "I trained for an elite guard unit. Beat out hundreds of others for the chance to learn." Pride made his voice fierce, though pain still pulled at it.

"You enjoyed it?"

"*Loved* it. The training was intense, brutal." Fire lit his expression. "I *mattered*. I was the best in our cadre and I was going to protect some of Bourshkanya's most important people." The fire quenched, and he picked up his toothbrush, scrubbing steel, his jaw muscles bunching. "I finally got my chance, and I failed."

She waited, barely daring breathe for fear he'd stop talking.

"I got sent on a mission and things went... wrong. I tried to follow orders, but there was an attack and I froze. By the time I—" An angry shake of his head. "I was too late."

She gripped his shoulder, not sure what to say.

He met her gaze, pain tightening his expression, though his hands kept working. "Everyone who depended on me. Everything I ever wanted. Everything I *was*—I failed."

"Is that why you're here?"

He picked up another piece of the gun, that antiseptic, hospital scent swirling around him in sousednia. "They couldn't trust me to do my job."

"From one mistake on your first mission?"

His jaw muscles worked like he chewed woody turnips. "What I told you before wasn't quite true. I was an Army cadet, but I commissioned. I'm a sub-lieutenant. This"—he waved a desultory hand at their surroundings—"I haven't deserted. I'm on assignment. Knife throwing to help recruitment wasn't Svoboda's idea, it was my commanding officer's." He scrubbed the gun in bitter silence. Celka waited, heart beating too fast. Sousednia smelled like pure Ctibor beneath that worried stink of sickness and hospitals. "I don't know if they'll let me go back."

"But you want to? Even with what happened to your sister? Even after"—she waved a hand at her illegal, disassembled pistol—"this?"

"I don't know. I want it to be like it was before." A self-deprecating laugh. "But how can it?"

Celka caught his hands, stilling their incessant scrubbing. When his dark eyes met hers, the contact jolted her entire body. "For what it's worth, I'm glad you're here."

Pain pulled at his expression, but he wrapped his large, grease-stained hands around hers and managed a sad half smile. "Sometimes I am, too."

CHAPTER THIRTY-SIX

GERRIT SAT ON a crate in the snake trailer. He'd skipped his morning run. There wasn't any point. The State would find him no matter what he did. His father would order his imbuements, and when Gerrit stepped out of line, he'd loose Tesarik to drive him storm-mad.

"Weren't you going to practice dislocations?" Celka asked.

He didn't lift his head. How could sousedni-dislocations matter? Maybe he'd be better off just going storm-mad here, in the circus, never giving his father a chance to use him.

"Hey." Celka crouched in front of him. "Come on. This'll help."

It wouldn't, but she would just keep pushing, so he sighed and slipped into sousednia. His mountain clearing had gone dark, moonlight barely glinting off snow. His mother's voice howled through the wind, *Don't be like him. Never become like him.*

In true-life, Celka vanished. Practice had increased her skill at pulling against concealment, though she hadn't yet figured out how to wall it off. It left her an incorrigible trickster, her control over sousednia giving her every advantage.

The expectation of her laughter brightened the night sky a little, but Gerrit turned his back on her, stepping away from his true-form.

Sousednia's icy wind tore tears from his eyes, and the night chill settled deep in his bones. Inky darkness cloaked the valley below. Gerrit stared into that abyss.

Then a feather brushed his neck.

He jumped and swatted at it, but the feather was already gone. Celka laughed behind him.

He edged away, but she brought the feather back, tickling along his neck so he couldn't ignore her, the sensation impossibly real in true-life. Not in a million years would he achieve a sousedni-disruption so realistic—even if he could figure them out.

When Gerrit twisted away, Celka vanished into the snow, changing their relative positions with a thought. He understood the mechanic, but theory and execution were entirely different. He tried to imagine himself at her side, but sousednia hadn't even rippled when she tickled him again. He yelped and leapt away. She reappeared behind him, stealth undermined by giggles.

As Gerrit searched for her, struggling to change sousednia ahead of her so she couldn't ambush him with imagined feathers, the sky brightened, as with approaching dawn. The more she tickled him, the more laughter overwhelmed his crushing emptiness.

Only when he'd lost his dislocation completely and could barely breathe for laughing did she show mercy.

Storm Guard training had never been like this. Part of him hoped Celka would never learn to build walls. But already, sousednia's sky darkened, and he knew his happiness couldn't last.

A scowl replaced Celka's mirth in true-life as she concentrated, scouring away the fluting trills of concealment from her core sousednia. Gerrit studied her sousedni-shape, wishing he had Filip's understanding of core nuzhdi to verify that she'd returned to herself. At least she ended the exercise in her high wire costume, concealment nuzhda no longer bluing her complexion. He hoped that was enough, hoped dangerous cracks weren't forming in her mind because he lacked the training to see them.

"It's still not working," she said.

"You'll figure it out."

She snorted. "Thanks."

It pulled a smile out of him. He rarely smiled in the Academy. He'd have to learn not to again. Fleeing that thought, he said, "I've been thinking about blocking the storms."

"Oh?" Her expression brightened. The weather forecasts showed this region irritatingly stormless, but no one was used to bozhskyeh storms yet, so the Storm Speakers could have miscalculated.

"Gods' Breath is somehow... drawn to nuzhda, or reinforces it," he said. "So maybe the key to ignoring a storm is to have no nuzhda."

She sighed. "Tried that. It helps, but not much."

"But did you eliminate *all* nuzhdi? Even your core nuzhda?"

Her head snapped up. "Is that possible?" He loved the way she latched onto ideas with a sniper's focus.

He shrugged. "I hear nuzhdi, so sousednia would have to go completely quiet, which it never does. I don't know how you block smells."

"Maybe a wind?" She wrinkled her nose. "But wind just blows stuff around. What if I stood in a—" She broke off, gaze distant and searching. Laughing, she focused back on him. "I have an idea."

"What?"

But she'd stopped listening, the concealment stone back in her hand, mischievous smile quirking her lips. She vanished, and he dipped into sousednia, anticipating her next prank. Instead, she drew a deep breath and spread her arms as though to take flight, feet aligning like she stood on a wire.

On Gerrit's moonlit mountaintop, Celka's civilian clothes bled into her high wire costume, sequins glinting in light from her own sousednia as she spun on one foot, lazy and graceful. The intensity that lit her face was pure Celka, but the playful trickster was gone, replaced by deep concentration. In true-life, she remained invisible.

«What did you do?» he asked.

«I don't know why it didn't occur to me before.» She

extended one leg into the air behind herself. Arching her back, she caught her ankle in both hands. Wobbling only slightly, she straightened into vertical splits, ankle clasped in both hands above her head.

Gerrit stared. Her high wire costume left bare the smooth sweep of her legs. Her neck arched like a swan's. She was power and control, distilled into something that burned so bright yet stayed somehow carefree.

Rattling metal yanked his attention back to true-life.

"Celka?" a voice called. The trailer door rattled harder, banging against the lock. "You in there?" They sounded angry or scared, and Celka's sousedni-shape faded as she focused on true-life.

"Ela? What's wrong?" She reappeared in true-life just before throwing the bolt, moving as though to step outside.

Celka's cousin bowled past her. "I can't *believe* Mom."

Gerrit pressed his back against the crates, but Celka still held the concealment imbuement. Before Celka could stop her, Ela stormed deeper into the trailer. Seeing him, she froze, mouth open. "Who are you?"

"Nobody," Celka said. "Ela, you need to leave."

"Riiiight." Ela studied Gerrit without even glancing at Celka. "You look famil—ooooh. You're the one they're looking for." She glanced back at Celka as Gerrit's hand dropped to his knife. "You've been hiding him all along?"

«What do we do?» Gerrit asked.

Celka slammed the trailer door closed and threw the lock. "Ela, this is Gerrit. Gerrit, this is my cousin." Irritation tightened her voice.

Ela gaped at her. "Your *cousin?*"

"He knows."

"Does he know...?"

"That my father, *Leosh*, was Storm Guard? Yes." She stressed her father's name oddly. "Ela, what are you *doing* here?"

"Ma was just... you know what? It doesn't matter." Ela bounced on her toes. Her face was rounder than Celka's, her hair lighter, but the family resemblance was clear. "I figured I'd interrupt you and Ctibor kissing, not you playing with a bozhk the regime is turning over all the rocks to find. Who are you, Gerrit?" The amused curiosity he loved in Celka brightened her cousin's eyes—but that curiosity could get them all killed.

"I'm someone you need to forget you saw." He stripped the threat from his voice, but made it a command.

Ela laughed. "Forget a handsome boy my sister's keeping secret? Not likely." She turned to Celka, grinning. "How *have* you been keeping him secret? And for weeks? This is sneaky, even for you."

"He can turn invisible."

"Yeah, right. *Oh*." Ela turned appraising eyes on Gerrit. "You mean with magic? Did he help you get the... crate?"

Celka moved to Gerrit's side, slipping the concealment imbuement, inactive, into his hand. She seemed more annoyed than concerned. "You have to swear to me, Ela, not a word about him—to anyone. Not even Grandfather."

"*Ob*viously. I don't want the Tayemstvoy questioning *me*." Ela's serious demeanor melted away. "But answer me this. If you're kissy-kissy with Ctibor, that means Gerrit's free, right? Can I have him?" She winked at Gerrit.

Gerrit couldn't let it go any longer. "Who's Ctibor?"

"Nobody," Celka said.

"The handsome sideshow knife thrower Celka's always sneaking away with," Ela said. "Well... when she's not with you, I guess."

Gerrit discovered his teeth grinding. He crossed his arms and glowered at Celka. "You have a boyfriend?"

"No, it's... ugh, Ela. You are *not* helping."

"What?" Ela feigned innocence. "Don't tell me you're playing with them both. Minx." Smirking, she turned to Gerrit. "Celka thinks anyone who wears a uniform is evil, but you don't look evil. And I suspect you're sleeting hot in uniform."

"All right, enough introductions." Grabbing Ela's arm, Celka dragged her toward the trailer door. "Out."

"Killjoy."

"*Now.*"

"Fine." Ela winked around Celka's shoulder. "You want friendlier company, come find me, all right? I can think of all sorts of things we could do while you're... *invisible.*"

Celka practically shoved her cousin outside. She kicked the door closed and leaned her forehead on it.

"So," Gerrit said, trying for calm. "Ctibor?"

"We haven't kissed."

"Not that it's my business," he said, for all that Celka would read the complete lie.

"Just... ignore Ela," Celka said. "Family, right? They know how to needle you."

He didn't want to think about family. Pushing that away, however, left him imagining some illiterate pretty-boy pawing all over Celka. "Knife throwing's useless, you know."

"Are you jealous?" Celka asked.

"Is that what you want? You're running around with some sideshow freak to make me *jealous?*"

"If I wanted to make you jealous, I would have told you about him myself," Celka snapped like he was being an idiot. And he was, he knew that, yet he couldn't let the issue drop. A mundane could never be worthy of her.

"How much is there to tell?" he asked. But he didn't want know.

His life was unravelling, and he wouldn't lose the one good thing in it. Catching Celka's hips, he pushed her against the wall. She gasped, and he twined his hand through her hair and pressed his lips to hers. Fire burned through him, sparking like storm energy, but hotter.

She made a small sound in her throat and caught his face, returning the kiss. For a moment, nothing else existed.

Then she tore away. "This isn't what you want."

"*Yes*, it is." He caught her again, kissed her again, hips pressing her hard against the wall. Her body felt so good against his, soft and warm, and imagining this kiss had been all that pulled him back from the swirling inevitability of storm-madness at his father's hands.

But the taste of her lips wasn't enough. He kissed her

harder, fiercer, needing her—needing to escape.

She pushed him away, breath fast. "You said it was too dangerous. You said we couldn't have this."

"I don't *care*." Worrying about the future only made sense if you had one. When the regime found him, he could release his grip on true-life, let storm-madness take him. He wouldn't let them use Celka to control him.

But when he tried to kiss her again, she turned her face to the side. He growled and turned her back, pinning her against the wall.

Celka pushed against his chest. "Gerrit, stop. This isn't you."

Every centimeter of contact between them burned like fire. He couldn't turn away from her, not now. "This *is* me—without duty, without the Storm Guard, without anything left in the world but *you*. Don't turn away."

The rise and fall of her chest against his made waiting agony. She'd leaned into that first kiss. She wanted him as much as he wanted her. He could kiss her again, right now, hold her and keep kissing her until her protests crumbled, until his darkness shattered beneath the heat of her mouth.

Part of him whispered that if he gave her time to answer, she might say no and she couldn't say no or he would fall back into that lightless pit. But Gerrit didn't move. His father wouldn't wait, would take everything he wanted, no matter her resistance.

Gerrit would never be like him.

Celka brought a hand to his cheek. "I do want you," she whispered, "but not like this."

Throat tight, Gerrit spun away, pressing his hands into a wall of crates, his back to Celka. The trailer seemed to contract, squeezing the air from his lungs. "I don't have a future, Celka. There's *nothing* but this."

"We'll find a way," she said.

He didn't believe her.

Heart pounding loud in his ears, Gerrit cast about for some way to fight the darkness, if only for a minute. Finally, voice choked, he asked, "You figured something out about walls?"

"Yeah. I don't need them."

That shook him. "What?

"My core sousednia's a high wire. I was trying to build walls like you do, but my world doesn't have walls. It has *tents*. I needed to shift out of my nuzhda-memory and under the big top, back to the high wire."

"That's... actually remarkably intuitive."

"I should have thought of it earlier." She caught his hand and squeezed until he found it a little easier to breathe. "Let's practice some more. You can work on sousedni-disruptions while I hold the concealment imbuement."

He nodded. It didn't matter what he learned, but at least, at her side, the darkness didn't subsume him.

CHAPTER THIRTY-SEVEN

CELKA COULDN'T STOP thinking about their last kiss. Sometimes she wished she hadn't pushed Gerrit away. When they snuck into Svoboda's trailer to type stencils, Celka couldn't help stealing glances at him, the concealment imbuement peeled back from his hands on the typewriter. In her bunk at night, remembering the feel of his body against hers made her struggle to concentrate on resistance mnemonics.

Yet, more and more, she was convinced that she'd been right to turn away. They still practiced together between her performances, but Gerrit had sunk into grim fatality. She wanted to pull him out of it but, much as Celka wished an imbued pistol would solve all their problems, the rational part of her knew it for desperate hope.

It left them at a strange impasse—Gerrit going through

the motions of training while convinced it wouldn't matter, Celka struggling to imagine a future where he survived. The effort exhausted her. Sometimes, she just needed to live.

Ela hadn't been wrong that she was sneaking off with Ctibor. The horse tack trailer no longer sent chills through her, but instead offered refuge. Each day, Ctibor greeted her with a hug then set about teaching her to shoot.

She'd expected the lessons to be brief since she couldn't risk actually firing the gun, but Ctibor insisted she had plenty to learn.

He had her practice dropping the gun's magazine, unloading it, reloading it, and sliding it back in place, drilling the motions until they became unconscious. He got her in firing position and explained how to line up the sights: she placed the front sight's flange dead center with the notch at the back, both overlapping her target. Then they worked on her trigger pull.

The gun a handsbreadth from the wall, Celka focused on the front sight as she pulled the trigger. The gun wobbled; the pistol clicked.

"See how you're not aimed at that knot in the wall anymore?" Ctibor said. "You missed." When he demonstrated, the pistol stayed rock-steady.

No matter how long she practiced, Ctibor never acted bored or frustrated. He offered encouragement and correction, gently nudging her arms up when the weight of the gun dragged them toward the earth.

She started spending more time with him, wishing

Ctibor were storm-blessed so he could teach her to imbue the gun as well as shoot it. When Gerrit demonstrated combat weaves, sousednia became a morass of blood and diesel smoke, but the resonances he claimed to create eluded her.

She kept searching for the key to translating Gerrit-weaves into Celka-weaves, but she left their practice sessions feeling wrung out and stupid. Even the way his weaves worked seemed wrong. They modified a weapon's material, making it stronger, straighter, sharper. As sure as Celka knew how hard to pull on her storm-thread, she knew combat magic could be so much more.

"Daydreaming?" Ctibor asked.

Celka startled, jerking the pistol. She concentrated back on the front sight and fired. The gun wobbled, but not as bad as when she'd first started.

"Remember to breathe out as you fire," Ctibor said, voice rumbling warm over her shoulder.

She focused on her breathing and fired.

"Better," he said.

Again. Again. Again.

Her hands started to ache.

"Take a break," Ctibor said.

She flipped the safety and set the gun on the workbench, muzzle carefully away from them, training the instincts that would keep her safe once the gun was loaded. She shook out her hands.

Ctibor handed her a water flask, his smile more reserved than the one he used in his sideshow act, private. "My turn."

She snorted. "Yeah, like you need the practice."

He tipped his head as though she might be joking. "Do you stop practicing on the low wire as soon as you've performed beneath the big top?"

"Of course not, we—" Her cheeks flushed hot. "Right."

He took position where she'd stood. "In training, we did dry fire exercises every day. It's cheaper than shooting real bullets, and it trains you differently. You don't worry about the recoil or the noise; you drill proper technique into muscle memory."

She watched him fire, faster than her, but no crazed flurry. He took his time, breathed.

"So, being a guard," she asked into the silence broken only by the gun's *click, click*. "Shouldn't that be a Tayemstvoy job?"

"I wasn't going to guard the Stormhawk."

Celka waited, curiosity eating her. "No?"

"Army officers, mostly. And elite bozhki."

Celka's stomach did a twisty flip. He fired five times before she managed, "Did you ever... train with the mages?"

"Sometimes."

She searched his profile, wanting to ask more but afraid he'd realize why. He stayed focused on the gun, and somehow the pistol's rhythmic firing made it easier to ask, "Did you know that boy the Tayemstvoy were looking for?"

"I met a lot of bozhki." He handed her the gun, butt first. "Your turn."

She tried to concentrate on her trigger pull while her mind churned. Ctibor stayed at her side, watchful, occasionally touching her elbow or reminding her to lean into what would be the gun's recoil. But the gun wobbled, no matter how she took in the trigger's slack or breathed out before pulling through the break.

"Ctibor, why are you helping me?"

"I don't want to see you hurt."

Sousednia smelled like truth around him, like it always did since he'd told her about the Army. Her throat tightened. "So you're just... being a guard?"

"No. Yes. I mean, not just." He sighed. "I like you."

"But?"

He shook his head. "And."

"And?" She focused on gripping her right hand hard with her left and pulled the trigger.

"I saw lightning hit the snake trailer," he said. "Twice."

The gun flinched hard to the side when she fired. Feeling like she was teetering on the high wire, she faced him. "What are you saying?" He couldn't know. No one could know.

"I read my gospel. You're storm-blessed, Celka." He spoke calm and even. "I've seen your storm-scar." He touched the base of his skull, mirroring where her scar branched out.

She pressed her hand over the scar. "I thought I could hide it."

That private smile quirked his lips. "I've spent a lot of time looking over your shoulder. I doubt anyone else has noticed." He reached out, sweeping back a strand of hair, fingers brushing her neck. She wasn't sure whether to flinch or lean into his touch. "Besides, I was looking."

"When the Tayemstvoy questioned you, what did you tell them?" Her voice shook.

"They were looking for that boy. If the lightning was you, it wasn't him."

"You lied to the Tayemstvoy for me?"

Solemn, he nodded.

Celka searched his sousedni-cues, trying to understand why he would risk his life for her. The springtime garden scent wrapped around him, warm and comforting but no less mysterious.

"It's why you got the gun, isn't it?" he asked. "To imbue."

She shook her head but couldn't voice the lie.

"It's not safe, Celka. The Tayemstvoy will follow the lightning strikes. That first time could have been a coincidence. Another strike wouldn't be."

Celka's pulse sounded loud in her ears, his warning echoing her own fears. She turned back toward the wall, locking her right elbow, pulling in with her left arm to prevent imaginary recoil from twisting the pistol to the side. She fired—once, twice—trying to decide what to tell him.

"Did someone ask you to get the gun?"

"This is for me." She fired again.

"Then don't. Practice shooting it, fine. That's good, that's useful. But if you imbue it, the Tayemstvoy will want to know where it came from. They'll question you until you tell them everything, then they'll arrest everyone who helped you. The State wants to *destroy* the resistance. If you give them a thread, they won't stop pulling until all that's left are corpses."

Her shoulders felt as hard as gunmetal, but she said, "I won't let them catch me."

"You're planning to run?" Incredulous, he caught her arms, pushing the gun toward the floor as he turned her to face him. "From this, from the circus, from everything?"

She made herself hold his gaze and strengthened her focus on sousednia, dreading some sign that he would turn her in. "Not yet."

"Alone?" he asked, swirling with the scent of hospitals.

"I can't tell you that."

He searched her face, desperate. "It only takes one mistake for them to find you."

"I'll be careful."

"Who's helping you? Who else is part of this?"

"You just said the Tayemstvoy would question everyone if they catch me. You know better than to ask."

He enfolded her hands, still clutching the pistol, in his. "Please, Celka. I'm asking. If you're going to do something reckless... tell me. Let me help."

Something about his desperation seemed off—too focused, too personal. She narrowed her eyes. "Why?"

He made a frustrated noise and spun away, pacing across the trailer. She watched his back, his breath harsh for a time before it slowed, the steel and old books scent of him pushing aside the antiseptic stink.

When he faced her again, he seemed as solid as a balance pole and as calmly confident as Grandfather on the wire. He took the gun, setting it aside before taking her hands again. "I can get you to Solniste. If you turn yourself in to the Storm Guard, they'll protect you."

She snatched her hands away.

"Please, Celka. I know it's not what you want—especially after your uncle—but it's the only way you'll be safe."

"Safe?" She shook her head. "The Tayemstvoy are driving bozhki mad."

A shadow crossed his face.

"You knew."

"It has to be better than being hunted."

"Tell that to the bozhk who ran."

"He ran, and they're hunting him like a resistance *dog*." Venom iced his voice. Sousednia exploded with blood and decaying leaves, and she could have sworn she heard the crack of blows.

Celka flinched, glancing toward the door.

"That's not what I—" He balled one hand in a fist and squeezed his eyes shut. As though wind scoured sousednia, the stench receded. His dark eyes snapped open, fear replacing anger. "It's how they think about the resistance. About you." A strained pause before he said, "About *us*. If we go to the Storm Guard, you'll be safe. Safer, at least. They're training all the State's storm-blessed to imbue. I could help protect you."

"You want to go back."

A muscle in his jaw tightened. "That's not why."

"The Tayemstvoy are monsters. I won't make them stronger."

He looked away, glaring at the empty pistol. "Maybe... we could help change things. From the inside."

She couldn't believe his naïveté. "Right. A sub-lieutenant recently escaped from the circus and a civilian?"

"There has to be a way."

"There is." She reached past him and grabbed the pistol. "It's not getting caught."

CHAPTER THIRTY-EIGHT

FROM THE MOMENT Celka woke, she felt a bozhskyeh storm building. Fear warred with excitement as dust swirled through sunbeams above her bunk. Fear won.

Despite what she'd told Ctibor, terror that she would imbue and the Tayemstvoy would track her paced like a tiger outside a rabbit hutch. She wasn't ready to flee into the resistance. Not yet, and not alone.

She tried to fight her fear by telling herself that Gerrit's plan to eliminate their core nuzhdi would work. Celka had discovered that, by morphing sousednia into an open field, grassy and featureless to the horizon, she could make it smell like nothing. Well, almost nothing. Three distant storms had broken since he'd had the idea and, holding her featureless field, she hadn't felt driven to imbue... but the Gods' Breath had been hundreds of kilometers away.

Today's storm jangled along her spine. It might not break directly overhead, but it wouldn't break far. If Gerrit's technique failed, she would imbue, the Tayemstvoy would come hunting, and she'd have to run.

Ignoring her family's mumbled good mornings, Celka dragged her steamer trunk from beneath her bed, wondering what to pack.

Ela crouched beside her. "What's wrong?"

"Nothing."

Ela sat on Celka's bunk and crossed her arms. "Uh-huh."

Celka couldn't fake nonchalance. Ela's familiar frown tightened her chest and she found herself memorizing her cousin's face. "A bozhskyeh storm's building."

Grandfather loomed over her. "You're certain?"

Celka could only nod.

"Too bad you're sick today," Ela said.

"I'm not—"

"Fever that high, you won't be able to leave the sleeper car."

Celka sat back on her heels as she realized what her cousin was suggesting. But it wouldn't be enough. Not if she lost control.

Except... she didn't have to stay in the railcar.

"Can you bring me some breakfast? And food for lunch... so you don't have to come all the way back to the railyard?"

Ela nodded, and Celka fought down her fear, dressing alongside her family. As the others left, Ela lingered.

"You want me to get Gerrit?" Ela asked, once they

were alone. She'd started helping them print resistance leaflets, and her attention had improved Gerrit's mood, if only a little.

"And my gun," Celka said.

Ela's jaw dropped. "You have a... *Sleetstorms.*"

Celka gave Ela instructions for digging it out of the tack trailer where she'd hidden it. "Don't let Gerrit see it."

Ela didn't ask questions, just hugged her. "Be careful, sis."

In that moment, Celka loved her cousin so fiercely she could hardly breathe. She returned Ela's hug, tears biting her eyes.

Invisible, Gerrit followed Ela into the Prochazka sleeper car. Bunks crowded the narrow walkway on both sides, laundry strung from every available surface. He felt like an interloper in Celka's private world, not sure why he was here. Ela squeezed down the aisle and shrugged off her pack, handing something surreptitiously to Celka.

"Can you tell Ctibor I don't want visitors?" Celka asked, low enough that Gerrit probably wasn't supposed to hear. He imagined punching the sleet-licker, but pretended not to notice the conversation. Celka must be planning to spend the day with Gerrit. That's what mattered.

Ela deposited some bread and cheese and a couple of carrots on the table. When Gerrit peeled the concealment imbuement away from his hand to add a purloined jar of peaches, she jumped.

Laughing, she grinned in his general direction, the active concealment imbuement making her not quite meet his gaze. "Good luck," she said, then skipped out.

Gerrit waited until the latch clicked closed. Ela still flummoxed him. She seemed too happy, too friendly. Maybe she just had some hope of a future. Trying to shake the thought, he stretched out, still invisible, on the bunk across from Celka's. «I miss beds.»

«Don't get too comfortable.»

He dangled his dirty bare feet off the edge. «Why not?»

«A storm's building.»

He sat up, smacking his head on the overhead bunk, surprised he'd felt nothing from his storm-thread. «How close?»

«I don't know. Close. We can't be here when it breaks.» She stuffed the food into a canvas rucksack.

Tamping down a familiar twinge of jealousy that she was better at some parts of imbuing than him, he stood.

Before they left the railcar, Celka activated her knife. Her lips skinned back from her teeth, then she walled off the Category Four nuzhda, the oily red sludge receding from her face as she extended her arms for balance.

«You're getting good at that,» he said.

In true-life, she grinned. «Let's go.»

With Gerrit taking point, his invisible reconnaissance second nature now after five excursions into Lieutenant Svoboda's trailer, they crossed the railyard and found the road north from town. When it diverged from the pull of Celka's storm-thread, they tramped across a sheep pasture.

Gerrit concentrated as they walked, searching for the jangle of storm energy. At first, he could have imagined it, but the sensation grew as the kilometers passed until the storm tugged against his spine.

He dislocated in sousednia and, to distract himself, practiced trying to tap Celka's shoulder—but she kept shaking her head. As his frustration grew, he expected her to snap at him, combat nuzhda leaking out until maybe she'd shove him and they'd fight. But she kept her calm as he progressively lost his. Sousedni-disruptions were probably useless anyway.

«Enough,» Celka finally said, swatting his hand from her shoulder on Gerrit's twilit mountaintop. «Let's talk about cloud animals.»

Gerrit followed her gaze to the sky, frowning. «I'm not five.»

Her withering glare made him laugh.

He kept the concealment imbuement up but said, "Fine." Their only spectators were sheep.

"That one"—Celka pointed at the sky—"looks like a hippopotamus."

It took him a moment to figure out which cloud she meant, not least because, "It looks more like a blob."

"No cloud looks like a blob." The eye-roll carried in her voice.

"Maybe a misshapen motorcar."

"Well, now it's more of a lion."

"How is that possibly a lion?" he asked.

"Squint and tilt your head sideways."

"That makes it blurry."

"No, that gives it *gravitas*. Lions have gravitas. Your turn."

"Um... all right." He checked that they were still alone, then peeled the imbuement back from his arm so he could point. "That one looks like a... bunch of idiots poking their heads over a rock so they can get shot."

"I think you meant to say a three-humped camel."

"No, it really looks more like—"

"A camel." Celka's tone brooked no argument. "So glad you agree with me."

"I don't think there's any way I can win this game."

"It's not about winning."

"It's always about winning."

She poked him in the ribs, the sousedni-dislocation effortless.

"Hey! What was that for?"

"I want to relax and not think about war or the Tayemstvoy throwing us in prison." She tried to say it lightly, but her voice caught. "Don't you know how to have fun?"

Great. No wonder she preferred Ctibor.

"Well?"

"I have absolutely no idea how to have fun," he said.

Her mock stern look didn't last long, laughter tugging at her lips. In the sunlight, her chestnut hair glowed like burnished copper, and the open neckline of her blouse revealed tantalizing shadows around her throat.

Gerrit caught her hand, and storm energy flared along his nerves, painful yet exhilarating. The pasture's greens saturated, the sky a searing cerulean. He managed to stop himself before he pulled her closer. Instead, voice rough, he asked, "Will you teach me?"

She wrinkled her nose, and he didn't understand how that little gesture could make him want her so badly. "You assume you can be taught."

"I'll work hard."

She narrowed her eyes as though unconvinced, then laughed and started walking again, keeping hold of his hand. "You'd better."

CHAPTER THIRTY-NINE

CELKA'S STEPS QUICKENED as her storm-thread tugged harder. Gerrit had done an admirable job learning to have fun, but their conversation had frayed during lunch, the bozhskyeh storm's first rumbles making it too hard to concentrate. Celka had dropped her knife's combat nuzhda, saving her focus for envisioning sousednia as an open field stretching to the horizon.

As they beat free of the thorny underbrush, thunder crashed, and rain sluiced down. They climbed a rock wall into another sheep pasture and, finding no roads or buildings in sight, called a stop to their trek. Dark clouds bulked overhead. Gods' Breath smeared Celka's vision, and circus tents sprung from sousednia's featureless field.

Fear threatened to overwhelm her, but she dragged in deep, slow breaths and forced the circus tents back into the earth. The big top went reluctantly, the band lingering with her family act's tremulous fluting. She could almost feel the high wire beneath her slippers, but she refused to believe it. She stood on solid, boring ground. She smelled only true-life's sheep manure; sousednia smelled of nothing.

"Can I have the pack?" Gerrit's voice startled her. He'd stopped holding himself invisible hours ago, saving his strength to imbue.

She handed him her rucksack then edged her attention inward. Green grass. Open sky. She needed nothing.

Until she caught a whiff of grilling meat. Her stomach rumbled, and she found Gerrit on his knees, straining upwards, leaning against something invisible in Celka's sousednia. The light shone wrong on him, faint and shadowy despite the sun and empty sky above her featureless field. A hunk of bread appeared in his upturned palms, and desperation screwed his features. She turned her back, striding away in sousednia. The dislocation pulled her focus. She needed nothing.

Slowly, she began to relax. Keeping sousednia featureless was hard, but it worked. The storm raged above her—she could taste its metallic sharpness— but it didn't pull on her. She touched the storm-thread reaching up from her spine. Numbness jangled through her fingers and she knew that if she pulled, Gods' Breath would come. But the choice was hers.

Then Gods' Breath flashed, its thunderclap deafening. The scent of grilling meat exploded through the air, and Celka gasped, turning to see spinach-green fire pour from Gerrit's hands into the bread.

A cry escaped Celka's throat, and she wavered, the high wire suddenly beneath her, her balance off, her body misaligned. She flailed, knowing she should recapture the empty field but not knowing how and then—

"Sleet!" Gerrit leapt to his feet, flinging the bread away.

«What—»

Before she could finish, the bread exploded.

In true-life, it tore itself apart. In sousednia, a green flare blinded her. Shrapnel lacerated her face and streamed tears from her eyes. Her back foot slipped. Her hip smashed against the high wire platform. Crying out, she twisted, flailing to catch the wire, the platform—anything.

Her hands caught nothing.

Terrified and blinded, she fell. Then her hand closed around something hard, and her feet hit solid ground. The impact should have hurt, but somehow, she'd forgotten the fall. A high-pitched keening cut the frozen air and, with one hand, her fingers numb with cold, she swiped at her eyes so she could see.

Whiteness blurred her vision, cut with dark slashes from winter-bare trees. She clutched an enormous knife in her too-small hand. She was herself but younger. Eight, maybe.

Pain cramps her stomach and the keening continues, pulling her attention to a white rabbit caught in a snare.

"Go on," says a voice achingly familiar. "It's our dinner."

She and Pa had spent three days alone in the forest with only snow melted in their cookpot to fill their aching bellies. Part of Celka panicked to hear Pa's voice, but that part felt distant and strange.

Her mouth waters, but Pa tells her to put the knife away. They'll break the rabbit's neck first. He'll show her how.

Hunger makes it hard to concentrate on anything except the gnawing in her stomach, but she tries, studying how Pa's hands move as he demonstrates in the air. She practices the motion until he nods, then she grabs the rabbit's head and shoulders. It thrashes, kicking, struggling, twisting to bite. Pa's hands cover hers, warm and strong, and together—

A hand gripped her shoulder, and she snapped around, startled. Gerrit stood incongruous in the frozen forest, wearing only battledress trousers and his tan undershirt. «True-life, Celka.» He sounded scared. «Remember the sheep pasture. Come back.»

The words buzzed like wasps. His form rippled and dulled, leaving her nearly alone with Pa and the rabbit. True-life? Sluggishly, she remembered.

Shifting her focus as though from near to far, the sheep pasture resolved, whipped by wind and rain. Her storm-thread threatened to drag her back into sousednia, but she crouched and dug her fingers into the muddy pasture. "What happened?"

"I filled the weaves wrong. The imbuement was unstable."

"It exploded," she said.

"I shouldn't have imbued so close to you." His dark eyes searched her face. "Are you all right?"

She nodded, but sousednia tugged on her, cold and bright with recent snowfall. She and Pa had snapped the rabbit's neck and drawn her knife to skin it. Something about those motions seemed wrong, but she didn't know why. "I think so. You?"

His jaw muscles bunched.

Making her voice light, she said, "I guess you imbued a weapon—of sorts."

His scowl deepened, and he paced like a caged tiger. Storm energy twinged painfully down Celka's spine, and she found herself staring up at the sky. If she reached out, just a little...

No. Not yet. She was in control. Except she was so *hungry*.

"Maybe they're right," Gerrit said.

Celka wrenched her attention back to him. In sousednia, she tried to turn the winter forest into an empty field. It resisted. "Maybe who's right?"

"The Tayemstvoy. The Stormhawk." He shook his head. "Maybe I need to be pushed or I'll never imbue anything useful." He tilted his face up, rainwater streaming down his cheeks.

"No," Celka said. "I don't believe it. Imbuing is a skill. It takes practice, that's all. You came closer this time. You just need more practice."

"My practice made a bread bomb."

Despite herself, Celka laughed. "Not the most fearsome weapon in the Stormhawk's arsenal."

Gerrit met her gaze without humor. "The imbuement *exploded*, Celka." He spoke like she'd missed something important. "It dumped its storm energy into sousednia. Into me. Into you. It could have—" His jaw tightened.

Catching on, Celka straightened. "It could have driven us storm-mad?" She edged into sousednia; the scent of grilling rabbit filled the air. Her mouth watered.

In the sheep pasture, Gerrit nodded.

"How strong was your nuzhda?" she asked.

"Category Two. I'm an idiot. I shouldn't have—"

"Gerrit, that's great."

He stared at her like she'd grown a second head.

"I'm serious. A Category Two imbuement exploded in your face, and it didn't pull you from true-life."

"It didn't dump all its energy into me. It—"

"Just most of it?"

He kicked at the weeds. Shrugged.

"So not only did you pull against enough storm energy to crystalize Category Two weaves—when last time you didn't have enough for Category One—but you held true-life despite the backlash of those weaves breaking. That's huge progress."

"'Progress' would be a stable imbuement."

Gods' Breath yanked Celka to crouch before the fire, ravenous. Maybe she could imbue the rest of their food.

"Great." Gerrit apparently misinterpreted her silence for agreement.

She struggled to concentrate on the pasture. "No, that's not—"

"I need to try again." Not waiting for her response, he pulled her rucksack open. "You didn't eat my carrot, did you?"

"No." But she wanted to now. Stormy skies, she'd eaten lunch, why was she famished? Wait. Gerrit's imbuement—a hunger imbuement—had exploded. "*Gerrit.*"

Her panic froze him. "What's wrong?"

"What's my sousednia supposed to look like?" Even asking the question felt wrong—she saw her sousednia right now, the winter forest, rabbit in the trap, her stomach so empty. But something about that world seemed indescribably *wrong*.

He blanched. "A high wire."

No, sousednia was a frozen forest. She faced him across the campfire.

"I'm an idiot," he said. "Your sousedni-shape's changed." Fear tightened his voice.

She looked down at herself. She wore layers of wool and fur to keep out the cold. "What else would I look like?"

Gerrit caught her hands, and both realities brightened. The smell of wood smoke and seared meat grew unbearable, but somehow his hold gave her the strength to think past it.

"You wear your high wire costume, gossamer sleeves and green sequined bodice." He kept talking, and his desperate intensity made her listen, made her struggle to understand even though every word sounded wrong. Her breath steamed the air and she'd skinned the rabbit and she wanted to eat it and yet... Everything he said felt *right*.

In sousednia, she dragged a slender branch onto the

trampled snow and stepped onto it as though it were the high wire. Eyes closed, she spread her arms and *reached*, struggling to believe the world he described. Nothing changed, so she pushed harder. Suddenly, with the crack of frozen river ice breaking, the air grew hot and humid, thick with the smell of horses and blood.

Gasping, Celka opened her eyes, blinded by spotlights. She inhaled air that tasted so sweet that tears streaked her cheeks. She felt strong and powerful and like *herself* in a way she hadn't known she could lose.

Gerrit flung his arms around her. She shifted sousednia so they stood on the high wire platform, the metal grating pressing into her slippered feet. Gerrit held her, strong and warm, his breath ruffling her hair. «I'm sorry,» he whispered.

She didn't try to control her exhausted, desperate tears, letting them dampen his shirt. «Thank you.» The thought of losing her big top left her colder than that winter forest.

Safe in her core sousednia, however, her tears quickly evaporated. The storm's nearness tingled through her fingers and tugged against her spine.

Pulling out of Gerrit's embrace, she wiped her face. «My turn.»

CHAPTER FORTY

GERRIT WATCHED CELKA rummage through her pack for something to imbue. Her sousedni-shape, graceful and sure, glittered emerald—a far cry from the desperate, wool-clad hunter she'd briefly become. He hated that he'd been so stupid as to imbue close to her, hated that he'd failed—again—and she'd paid the consequences. But he tried to accept her spin on the failure—he *had* done better; and she was safe, free of her hunger-warped sousednia.

He tried to be buoyed by his own small success in that imbuement—returning to his core sousednia's sunbright mountaintop without Filip's help. Endless hours practicing sousedni-dislocations and attempting disruptions had apparently anchored him in true-life.

For all it would matter.

Celka pulled something out of her pack, and her

posture shifted, rageful. Her sousedni-shape sharpened, high wire costume vanishing beneath a child's short pants and blouse. She stumbled as though grabbed by someone stronger. Her building combat nuzhda made Gerrit's sousednia echo with gunfire, so he tore his gaze away, squinting up into the sky, face stung by wind-whipped rain. No hail yet, which was fortunate since they lacked protective gear.

Since trying to imbue, his storm-thread no longer yanked on his spine, and his mouth was free of the battery-sucking taste. Even staring upwards, the storm felt distant, the lightning dim and the thunder rumbling as though from behind thick glass. He wondered if he could pull Gods' Breath again. He'd been hiding for nearly a month and had no imbuements to show for it. If he could just prove his control...

It wouldn't matter, not to his father.

He fled that thought, Celka drawing his gaze like a lodestone. Before he could think, he'd crossed to her side. He realized his mistake as she spun, snarl curling her lips, pistol aimed at his chest. He threw his hands up and stumbled back. "How did you get a Stanek pistol?"

Strain tightened her features, and she shifted her aim off him. Free of the immediate danger of being shot, he touched sousednia. Gunshots shattered his mountain stillness. "Celka, no!" He reached for her. «Your nuzhda's too strong.»

Snarling, she shifted her aim back to him, control overwhelmed by her powerful nuzhda. He lunged, grabbing her hands, twisting the gun from her grip and flinging it behind him before she could fire. Touching her skin flared Gerrit's senses.

For seconds or maybe centuries, sousednia fell silent. No gunshots, no truncheons on flesh, no wind, no screams.

The glass partitioning Gerrit from the bozhskyeh storm shattered, and sensations poured from his grip on Celka hands, echoing between true-life and sousednia. But where the storm had overwhelmed him before, now everything seemed perfect.

Celka's eyes widened. «What...?»

When he'd attempted to imbue before, he'd struggled to see both true-life and enough of sousednia to hold his weaves. Now rain stung his face and he smelled the pasture's loam as clearly as he heard the grunts and blows from the disguised Tayemstvoy attacking his mother.

His sousednia had warped, Celka's combat nuzhda calling his own. He should have been terrified, but somehow, it seemed right.

«I need the gun.» Celka's voice carried deadly threat, though Gerrit knew it wasn't for him.

He released one of her hands, reaching for the pistol.

No. He balled his hand into a fist at his side. The nuzhda was calling for the weapon; he needed to regain control. Stone by painful stone, he walled off a tiny portion of his mind that wasn't combat-warped and, from that sanctuary, focused back on Celka. «This nuzhda? It's Category Five, maybe higher. If anything goes wrong—»

«I won't let it.» She lunged toward the gun.

He caught her. He couldn't lose her to this. «Celka, look at me!» Touching her cheek, he tried to turn her from the gun.

She fought him. He struggled to hold her without hurting her, but the fight flared her nuzhda, and the humanity that had resurfaced at their contact drained away. She bared her teeth.

He had to do something—*now*, before she imbued again at a distance, as she had with his knife.

Concentrating on that terrifying expanse of his mind beyond his protective walls, Gerrit coaxed impossible rain from winter's iron-gray sky. The white noise drowned some of the sound of blows. «You're out of control, Celka. Build your big top. Step onto your high wire.»

She blinked, focusing on him as though shaking off a dream. «How are you... You're changing my sousednia.»

He couldn't stop to understand how that was possible. «You stand in a spotlight,» he told her, «the crowd far below. Step away from the nuzhda.»

She drew a deep breath through her nose, stance shifting until her feet formed a line, hands still clasping his. «Everything's so much clearer, so much easier.» Her costume's sequins glittered as the sun rose on his mountaintop. «How are you doing that?»

«I'm not.» With a conviction that frightened him, he released her—in sousednia and true-life.

His focus stuttered. Storm energy jangled painfully through his hands, and true-life vanished.

Celka stumbled.

He caught her before she could fall—before *he* could fall—and both realities sharpened. He felt like he finally saw as he was meant to see. Lines so crisp, colors so bright.

Reaching through his walls into sousednia's combat-warped expanse, he shaped the sound of boots striking flesh into a resonance to straighten a Stanek pistol's barrel. Forming a weave had never been easier. «Celka, this is incredible.»

«Do you think we can call the storm together?» Wonder softened her voice.

Gerrit's control flickered. What were they *doing*? «Joint imbuements are rare. Dangerous.» But despite the dire reports, he *wanted* to imbue with her. Was the nuzhda warping him?

Even in the walled-off corner of his mind, he wanted to imbue. He'd never felt so in control during a storm. Focusing back on Celka, he said, «A single mistake, and we could both lose true-life.»

«We won't.» Confidence suffused her expression. «Gerrit, I feel incredible! This must be how sousednia's supposed to feel. How *imbuing* is supposed to feel.»

Her enthusiasm threatened to make him smile. He quashed the emotion. He was in control. «You're certain?»

She nodded.

«Then we need a weaker nuzhda. Category Two. Something safe.»

Closing her eyes, she drew a slow breath. Rain sheeted harder from his impossible clouds, further dampening the sound of blows. «How's that?»

Gerrit listened for a moment, less of his mind locked in a combat fugue than before. «Closer to Category Three.»

«Good enough. Now—» Pistol reports joined the grunts and blows, but chaotically.

«Here,» Gerrit squeezed her hand, «let me.» He shaped a disguised Tayemstvoy's snarling into a rhythm that would keep the pistol's action clean and smooth, even after years of neglect. The crack of wood on bone he formed into a simple accuracy weave, aligning the gun's sights with its barrel.

Celka inhaled deeply through her nose. «*Those* are the weaves you keep talking about?»

This time, he did smile. Before, the storm had made concentrating on anything but his weaves a strain; these he could hold with barely a thought.

«There's still nuzhda left over,» Celka said. «Your pot's complexity isn't matched to the amount of clay. What about...»

Her posture shifted, aggressive, and fire buzzed through his arms, the sound of blows erupting around him. Gerrit clutched her hands, worried she'd expanded the nuzhda. But, after a second, the clamor dampened to fit their unused nuzhda. Still, he couldn't see how she could possibly have created a stable weave out of such chaos.

«There.» She sounded satisfied, her sousedni-shape shifting back onto her high wire.

Frowning, Gerrit struggled to make sense of what she'd built. At first, he thought the grunts and scuff of boots was random. He couldn't tease any pattern out of shouts and punches, but Celka smiled like she'd done something brilliant, and he concentrated harder, focusing on the aural interplay.

Academy weaves were straightforward, reproducible. They used minimal components so mages could ensure they made no mistakes. Compared to Celka's weaves, Gerrit's were a geometric painting of a house. He'd drawn a triangle atop a square. Anyone could copy it.

Celka's weaves were a riot of color—abstract art that drew him in circles and tied his perceptions in knots. The weaves were beautiful and subtle and, the more he listened, the more sense they made. Her weaves would interface the mage to the gun, letting them aim steadily and control the recoil easily.

«It's beautiful,» he said.

Celka grinned, combat nuzhda giving the expression a cutting edge. She released one of his hands, and the pistol appeared in her grip. Before he could shout for caution, she called the storm.

Gods' Breath exploded down Gerrit's neck, euphoria riding the heels of agony. The lightning leapt so cleanly, so *beautifully* into the pistol. Combat's hot coals glow flared through the gun, settling into a complex rhythm as the weaves crystalized.

In the silence following the thunderclap, Celka looked radiant, rainwater plastering her hair to her face. Gerrit's back burned with a fresh storm-scar. Still clutching her hand, sousednia and true-life remained vivid.

"We did it," he said, feeling invincible. "We imbued."

CHAPTER FORTY-ONE

CELKA KEPT HOLD of Gerrit's hand while they walked back to the railyard. After imbuing together, the strange clarity that came from contact seemed right, and she resented when brambles and woods forced them to part. The first time they separated, she expected him to retreat back into grimness, but once they regained open pasture, he reached for her hand with a small smile.

When she took it, he said, "I still can't believe that worked."

"I can't believe it took us so long to try," Celka said.

His grin transformed him, softening the planes of his face. Imbuing gave them power like Celka had never imagined. Her first imbuement, Celka had felt strong and deadly, but terrifyingly out of control. Imbuing had felt inevitable—like impact with the ground if you fell from the high wire.

Today, Gerrit had controlled her fall. He'd expanded her awareness, helped her understand how to shape her nuzhda. This was no 'useless' imbuement. Every gram of the pistol's magical clay served a purpose and, carrying this gun in the resistance, she would be powerful.

Uncertainty twinged her at the thought, but Celka shoved it aside. She could worry about the future later. The storm had dissipated and, as they crossed a clearing's dappled sunshine, she stretched. Satisfaction mingled with fatigue, and she felt like a cat curled in a sunbeam.

Gerrit's gaze swept her, hungry.

She searched for the nihilistic desperation that had driven him to kiss her before, but his eyes were alive and bright, his attention sparking like Gods' Breath along her nerves.

Still holding his hand, she laid her other on his chest, feeling the heat of him through his rain-soaked shirt. His smile vanished, replaced with desire that made her unsteady.

His fingers slipped around her neck to touch her storm-scar. Celka gasped as sousednia, already vivid, brightened. She could barely breathe, staring at his mouth, craving more of his touch.

"Celka," he whispered. Raw desire sluiced fire through her.

The distance between them became agony. She slid her hand up his chest and around the back of his neck, palm settling against the mirror of her own storm-scar. Stepping close, she pressed her body along the length of him.

Gerrit groaned. "I want you." His other hand slipped to her hip, pulling her hard against him.

She tilted her head ever so slightly, his lips centimeters from her own, their breath mingling. Shoving aside her terror of the future, she whispered, "Yes."

His mouth tasted of stolen peaches, and the air whispered with his sousednia's pine bough chill. She lost herself in his embrace, flush with success and power. He understood her at a level no one else could. They shared a secret world.

Then Gerrit stiffened in her embrace. She drew back enough to look him in the eye and found him drowning.

"I don't want to wake," he whispered.

"This isn't a dream," she said. But facing his fear, she couldn't believe it.

CHAPTER FORTY-TWO

CELKA STRAINED TO spot light in the dark landscape passing the circus train, the steady *clack-clack*, *clack-clack* drooping her eyelids. Midnight had come and gone, but her family was wide awake.

In the tangerine warmth of a mostly shuttered dark lantern, Aunt Benedikta and Uncle Andrik tied ropes about Demian's waist and shoulders, building a secure harness. Celka kept watch on one side of the train, Ela the other.

"You'd think if someone could manage a dead-drop in Dolni Bezdyekov they could sneak on board at its railyard," Demian said, tying a rope to one of the posts supporting Ela's bunk. He sounded excited, though. They would perform a moving pickup tonight, a feat they'd never attempted. The train climbed a steep grade, engine laboring, but they were still going faster than a person could run.

"Maybe they didn't drop the note," Celka said. "Our schedule's set months in advance; whoever we're picking up could have prearranged a time, had someone from the local cell inform us."

"What would be so dangerous they couldn't come into town, but would risk leaping onto a train?" Ela asked.

"Maybe we're picking up the Wolf," Demian said.

Excitement tingled Celka's storm-scar at the thought, even as Aunt Benedikta said, "We're not picking up the Wolf."

"How do you know?" Ela asked.

"Enough," Grandfather said. "Concentrate on your tasks."

Celka could practically hear Ela's eye-roll and swallowed a laugh as she studied the darkness for... "There!" Around a leftward turn, a farm house appeared, candlelight flickering in its dormer window. "Pickup's still on."

"Lines in place," Uncle Andrik said, and Demian flung wide the door.

Chill wind buffeted the compartment. Celka cupped her hands around her eyes as Ela lifted the dark lantern's shutter to silhouette Demian reaching into the darkness. If the catch went poorly, the harness and anchor lines would save Demian from getting chopped to pieces by the train—but it wouldn't help their target.

"Youthful madness," Grandfather muttered, crouching beside Celka to peer through the window. "These reckless heroics endanger us all."

"It'll be thunderclap if it works," Demian said, leaning out of the compartment, Uncle Andrik and Aunt

Benedikta on his anchor lines, ready to haul him and their target inside.

Celka shifted her focus to sousednia, sweeping aside trees and underbrush and directing a spotlight ahead, searching for a running smoke-form. She blew a breeze toward her, expecting desperation like she'd smelled from the last rezistyent to steal her bunk.

"I think I see someone," Demian said, and Celka strained harder.

The air seemed to ripple, and Celka caught the scent of roasting chestnuts. She swept the spotlight around again—there was *some*thing, but vague enough that she had a hard time resolving it into a person, especially with the clacking train changing the distance.

Frustrated, Celka focused back on true-life's moonlit landscape. Ahead, a figure sprinted flat out, the train rapidly gaining. The target stumbled but recovered, still running. They were three railcars ahead, then two, then one, and still they didn't look back. Sleet, if they didn't reach out, Demian wouldn't be able to grab them.

At the last moment, the target jumped, catching Demian's forearms. Their inertia slammed him to the side, ropes jerking taut. Demian grunted but held on.

Uncle Andrik and Aunt Benedikta heaved against the anchor lines, and their target twisted like a cat, catching the door frame and swinging inside.

Demian fell backwards into Celka's aunt and uncle, and they all landed on their asses. The rezistyent reached out and pulled the door shut, breathing hard but grinning.

"The Amazing Prochazkas." They tipped their cap, eyes dancing like leaping onto moving trains was great sport. They were about Celka's age but a little taller and substantially bustier. Simple red enamel earrings brightened both ears, and the rezistyent wore a satchel over her patched jacket. Celka would bet money that the bulge beneath her right arm was a pistol. "Thanks for the lift. Ah, beds. *Brilliant*."

Grandfather glowered while they exchanged hand-signals, and Celka focused on sousednia. The rezistyent smelled of chestnuts and mulling spices, an acrid whiff of cordite drifting through, like a shelling had interrupted Darknight festivities. A faint blue glow caught Celka's eye near the rezistyent's collar, and only then did she realize what should have been obvious from the start: the girl was too well-defined in sousednia—not a smoke-form, but a human-shaped ripple. She was a bozhk, the glow about her neck a concealment imbuement.

Celka flung herself off her bunk, yanking open her trunk and shoving her clothes aside, digging for her imbued pistol as she stoked her fear into anger. The State controlled all imbuements and trained all bozhki. If the girl knew the right hand-signals, it just meant that someone in the resistance had broken.

Opening her trunk's false bottom, Celka grabbed her pistol. Since imbuing it, she couldn't stand the thought of it out of reach in the tack trailer, despite the risk of the Tayemstvoy finding it. Yanking back the slide, sousednia's blood and gun oil flaring, Celka leapt to her feet, aligning the bozhk's chest in her sights as she activated the imbuement. "Hands up."

Rage insisted she fire before the bozhk could disarm her. Celka struggled to contain the nuzhda's violence, but she refused to divert enough attention to shift sousednia back to her big top. "Everyone get away from her. She's a bozhk."

The mage put up empty hands, eyes wide. "Don't shoot. I'm not your enemy." That came out cold and menacing, and Celka struggled to disentangle what was real from how the combat nuzhda twisted her perceptions.

"Ma, take her gun—it's beneath her right arm." To the bozhk, she said, "If you so much as twitch, I'll shoot."

The State boot-licker gave a tiny nod, hardly moving. While Aunt Benedikta opened her jacket, she stood motionless, holding Celka's gaze. Sizing her up. Preparing to attack. Sleet, Celka needed to step away from her nuzhda.

"She has an imbuement on her chest," Celka said once Aunt Benedikta had handed the gun to Uncle Andrik, "probably a necklace." Near the door, Demian worked fast, untying the knots to free himself from the anchor ropes. Even through her combat nuzhda, she could sense her family's shock at seeing her with a gun. If they survived tonight, Grandfather would have sleeting plenty to say about it—but for now, they had bigger problems.

"It's the jade carving," the bozhk growled—or maybe she whispered it, Celka couldn't be sure.

Aunt Benedicta pulled the carving from beneath the bozhk's shirt, keeping Celka's line of sight clear. When her aunt held out the necklace, Celka nodded. "Ma, back away from her."

"Please," the bozhk said, "wall off your nuzhda."

"If you move—" Celka kept her aim steady, grateful for Ctibor's instruction and her weeks of dry fire practice.

"I won't."

Struggling to keep some attention on true-life, Celka shifted sousednia so she stood inside the big top rather than watching the Tayemstvoy beat Pa. Transitioning while keeping an eye on the bozhk knifed a headache into her temples, but she refused to provide the slightest opening. Once Celka had steadied on her high wire, she drew a slow breath of hay and sawdust and returned most of her attention to the sleeper car. "Who are you?"

The State-trained mage released a shaky breath. "Lucie. The Wolf sent me. Can I—"

"The Wolf?" Celka's stomach did a terrified lurch. If the State had sent one bozhk to glibly infiltrate the resistance, how many others had sweet-talked their way in, carrying concealment imbuements so they could sneak off and report to the Tayemstvoy? Celka edged deeper into sousednia, trying to read how much the bozhk knew about them. Over the Darknight warzone of Lucie's core, she caught the faint urine stink of fear. "Try again."

"I don't understand." Lucie did an impressive job of sounding confused. "With the bozhskyeh storms' return, you must have expected he'd send someone."

"Take her bag," Celka said. Whatever angle Lucie was trying to play, it would take more than an innocent act to lull Celka into releasing her. "Demian, use some of that rope to tie her hands."

"Wait!" Lucie handed over her bag without a fight, but when Demian came toward her with the rope, she backed away. "You must know the resistance has bozhki. I'm here to help. Look in the bag. I brought—"

"Enough," Celka snapped.

"Celka." Grandfather raised a quelling hand. To the bozhk, he asked, "What did you bring?"

"You reported that we needed better access to blank identification folios. I stole engraving dies—official ones—for printing them. I grabbed some blank folios, too, so the printer can match the inks."

Demian dug in Lucie's pack and pulled out a heavy, cloth-wrapped parcel containing two copper plates, one bearing a raised seal and type, the other its reverse, hollow where the first was raised. The paper must get pressed between them to emboss identification folios.

Impressive—but Celka didn't believe her story. "They must leave some mark the State can use to identify the folios." She glanced at Grandfather. "This is bait. No one steals official engraving dies. The Tayemstvoy *gave* them to her so we'd swallow her story."

Lucie's expression darkened, and her warzone scent strengthened. "I risked my *life* to get those plates. You're right that no mundane could get them—but I have a concealment imbuement. I—"

"Had," Celka snapped. "Demian, tie her hands."

"No," Grandfather said. "Celka, lower the gun."

"*What?*"

"I trust her," he said. "She's one of ours."

"She's a *bozhk*."

Grandfather's shoulders slumped, and he sat heavily. "We have mages."

If Celka hadn't walled off her combat nuzhda, she would have lost it. "What are you—No. You said we didn't have any. I *asked* you, and you said we had *no one*."

"No one who could teach you," he said. "Lucie is storm-touched. We have no one storm-blessed."

"No one but you," Lucie said to Celka.

Celka's throat tightened, but she kept the pistol aimed at Lucie, unwilling to trust a State-trained bozhk no matter what Grandfather said. Yet at the same time, she wanted to grab Grandfather and scream at him. "How could you decide that for me?" To Lucie, she asked, "What's your bolt-level?"

"So far as the State knows?" A smirk pulled at her lips. "Only silver."

Celka turned to Grandfather, shaking her head. "There's so much a trained bozhk could teach me."

Grandfather turned his hand palm-down until Celka lowered the gun, betrayal twisting her stomach. She kept the imbuement active, though, nuzhda raging outside her big top. "They could not teach you what you must learn," Grandfather said. "They could not teach you to block the storms."

"Why would she—?" Lucie began.

Grandfather cut her off with a glare. "Celka, put the weapon away. Lucie has done as the Wolf directed.

These printing plates will save many lives." To Lucie, he said, "You must be tired. Celka will loan you her bunk for the night. I expect you must depart tomorrow." His usual gravitas carried a hint of menace.

Lucie frowned, taken aback, but smoothed over the expression as fast as Gerrit ever had. "Of course."

Celka had never known Grandfather to chase a rezistyent off so quickly. Maybe he didn't trust Lucie as much as he claimed... or maybe he didn't want to give Celka the chance to talk to her.

"I'll go as soon as I get the rifle training manuals," Lucie said. "You printed them, right?"

Celka turned to Grandfather, still unable to trust the bozhk.

Ela said, "They're almost ready. We have to print the last page, but Celka finished the stencil."

Lucie's face softened with relief. "That's good. Thank you."

Silence settled over the car, awkward, as everyone climbed into bed. Before Ela extinguished the dark lantern, Lucie caught Celka's gaze and mouthed, *tomorrow*. Silent, Celka nodded. Whatever Grandfather's plans, Celka would make sure she and Lucie had time to talk.

CHAPTER FORTY-THREE

"UGH, YOUR TURN." Ela dropped the mimeograph's handle, making space for Gerrit to take over. She shook out her arms.

Gerrit swept the crank through a full rotation, Ela holding the paper aligned on the stencil tacked to the ink-filled barrel. The heavy scent of castor oil lingered over the press. Ela set the completed page on a snake cage to dry then aligned a fresh sheet. *Crank, crank, crank.* Running the paper between the barrel and pressure rollers squeezed ink through the stencil. Gerrit kept turning, ignoring the discomfort in his arm as they printed Celka's last pages of treason.

He should be horrified, but the thousands of pages of treasonous text made him vindictively proud. His father would find him and chain him, but at least these rifle manuals meant someone would fight back. Even if they'd fail.

"So, Celka imbued a gun," Ela said as she fed another page into the rollers.

"*We* imbued it," Gerrit corrected. "Together."

"Except joint imbuing's not supposed to be a thing?" Ela asked. "How's that work?"

"It's dangerous," he said.

"But Celka's special?"

He nodded before noticing Ela's smirk. "Not—I mean. She is, but—" He shook his head.

"Mm-hm." They printed another page in silence before Ela gained a mischievous smile. "Do you suppose Celka's off with Ctibor right now?"

Jealousy made it easier to ignore the ache in his arm as he twisted the mimeograph's crank.

"Ludvik said he's a really good kisser," Ela said with a wistful sigh, as though it were an idle comment.

"Stop." He snapped it like a command, and Ela straightened, surprised. Feeling like sleet-licker, Gerrit cranked hard on the mimeograph, forcing a slow breath. "Just stop, please."

"Fine." She rolled her eyes, not intimidated. She stacked several dry pages before returning to press a fresh sheet to the rollers. "Your claws come out easy."

"I just..." He didn't know what to say.

She shrugged. "Celka always talks about you like you're a tiger."

Heat and cold twined through him. "You talk about me?"

"Duh. And tigers, for your reference, are vicious wild beasts, dangerous even to their trainers—unlike lions, which can be total kittens once you know them."

"So the knife thrower's her lion?" Gerrit really hated the sleet-licker.

"You're so cute. No. Apparently Celka likes tigers."

Gerrit imagined Celka facing a dozen snarling beasts in a circus ring, so ferocious they wouldn't dare attack. The image almost made him smile, but darkness pressed it down. "You just want a chance at Ctibor."

Ela blew on a completed page to dry its ink. "He's not really my type."

"What is your type?" Maybe he could get her talking about herself.

"Someone *not* head-over-heels for my sister."

Gerrit drove the mimeograph through another rotation even as his attention slipped to sousednia's night-dark mountaintop. He stood at the edge of a cliff, the abyss yawning below him.

"I don't get you, Gerrit," Ela said. "Celka likes you. You like her. What's the problem?"

He wrenched his attention back to the snake trailer. They had only a few dozen pages left to print, and then the one thing that had given him focus would be finished. He didn't know how much longer he could make himself practice sousedni-disruptions, as if anchoring himself in true-life would matter.

"She should date Ctibor," he made himself say. "He has a future. I don't."

"Aren't you the wounded bird?" Ela waved the next

page through the air. "Of course you won't have a future if you believe you won't."

Like belief was all that mattered.

Ela leaned close to whisper in his ear, and Gerrit found himself holding his breath. "You're a tiger, Gerrit. Tigers fight until the end."

CHAPTER FORTY-FOUR

CELKA EASED THE sleeper car door shut, blocking the afternoon sun. The supposedly resistance bozhk, Lucie, had pushed the table and chairs aside and moved through an empty-handed combat form. The matinee sideshow had just ended, and Celka had slipped away before Grandfather could stop her.

His insistence this morning that she practice with the family on the low wire made Celka wonder what Lucie knew. Maybe the resistance had more resources than Grandfather claimed. If they had mages, maybe they could already protect her.

She struggled not to let hope make her stupid. Grandfather might believe that Lucie was resistance; Celka still wasn't convinced.

"Where did you learn storm magic?" Celka asked. She didn't really expect to recognize the name of Lucie's school; the State had plenty of regional academies for children with storm-affinities—schools slightly more respected than their non-magical counterparts, sprinkled with bozhk training and heavy doses of State propaganda. But the way Lucie had insinuated she was more skilled even than a regular silver-bolt made Celka wonder if she'd studied somewhere prestigious. Not that a resistance bozhk would necessarily answer any question that could link back to her real identity—'Lucie' had to be a false name.

Lucie wiped sweat from her brow with a ragged handkerchief, stopping her combat form to study Celka. In sousednia, over her core scent of chestnuts and battlefields, Celka caught a hint of humus and rotting leaves, as though Lucie watched her from a blind in the woods. The scent seemed evaluative rather than evasive. Warily, she said, "The Storm Guard Academy."

Celka tensed, but drew a slow breath in sousednia, searching for deception. Lucie seemed to be telling the truth. "So why aren't you a fancy Army officer?"

"They threw me out."

Celka's stomach tightened like she'd slipped on the wire. Gerrit had mentioned that over half the people who entered the Storm Guard Academy washed out, either unfit for the strenuous academic curriculum or unable to control their storm-affinity to the Guard's high standard. He'd dismissed them as weak or incompetent. Celka wondered how much that was true and how much it had been his justification to endure.

"I didn't fail," Lucie snapped. "I got high marks and

earned my silver bolt young. I'd be a gold-bolt and probably kissing regime boots if I hadn't befriended the wrong person."

Celka wasn't sure if the bitter edge to Lucie's tone was from not living that life or from the thought that she could have. "Who'd you befriend?"

Sousednia exploded with a tangle of scents Celka couldn't sort out, some sweet, some acrid. "Someone with an important family and not enough sense. He pissed off some staff officers, so they dragged *me* away in the middle of the night because they couldn't touch him. Probably told him they sent me to a labor camp."

The idea chilled Celka, recalling Gerrit's insistence they not get too close. "Did they? Send you to a labor camp, I mean."

Lucie shook her head. "Just some hail-bitten factory job. Stripped my bolt-rating and dumped me there with no savings or family, so I couldn't get out." Copper-bolt bozhki or even black-bolts, who couldn't control their storm-affinities at even a basic level, still got more opportunities than everyone else—the mere existence a storm-affinity was a mark of the Storm Gods' favor. Celka could only imagine what a shock it must have been to go from one of the State's most elite academies to endless days of fourteen-hour factory shifts. Yet Lucie's story didn't quite add up. "If you were so skilled, why would they just dump you? The State needs bozhki."

"Bozhk doctors, maybe, but the Storm Guard Academy trains mainly combat affinities. During the war, pretty much any imbuement useful on the battlefield got overdriven and destroyed, so there's not much real call for combat-trained bozhki. Or there wouldn't be if the bozhskyeh storms hadn't returned." Lucie shrugged. "The Storm Guard mostly exists to mold the State's elite into perfect regime toads—with shiny bolts on their throats so everyone *knows* how superior they are." She rolled her eyes.

Celka hadn't thought of it that way, had always assumed that the Storm Guard Academy and all the other top schools—bozhk or mundane—were so elite because they took only the best students. "Then how'd you get in?" If Lucie's family was so unimportant that the State could toss her away without consequences, by her own reasoning, she shouldn't have been there in the first place.

"Elite doesn't just mean regime connections," Lucie said. "Though it helps. The Storm Guard Academy draws top students from regional bozhk schools, too, the better to keep the Storm Gods' blessings close to the State's rotten heart."

Even amongst other rezistyenti, Celka had never known someone to so openly criticize the regime. "So you're doing this why? Revenge?"

Lucie heaved a sigh and sat on Celka's bunk. She pressed thumb and forefingers to the bridge of her nose and shook her head. When she spoke, the bitter edge was gone. "I believe Bourshkanya can be better."

Celka drew a slow breath in sousednia, but Lucie's spice-and-cordite scent only intensified. Assuming she couldn't control her sousedni-cues, she'd told the truth this whole time. "So why are you really here?"

"The rifle instructions and printing plates—"

"Aren't the whole story."

Lucie smirked. "I knew I'd like you." She grabbed her jacket off the bed. Celka tensed, and Lucie froze, as though Celka had drawn a gun. Carefully, she said, "The Wolf gave me a letter for you."

"The Wolf doesn't know about me." Or so Grandfather had claimed.

Lucie's expression went carefully neutral. "May I?"

Celka nodded, and Lucie handed her an envelope made of brown leather. The paper inside was oddly thick. Unfolding the page, Celka read. "A dumpling recipe?" Was this some kind of joke?

"Look closer," Lucie said.

Celka read the instructions more carefully, wondering if she had to decode them. But Grandfather hadn't taught her any code that would transform this into sense. Only then did she realize that the page glowed a blue so faint she'd dismissed it as part of the paper.

"Careful when you activate it," Lucie said. "It's a staged imbuement with a combat trigger."

Celka didn't know what that meant. Apparently it showed.

"Here, watch me." Standing, Lucie touched the page with one finger. "If you activate it improperly—or just pull on the combat trigger—it'll burst into flames. The envelope's a darkbag—it hides the imbuement."

Lucie didn't give Celka time to be impressed. She

cringed, her wavery sousedni-shape twisting in agony. Celka was about to ask if she was all right when the paper's blue glow brightened. Of course. The girl was Storm Guard-trained; her concealment nuzhda would arise from some horrible brutality.

Slipping into sousednia, Celka watched the imbuement brighten, the air redolent of cheap perfume and musty canvas. Lucie stopped there, breath fast and panicky, meeting Celka's gaze to make sure she'd seen. Only then did Celka spot a red flicker of combat nuzhda, its blood-and-gun-oil scent faint. Lucie's jaw tightened, and the combat component flared then vanished from true-life as she activated its weaves. Lucie's expression twisted again, and she curled in on herself, activating the remaining concealment weaves. The imbuement's glow disappeared completely from true-life, though it rippled brighter in sousednia, revealing hidden complexity.

Eyes squeezed shut, Lucie walled off her nuzhdi. Given the imbuement's glow, Celka guessed it was Category Two or Three, but it took Lucie only a few seconds to partition off.

Walls in place, Lucie straightened. Gerrit always looked embarrassed after Celka saw him pull against concealment, but Lucie met her gaze unflinchingly. "Read it."

The biscuit recipe had vanished, the page filled with a small, cramped script that Celka recognized immediately as Pa's.

Hello, little lightning rod, the letter began.

Feeling like the air had been sucked out of the room,

Celka sat on her bunk. She heard Lucie retreat, but couldn't look away from the page.

I guess you're not so little anymore, are you? I'm sorry I've missed so much. You, your mother, the circus—you kept me grounded as the bozhskyeh storms neared. But that only delayed the inevitable.

I'm going storm-mad, Celka. By the time you read this, the bozhskyeh storms will have returned, and they will have taken my mind.

Celka reread the lines, struggling to understand. Pa was alive—alive but going storm-mad?

Wait, Lucie had said she'd gotten this letter from the Wolf.

Churning with questions, Celka dove back into the letter.

During the war, I tried to imbue. The bozhskyeh storms were still decades off, but we were losing. I abandoned true-life, but still failed.

No matter how a storm calls or how desperate your nuzhda, always keep one foot in true-life. Always. I didn't, and that's my greatest regret. If I had, I'd be with you right now.

This page is only so long, so I must get to the point. Since my 'arrest,' I've been leading the resistance. We started by spreading the truth. We'll end by destroying Kladivo's State before he can start another war.

Sleetstorms. Pa was the Wolf.

Lucie flowed through an unarmed combat form a few meters away. "You saw him? The Wolf? My... pa?" Her voice choked.

"It's been a few months. And he gave me that letter almost a year ago."

"Is he really storm-mad?"

"The bozhskyeh storms hadn't returned yet when I saw him."

Celka's throat closed off. Pa was alive and free, but going—or already?—storm-mad. Pa was the *Wolf*. Why hadn't Grandfather told her?

Despite the regime's claims, we started the Lesnikrayen War. Bourshkanya, not Lesnikraj. No foreign assassin stole into the palace that fateful night. Artur Kladivo arranged the king's assassination and the simultaneous murder of top members of Parliament. They stood in his way.

The old elites who didn't rally to Kladivo's war cry fell soon after, victims to 'foreign assassins' or 'war protestors,' whomever Kladivo deemed most convenient to demonize. Then he used our victory at Zlin to convince the public that the Storm Gods favored his rule.

After Lesnikraj surrendered, Kladivo slaughtered hundreds more, blaming the deaths on Lesnikrayen sympathizers and bleaching news reports to paint the Tayemstvoy as heroes rather than axemen. Most people were so relieved to have survived the war—or so stunned by their losses—that they swallowed his propaganda gladly.

That the Tayemstvoy patrolled in gangs and we'd become a police state while everyone focused on the front lines—well, wasn't anything better than foreign occupation?

A hundred thousand Bourshkanyans died so Kladivo could seize power. He intends to rule the world and, as soon as he thinks he can win another war, he will start it. With the bozhskyeh storms' return, he won't wait much longer.

I'm sorry I couldn't take you with me when I had to disappear. The life of a resistance leader was not one I could force on my child. That doesn't mean I've forgotten you. Not for one day.

The people need to see that the Storm Gods have not forsaken them. You can give people the strength to fight.

I wish I could touch Gods' Breath as you do, but I barely returned to true-life after Zlin. As I write this, my storm-thread pulls me ever closer to madness.

If you're ready to help, speak to the girl who brought this letter. She can get you to safety and protect you while you imbue.

If the State finds you, my people will create an opportunity for you to escape. Watch for it, and learn what you can until it comes. The Storm Guard intends to control Bourshkanya's imbuement mages, so you'll likely be brought to

*their fortress. Amongst their number, your only
ally is Karolina Vrana.*

Celka froze on that impossible name. Before that line,
she'd devoured Pa's words, struggling to wrap her mind
around the implications. But this... she couldn't believe
this. Vrana had dragged Pa away. Vrana had led the
Tayemstvoy who'd arrested him.

She squeezed her eyes shut, that horrible day welling
over her. Vrana couldn't be an ally. She couldn't.

> *Please trust me. I know what you saw and how
> hard these words must be to believe. But Kaya has
> saved my life more times than I can count. That
> charade was necessary to protect you. As far as
> anyone else knows, Captain Vrana arrested Storm
> Guard deserter Leosh Kratochvil. He was shot for
> treason.*
>
> *If the State realizes what you are, claim him as
> your father and hide your abilities. Take your time
> 'learning' to imbue so you give the regime as little
> as possible.*
>
> *The Storm Guard overflows with venom and
> lies. My people have been doing their best to
> pluck a few flowers from that soil before they are
> irreparably poisoned, so we have skilled bozhki to
> use your imbuements. Though we have precious
> few—far fewer than the State.*
>
> *You are clever and resourceful, my little lightning
> rod. The resistance needs you.*

Ensure you can pull this letter's failsafe. Allow no one else to read it.

I love you. Goodbye.

Tears filled Celka's eyes, but she blinked them away and read the letter again, fingering her storm pendant. Then again, the world reeling. Finally, she tore her gaze from the page. She asked Lucie, "Did you read it?"

The resistance bozhk sat beside Celka. "Yeah."

"Why did he give it to you?" Celka asked. Lucie said she'd carried this letter for a year. Why hadn't Pa contacted Celka himself? Why hadn't Lucie found her earlier?

"He said I reminded him of you."

Jealousy knifed her chest, and Celka turned away so Lucie wouldn't see it. The unfairness of this stranger seeing Pa when Celka hadn't even known he was alive made her want to scream.

Lucie let the silence stretch, but Celka could feel the other girl studying her.

"You hide your sousedni-cues really well," Lucie said. Celka snapped around to face her, plunging into sousednia. Had she misread the bozhk? She would have sworn Lucie was only storm-touched, her sousedni-shape a heat-shimmer.

"I always caught glimpses of sousednia," Lucie said at her scrutiny. "The Wolf taught me to use the background rumble around people to read the basics—truth, lies, that sort of thing. Sometimes I can do more. He trained me for an intense week last year, which was when he gave me that letter—and how I know him. But I haven't been able to read anything from you, though I sometimes catch your sousedni-shape from the corner of my eye." She made a face, like she was trying to keep from smiling. Finally, she gave up. "It's so amazing to finally meet you."

Celka frowned. "Why?"

Lucie laughed. "You're Celka Doubek!"

It felt like Lucie had shoved a knife in her ribs. "Don't say that name. *Never* say that name."

The last time she'd heard it aloud, Captain Vrana had been looming over her while the Tayemstvoy beat Pa. Celka's family never used the name, not ever. It was too well known. Major Doubek had saved Bourshkanya at Zlin, and everyone thought he was dead. Everyone.

Pressing her hands over her eyes, Celka struggled to think. Everything she'd thought about Pa's arrest could be wrong. If it had been staged... stormy skies, she couldn't believe Pa would have set up that beating. That must have been Vrana's idea, the sadistic sleet-licker.

No, Celka couldn't afford to cling to her old narrative. Something had been wrong that morning, even before Vrana and the Tayemstvoy had arrived. Pa had chased the rest of their family off so that he and Celka could practice on the low wire alone. He'd been acting strange, his balance off, and he'd hugged Celka and told her he loved her like he might never see her again. She bit her lip, fighting against tears.

Pa had known. He'd known the Tayemstvoy were coming—because he'd planned it. With Vrana.

Vrana, who'd ordered a dozen soldiers to beat Pa until he couldn't stand, until he was covered with blood and too broken to even look at Celka as they dragged him away. Vrana, who'd beaten Celka herself.

But Vrana hadn't dragged Celka away, despite saying her true name. Vrana would have seen Celka's sousedni-shape, too well-defined for a storm-touched bozhk, no matter how strongly Celka held true-life. The more Celka thought about those fractured moments, the more her assumptions broke down. Vrana hadn't been using Celka to blackmail Pa into imbuing for the State. If Celka believed Pa's letter, Vrana had helped him disappear to lead the resistance.

And Gerrit... Vrana had helped Gerrit escape the Storm Guard.

Celka scrubbed her hands over her face. Just before kicking her so hard she couldn't stand as they dragged Pa away, Vrana had said, "His lies might yet protect you."

Had it all been an act? Had Vrana beaten her... to keep her safe? The thought made Celka sick. No matter how Pa trusted that hail-eater, Celka couldn't believe that had been part of his plan. Celka had been *thirteen*, a child. Bad enough that she'd seen Pa's blood flying from Tayemstvoy truncheons. Pa would never have planned for Celka to be hurt.

Lucie caught her hand, and Celka tensed. The other girl squeezed reassuringly. "I know. I couldn't believe it at first, either. I always thought the Stormhawk was the greatest Bourshkanyan alive." A mischievous smile.

"But your pa's the real hero." Her smile grew, and she practically bounced on the bunk. "And you're... you're *his* daughter! You're *storm-blessed*. And one of *us*. That gun you imbued is really amazing!"

Despite herself, Celka found her mood lightening. Lucie's enthusiasm was infectious and, around her, Celka's big top smelled like spiced cider and happiness.

"I studied its weaves last night—I hope you don't mind. I just"—this time Lucie did bounce a little—"it's thunderclap! I've never seen an imbuement that interfaces with a mage like that."

Celka's cheeks went hot, but she smiled. "Thanks."

"So, are you ready to go?"

Celka glanced back at the page, a roaring in her ears. Pa was the Wolf, and Grandfather had lied to her. She could imbue and be safe. She could escape the State.

She focused back on Lucie. Grandfather might not want her to leave, but he must have good reasons. "Can the resistance really protect me? If we're chasing storms, the Tayemstvoy and Storm Guard will be there. They'll figure it out."

"We'll form a team. I'll be your strazh mage—you know what that is?"

Celka nodded. Gerrit had explained it, sousednia gusting loss and pain while he described Filip's role in his first imbuement.

"We'll pick up another bozhk and a couple of mundanes who know their way around weapons and explosives," Lucie continued. "We'll form a mobile imbuement team. The Wolf arranged safe-houses all across the country to hide us between bozhskyeh storms." Lucie searched Celka's expression, her hazel eyes bright and determined. "He walked me through his plans a couple months ago. You're important, Celka. We'll keep you safe."

Safe. While imbuing. She wanted to say yes, pack her things and follow Lucie into this world that seemed the answer to everything she'd wanted. But what about Gerrit?

"I need to... to think about it," Celka said. She needed to talk to Grandfather, find out how much he'd known and why he didn't want her to follow Pa's plans.

Lucie blinked in surprise then leaned back, playing casual. "Sure. Um. I'll just..." She shrugged. "Sleet, you have *beds*. I'll be in bed."

CHAPTER FORTY-FIVE

CELKA'S BOOTS SQUELCHED through mud as she sprinted toward the big top, hoping to catch her family before they entered the ring. She skidded to a stop in the performers' entrance only to find them crossing the hippodrome track. She'd have to wait until after their act. *Their* act, not hers.

Her stomach twisted—panic, excitement, fear... she was so mixed up it was a wonder she could remember her own name. A burble of hysterical laughter threatened to escape. Even her name wouldn't be her own soon. In the resistance, she'd have to use a false identity.

Celka struggled to rein in her emotions. This might be the last time she ever saw the circus.

The thought tightened her chest. While Evzhan, Ludvik, and the other tumblers built a human tower, the rope ladder to the high wire swayed as her family climbed. The visceral memory of wooden rungs beneath her hands and performance jitters in her stomach heightened her loss. She was leaving this world—perhaps forever.

A group of clowns loitered a couple meters away, chatting and laughing. She couldn't make out their words, and an invisible wall seemed to turn them into strangers—though she'd known them all her life.

"You miss it." Ctibor's voice made her_ jump. His shoulder bumped hers, the contact supportive, comfortable.

Her family reached the platform high above, and Celka felt the wire grate pressing into the soles of her feet—from sousednia or memory, she didn't know. In the center ring, the tumblers bowed to thunderous applause. The clowns dispersed to amuse the audience while the Prochazkas prepared for the circus' finale.

Alone with Ctibor, she said, "I do miss it. Though performing up there feels like a different life."

High above, Grandfather climbed onto a bicycle, balance pole across his lap. Almost half way across the wire, he wobbled. The crowd gasped. He'd performed that trick a million times and always 'lost his balance' at the same point.

"I wish I'd had a chance to see the act while you were in it," Ctibor said.

"Why?"

"It was important to you."

Celka nodded—then her stomach clenched. "'Was'?"

"What?" he asked.

"You said 'was,' not 'is.'"

When Ctibor didn't respond, Celka turned to find him studying her with solemn intensity. "You're leaving soon, aren't you."

She turned back to the wire. How could Ctibor read her so well after having known her barely a month? On the wire, Grandfather stabilized and edged the pedals forward. The audience released their collective breath.

"When you were sick," Ctibor said, "you missed a major storm. Dozens of lightning strikes."

"Must have been quite the show. I'm sorry I missed it." The band broke into a peppy waltz, and Aunt Benedikta and Uncle Andrik danced across the wire. Celka could feel Ctibor waiting for more.

Rather than push for an admission she couldn't make, Ctibor's hand slipped into hers. Together, they watched the rest of the act in silence. She would miss this when she escaped into the resistance—would miss him.

Finally, beneath the drumroll for her family's pyramid finale, Ctibor said, "This isn't the solution."

Her throat tightened, but she kept her gaze determinedly upward as Demian steadied the chair between Uncle Andrik and Grandfather's bicycles. When he climbed atop it, the feat looked miraculous.

She released Ctibor's hand. He'd helped her, but he still carried his Army papers, still wanted to serve the State. Grandfather was right that she couldn't risk trusting him.

Her storm pendant pressed into her chest, a weight or a lifeline, she couldn't tell. She felt like she teetered on the edge of a precipice. Pa's letter changed everything. She couldn't turn back, but if she stepped forward, would she fly or would she fall?

AFTER GRANDFATHER CHANGED out of costume, he and Celka grabbed canvas chairs and left the fairgrounds behind. They crossed a field, a grassy crop whispering around their calves. Afternoon sun glared in Celka's eyes, and the moist earth plus the town's pall of coal smoke lent the air a gritty humidity.

Out of earshot of the back lot, they sat. "Lucie gave me a letter from Pa," Celka said.

Grandfather grew very still, his blue eyes darting as he studied her. Around them, insects chirped and buzzed.

"You knew." Celka hadn't wanted to believe it, though it seemed impossible he wouldn't have known. "You knew he was the Wolf. That he was alive."

Grandfather sighed, staring toward the big top. It looked like a dirty brown mushroom, its fungal brothers spreading across the field. Colorful trailers dotted the grounds, too distant to make out the exotic creatures painted on their sides. "I knew."

"And *Vrana?*" Celka couldn't help but twist the Storm Guard officer's name. "When I ran to you, crying after she beat me—did you know they'd staged the arrest?"

"Your father thought you too young to understand."

"But not too young to see him beaten and dragged away by the Tayemstvoy?" Her voice came out choked.

"I am sorry you saw that."

"Do you know where he is?"

"No."

Celka hadn't realized she'd dipped into sousednia until she caught the faintest whiff of something foul and out of place. She swirled a breeze around Grandfather, wondering if she'd imagined the stench. Concentrating, she picked out an oily grittiness, like a motorcar's exhaust. "You're lying." Even as she spoke the words, she could hardly believe them.

"A great many people would like your father found. Just as I have taught you not to ask dangerous questions"—his stern expression made her want to stare at her boots—"I have not asked."

"Asked?" The pieces clicked. "*Vrana* knows where he is."

"Karolina helped him escape the State's noose. That is all."

In sousednia, Celka drew a deliberate breath. The stench was faint, and she never would have noticed had she not been searching. Grandfather's expression remained as solemn and truthful as ever, and years of deferring to him made Celka want to accept his wisdom. But Pa had taught her too well. "What else have you lied to me about?"

"Do not be a fool. I am not—"

"Don't." She bit off the word the way Gerrit might. She felt sick turning against Grandfather like this, but she couldn't hide behind him any longer. She was storm-blessed and about to leave the circus. His lies could get her killed. "You can't lie to me. Just like you couldn't lie to Pa." The last was a guess, but Grandfather straightened.

A sigh deflated him. "Karolina knows. But she resides within the Storm Guard fortress. Trying to speak with her—"

"*You* do."

"She sends the occasional letter. More is not safe."

Exhaust fumes—not as strong as before, but he was still dodging the truth. Stormy skies, how often had Grandfather lied to her? She held his gaze, refusing to back down.

He twisted his shirt cuff. "She found me in Solnitse—as she used to find your father when he was in the troupe."

Celka shook her head. "Pa was terrified of Solnitse. He always pretended to be sick."

"Illusions and misdirections. Your father has always played a dangerous game. Magic made Karolina invisible. In the old days, she brought imbuements for your father so they could spend the day together."

No. Vrana might have saved Pa from the Storm Guard, but they weren't friends. They couldn't be. Yet much as Celka searched the air for deception, sousednia carried only Grandfather's core scents of boiled cabbage and sweat.

Celka forced herself to keep breathing. She wasn't a child anymore to ignore inconvenient truths. "What did she tell you?"

"Your father has deteriorated rapidly since the bozhskyeh storms returned. She seemed surprised that he still held true-life at all. He has a strong will." A bitter smile. "Like you."

"What else?"

"She sent a storm-blessed bozhk to find you. She wanted him away from the Storm Guard before he could imbue."

Celka tried to keep her face blank. "Did she tell you his name?"

"No. This boy, Ctibor, he is the bozhk?"

"Ctibor?" Was that why Grandfather had been so awkward about him? "He's not Storm Guard."

Grandfather frowned. "You're certain?"

"He's not even a bozhk. I'd see him in sousednia if he was."

"So all this time you spend with him? I assumed he was Karolina's mage. If this is not true—why are you wasting your time?"

"I *like* Ctibor."

"Celka." Grandfather took her hands. "I know this is difficult at your age, but you must forget him. You are storm-blessed, special. There will be other attractive young people—ones more worthy. If anything, the trials you will face will only get him killed."

She snatched her hands away, but his words chilled her.

"Save your coal for the steep grade ahead."

It didn't matter. Whether or not she agreed with Grandfather, she'd be leaving Ctibor behind when she disappeared into the resistance. "Lucie says she can get me out—keep me safe." Better that she divert the conversation before Grandfather could ask dangerous questions about who Vrana had actually sent. "She said Pa prepared a place for me."

Grandfather looked as though he'd watched the Tayemstvoy execute a friend. "Your father... we disagreed over many things."

"I *want* to imbue. And the resistance needs me. The *Wolf* needs me."

"The Wolf *cannot* help you." His gravitas crumbled, leaving an old man, bitter and afraid. "Whatever he thought he prepared, the Tayemstvoy will follow the lightning strikes—"

"Which is why I can't be *here!*" She could hardly believe she was fighting with Grandfather. All her life, he'd never been wrong—not about the important things. "I have to *go*. Before I lead the Tayemstvoy to you."

"No. Resist the storms. Their power seduced your father, and their return has taken his mind. What Lucie thinks he has in place—it is not enough. You will not be safe if you leave here. You will *never* be safe if you imbue."

Celka felt as though he'd shoved her from the low wire. "Never?"

"*Never*. Stay and resist the storms. You are helping the resistance. With us. With your *family*."

"The resistance needs imbuements," she said.

"The *State* needs imbuements. You think that pistol you imbued makes you safe? The Tayemstvoy are more numerous than roaches. Shoot two, and five more take their place. If you continue imbuing, they will *hunt* you and *destroy* you."

Stomach churning, Celka wanted to curl into a ball, wanted to tell Grandfather that she'd do as he asked and have him wrap her in his strong arms. But remembering Lucie's confidence steadied her, and she breathed past her fear. For two decades Grandfather had fought a quiet war, hiding rezistyenti and transporting information. Maybe that had been enough, once.

But now that the bozhskyeh storms had returned, the resistance couldn't just slink along in the shadows. Supreme-General Kladivo wanted another war. If the resistance didn't stop him, he would get hundreds of thousands of people killed—again. Pa had fought in the Lesnikrayan War. He understood the importance of risk.

Pa wouldn't put her in danger without good reason. To protect Celka, he'd let the Tayemstvoy beat him senseless. He'd had four years to plan for the returning bozhskyeh storms. Grandfather was afraid, but Celka trusted Pa.

CHAPTER FORTY-SIX

GERRIT SUPPORTED HIMSELF on fingertips and toes, body straight as a plank, muscles straining while he shifted from sousednia to true-life and back again. Spotting Celka's approach, her sousedni-shape wavering like a reflection in water, he leaped to his feet and opened the snake trailer door. «I think I've figured it out.»

«Figured what out?»

While Celka strode deeper into the trailer, Gerrit stayed near the door. His true-form motionless, he laid a hand on Celka's shoulder from sousednia.

She cocked her head. "That was pretty good. It almost felt real."

Gerrit tried not to be disappointed by the "almost." He'd practiced with a mule after he and Ela finishing mimeographing, and was pretty sure he'd made its ear twitch.

"What changed?" she asked.

"I'd been focusing on touching a sousedni-shape, but that's not the whole person. Instead, I've been trying to see the true-form from sousednia. Almost like I'm bringing the true-form and sousedni-shape into contact, and then touching the true-form *from* sousednia."

Celka smiled, but sobered too fast.

"What is it?" he asked. When she hesitated, his own words tumbled out, too urgent to keep locked inside. "This morning, I realized I haven't been thinking about things right. I was so scared and angry that I forgot who I am."

Celka frowned, and Gerrit struggled to put his swirling thoughts into some semblance of order. He didn't quite know where this path would lead, but he felt hopeful for the first time in weeks. "My father doesn't realize what I know about him. He'll find me, but that doesn't have to be the end. He trusts my brother and sister, he's groomed them to stand at his side and he *must* want that from me, or he would have just murdered Mother quietly, rather than using it to warp me. That means I have a chance. In the next storm, I'll imbue again—I *know* I will. It made so much sense when we imbued together that I'm certain I can imbue on my own.

"And then, instead of waiting for regime dogs to find me, I can return to the Storm Guard."

"What?" Celka cried. "Gerrit, no! That's a terrible idea."

He clasped her hands. "Hear me out. The Stormhawk wants imbued weapons and is willing to destroy mages to get them. But once I prove I can imbue, my father will respect me and I'll be able to"—he scrabbled for a way to explain without admitting his father's identity—"use his influence to make the Tayemstvoy back off of the Storm Guard. I have friends in the Storm Guard, Celka. If I go back, I might be able to protect them."

"How can you possibly believe that'll work?" she asked. "Even if your father's that powerful, he's not just going to trust you because you made him a shiny gun. And if he does? How could you even consider licking his boots? He *murdered* your mother."

Gerrit struggled to cover the wince. He had to crush that knowledge down so it couldn't betray him. He'd thought this through, practiced the words—"It's better than being hunted and driven storm-mad."

"What if there was another option?" Celka asked.

He tried to pull his hands away, but she tightened her grip. "We've talked about this," he said, frustrated. "The resistance—"

"Is stronger than I thought." Belief lit her expression. Before, she'd been frightened of the future, had seen the resistance as a desperate chance.

He shook his head, but hope lit in his chest, a painful ember he tried to quench. "What changed?"

"I got a letter from the Wolf," she said.

"The one on the leaflets?"

"Our leader. He arranged safe-houses to hide us while we chase the storms and strazh mages to protect us while we imbue."

"Us?"

"Me." She shook her head. "But it could be *us*. If you come with me."

"One letter, and you believe we'll be safe? It sounds like a trap."

"I know the Wolf," Celka said. "I trust him."

"You *what*? How?"

"I can't say." She squeezed his hands. "Trust me?"

He paced away. He wanted to say yes and leap after this chance. His mother had been moving to stand against his father; he could pick up where she'd left off. But it would mean abandoning his friends. Filip, Hana, and all his squadmates and the younger cadets; could he leave them to be brutalized? Every day fear sickened him that the Tayemstvoy had punished his friends for his disappearance. He'd finally started to believe he could make this right.

But was he deluding himself? Was he clinging to a thread that he could influence his father where his mother had failed? In the resistance, he could fight the regime head-on. The anger that had nearly subsumed him these last few weeks burned for that destruction.

"My father wanted me to become a weapon." He hadn't intended to speak aloud, but the words helped clear his head. "Mother believed in rebuilding." He turned to face Celka. "What happens if we tear down the State? Does the resistance have a plan to make things better? Will they put the Wolf in charge?"

"Not the Wolf." Pain pulled at her expression, and she looked away.

"Why not?"

"It's... complicated."

"Fighting the regime could lead to chaos. Civil war. Without a strong, unified Bourshkanya, the Lesnikrayens will sweep in and conquer us."

"There's probably a plan," Celka said, "I just don't know it. Maybe Vrana does."

That snapped his attention to her.

"She's an ally." Celka's rage had transmuted into quiet intensity. "I just found out."

"She arrested your father."

"They arranged his arrest so he could vanish into the resistance."

Gerrit gaped at her.

"In Solnitse, she told Grandfather she was sending an imbuement mage to us. She wanted him out of the Storm Guard before he could imbue."

Gerrit shook his head. "I don't understand."

"Vrana sent you here. She wanted you to join us."

Head reeling, he slumped down the wall to sit on a crate. If his mother had started moving against his father, was it so hard to believe that Captain Vrana had as well? Wrongness gnawed at him. He looked up at Celka. "What, exactly, did she say to your Grandfather?"

"He told me, 'she wanted him out before he could imbue.'"

"Not 'before they could *force me* to imbue'?"

Celka shook her head. "Maybe Grandfather didn't understand the difference?"

"Maybe." It chewed at his thoughts, though he couldn't quite grasp why.

Celka crouched before him, taking his hands. "You have a chance to be free, Gerrit. To control your own life. Your friends would want that for you." Her grip tightened, matching her fierce belief. "Come with me."

He wanted to say yes. Wanted it more than anything. But his mind still churned. "Let me think about it."

She touched his cheek then stood. "Don't take too long."

CHAPTER FORTY-SEVEN

Ctibor's Army papers got Celka through Bludov's outer checkpoint without question, despite her heavy picnic basket—supposedly a gift for one of Grandfather's old friends in town. The two bottles of wine and wedge of cheese were hard to come by but not illegal, and their weight would cover Lucie's engraving dies in the basket's false bottom.

Lucie herself had leapt from the train last night, reams of rifle manuals in her pack, off to arrange Celka's disappearance. When Celka had mentioned that she might bring someone from the circus, Lucie hadn't been happy, but she'd agreed to make it work.

Tonight, Lucie would sneak into the Prochazka sleeper car before they departed Bludov. At dawn, in the next town, they'd vanish together into the resistance.

The sideshow had seemed different today, the half-light filtering through the tent canvas portentous, Nina's weight like a burden of responsibility. The other performers' disdain had felt distant, the circus's fraying glitter as precious as Ma's kiss on her cheek before Celka left Mirova each spring.

Despite Lucie's confidence, Celka feared being alone and hunted. Worse, Gerrit had still given her no answer. This morning, she'd found the snake trailer empty except for his note, *See you this afternoon*. She didn't understand how this decision could be so hard.

"You seem worried," Ctibor said as they passed one of Bludov's empty lots, weeds clotting rubble from buildings destroyed during the war. He lifted his gaze to the storm clouds bulking south of town. "Maybe we should let someone else take care of the soup kitchen today."

The building storm was a risk, Celka's storm-thread already buzzing, but she'd blocked the last one fairly well until Gerrit's imbuement had exploded. "I don't melt, remember?"

Ctibor frowned down at her. "I wasn't worried about you melting."

She looped her arm through his, his concern warming her like tea on a frosty morning. "I'll be all right."

"I just—I think it would be safer."

She wrinkled her nose, twining a wind about herself in sousednia to leave behind only confidence. "Seriously. I'll be fine." She lifted her basket. "Besides, I have errands to run. Meet you at the storm temple?"

His jaw tightened, the gesture so small she wouldn't

have noticed if they hadn't spent so much time together. "They can make soup without our help today."

"No it's..." She trusted Ctibor, but not enough. Not to let him see where she went—even if he didn't watch her hand over the printing dies.

His pace faltered and his gaze slipped to the basket. Then he smiled like he did when throwing knives. "It's personal. Of course." Seeing that carefree mask instead of his intimate smile felt like reproach. They both knew she wasn't fooling him. "How about I find a café and wait for you? That way, if there's trouble, I'll be nearby."

Ctibor's willingness to help made her feel even more guilty about using him—and that she wasn't planning to tell him goodbye. "That'd be perfect," she made herself say.

He winked. "Consider it a date."

Lungs burning, Gerrit slowed to a walk in the open field and wiped his face with his shirt. Exhausted from fitful sleep, he'd left the railyard as soon as the circus train had stopped in the pre-dawn darkness. Since then he'd been running. It was a fitting metaphor; another time, that might have amused him.

Legs shushing through some knee-high crop, Gerrit crested a low hill. Behind and far distant, a pennant flapped from the big top's peak. Ahead, lightning licked the clouds. A mild sousedni-dislocation and a rainstorm over his mountaintop kept the bozhskyeh storm from tugging at him—and let him bide his time.

Temple meteorologists had predicted this storm. The Storm Guard would likely have bozhki in place to attempt their own imbuements, and Gerrit couldn't risk being observed. Instead, he kept away from roads, circling the storm's edges. He'd give the State's bozhki their chance, then he'd imbue alone.

Staring out at the storm, Gerrit imagined Celka's bright laugh, bubbling out of nowhere. She was the circus distilled into one perfect, frustrating person—colorful, intense, and free. Was he really considering turning his back on her to return to his father's manipulation and Storm Guard brutality? What was wrong with him? She said they'd be safe in the resistance. He trusted her, mostly. So why was he still running? Why weren't they imbuing side by side today?

Crouched beneath the spreading branches of a chestnut tree, Gerrit watched lightning flicker through the dark clouds. Captain Vrana had given him a chance to escape. Captain Vrana, Hero of Zlin, supported the resistance. She wanted him to stand up to his father. She'd wanted him out before he could imbue for the State.

Gerrit froze, feeling like he'd walked into an ambush.

He'd been so certain he would imbue in that first bozhskyeh storm. But moments before he'd called the storm, he'd noticed something—a flicker in the corner of his eye, forgotten in the blaze of Gods' Breath. Then his weaves had shattered. But he'd double-checked his weaves; they'd been perfect.

The double dissonance Jolana had sensed—one for his weaves, one for Filip's—what if it had been deliberate?

Before he'd met Celka, Gerrit had thought he understood sousednia. But her sousedni-disruptions, the way she read sousedni-cues—sleet, even the ease with which she stepped away from her true-form—all proved how little he understood. And he was certain Captain Vrana's control was closer to Celka's than his own.

Gerrit and Celka had imbued together, shaping each other's nuzhda. And, he suddenly realized, he'd shaped Branislav's nuzhda right before his friend's fateful imbuement.

If Gerrit could affect someone's weaves, Captain Vrana could, too.

Fingers digging into the soil beneath the chestnut tree, Gerrit struggled to get enough air. Captain Vrana had sabotaged his imbuement. She'd damaged his weaves so they shattered when he filled them with Gods' Breath. And she'd destroyed Filip's weaves just as subtly, ensuring that the storm energy drove Gerrit from true-life.

He wanted to dismiss the theory as madness, but it fit too well. If not for Captain Vrana, Gerrit would have created the first imbuement of the storm cycle and earned his father's respect—just like he'd always dreamed.

His difficulty imbuing wasn't base incompetence, but fear insinuated deep within him by his most-trusted instructor. In the circus, his first imbuement had failed because he hadn't pulled hard enough on the storm, afraid of losing true-life. In his second, he'd filled his weaves wrong, nervous about handling storm energy. But imbuing with Celka, her confidence had left no space for doubt. Celka, a civilian with a fraction of his training, had handled the storm energy naturally, intuitively. Because she was storm-blessed.

Imbuing today, alone, he would feel that clarity and rightness again. And it would damn Vrana.

He let Gods' Breath lash the heavens for a good twenty minutes, then leapt into a run, closing the distance between himself and the storm. If Storm Guard mages were going to imbue, they'd had their chance. With each pounding step, he let his sousednia rainstorm fade. Today, he would imbue. Nothing—no one—would stand in his way.

After Branislav's imbuement, Vrana had played on Gerrit's fears. Her warnings had convinced him he'd lose true-life in his next storm, convinced him Tesarik would force him to imbue. Had those been lies? Tesarik was a sleet-licker, but for all Gerrit knew, Branislav would imbue only once or twice more before creating something so powerful that he killed himself and everyone around him. Maybe the Stormhawk wasn't so reckless as Captain Vrana had painted him. Gerrit's father was smart. He didn't waste resources.

But Captain Vrana had her own agenda. The one person he'd trusted most, and she'd puppeted him as coldly as his father had.

Thunder crashed overhead and anger simmered through Gerrit. Was he just a bullet for someone else to fire?

In sousednia, combat nuzhda flattened his mountain peaks into the hills around his family estate, frozen branches bare. His helplessness boiled into rage.

Gerrit forced a slow breath. He couldn't lose control. Whatever he did next, he needed to prove he could imbue dispassionately.

Drawing his unimbued combat knife, Gerrit laid it across his palms. He squeezed his roaring combat nuzhda down to a safe Category Two, then shaped gunshots and cries into a sharpening and strengthening weave—the big brother to what he'd attempted during his first imbuement. Captain Vrana's trick had shaken his confidence, but he refused to let her manipulation curtail his power.

After triple-checking his weaves, Gerrit pulled Gods' Breath down from the sky.

CHAPTER FORTY-EIGHT

THE FRONT ROOM of Lukska's Print Shop and Photo Studio had been painted the color of fresh cream, black and white photographs hanging next to sepia-toned daguerreotypes. Engraved wedding invitations and elaborate stationary decorated the wall across from yellowing posters and handbills.

Mr. Lukska invited Celka inside, smiling, and Celka asked about getting a new photograph to use for sideshow postcards. At the same time, she rubbed her right thumb across the back of her left knuckles.

Lukska straightened his collar and asked for details about the print run.

Satisfied with the resistance signals, Celka dropped the ruse and opened the picnic basket. "Grandfather thought you might enjoy a bottle of wine."

"Your grandfather is a true Hand of the Storms."

Laugh lines crinkling around his eyes, he beckoned her through a door behind the counter. "And you have grown since I last saw you. It must be... four summers since you and your sister played in the fountain while your grandfather and I spoke of the old days."

Celka relaxed further. Her memory of Lukska was vague, but Grandfather had told her to expect this reminiscence and, only then, to give Lukska the engraving dies.

The workroom smelled of metal and ink, and stacks of paper covered the workbenches and shelves. Turpentine's piney bite wrinkled Celka's nose. Lukska waved her toward a scuffed table blotched with ink, and Celka unloaded the wine. When she unwrapped the engraving dies, Lukska stared in mute astonishment. "They're official," Celka said.

Lukska wrapped her in a hug. "Bless you, little Prochazka. Bless your family."

Her heart light, she waved goodbye and hurried to the bakery where she'd left Ctibor. She'd be leaving her home, but the resistance was its own sort of family.

The storm had broken some ten klicks to the southwest but, holding her sousednia as a dull field, she felt only the faintest tug against her skull. By the time she spotted Ctibor, lounging at a bistro table in the shade, she was smiling. Elsewhere, the pall of coal smoke had crushed Bludov's spirit, but purple and yellow pansies sprouted from the bakery's window boxes. The scent of butter and cardamom quickened her step.

She fingered her storm pendant beneath her blouse.

Everything was about to change, but she could do this. Pa had built the resistance to protect her, and she wouldn't disappoint him. She'd imbue and give the people something to believe in. Supported by Pa's planning, they would destroy the regime.

Ctibor didn't notice her approach, staring at the wall, expression strangely intent—like he was trying to remember something unpleasant.

Celka pulled out the wrought iron chair across from him, and he turned with a start. "Taking a nap?" Celka asked, hoping to lighten his mood.

"No. I mean, yes. No." His jaw tensed and he glanced off to the side again before seeming to shake himself. "That was fast."

"Didn't want to keep my date waiting."

He rewarded her with his small, private smile but, beneath it, he looked exhausted and... afraid?

"Is something wrong?" she asked.

"Of course not." The exhaustion vanished beneath his circus smile. With a flourish, he folded back the napkin covering a small basket. "At least, nothing butter and sugar won't fix." Steam wafted from two plump loupak, their flaky, buttery tops crusted with poppyseeds. Celka's mouth watered. Ctibor poured coffee from a metal pot and, when he offered her a little porcelain cup of cream, her jaw dropped.

"How did you afford all this? And the ration coupons?" She shook her head, unable to pour the cream into her coffee. "Are you sure?"

"The circus has my civilian ration book, but the Army

let me keep my A3 book, too. Extra butter and sugar coupons, and nowhere to spend them."

"I haven't seen fresh cream since... I don't know when."

Ctibor grinned, finally genuine. "Take it all."

"You're sure?"

When he nodded, Celka upended the cup over her coffee. Closing her eyes to concentrate on the creamy deliciousness, she sipped.

When she opened her eyes, she found Ctibor frowning at a spray of bullet holes chipping the stone wall.

"You think that's left over from the war?" The question sounded idiotic as soon as it left her mouth. They'd walked past plenty of rubble and even a statue of proud Bourshkanyan soldiers inside the blackened stone of a storm temple burned by the Lesnikrayan Army.

"Bludov saw brutal street fighting," Ctibor said. "The Forty-Second Battalion tried to stall the Lesnikrayans here long enough for the rest of the Army to regroup and mount a counteroffensive."

"Did it work?"

Ctibor shook his head. "The Lesnikrayans uncovered the plan. It was a slaughter."

"I'm surprised they taught—" Celka caught herself before she could say something bordering on treason.

He inclined his head, silently asking the question.

Celka nibbled the corner of her loupak—it proved just as buttery and amazing as it looked—while Ctibor waited. "In school they only talked about victories. And a few heroic sacrifices."

"It'd be poor officer training if we didn't study defeats."

"I've always wondered..." Could she ask this? She didn't want to sound suspiciously curious. Ctibor already knew too much about her, and he would eventually put back on his uniform and become the enemy. Yet Pa had never talked about what he'd done to win the war, and if Grandfather knew, Pa must have sworn him to silence. "How did we win? What happened at Zlin?"

Ctibor's jaw tightened. "Bloody battles recounted over loupak?" His levity sounded forced. "Wouldn't you rather enjoy your coffee?"

She took his hand across the table's mosaic tile top. "What is it?"

He stared down at his loupak for a long time. "My father died at Zlin."

"I'm sorry. I didn't... We don't have to talk about it."

"No, it just... surprised me."

"Were we really losing?" The history books painted Bourshkanya's victory as a sure thing, but a sure victory didn't require a Miracle.

"We'd been losing for months, our generals just didn't want to admit it." He paused, giving her a chance to divert their conversation, maybe, or rallying his strength. She nodded encouragingly. "We'd surrendered all our early gains, and Lesnikraj was pushing toward the capital. That counterattack I mentioned, the Battle of Oleshka, it was a disaster. We lost two thirds of our fighting force and—" Ctibor's head jerked up, his gaze slipping past her.

She turned. Three Tayemstvoy marched toward them, their leader's hand on their truncheon.

When the red shoulders neared, Ctibor asked, casual as could be, "Something we can do for you, Corporal?"

"New to town?"

"Just arrived on the circus train this morning."

Celka stared at her loupak. The half-eaten pastry suddenly smelled of blood and gun oil. Edging into sousednia, she concentrated, forcing the circus tents back into the ground, struggling to see only an empty field that smelled like nothing. She couldn't fight. Fighting would make this worse.

"Circus, huh?" the corporal said. "Why aren't you performing?"

"I'm taking my friend here on a date between shows." Ctibor still sounded calm and reasonable, as if he hadn't heard the corporal's menace. "It's nice to get away from the circus now and then—especially on such a lovely day."

"You celebrating something?" The corporal sounded increasingly suspicious, and Celka dared a quick glance. Her attention snagged on the waterfall of bright glass beads that dangled from one of his ears, then skipped to his sneer. Her throat tightened; she could practically feel the sleet-licker despising them for buying loupak with 'money stolen from hardworking families.' Like circus folk didn't work for a living. Like they were parasites worse than the Tayemstvoy.

Celka dropped her eyes, clenching her hands in her lap.

A private picked up Celka's picnic basket. Her chest tightened. If they noticed the false bottom, they'd have questions. She thought frantically for an innocent reason for a secret compartment.

"Just trying to woo Miss Prochazka here." Ctibor's chummy tone made her sick, but she dislocated across sousednia's featureless field, hoping distance would stop her from reacting to the soldiers' threat.

"You seen this before?" A rustle of paper, and the corporal held a page out to Ctibor.

Ctibor shook his head. The corporal thrust the page in front of Celka's nose.

The Stormhawk was sketched fat with heavy jowls, truncheon hanging off a belt that struggled to contain his girth. He stomped amongst houses like they were children's toys, gathering up grain silos while farmers toiled, small and downtrodden at his feet. Children with gaunt faces begged for grain. The caption read, *Rationing serves the State.*

Typed text filled the bottom half of the page, but the corporal snatched it away. "Familiar, huh?"

"No!" Stupid. Why couldn't she have done like Ctibor—glanced at it and shaken her head?

The corporal slammed his hands down on the table, making the plates jump and coffee spill. He put his face right up in Celka's. "They showed up all over town this morning. You want to tell me why?"

Celka recoiled, but another soldier caught her chair so she couldn't back away. She shook her head. "I don't know. I've never seen it before."

"But you've seen others like it. In other towns."

She shook her head, heart hammering.

He caught her chin, grip bruising. "Who's responsible for these? Give me names, and I'll let you go."

"I don't know. I've never seen them before!"

"Convenient they showed up right when you came into town."

"What better way for a local resistance cell to hide," Ctibor said, "than to cast blame on travelers?"

"What better way to get this *filth*"—the corporal slapped his free hand down on the flyer, clanking the cups again—"into town, than by circus train?" His bulging eyes never left Celka's. "Give. Me. A name."

She tried to shake her head, but could only tremble in his grip. She clenched her chair's wrought iron arms, struggling to keep sousednia featureless. She couldn't fight. Couldn't struggle. Anything she did would make this worse.

"Maybe we'll take you to the station. Maybe you'll be more willing to talk there."

"Please, I don't—"

Ctibor shoved back his chair. It crashed to the paving stones. "Leave her alone." Gone was his calm reserve; instead, a military snap made his words an order.

Celka's stomach dropped. The storm was affecting them, it had to be. *Don't fight back,* she wanted to scream. *Don't give them a reason to make an example out of us.* "Ctibor, don't."

But everything happened too fast. The corporal released her, and one of the others dragged her up out of her chair. They flung her down, her hands and knees hitting the cobblestones in a flare of pain, then their weight landed on her back and they wrenched her arms behind her. Metal restraints clapped cold about her wrists.

The soldier dragged her to her feet and shoved her against the wall. Granite dug into her shoulders, centimeters from her face, and they gripped the back of her neck, pinning her.

Past their table, Ctibor stared down the corporal, his hands up in a pose that might have seemed non-threatening if the rest of him didn't look like a tiger ready to pounce.

The corporal slipped his truncheon free. Celka couldn't see his expression, but she'd swear he was smiling. "Get on your knees."

Ctibor complied slowly, holding the corporal's gaze. "Look at our identification papers. You still want us to go with you to the station, we will. No trouble."

"*Papers*. The circus rabble wants us to check their papers."

The two other soldiers snickered, cracking with tension. Ctibor didn't look any less intimidating on his knees, and Celka suspected that if he decided to fight, he'd be just as deadly starting from there. She swallowed hard, twisting her wrists against unyielding steel and silently urging Ctibor not to do something stupid, even as the storm's iron taste burned her tongue, and the big top surged from the ground.

She couldn't let the Tayemstvoy arrest them. Whatever

it took, she needed to disappear into the resistance tonight.

High wire pressing into the soles of her feet, Celka touched her storm-thread. It felt too thin to carry Gods' Breath, but it tugged on her. Could she reel the bozhskyeh storm closer? Fingers tingling, she gripped the filament and began to pull.

GERRIT'S WEAVES WORKED perfectly.

Gods' Breath burned down his spine to cascade, crimson, through his weaves. Combat's rage faded as the weaves crystalized, and the knife pulsed blood red.

Exhaling a shuddery breath, Gerrit returned completely to true-life. The transition felt good, like stretching stiff muscles after a hard workout.

In the eerie post-imbuement silence, burning lines sparked along Gerrit's right shoulder blade. He rubbed it, imagining the fernlike patterns from his imbuement with Celka darkening from the extra storm energy.

He'd done it. He'd imbued on his own and it had been *easy*. Curse Captain Vrana to clear skies.

The wind picked up, and rain turned to tiny hail. Ducking his head, Gerrit opened the canvas umbrella he'd stolen, invisible, after imbuing with Celka in the sheep pasture. He'd left a couple of myedyen on the shop counter, so it maybe it wasn't stealing. Getting wet was one thing, but he'd rather avoid a hail-induced concussion.

Fatigue made Gerrit want to return to the circus where

he'd be safe from the worsening hail and lightning, but he had work to do. Category Two combat had been easy. He didn't carry any other weapons, but the hail hammering his umbrella gave him an idea. Strong winds risked the umbrella's wooden struts, and big enough hail could tear through the canvas. He hadn't seen any strengthening imbuements applied to something so flimsy as an umbrella, but why not? If he escaped with Celka into the resistance, it'd be nice to know they carried sturdy protection from a storm.

Giving himself one minute to rest, he sat cross-legged in the mud and watched coppery Gods' Breath weave through electrical lightning overhead.

As the sound of hail hammering his umbrella returned to his imbuement-muffled ears, Gerrit stood. He hadn't practiced as much with strengthening nuzhdi, so he moved in true-life to match the memory of bracing a flimsy door, struggling to hold it against his attackers pounding on the other side. Barely had the memory started to coalesce when the hail ceased. Grumbling thunder, the storm clouds raced away, and his storm-thread unraveled.

Frowning, Gerrit tipped the umbrella back in time to see the clouds come to an unnatural halt over the city. His stomach clenched. Clouds shouldn't move like that. Unless...

Dimly, he remembered reading about mages desperate to imbue pulling storms across the sky. Usually, those mages ended up dead, pulling the storm causing Gods' Breath to lash down into ill-formed weaves. No one with a lick of training would try something so suicidal.

"Celka." Fatigue forgotten, Gerrit broke into a run. She wouldn't know the danger. But she also wouldn't risk drawing attention. Not unless she'd lost control or...

Something was wrong. Terribly, horribly wrong.

THE STORM CAME at Celka's call, the clouds rushing across the sky to blot out the sun in the dead-end alley. In true-life, Ctibor said something about papers, reaching toward his pocket. His motion shattered the impasse, and the Tayemstvoy corporal lunged, truncheon driving down in a terrible arc.

Celka's grip on her storm-thread slipped as her sousednia changed, spot-lit big top snapping into the springtime back lot, Tayemstvoy truncheons raining down on Pa.

"*No!*" she screamed, expecting that same horrible *crack* as the corporal beat Ctibor. The private holding Celka against the wall tightened their grip on her neck.

Instead, Ctibor's hands flew up, and the corporal twisted like he'd slipped on ice. His truncheon clattered against the cobblestones, and the corporal flopped, loose-jointed, as Ctibor wrenched one of his arms behind his back.

The air around Celka stunk of blood and mud and gun oil, and the corporal snarled in Ctibor's hold. The third soldier snapped their rifle to their shoulder, and the one holding Celka cursed and jabbed a pistol against her skull. Gods' Breath flashed overhead.

One wrong move, and the Tayemstvoy would kill them.

Celka wouldn't let that happen. Balanced between true-life and her combat-warped sousednia, Celka imagined her hand restraints clattering to the cobblestones as she twisted free, Stanek pistol no longer pressed to her skull but heavy and deadly in her palm. She would turn, and three beautiful, clean shots would ring out.

The Tayemstvoy would never drag her away, limp and beaten. They would never force her to imbue for the State.

She reached for her storm-thread again, hot iron searing her tongue, but true-life filtered in. The shouting had stopped.

The corporal spoke, urgent, anxious. "Let her go. Now." And the pistol pressing into Celka's head disappeared.

On the sunlit back lot, the gun that had felt so real in her hands wisped into smoke.

"Release her," the corporal ordered, and her wrists fell free of the restraints without magic.

Combat nuzhda locked her hands in fists as she turned, but the two other Tayemstvoy retreated, rifles slung over their backs.

Cringing, the corporal handed Ctibor back his identification folio. "Our apologies, sir."

Gods' Breath flickered overhead, but sousednia's stench of blood grew patchy, uneven, no longer a blanket to wrap around a weapon. A raindrop splattered her cheek. Boots clumped away. The Tayemstvoy were leaving?

She stared at their retreating backs in the thunderstorm's bruised light. Someone touched her arm. She turned with a snarl, ready to strike.

"Are you all right?" Ctibor asked.

Her fist fell back to her side, and she searched his face. Sousednia still resembled the back lot, but horses whickered. Pa and the Tayemstvoy had disappeared. "What just happened?"

"They finally remembered to follow regs."

She frowned, uncomprehending.

"Tayemstvoy are supposed to check the identification papers of anyone they stop. And they can't arrest Army officers without evidence. If I'd been in uniform, this never would have happened."

"Lucky you." The words dropped like stones into a well. Her combat nuzhda lingered like a violent aftertaste. Part of her wanted to chase the Tayemstvoy down and imbue the pistol, shoot them all.

Then what? An imbuement would storm-mark the ground, and dead Tayemstvoy would kick the rest of Bludov's red shoulders into a frenzy. Dead Tayemstvoy would suggest an imbuement mage working for the resistance.

They'd search house-to-house. They might find Lukska and his engraving dies.

Major Rychtr would return. They'd close the railways and the roads. Suspicion would redouble on the circus. The red shoulders might find the hidden compartments in her family's sleeper car. Lucie would return to a trap.

In one desperate moment, she could have ruined everything.

Ctibor touched her cheek and she flinched, the need to attack still simmering beneath her skin. "I'm sorry I didn't stop them sooner," he said.

"They could have shot us."

"I wouldn't have let them. I would never let them hurt you." His dark eyes held hers, his thumb brushing her cheekbone.

A shivery tingle traveled from her cheek to her belly. Sousednia dimmed, chased by the scents of butter and cardamom. Ctibor drank her in like she was the only thing that mattered in the entire world. Catching her waist, he pulled her against him.

She touched his chest, felt his heart pounding. Part of her shouted that they were sparking, but suddenly the horror of nearly having shot three Tayemstvoy and gotten her family killed didn't matter because his fingers slipped into her hair. She tilted her face up, and he kissed her, the heat of his mouth stealing her breath. Pleasure tingled through her, chasing away the storm's buzz.

Eyes closed, she saw only darkness, felt only his lips against hers and the exquisite touch of his strong hand against the small of her back. Thunder crashed, and rain poured down, icy rivulets tracing her spine. Ctibor pulled her closer and, pressed against him, she felt as though the rain must boil to steam on their skin.

CHAPTER FORTY-NINE

CELKA DIDN'T KNOW how long they kissed. Gods' Breath flashed through the clouds, red-gold when she opened her eyes, but a breeze had cleared the air until the alley smelled only of rain and loupak. Ctibor tasted of cardamom and coffee, and while he held her, nothing else mattered.

"You're incredible, Celka," he whispered.

She'd never noticed how long his eyelashes were or that the left side of his mouth quirked up a little more when he smiled that private smile she loved.

Rain poured down harder, and Ctibor glanced up, as though only just noticing the deluge. "Maybe we should go."

In the window boxes, pansies shuddered, and copper drainpipes gushed rivers onto the street. Celka grabbed her picnic basket, inhaling the rainstorm's freshness. Her mouth tasted of loupak, not hot iron and dried leaves. She made a fist, expecting storm energy to numb her fingers, but only rainwater chilled her skin.

Ctibor wrapped an arm around her shoulders, and she fell into step beside him, feeling strangely, wonderfully grounded. Had the answer to blocking the storms been standing in the sideshow all these weeks? Laughter threatened to bubble free, and she barely caught it.

Madness. She was still sparking. Distraction seemed to help ignore a storm's pull, and kissing Ctibor had certainly been... distracting. She thought of Gerrit then—the times they'd kissed and almost kissed—and confusion churned her stomach. She pushed it away. Celka was leaving soon, and Ctibor wasn't. This kiss had been no more than a kiss, though it had felt so... right.

She loved how Ctibor seemed happy to spend time with her no matter the drudgery of their task, how he listened without making demands. Around Ctibor she felt like a better, truer version of herself. That thought tightened her throat, made her wish she dared ask Ctibor to come with her into the resistance.

But Ctibor was a soldier, committed to guarding members of the regime. He cared about people, but he wanted his old life back. He helped her only because he didn't want to see her hurt; she could tell he didn't believe in the resistance, didn't want that life.

She couldn't blame him. She'd seen rezistyenti with haggard, hunted faces. That could be her in a year, if she survived. She had no guarantee that she'd succeed at freeing Bourshkanya, even with Pa's planning behind her.

This was her fight, not his. They'd had fun together, but their kiss was an ending, not a beginning. The storm temple and today's soup kitchen loomed before them. Time to stop stalling.

She pulled Ctibor to a stop and took his hands. "You were right," she said. "I'm leaving the circus. My aunt's health is failing, so I'm going to help take care of her."

Ctibor searched her face. "When do you leave?"

"Soon." Even telling him this much was risky; she wasn't fool enough to say more.

Emotion washed his features, but she couldn't read it. He was struggling with something, but sousednia's confused mélange gave her no clues. "I don't want to lose you."

Her chest tightened, and his eyes trapped her like a fly in amber. She was still trying to find words when his attention jerked off past her shoulder.

"Sleetstorms, no," he said.

She spun, expecting more Tayemstvoy. But Ctibor stared at an empty alleyway.

His hands still clutched hers, but he squeezed his eyes shut, concentrating. "Not now," he growled. "Not *sleeting* now."

"Ctibor, what—"

Tense, he focused back on her. "Celka—" He pulled the steel ring off his thumb, gripping it angrily before jamming it back on. "Freezing sleet, I'm sorry. *Please*, find me before you go?"

Before she could ask what he was talking about, he sprinted away, disappearing around gray stone apartments.

Reeling, she stared after him. When he didn't reappear, she turned in a slow circle, rainwater plastering her hair to her cheeks. Townsfolk straggled past, eyes on the cobbles, bowls in hand as they scurried to the storm temple. Shops around the square had closed for the day, everyone headed to the circus.

Coming full-circle, she stared back down the street, hoping Ctibor would return to explain. Finding only strangers, she edged into sousednia. No matter how she swept the spotlights around, the smoke-forms were all unfamiliar.

Recalling the vicious Tayemstvoy corporal going from superiority to servility at the sight of Ctibor's papers, her stomach twisted. No matter how Ctibor had helped with the soup kitchen and her illegal pistol, he was an Army officer. What if his exile in the circus covered something more dangerous? What did that ring represent to him? Duty—but to whom?

She should never have told him she was leaving. What better way to regain his place in the regime than to hand her to the Storm Guard?

Gods' Breath arced through the sky, jangling down her storm-thread, and the sky opened, shitting hailstones. Cursing, Celka tented her arms over her head and sprinted for the temple. As she ran, she struggled to imagine sousednia featureless. She'd been a fool. Ctibor could destroy her.

Safe in storm temple—not that safety from hail meant much now—Celka leaned over her knees, gasping for breath, trying to figure out what to do. She could run, but that would break her rendezvous with Lucie, and might not even save her. She clutched her storm pendant, wishing she could ask Pa for advice.

Maybe Ctibor's weird behavior hadn't been about her. She didn't believe it, but the possibility helped her breathe a little easier.

If she ran now, she'd be running blind. Better to act normal. Ctibor had just faced down the Tayemstvoy to protect her; he wouldn't really betray her, would he?

Stomach still knotted with fear, she nodded to Anastazie, one of the circus roustabouts who often helped at the soup kitchen. Cutting stale bread, Celka warily eyed the temple for red shoulders. If they came after her now, at least she could imbue one of their guns. Maybe she could even shoot enough of them to escape.

Barely had she sawed through a half loaf when a lake-blue form dodged through the crowd. «Celka!» Even in sousednia, Gerrit's breath came hard. «Celka, are you all right?»

Focusing on her featureless field, she threw her arms around him, struggling to keep her true-form cutting bread. Surprised, he stiffened, then returned the embrace.

«What happened?» he asked. «You didn't imbue?»

She released a shaky breath and told him about the Tayemstvoy in the alley, the leaflet, how they'd handcuffed her and put a gun to her head. «So I pulled on the storm. I didn't know if it would work, but I couldn't let them arrest me.»

«You imbued a Tayemstvoy pistol?» Worry tightened his voice.

She shook her head and told Anastazie she'd be right back, then pulled Gerrit into the back alley. The hail had given way to rain, and flaking stucco walls, black with coal smoke, broke most of the wind. «Ctibor talked them down, got them to leave.»

Suspicion twisted his sousedni-shape. «How could a knife-thrower—»

But Celka didn't want to pick that scab. A cherry glow at Gerrit's side distracted her. «You imbued!»

«My knife.» He shrugged like it was nothing.

Forcing Ctibor from her mind, she asked, «How was it?»

«Great.» He didn't smile. «Celka...»

Hope warring with fear, she searched his expression.

«Do you still want me to come with you?» he asked.

«Of course I do.»

A muscle in his jaw tensed. He peeled back the concealment imbuement, his hand appearing in true-life. In it, he held a blood-red identification folio.

Celka shook her head. «It doesn't matter who your father is. I—»

«It *does* matter.» He pressed the folio into her hand. «The Tayemstvoy will *never* stop hunting me. If I go with you, I put you in danger.» She tried to object, but he didn't let her. «Celka, my father is the Stormhawk.»

CHAPTER FIFTY

CELKA STUMBLED BACK in both sousednia and true-life, her high-wire slippers splashing the slushy snow of Gerrit's mountaintop, her boots squelching mud. She stared at him like he'd pressed a pistol to her head. «The Stormhawk?» She opened his identification folio, staring wide-eyed at the page. «I must have sounded so stupid.» She shut the folio, squeezing its cover between her palms as if she could make it disappear. «No wonder you...» She shook her head, angry. «Of course you'll return to the Storm Guard.» She squared her shoulders and handed back the folio. He'd never seen her so scared. Never seen her fear leashed so tight.

«Celka, I'm—»

«My family, you won't—» They spoke at the same time.

«Go ahead,» she whispered.

«I'm sorry I didn't tell you.»

«Of course you didn't.» She searched his face with desperate eyes. «You won't tell them about my family? I'll do anything, just... *please*.»

He wanted to tell her that nothing had changed between them, but he knew it was a lie. If he could so easily escape his father's shadow, he wouldn't have hidden the truth for so long.

Captain Vrana was wrong. She'd wanted Gerrit to join the resistance; she'd never considered that the resistance wouldn't want him.

Drawing a deep breath, Gerrit steeled himself to return to his old life. «I'll keep your secret. Buy you as much time as I can. I'll try to make things better from within the regime.»

Celka searched his expression, her own feelings buried deep. He wished he could read her in sousednia, then was profoundly grateful he couldn't. She was terrified of him. Of course she was terrified. All the trust they'd built over the last month had gone up in flames.

«Do you really want to join me?» she asked.

He frowned, confused until he realized what she was really asking. «I won't betray the resistance.»

«You could,» she whispered. «It would make your father trust you. It might give you the power to help your friends.»

«It would destroy you and your family. I'm not like my father. I'm *not*.» He held her gaze for a moment, wishing he could make her believe him. He hated seeing her so afraid.

Turning away, Gerrit crouched, scooping up a handful of snow and crushing it into a slushy ball. He stared down into sousednia's forested valley, icy water dribbling down his forearm.

The sun still hung high in sousednia's cloudless sky but, as he imagined returning to the Storm Guard, the shadows slanted longer. Immersed in the regime's grim brutality, how long until night fell permanently over his sousednia? Still staring into the valley, he said, «When you first asked me to come with you, I hesitated because I'm worried the resistance doesn't have a plan past destroying the regime. Everything I've been taught tells me that without the Stormhawk to direct us, the Lesnikrayens will destroy Bourshkanya.» He glanced up at her, beautiful in spotlit sequins. «But until you locked me in that stinking trailer, my father and the Tayemstvoy had controlled everything I knew.» He threw the snowball, watching it plummet until he lost it in the distance.

When he turned back, Celka was watching him, uncertain. He stood to face her, shoving his hands into his pockets. «Captain Vrana manipulated me into coming here—she damaged my weaves during my first imbuement and lied to make me think I couldn't hold true-life. I don't know if I can trust her any more than I trust my father, but...» With a shaky breath, he reached out, hoping Celka would take his hands, certain she wouldn't. «But I trust *you*. I'm willing to help the resistance—at least long enough to find out if they really have a plan. All my life, other people have controlled me.» She hadn't taken his hands. He dropped them to his sides, quashing his disappointment. «For once, I wanted to make my own choice.»

Celka glanced back at the storm temple like she wanted to run. Like she was hoping for rescue.

Gerrit kicked at the slushy snow. «I understand. I wouldn't trust me, either.»

«Gerrit, I...» She shook her head and fell silent.

He tried to smile like her rejection hadn't cut. He'd meant what he'd said. He did understand. He'd just... hoped. «Good luck.» He moved to hug her goodbye, but stopped. He was the Stormhawk's son. She didn't want him to touch her. «Goodbye.»

Turning his back so she wouldn't see him struggling for control, he sloshed barefoot through a true-life puddle. Gods' Breath still flashed through the sky. He needed to imbue a second time. With Celka leaving, he had no reason to keep hiding from the State.

CELKA WATCHED GERRIT'S blue-limned sousedni-shape walk away down the alley, leaving behind muddy footprints quickly washed away by the rain. Part of her screamed that she should flee before he called the Tayemstvoy—but he'd sounded so sincere. He didn't know how to control his sousedni-cues; she knew he wasn't lying.

And yet. How could she possibly trust him? Gerrit was the *Stormhawk's son*. Sure, he was angry at his father now, but the State had raised him, shaped him.

Just yesterday he'd told her how he could stand at his father's side and restore Storm Guard autonomy. She'd seen a spark in him that she'd felt from the beginning: he wanted power. He would invent a neat explanation for his mother's murder. A year from now, he'd be clicking his heels, stars covering his red shoulders, proud that his father had contrived to make him so strong.

The image sickened her, and she started to turn away.

But Gerrit had read the resistance leaflets she'd given him and helped print the rifle instructions. Part of him hated his father, hated Tayemstvoy brutality.

If Celka trusted Pa, Vrana was an ally. Vrana had trained Gerrit before sending him here. She knew who his father was, yet she still believed Gerrit could help the resistance.

Maybe he deserved a chance to decide his own fate. «Gerrit, wait.»

Half a block from her, he froze. She waited for his sousedni-shape to turn, but he didn't.

«If you come with me, you'll be hunted.» She closed the distance in true-life until only a meter separated them. A quick glance over her shoulder showed the alley still empty, its windows shuttered. «No plush motorcar driving you to every storm. No fancy State dinners.»

In sousednia, a featureless field stretched around them. Gerrit spoke with his back to her, voice tight and guarded. «No Tayemstvoy watching my every move, ordering my every imbuement.»

«You said you could influence the regime if you went back. You'll stand at the *Stormhawk's* side. His *son*. You *wanted* that power.»

He turned, honey-brown eyes so sincere. «I *want* to be with you.»

Celka's stomach flip-flopped. «Even if it's hiding in a root cellar while jackboots stomp overhead? Even if it means the Tayemstvoy capture us and torture us because we imbued for the resistance?»

«You said they could keep us safe. You *believed*.»

She swallowed hard. She had believed. Before she'd known he was the Stormhawk's son. How could her trust survive that? Everything she'd thought about him was a lie.

«When the storm raced away from me,» Gerrit said, «I was terrified. Pulling storms gets mages killed. But worse, if you were willing to pull that recklessly—I was afraid the Tayemstvoy had found you. I was ready to do anything to get you back.» He kicked at sousednia's green grass, jaw locked. «I've seen my father interrogate prisoners. He enjoys it. I don't. I'm *not* like him.»

She searched his face for a likeness to the Stormhawk's portrait that hung in every shop and home. Gerrit and his father shared the same strong jaw, the same nose. His eyes were completely different though, and his build. Was that enough?

Fear sat heavy in her stomach, yet sousednia smelled like pure alpine honesty around him. *Storm Guard Cadet Gerrit Skala Kladivo.* His identification papers had been so stark, so damning.

Yet if Gerrit had wanted to infiltrate the resistance, he could have accepted her offer yesterday. He could have kept his name secret. He'd told her. He'd trusted her.

She took his hands despite the risk of someone spotting her holding empty air in true-life, and the burst of storm energy stole her breath. In sousednia, she met eyes that weren't the Stormhawk's eyes. Bad enough that Gerrit had been raised by the Storm Guard, that he'd lost his mother to his father's treachery, she couldn't imagine growing up with the Stormhawk for a father. No wonder he flinched whenever his icy control slipped. Could he really escape that training, those expectations?

Gerrit tensed beneath her scrutiny, urine and damp stone wafting around him. Gods' Breath still brightened Bludov's sky, but Celka kept her sousednia empty. When he'd held her hand during that last storm, the world had brightened into such exquisite clarity. Imbuing together had felt so right. And the anger and hopelessness that had subsumed him—he'd felt that towards his father. The vicious tiger was a mask he wore to survive, but the regime's brutality hadn't warped him irreparably. She'd believed that before; his name shouldn't change what she knew in her heart.

Taking a deep breath, she said, «I don't care who your father is.»

Hope and fear warred in his expression.

«I trust you.» Saying it released some of her tension. They'd spent so much time together this last month. They'd imbued together. She *knew* him. This was Gerrit. He'd proven again and again that he wouldn't betray her.

CHAPTER FIFTY-ONE

GERRIT'S THOUGHTS SPUN as they walked back toward the circus, and he kept stealing glances at Celka, hardly daring believe her trust. Outside the city, Celka pulled a brown leather envelope from her pocket. She concentrated on the paper inside, her sousedni-shape rippling into civilian clothes, laughter brightening her eyes as though she activated a concealment imbuement.

The page flared blue, and she handed it to him. «The Wolf sent me this.»

He took it eagerly, thrilled to learn what had renewed her faith in the resistance. After the first few lines, he stared at her. «Your father is the Wolf?»

She grimaced. «I just found out.»

«I can read while we walk.» Yet they quickly discovered a problem: he couldn't wrap the concealment imbuement around the page and still read it, but with the imbuement hiding him, the paper appeared to float in midair. To solve the problem, Celka held the letter, Gerrit walking arm-in-arm with her, reading over her shoulder. The arrangement suited him just fine. Even soaked and worried, she was radiant.

Focus. She'd offered this letter as proof of her trust. He needed to read it, not ogle her... though her rain-soaked blouse clung distractingly to her curves. *Focus, Gerrit. Invisibility doesn't give you license to stare.*

Artur Kladivo arranged the king's assassination...

Gerrit froze, jerking Celka to a halt. He stared at the page. Not believing, not wanting to believe.

«Gerrit—»

«Keep walking.» He needed to finish this letter. Stormy skies, what else did her father claim to know?

The world faded beneath the Wolf's accusations. They reached the circus, and Celka left him outside the dressing tent, taking the letter with her. He poked the weeds with his umbrella, mind churning. Parts of the letter he believed. His father often talked about reclaiming Bourshkanya's lost empire, and Gerrit had spent his youth learning about Lesnikrayen aggression. What if Celka's father was right? The Stormhawk's drive for imbued weapons fit if he was planning an expansionist war.

Celka emerged from the dressing tent, but he hardly saw her. She held the letter out, and he caught her arm again to reread the damning words while she led him somewhere.

A glassy distance separated Gerrit from the world. He wanted desperately to dismiss the letter as sleet, but someone who'd arrange his wife's murder wouldn't hesitate to assassinate a king. Wouldn't hesitate to start a war. And Celka's father was a Storm Guard-trained imbuement mage, not some ignorant cowhand.

They entered the snake trailer, and Celka set the letter on a crate. Gerrit skimmed the page until he found the line he wanted. *Kaya has saved my life more times than I can count.* Celka's father knew Captain Vrana well enough to call her by a nickname. And he'd fought at Zlin.

"Stormy skies," Gerrit whispered as the pieces fell into place. "Your father is Major Doubek."

She gasped, but he couldn't tear his eyes off the page, rereading as if something would change. He felt like someone held his head underwater.

Celka grabbed his arm and pocketed the letter, dragging him out of the trailer, Nina looped over her shoulders. Celka led them into the empty sideshow tent while his thoughts churned.

Major Doubek, Hero of Zlin, had accused his father of starting the Lesnikrayen War and getting a hundred thousand Bourshkanyans—and nine out of every ten bozhki—killed so he could gain power. From anyone else, Gerrit might have been able to dismiss the accusation. But Major Doubek had saved Bourshkanya. He'd been Captain Vrana's best friend. Freezing sleet, no wonder she supported the resistance. She'd probably helped *build* it.

Gerrit's mental walls crumbled. In true-life, he crumpled on a sideshow platform; in sousednia, the concealment nuzhda locked him in a cell, wrenching his bound hands above him. Blood dripped down his back from his last whipping. A terrified, animal noise escaped his throat, and his control over the imbuement shattered. He stared at his bare feet in true-life's trampled weeds.

"Gerrit!" Celka knelt before him, eyes wide, terrified. «Activate the concealment stone before someone sees you!»

Feeling like someone else was puppeting his body, he pulled the stone from his pocket, but he couldn't control sousednia's fear and agony. Choking down sobs, he reached for his mountaintop, letting the mournful wind tear the concealment nuzhda to shreds. "No wonder you're so strong," he said. "Major Doubek—"

"Don't say his name," Celka whispered. "You have to promise never to tell anyone. *Ever*."

Her concern seemed distant. He stared at a rack of combat knives, fixating on that detail as the world unraveled. He must be on the knife thrower's platform. "Ctibor uses combat knives? They're terrible for throwing."

"Focus, Gerrit." «You have to activate the imbuement.»

He pulled a knife from the rack, finding its edge blunted. "How did your father survive the explosion?"

"What explosion?"

"At Zlin, up on the wall."

She opened her mouth on another question, then snapped it closed. She held one of her sideshow postcards,

Nina wrapped around her shoulders. «I would love to hear everything you know about Zlin, but right now, you need to concentrate. We can talk about all of this— but not here. Not where *anyone* could see you.»

"Don't think I could take your smarmy knife thrower?"

"This isn't a joke, Gerrit."

He thought about his father, the war. A hundred thousand dead. "I'm not laughing."

Celka straightened, sousedni-shape smiling incongruously before the concealment imbuement's tingly, slimy magic coated his skin. She'd activated the stone herself and wrapped the imbuement over him.

He stared at her as she concentrated, sousedni-shape rippling back into her high wire costume. Stormy skies, she was Major Doubek's daughter. No wonder she trusted the Wolf; he'd saved Bourshkanya. Would he be able to save it again?

«Come on, we're going back to town.» She grabbed him by the arm, hauling him to his feet. Nina flicked her tongue at him. «You want to talk, do it in sousednia.»

CELKA WAS GLAD for Gerrit's umbrella while she pounded on the door to Lukska's Print Shop, her knuckles smarting. Shutters covered the windows and a 'closed' sign hung on the door. Her stomach churned with the fear that Lukska might be out.

They hadn't run into Ctibor at the circus, and no Tayemstvoy had lurked around the dressing tent to throw her in irons, but Celka felt far from safe. She tried to calm herself with the knowledge that, before tomorrow's dawn, she and Gerrit would escape into the resistance. Ctibor and his secrets wouldn't matter. Yet her fingers drifted to her lips, the memory of their kiss welling up like circus tents from her featureless sousednia.

She banged on the door again, trying to drive Ctibor from her thoughts. If Lukska didn't answer, she wouldn't be able to get false papers for Gerrit before they left. With a disguise and a false identity, Gerrit could move in relative safety; without civilian papers, he'd have to use the concealment imbuement constantly—or someone would. Celka was still holding the imbuement active, since Gerrit had been too blindsided by Pa's letter to care about self-preservation.

Angry at herself, Celka knocked harder. She was sleet-stupid for having shown him that letter. All she'd thought about was how he'd admitted his parentage, so it seemed right to tell him hers. She'd wanted to show she trusted him. She hadn't even *considered* that the knowledge would crush him. What was a king's assassination added to the list of the Stormhawk's crimes?

«Maybe we should go,» Gerrit said, grim. «It doesn't look like they're going to answer. And you're getting strange looks.»

Needing new sideshow photographs gave Celka a reason to be at a print shop, but the snake would also make her memorable.

She banged on the door again. Once they disappeared into the resistance, it might be months before she could contact a forger as good as Lukska. Gerrit risked everything in joining her; she refused to start him with a handicap she could fix.

Finally, the bolts slammed back, and the door cracked open. A child maybe twelve years-old peered out. "We're closed. Haven't you heard? There's a circus today."

Celka maneuvered Nina's head into view. "I'm *from* the circus. I need a photograph taken."

"With the snake?" The child made a face, but the door opened a little wider. "Snakes are gross."

Celka made herself laugh, cajoling the child into petting Nina and letting her in, Gerrit invisible at her heels.

Lukska emerged from the workshop, fingers blue with ink. His eyes widened when he recognized Celka, but he covered it with a smile. "I see you've charmed my gatekeeper." He shooed his child, Darya, into the workroom, and his smile dropped. "Is there a problem?"

"I need papers." Celka dropped the concealment imbuement so Gerrit blinked visible.

Lukska jumped back. "Sleetstorms." He focused on Gerrit's face, and his expression sobered. "Well. That explains why they want you so bad."

Celka felt Gerrit tense, and the cook tent poked up from her field with a whiff of blood.

Lukska touched forehead then heart as if in prayer. "Welcome to the Wolf's fold, young man. May the Storm Gods bless your travels." He stared at Gerrit for a moment longer, then seemed to shake himself. "Papers, yes. You need a photograph, I assume. And a disguise—unless you have your own?"

Gerrit shook his head. "We were hoping you'd have something."

Nodding, Lukska fetched a curly brown wig, a false moustache, and a bottle of adhesive. "You'll need to learn to act like a civilian." His shrewd eyes swept Gerrit as he adjusted the wig and helped attach the moustache.

"How long will it take to prepare the folio?" Celka asked.

Lukska waved Gerrit to a stool. "An hour." He plucked a pair of spectacles from under a counter. Once Gerrit donned them, Celka hardly recognized him. He looked older and bookish—though his stiff posture ruined the effect.

"Maybe you should smile," Celka said. "And slouch."

"No one smiles in identification photos," he said.

"None of *your* friends, at least."

Gerrit grimaced but managed a skeptical smile and a reasonably convincing slump. With a satisfied nod, Lukska adjusted something on his camera then ignited a flash-lamp.

As the smoke dissipated, Lukska pulled the plate from his camera and waved them into the workshop.

Darya stood at a narrow cabinet, sorting letters into their compartments. Seeing Gerrit, they frowned. "Where'd he come from?"

"He's my friend," Celka said.

The child shrugged and edged toward Celka. "Can I pet your snake again?"

Lukska disappeared into a darkroom and, while Darya pet Nina, Celka focused on sousednia, dropping the concealment nuzhda and reintegrating her mind. Gerrit might be able to hold the imbuement active for hours but, despite Celka's tent walls, if she held it much longer she'd start tickling someone.

Gerrit slumped into a chair and dropped his head into his hands. An hour's delay meant she'd miss the evening sideshow, but it couldn't be helped.

"Have you ever ridden an elephant?" Darya asked.

At the child's eager questions, Celka described an elephant's leathery skin and lumbering walk. Before she knew it, she found herself talking all about the circus she loved.

Pounding on the front door interrupted, and Darya made a face. "Can't *any*one read the sign?"

"Wait." Celka caught the child's arm. A shift of perception put her on sousednia's empty field. A smoky chill steamed her breath, and the air carried a whiff of rotting meat. The big top surged from the ground, and she struggled to force it back down.

Darya slipped free and disappeared into the front room.

"Don't." The word came out a whisper as Celka focused back on the workshop. Bolts slammed back, then Darya cried out, and wood banged against wood.

"Gerrit." Fear made Celka's voice squeak. She reached for the concealment imbuement, but neither had time to activate it if the newcomers were what she feared. «Tayemstvoy.»

Gerrit reached for his knife, cursed, and met Celka's gaze. «Maybe it's not.»

A gruff, muffled voice filtered in from the front room.

Across the workshop, another door led out the back. «We could run.»

«They'll have posted a back guard.» His jaw muscles tensed. «We stick to the cover story. You're here for a postcard photograph. I'm a circus... accountant.»

Though he still wore the wig and spectacles, the ruse felt horribly thin. She'd stuffed her costume in her rucksack, but hadn't changed into it. Lukska was in the darkroom, and if the Tayemstvoy got a look at the photograph—

The door into the front room slammed open.

"Pa!" Darya cried. A Tayemstvoy soldier held the child by the hair, a pistol to their head. Five more Tayemstvoy stomped in after them. Tears brightened Darya's wide, terrified eyes. "Pa!"

Two soldiers waved pistols at Celka and Gerrit, ordering them up against the wall. Celka's chest tightened, and storm energy buzzed through her hands. Hobnailed boots clumped up the stairs as two more went to search the apartment above.

The darkroom door slid open, and Lukska stepped out, wiping his hands on a stained apron.

Darya made a strangled noise, and Lukska paled. His mouth opened, but if he made any sound, Celka couldn't hear it with the soldiers stomping around. Heavy thumps sounded upstairs. The sub-lieutenant in charge prowled over to Lukska. In a single, fluid move, she drew her truncheon and rammed it into his stomach.

Lukska folded with a grunt, and the sub-lieutenant cracked her truncheon against the side of his head.

He collapsed like a marionette with cut strings. Darya screamed.

Gerrit shifted, and a Tayemstvoy aimed their pistol at his head. "Don't move."

The corporal who'd been holding Darya shoved them toward Celka. She caught the child, hugging them tight.

The sub-lieutenant landed a kick in Lukska's ribs. "Start talking."

"What do you—?" Lukska's voice shook.

The sub-lieutenant dropped a knee on his back and grabbed his hair, forcing his head up as she shoved the resistance leaflet in his face. "You printed this."

"No! I've never seen that before."

Celka swallowed the storm's taste of hot iron and hugged Darya tighter. Maybe the red shoulders were fishing, kicking over anthills to see if anyone admitted resistance sympathies. Surely Lukska wasn't fool enough to print leaflets, not when he also forged false identities. The former was too public, too risky. A mimeograph machine in a cellar could make leaflets; it didn't take a professional printing press.

Behind Celka, hobnailed boots clumped down the stairs, and one of the soldiers handed a bound stack of letters to the sergeant guarding Celka and Gerrit. The sergeant jerked her chin, and the private started banging open cupboards and dumping out drawers. They shoved aside a stack of paper, sending pages fluttering across the wood floor.

Celka caught Gerrit's hand, and the print shop brightened. Lightning tugged against her spine, and she struggled to drive the circus tents back into the field. The big top resisted. The air stunk of blood. She prayed Lukska had hidden the engraving dies and false identity documents somewhere safe.

Two Tayemstvoy shoved Lukska into a chair. "Where are the image plates?" the sub-lieutenant asked.

"I don't have them. I didn't print that. I don't even have that font. Please, look through my type cases, the letters won't match!"

The sub-lieutenant punched him in the jaw. "Where did you hide them?"

Lukska shook his head, desperate, as one of them tied his wrists to the chair's arms. "No, no, please. Please listen to me. I have letterpresses—that page was mimeographed."

The sub-lieutenant hit him again, and Darya whimpered, fists balled in Celka's shirt.

The scripture Gerrit had quoted tumbled through Celka's mind: *A palm becomes a fist, a fist a knife, and the blade strikes a killing blow.* How much worse would the Tayemstvoy become with a storm sparking their violence?

"Please," Lukska begged, "I can show you my typefaces, I can show you my inks. None will match, I swear! I would never work against the State. Please, I have a child." His voice choked as the soldier finished binding his ankles to the chair.

Celka couldn't get enough air.

No matter how she tried to control her sousednia, she breathed in blood and gun oil. Beneath her combat nuzhda, a twisted, rotting scent poured off the Tayemstvoy. She shuddered, the storm tugging harder as the sub-lieutenant barraged Lukska with questions.

"You choose when this ends," the sub-lieutenant said, metal glinting in her hand.

An anguished scream, and Lukska jerked in his chair, straining against the bonds. The sub-lieutenant flicked a hand casually behind herself, splattering blood across Nina and the table. Pliers. She was holding pliers. Stormy skies, she'd torn off one of Lukska's fingernails.

Celka's stomach lurched, and she swallowed hard, struggling not to vomit.

Lukska panted quick breaths, eyes too white.

"Pa." The agony in Darya's voice filled the workroom.

Celka's horror transmuted into rage, and she gritted her teeth, sousednia's blood and gun oil overwhelming the workroom's turpentine and ink. She struggled to shift sousednia to her big top, struggled not to feel Vrana dragging her by the hair and demanding whether Pa was her father.

"Where?" the sub-lieutenant repeated, catching Lukska's hand again. When Lukska shook his head, desperate and animal, the Tayemstvoy officer ripped off another fingernail.

"Pa!" Darya tore free of Celka's hold. When the child pounded fists against the sub-lieutenant's arm, the hail-eater struck them across the face. Lukska begged them not to hurt Darya, but the red shoulders tied the child to another chair. Darya kicked and flailed and screamed until a truncheon clipped their jaw.

"Stop!" Gerrit cried.

The sergeant guarding them smiled. "You want to be next?"

"We're not involved." Celka's voice shook. She caught Gerrit's arm with both hands—to restrain him or herself, she didn't know. "We're just waiting for a photograph."

The sergeant's lips twitched like she hoped they would fight. "We'll see."

In sousednia, Vrana's casual slap smeared Celka's vision. She dug her true-life fingers into Gerrit's arm, struggling to think. Six Tayemstvoy had come in through the front. There must be more outside, ready in case anyone tried to run. Grandfather's warning that a pistol would not protect her spun through her mind. If she shot these Tayemstvoy, more would climb over their corpses to arrest her.

«We can't just stand here,» Gerrit said.

With supreme effort, Celka shifted sousednia until she balanced on her high wire. Breathing sawdust and hay made thinking a little easier. «Even if we both imbue—if we kill them—what then? The storm-marked floor will point to imbuement mages, and dead Tayemstvoy will implicate the resistance. They'll lock Bludov down. No one will escape the city until we're found.»

His hands clenched into fists at his sides. In sousednia, rain plastered his hair to his skull as he tried to control his own nuzhdi. «If we do nothing, they'll question us next.»

«Not if Lukska doesn't break,» Celka said, praying it was true.

«They're sparking. This isn't an interrogation, it's *play*.» His sousedni-shape wavered as he focused on true-life. "The Stormhawk issued an edict," he shouted over Lukska's screams. "Interrogations during storms are strictly forbidden."

The sergeant guarding them smashed her pistol across Gerrit's face. He stumbled. Another blow, and he dropped.

"No!" Celka clutched him as he fell.

Gerrit was right. They had to save themselves. Pa's words echoed across the back lot in the sound of Tayemstvoy blows.

You can give people the strength to fight.

The red shoulders kept kicking Pa though he'd fallen to the ground. They would do the same to Gerrit and her resistance allies. Unless she stopped them.

In the print shop, Celka let Gerrit slump to the ground, dazed. The sergeant who'd attacked him smashed her pistol across Celka's face. Pain flared Celka's nuzhda, and crimson smoke coiled through sousednia's back lot.

Celka envisioned the gun in her hands and, as combat nuzhda flowed over it, she snarled. The sergeant slammed her pistol into Celka's kidney. The pain should have driven her to her knees, but she poured that power into her nuzhda, tying the weapon to her with blood and mud and screams and the crack of blows.

Some small part of her mind told her to step away from the need to destroy. It spoke of a high wire and spotlit darkness. She reached for that place of calm control even as she gripped the gun in her sousedni-hands, even as Gods' Breath yanked on her skull. The back lot began to darken, and she shifted her stance, aligning her feet to balance on a wire that seemed to quiver just below the ground.

But another Tayemstvoy drew their truncheon in the print shop, striding towards her. The blow snapped Celka's head to the side, and the big top vanished. In sousednia, she saw only the horror of the red shoulders beating Pa, heard only Vrana's cold voice. Oily combat nuzhda flowed over Celka's hands as she gripped the sergeant's pistol. The object's location in true-life didn't matter. Celka knew this gun in the blood running down her cheek, in the distant ache in her back.

Another blow to her jaw, and Celka fell. The back lot's mud squelched beneath her knees, but it didn't matter. Her weaves were ready. Grabbing the rope connecting her to the storm, she *pulled*.

CHAPTER FIFTY-TWO

FIRE BURNED DOWN Celka's arms before a bright, euphoric thrill washed away the agony. The pistol coalesced in her hands like she'd been born holding it. The workroom still bright with Gods' Breath, Celka pulled the trigger.

One shot, two. The Tayemstvoy who'd beaten her fell.

Three shots, four. The sub-lieutenant and her underling—both still cringing from the flash—dropped to the ground.

Five shots, and the private who'd been searching the workroom dropped.

The Gods' Breath faded, but Celka saw in a way she'd never seen before. At the top of the stairs, a ghostly shape glowed red. Boots thumped, and the burning shape of a rifle poked through the banister rails.

Raising the pistol felt as natural as breathing. She fired. Six.

The soldier slumped against the banister, then their corpse bumped partway down the stairs with three dull thuds. Celka was already turning away.

Another ghostly shape glowed red in her periphery. The door to the back alley should have blocked her view, but the imbuement extended her senses to reveal the enemy beyond. The door's handle turned, and Celka crouched behind a printing press, nosing her pistol out in a comfortable, two-handed grip. The door opened with a sudden bang, kicked back, and Celka fired before the soldier's eyes could adapt to the dimmer light inside.

Their body fell, propping the door open. Seven.

The pistol locked open, empty. She dropped the magazine like Ctibor had taught, grabbed another from a corpse even as a humming tug on her spine made her turn: another enemy. She locked the fresh magazine in place.

This enemy approached more warily, already inside the shop's front room and cautious as they neared the workroom door. Celka saw only the figure's red outline through the wood, her imbuement coloring the threat.

Celka strode across the scarred wooden floor, skirting a crimson stain spreading from one of the Tayemstvoy. More than their shoulders were red now.

She reached the door to the front room at the same time as her enemy. The soldier nudged it open a few centimeters. "Sir? Should I go for backup?"

Backup would be a problem.

"Sir?" the soldier called again.

Celka hooked the door open with her foot, catching a glimpse of the soldier's face. Their eyes were fawn brown, wide and startled. Their mouth opened in a perfect O as Celka pressed the pistol to the side of their head and pulled the trigger. Eight.

Celka wanted to scream. She didn't.

Her stomach twisted, trying to vomit. She couldn't.

The enemy collapsed, no longer glowing, the only red now from their shoulders and their blood. Celka scanned the workroom. Two more figures sat in chairs, bound. One made a high-pitched keening. They didn't glow red. They weren't threats.

Another figure lay belly-down on the floor, his hands on his head. He said something, but Celka couldn't parse the words.

"Quiet," she snapped. How could she hear approaching bootfalls if people were talking?

Returning to the sergeant whose gun Celka had taken, she unclipped the pistol's holster from their black leather belt and settled it against her right hip. She holstered the gun and pocketed three spare magazines from the corpses.

"Drop the nuzhda, Celka," said the person laying on his belly. "It's over. You're safe."

She leveled her gun at his head, but he didn't glow red.

Keeping a wary eye on him, she crouched next to another corpse, searching for more ammunition, still listening for pursuit. The world had gone strangely silent.

Good. She'd bought herself time.

More Tayemstvoy would come, though. She needed to be prepared. She pulled a second pistol and holster off a corpse. This one felt heavy and dead, but she holstered it on her other hip anyway. The Tayemstvoy were like cockroaches. She'd killed the ones she could see, but others would scurry from the woodwork.

She glanced at the prisoners. They'd been beaten. She remembered that dimly, the knowledge abstract.

She waved her pistol to the boy still laying on the floor. "Cut them free."

He climbed to his feet and put his hands up, wavering as he walked. Blood darkened one side of his face. Her stomach twisted, and his name bubbled up. Gerrit.

She'd kept him safe.

A pounding, shuddery feeling shook Celka's chest. What had happened to her? She'd killed people, she—

Irrelevant. More enemies were on their way.

Gerrit crouched next to the dead sub-lieutenant and pulled the knife off her belt. Celka's grip on her gun tightened, but she managed not to raise it. Gerrit was her ally.

A humming in her mind snapped her around to face the door into the back alley just before a light knock sounded. She raised the pistol, but the figure glowed blue except for a red knife strapped at its ankle. "Celka, it's Ctibor. Can I come in?"

"Fine," Celka said, at the same time as Gerrit said, "No."

The door swung open and Ctibor edged in, hands above his head, unarmed. Something deep within Celka urged her toward him, but he was a complication, not a threat, so she turned away.

* * *

GERRIT FACED AWAY from the door, cutting free Lukska's bonds while his mind raced. Maybe his disguise would prevent the knife thrower from recognizing him from Tayemstvoy photographs, but nothing would hide the corpses littering the floor, the storm-marked ground, or Celka arming herself for war.

He ground his teeth as he worked on the last rope. Darya, already freed, clutched their father's unbloodied hand, whimpering. As soon as the last hempen strands parted, the child threw themselves into Lukska's arms.

No more time to think of a plan. Gerrit would face the knife thrower and hope he didn't do something stupid and get himself shot. Celka was combat-warped, and Gerrit couldn't pussyfoot around some illiterate showboy while he tried to pull her back to herself. He only hoped he could.

As he turned, Ctibor finished dragging a corpse fully inside the workroom. He kicked the door to the back alley closed. "Good," he said, "it locks."

Ctibor straightened, and his eyes met Gerrit's over Celka's battle-edgy form. Woozy from his blow to the head, Gerrit scrubbed his eyes, certain he must be hallucinating. "Filip?" Except it wasn't. The storm yanked Gerrit into sousednia, and he frowned, confirming Ctibor's mundane smoke-form. "What—?"

The other boy's jaw tightened, and the almost imperceptible shake of his head erased Gerrit's doubts. Somehow, Filip looked like a mundane—and he didn't want Gerrit to question why.

Reeling, Gerrit searched Filip's face for answers.

"Celka," Filip said gently, "you're safe now. You can holster the gun."

Gerrit shook himself. Filip was right. Celka was on the edge of storm-madness—he refused to believe her lost. But if Gerrit brought up the Storm Guard or revealed that Filip had lied to her—*why?*—she might shoot them both.

Lukska stumbled toward Celka and, too late, Gerrit called, "Wait."

But Lukska dropped to his knees. Celka straightened, surprised but not murderous. "Thank you, Storm-blessed Prochazka."

Celka cocked her head even as her combat-warped sousedni-shape folded beneath an invisible blow. The memory of Branislav succumbing to attacks that Gerrit couldn't stop tightened like a vice on his chest. Celka couldn't be storm-mad. He cast a desperate glance at Filip, who nodded almost imperceptibly. Whatever had brought Filip to the circus, whatever had kept him from Gerrit and hidden his sousedni-shape, right now, it didn't matter. Celka was dangerously combat-warped, and having a strazh mage would improve their chances at saving her.

THE REZISTYENT WHO'D been tortured gripped Celka's hand, his fingers sticky with blood from where four of his nails had been torn off. The contact jolted her and, dimly, she recalled his name. Lukska.

"It's like the Wolf said." Screaming had torn his voice, but Lukska spoke with wonder. "The storm-blessed will turn from the State."

Celka frowned, the words tugging at something deep within her. "What did you say?"

"You protected—"

"No. The name."

"The Wolf."

Lukska's child tugged at his sleeve. "Pa, we have to go."

«The Wolf is your father, Celka.»

Her head snapped around, and she studied Gerrit, wondering why he would say that, what relevance it might have. On the circus back lot, Vrana's boot landed in Celka's stomach; Celka had to struggle not to raise her pistol and fire.

«You're Celka Doubek Prochazka,» Gerrit whispered as he approached, hands open and empty. «Drop the imbuement, it's—»

«You need to imbue, Gerrit, not talk,» she said. Vrana stood once again by the Tayemstvoy. At the Storm Guard officer's signal, the red shoulders spread out, circling Pa like wolves, truncheons swinging from their hands. Celka struggled to focus past her need to kill every one of them. «We need to move.»

«Drop the gun's nuzhda and I will,» Gerrit said.

«We need to be armed.»

«We will be,» he said, «just save your strength. Let the nuzhda go and I'll imbue a dark holster so no bozhki can spot your gun.»

His words buzzed, losing their meaning as Pa fought

the Tayemstvoy. Concentrating back on the workroom, Celka pulled free of the older rezistyent's grip. She crouched and wiped his blood on the sub-lieutenant's jacket. She needed to get these civilians to safety. But the world looked wrong.

Wrong? No, changed.

"Darya, go into the darkroom," the rezistyent said. "Storm-blessed Prochazka, the photograph you wanted, it should be finished. We don't have time to insert it into the folio, but you can at least take it."

Celka frowned. A photograph shouldn't have mattered, but somehow it did. She shuddered, her eyes drawn to the sub-lieutenant's forehead where a ragged hole appeared between her brown eyes. Blood oozed around splintered bone and something grayish pink.

Nausea flashed over her. Olive drab uniforms littered the floor—but they weren't just uniforms. They'd been soldiers. People.

Elephants played tug-of-war in her chest. She tasted bile. Storm Gods, what was happening?

She shook her head and, instead of people, she saw dead enemies who couldn't threaten her.

Gerrit. She turned to him, gripped by sudden desperation.

A buzzing energy jerked her attention toward the door into the back alley. It was limned in blue—her escape route—even as color drained from the rest of her surroundings. Why was she wasting time? In her hand, the gun hummed urgency. It made her strong. It gave her purpose. She had to go.

The child she'd rescued ran up, holding out a small, glossy photograph of Gerrit. Droplets of the real world leaked past the floodgates of blood and gun oil that kept her on her feet and ready to move. She'd imbued. Combat. Celka still held the gun's nuzhda. It filtered her perceptions. Warped her.

She tried to throw the gun across the room. Instead, she clicked off its safety and started for the alley.

Someone caught her, strong hands on her shoulders. She wanted to fight, but he was limned in blue.

"We have to move," she said, but Ctibor didn't release her.

He spoke words she didn't quite hear. Behind her, Gerrit was talking and Lukska was talking, but none of it made sense. She stood in the back lot, the practice wire behind her, Pa's cries and the crack of blows drowning everything out.

Ctibor's thumb brushed her cheek, and he cupped her face in his hands, staring into her eyes as he spoke. Then he began to glow the same hot-coals red as her pistol. She stared at him, not understanding but unable to look away.

«Let the pistol go,» Gerrit said at her side. He touched her hand and she flinched, gripping the gun harder. But she couldn't look away from Ctibor.

Was he changing? The combat reds seemed to ripple, other colors skittering across him like the reflection of birds on a lake. Watching him, her chest went shuddery, and she felt something in the distance, something she'd lost but could barely recall.

«Remember your high wire costume?» Gerrit asked, and it worsened the ache. «Its green matches your eyes. The sleeves float like smoke, and the bodice glitters with sequins.»

«No,» she whispered, but she remembered, dimly. It terrified her.

Gerrit eased the pistol from her hand and set it out of sight, thinning the smoke twining between it and her. She wanted to reach for it, but Ctibor pulled her closer.

«You always look so confident,» Gerrit said, «so natural balancing up on the wire. You don't need a gun to be strong, Celka. You don't need to become a soldier. The circus is part of you.»

A strangled sound tore from her throat, and Ctibor's voice filtered through. He described her family's high wire act, Ela stepping delicately across the wire, Demian holding the chair for her.

«Reach for it, Celka,» Gerrit said. «Feel the high wire beneath your slippers, the spotlight shining on you and the air bright with sawdust. Do you hear the band?»

Those things should have been far away. She stood in the back lot, the mud churned where the Tayemstvoy clustered around Pa, blood flying from their truncheons. She screamed and tried to reach for the gun, but Ctibor tilted her face back toward him, his touch ghostly, more like a memory than a touch, his form shading blue like a lake in summer beneath the combat reds. When Ctibor spoke, she smelled sawdust and heard tremulous fluting.

«No,» she choked. «I can't. They'll find us and I killed them and I *can't*.» She jerked free, stumbling back, her sleeves rippling, gossamer green fluttering over her linen shirt.

But Ctibor touched her cheek again, and Gerrit stood at her side, and this time—though she didn't want to—she reached for the world they described. With an agonizing tearing in her mind, the back lot sundered, and she stood on the high wire.

She cried out and nearly fell, but Ctibor caught her. Somehow they stood together on the platform's metal grating. She slumped into his arms, her legs too weak, her mouth tasting of bile. Ctibor cradled her as she dropped to her knees, his words changing. Gerrit, too, talked about printing presses and turpentine, papers strewn about the floor and... bodies.

Gasping a breath that seemed to fill her lungs with water instead of air, Celka opened her eyes to a dim, narrow room. Bare brick walls and overturned cabinets surrounded her. Papers littered the floor, soaking in blood.

Celka lurched over and emptied her stomach. Her vomit splashed a Tayemstvoy soldier's uniform. A person she'd shot.

She pressed a fist to her mouth, trembling. She felt hot then cold. Stormy skies, what had she done?

Gerrit caught her shoulders, pulling her gently toward him. "You did what you had to. You saved us."

She shuddered against him, her tears soaking his shirt. Ctibor rubbed her back, his palm stroking down the storm-scar burning her spine. Gerrit shifted beneath her and, distantly, she wondered what the two boys thought of each other—Gerrit with his jealousy, Ctibor to see a hunted fugitive. Horror at the corpses submerged those thoughts. Over the ink and turpentine, the air smelled of shit and blood.

Some part of her urged her to think, to move. "I storm-marked the floor." Her voice came out small, but she needed to say the words. "They'll connect this imbuement to the resistance. We have to go."

"Running won't help," Ctibor said softly.

She frowned, but Ctibor was wrong. He didn't know the resistance could protect them. Lifting her head, she wiped away tears—her hand coming away pink with blood from a wound she barely remembered. "Where are Lukska and Darya?"

"I told them to run," Gerrit said.

She squeezed his hand, relieved. "We need to, too. Gather weapons. Go."

"Celka," Ctibor said, "I know you're afraid of the Storm Guard—"

She stumbled to her feet, silencing him with a glare.

Ctibor raised his hands in surrender, and she struggled to draw slow breaths. He started singing the Song of Calming, but something in her resisted its soothing rhythm.

"We don't have time to waste," she snapped.

"She's right." Gerrit stood at her side. He clasped her hand, and true-life sharpened. It made her sick, but somehow she breathed a little easier. "We're joining the resistance, Ctibor. Come with us."

Ctibor stared up at them with a level of shock Celka

didn't understand. "You can't," he said, focused on Gerrit, not her. He flowed to his feet, as graceful and deadly as he had been fighting the Tayemstvoy outside the bakery. "Are you *crazy*? Your father will *hunt* you."

His myriad inconsistencies crashed together, a tidal wave overwhelming Celka's horror. Peering more closely at him, she realized he looked wrong. She'd assumed the storm had warped her perceptions, but no. His clothes rippled as though with light reflecting off water. She shifted into sousednia, and a bozhk's heat shimmer stood before her, a lake-blue glow ringing his thumb.

She stumbled back, wanting to activate her gun's imbuement. She stopped herself—barely—distantly certain she couldn't risk pulling against combat. Instead, she fumbled for the unimbued pistol holstered at her hip. She leveled the gun on Ctibor. "You're Storm Guard."

Ctibor's jaw tightened, but he raised his hands, palms out and open. "I'm sorry I couldn't tell you."

Betrayal cut her. She wanted to scream, barrage him with questions. How? Why? But the world seemed to slip, twisting. Sousednia brightened. She struggled to feel the high wire beneath her feet and the big top shading the sky, but they unraveled into the weedy back lot, the stench of blood and the sound of blows cracking the air. Vrana grabbed her by the hair, and she stumbled.

"Celka, no, please!" Ctibor snarled. Her combat nuzhda rose like a storm front. She screamed, trying to fight it, but the nuzhda warped her scream into rage. Ctibor kept speaking, but she heard only a tiger's snarl.

Instinct overwhelmed her. Fight or die. Kill before he could drag her to the Storm Guard.

Her nuzhda twined around the unimbued pistol, power coursing through her, shaping weaves as she imagined the gun an extension of her hands. "I will *never* serve the State!"

«Celka, no!» Gerrit caught her wrist, and true-life sharpened before popping like a soap bubble on the tip of a knife. «You're already storm-warped. You can't imbue again!»

But she could. She would imbue and kill Ctibor. He would never drag her to the Storm Guard.

CHAPTER FIFTY-THREE

GERRIT GRIPPED CELKA'S wrist, forcing the pistol down before she could shoot Filip. Contact sharpened true-life's stench of ink and death, and sousednia's icy wind seared his sinuses. The storm yanked against his skull, smearing his vision. «Ctibor's not the enemy, Celka, please. He's my strazh.» Clouds boiled out of the alpine sky and, with a *crack* like breaking ice, the cold deepened, cutting through his uniform. He remembered being warm moments before, huddled with his mother beneath furs in the back of the motorcar.

He raised a revolver in sousednia now, aiming at the sleet-lickers beating his mother. Though his arms should have been bound, his right hand gripped Celka's wrist, slick with combat nuzhda.

«You don't need to fight,» he told her, but the words felt alien and salty on his tongue. Lies. Filip had lied to him. He wanted to drag Gerrit back to the Storm Guard and his father. Part of him screamed that Celka's combat nuzhda was sweeping him away. He had to stop. He couldn't imbue—couldn't let *her* imbue, not while so out of control.

But the nuzhda pounded against his senses, the crack of blows, his mother's cries tearing away reason.

They would imbue, together. Something more powerful than the world had ever seen. They would destroy their enemies.

"No!" Gerrit flung her hand away, stumbling back. Filip caught him as he reeled, printing presses jutting through the disguised Tayemstvoy beating his mother. "No!" he cried again, struggling to see his alpine clearing. Filip caught his face, pulling on Gerrit's core nuzhda to give him a beacon back to himself. "I can't," Gerrit gasped. "She changed my sousednia. Her nuzhda's too strong. She's not holding true-life." The words poured out. "It's like Branislav again."

Fear brightened Filip's eyes, his calm cracking for an instant before he squeezed his eyes shut, sousedni-shape crouching and pressing hands to the earth as he pulled against a protection nuzhda. "I don't know if she'll trust me to help her, but..." Releasing Gerrit, he strode toward Celka.

Celka smashed her gun across Filip's face. "Never!"

Filip stumbled, blood slashing his cheek. Desperate, he raised his hands in surrender. "Please, Celka, you can't imbue more combat!"

With Filip's words, time seemed to freeze, a foolish,

suicidal plan blossoming in Gerrit's mind. Celka's first combat imbuement had warped her close to breaking; another imbuement this strong would lock her in that brutal fugue as surely as it had Branislav. Gerrit couldn't stop her imbuement: her weaves were nearly complete, her nuzhda too powerful to disperse, her control too far gone. She would imbue, and if she imbued alone, he'd lose her to storm-madness.

But Celka was strong. Maybe she *could* survive a second major imbuement—if it wasn't combat.

The thought terrified him, but he grasped at the hope. When Branislav's combat nuzhda had warped Gerrit's sousednia, he'd fled rather than risk joint-imbuing. Celka's nuzhda was more powerful than Branislav's had been, and already it had overwhelmed his control. But he had to try.

Gerrit finally understood what Captain Vrana had meant about a true-life anchor. He'd found her. He refused to abandon Celka now—no matter the cost.

Gerrit caught Filip's arm. "Ground us."

"'Us'?" Filip cried. "You can't—"

"It's her only chance." Either Filip helped them or both Gerrit and Celka would end this imbuement mad, but Gerrit didn't have time to convince his strazh. Involving Filip risked all their lives—but Filip's strazh weaves would at least give them a chance.

Trusting Filip to do his job, Gerrit caught Celka's hand, gritting his teeth against sousednia's piercing cold and the crack of pistol reports. Celka returned his grip, her other hand holding the Stanek pistol that she'd drawn from true-life into sousednia. She grinned a vicious snarl, combat nuzhda slicking her teeth blood-red.

Gerrit returned her grin-snarl as he fired at the disguised Tayemstvoy. He would save his mother. He would kill them all. Nothing else mattered.

Then Filip gripped the back of his neck. Contact drove the scent of turpentine and ink into Gerrit's nostrils. For a heartbeat, the gunfire ceased. "Don't do this, Gerrit." In sousednia, Filip glowed violet with protection nuzhda, weaves twittering birdsong.

Filip's touch and that heartbeat of silence let Gerrit claw back into control, though he didn't attempt walls. He had to shift Celka's nuzhda—and his own. Maintaining a fingernail hold on true-life through Filip's touch, Gerrit focused on his mother. Not on the moments when he'd fought to save her, but after, when he'd held her, bloodied and broken.

Silence stilled the frozen air. Then his mother's voice, faint, so faint. *Don't become like him. Never become like him.*

Eyes burning, Gerrit reached deeper, into the empty mountaintop where he'd retreated after her death.

Gods' Breath flared like a hot poker against the base of his skull as Celka pulled on her storm-thread. But, beneath the force of Gerrit's will, her combat nuzhda shifted, twisting toward the muddied, combat-tinged complexity of Gerrit's core.

If he'd had more time, he would have pulled against a different nuzhda—protection, maybe—but he didn't have time. The only nuzhda he could pull hard enough against to have any hope of shaking Celka's combat warping was the one so fundamental to his *self* that he pulled on it without thinking. And Celka's core nuzhda was similar, from what he'd seen of Filip's shifting colors as he'd drawn her back to herself minutes before.

Even pulling against his core nuzhda, the move was stupid, dangerous. An imbuement's weaves had to match both nuzhda and object or the cascade of storm energy would shatter them. He had fractions of a second to reshape weaves he barely understood.

Gods' Breath tore down his spine, down his arm to where he gripped Celka's wrist. Heat seared his sinuses, burned his lungs. «Never become like him!» he screamed at the oppressive, overcast sky as he clutched his mother's motionless body to his chest.

Their nuzhda shifted too slowly, the strength of Celka's combat need giving it powerful inertia. But Gerrit refused to lose her. As fire tore through him, he believed the impossible: he and Celka and Filip stood on his mountaintop as it should be, bright with sunlight, his mother's last words keening through the wind.

At the same time, in Lukska's workshop, Gerrit reached out. An object had to fit its imbuement, and a pistol could never hold his mountainscape's emptiness. The right object would reshape the weave's edges, would pull the imbuement further from combat.

In the print shop, Gerrit's free hand touched something. Beneath the glaring alpine sun, the pistol stretched and writhed.

Screaming, Gerrit pulled the storm energy out of

Celka, channeling it through himself and into the new object. Filip gripped the back of his neck, his palm a burning brand as fire consumed Gerrit's flesh and agony shredded his mind.

CHAPTER FIFTY-FOUR

DARKNESS FADED INTO a nightmare.

Gerrit stumbled, barely catching himself with a hand flung out against a table. Filip's hand slipped from his neck, and Gerrit's stomach lurched. Silence suffused the workshop, thick like mud in his ears, broken only by the golden *lub-dub* of his heart.

He stumbled again, tripping back against a workbench, falling in an avalanche of paper.

Celka!

He'd lost his grip on her hand. He sought her in the blurring workshop, finally focusing. She still stood, and he struggled to go to her. But he only flailed, pinned as if a field gun rested on his chest. Each breath came slower than the molasses thump of his heart.

The pistol had fallen to the floor. Instead of holding it, Celka now wrapped her hand around Filip's neck.

Filip's fingers twined in her hair, his other arm encircling her waist—while they kissed.

Gerrit struggled to draw enough breath to call out. Fought against the weight of his body. His throat felt raw, scalded, and darkness pressed on his eyes, the workshop's every shadow like an advancing tide.

Desperate, he fought the darkness. True-life slowly righted. He pushed upright just as Celka's hand dropped from Filip's neck. Her knees buckled, and Filip hugged her against him as she collapsed.

Gerrit stumbled forward.

Filip glanced at him as he lowered Celka to the floor, his expression a jumble that Gerrit couldn't quite read: fear, uncertainty—was that guilt? It better sleeting be guilt.

Filip turned back to Celka, saying her name, voice distorted like he spoke underwater. She didn't respond. Unconscious. Or...

Gerrit didn't know how he moved so quickly, but suddenly he knelt at her side, heartrate ratcheting. She wasn't dead. She couldn't be dead.

Catching one of her hands, he squeezed. Nothing. He pressed two fingers to the side of her throat and released a shaky breath. Her pulse raced beneath his touch, her skin feverish. Not dead, but... storm-mad?

"She wasn't holding true-life," Filip said.

"So you *kissed* her?" The words tasted like blood and the workbenches' straight lines went bendy.

"It helped before. It's the closest connection we have. I thought it might—"

"You *thought*." Gerrit launched to his feet, hands

fisting. "You thought I liked her so you'd better get there *first*." Distantly, Gerrit felt the combat nuzhda he hadn't fully turned away from driving his belligerence, but exhaustion shattered his control. The nightmare of Filip kissing Celka made him want to smash his strazh's face. "You thought she'd be fun to play with while you hid from *me!*"

Filip stood to face him. "It's not about—"

Gerrit shoved him, and Filip stumbled back, tripping over a corpse and barely catching himself. "You thought you'd waltz in here after she imbued and drag her to the Storm Guard!" Gerrit closed on his strazh, stepping over the dead Tayemstvoy. "What about *me?*" Gerrit shoved Filip again. "You're *my* strazh. You're supposed to protect *me!*"

Another shove, but this time Filip caught Gerrit's wrist, twisting him off-balance. The strazh drove his shoulder into Gerrit's chest and slammed him up against a cabinet. Metal typefaces scattered across the floor beneath their feet.

"While you joint-imbued with a civilian out of control?" Filip snarled. "While you shifted a powerful nuzhda *after* pulling down Gods' Breath? Did you *want* to get us all killed? Or did you just not care about my life?" Filip bunched Gerrit's shirt in his fists. "I'm just your strazh. A thing to use. To throw away when it breaks."

"You don't want to risk your life for me?" Gerrit said. "No wonder you've been hiding. You're a pathetic excuse for a strazh."

"I *did* risk my life. For both of you. For that." He jabbed behind him. "Whatever it is."

Gerrit wasn't fool enough to take his eyes off the enemy. *He's your best friend*, something within him screamed, but he barely heard it.

As if jolted by a sudden shock, Filip released him. "I'm sorry, I..." He pressed his back against the cabinet at Gerrit's side, chest heaving, eyes squeezed shut. "Sleet." He slumped down the cabinet to the floor. "I lost control, I'm sorry."

Gerrit stared at his strazh, reeling, trying to cling to his anger, strangely unwilling to release it. But it spooled away as Filip dropped his head into his hands, knees pulled to his chest.

Exhaustion landed like a sack of bricks on Gerrit's shoulders, and he slid down the cabinet at his best friend's side. The cut on Filip's face where Celka had pistol whipped him had fully healed—only overflowed storm energy could have done that.

They were sleeting lucky to have survived. And, as Gerrit's combat-warping eased, he realized Filip was right to be angry at him. Gerrit had risked his friend's life over his protests.

Despite that sickening knowledge, having Filip at his side loosened a painful knot in his chest. Filip's absence had been like a toothache he'd taught himself to ignore. Only now, with the pain gone, did he realize how much it had strained him.

That didn't make their situation any safer. Someone would have heard the shots. More Tayemstvoy would be on their way.

He turned to Celka, hoping she'd stir. He'd been so combat-warped before he hadn't even thought to check her sousedni-shape for nuzhda-warping. She lay unconscious, but her high wire costume's billowing green sleeves showed ghostly over her true-life blouse. He released a shaky breath. The combat oilslick was gone, only a frown marring her beautiful face.

Only then did he manage to turn to Filip. But his apology stuck in his throat, too many unanswered questions between them. "Thank you," he managed. "We wouldn't have survived that imbuement without you."

Filip's jaw tensed, and he held Gerrit's gaze for only a second before looking away. "What does it do?"

Gerrit frowned, following Filip's gaze toward the table. As if sensing his attention, the python raised her head to stare unblinkingly back at him.

"Nina?" Gerrit said, unbelieving. But the snake's sousednia bleed-through erased any doubt. Over chestnut and sand-colored scales, the snake rippled with the shifting fires of crystalized nuzhda. Combat reds formed her base, but rainbow hues flowed across her, the colors twisting and shifting so rapidly that Gerrit couldn't find a pattern.

She coiled as though ready to strike, her tongue tasting the air. If Gerrit hadn't known better, he would have sworn she watched them with more than a snake's predatory instincts behind her vertical slit pupils. Shaking his head, he turned back to Filip. "Why are you here?"

"Captain Vrana sent me to watch your back." Only then did Gerrit notice the exhaustion slurring Filip's words. Sleet, Gerrit could barely hold up his head and he'd imbued before, developed some tolerance. How much storm energy had they overflowed into Filip? How close had they all come to madness?

Filip twisted the iron ring on his thumb. "She gave me a concealment imbuement to hide my sousedni-shape. Another"—he tugged at the cord around his neck, revealing what had to be a storm pendant, though it hung inside a bag usually reserved for the charging cloth—"to sharpen my senses."

"In a darkbag?"

Filip nodded.

"Why?"

Filip understood the real question. "She said you needed space to imbue on your own. Though you were hardly on your own." Venom drove back some of his exhaustion, and Filip pushed himself to his feet, stepping over corpses to crouch at Celka's side. He took her hand, tender in a way that made Gerrit want to shove him again.

Gerrit fought the instinct, controlling his combat-warping if not his jealousy. He knelt on Celka's other side, taking her other hand.

"I had orders not to reveal myself unless I needed to protect you," Filip said. "I was outside, down the block when I felt the imbuement and heard the shots. At first I thought you—" He met Gerrit's gaze, expression raw with fear. "But you were alive. I *couldn't* stay away after that.

You didn't feel combat-warped, so I knew the imbuement was hers. But it was too powerful. I should have been here—I should never have left her." He scrubbed a hand across his jaw, his soldierly mask broken in a way Gerrit hadn't seen in years. "I was afraid that if we didn't pull her back right away, she'd end up like Branislav; but I made it worse, didn't I? Bursting in." He hunched over Celka. "No wonder you didn't tell me you were leaving. No wonder you don't trust me."

Gerrit grimaced. "Celka ambushed me. If I was going to run away, I would have told you."

Filip lifted his head. "Ambushed you?"

"Knocked me out with a board and tied me up. By the time I could escape..." He shook his head. The story was too big to tell right now. His brain lurched into motion, like a railcar finally coupled to a steam engine. They needed to get out of here, but Filip looked so lost. "Stormy skies, Filip. We made our plans together. I kept expecting you to come find me. I was terrified the Tayemstvoy had arrested you."

"Captain Vrana *ordered* me not to make contact. She went through some serious contortions to put the Tayemstvoy off your trail. Got me a commission and convinced the Storm Guard General to send me after you on my own. But she ordered me to stay out of sight until you'd imbued combat at least twice—at a minimum, Category Three—unless I needed to keep you safe." Filip's dark eyes searched Gerrit's face. "You want to tell me why?"

The answer came sickeningly fast. Captain Vrana had

wanted him scared and alone with no one to trust but Celka. Keeping Filip away had been another play to turn him toward the resistance. "We need to get out of here. I'll explain when we're not—" He gestured at the corpses.

"You're serious about joining the resistance?" Filip asked.

Gerrit nodded. "Will you help us?"

"You know how crazy this sounds? How suicidal?"

"I do. Trust me?"

Filip clasped his shoulder. "I've always had your back. I always will."

With a nod, Gerrit focused on trying to wake Celka. But she lay limp and unresponsive—in true-life and sousednia.

"I could carry her," Filip said, "hold your concealment imbuement active so we don't look suspicious."

Swallowing bile from clawing out of sousednia, Gerrit nodded. "Take the snake, too. She's too memorable."

With the ease of long practice carrying wounded cadets out of field exercises, Filip settled Celka across his shoulders. Gerrit looped Nina around them then handed over his concealment stone. Filip activated it with barely a twitch, vanishing Celka and the snake.

"You've gotten better at concealment," Gerrit said, forcing his leaden limbs toward the back door.

"Had to hold that sleeting ring active whenever I was awake. You might have noticed me otherwise." Betrayal and guilt laced Filip's voice.

A dead private was slumped near the back entrance,

though Filip had dragged them inside and shut the door. Blood left the floor sticky. Gerrit pressed his back to the brick wall, ready to peer out and check that they were alone.

«*Stop.*»

Gerrit froze. The voice in sousednia wasn't Celka's.

He held up a fist to tell Filip to wait, but a glance showed his strazh motionless and frowning.

What was that? Filip mouthed.

Gerrit shook his head. It had sounded like his mother.

Leaning heavily against the wall, Gerrit fought past his exhaustion to edge into sousednia.

«*You're too late,*» the voice said.

Gerrit tried to identify the speaker. Celka hung motionless across Filip's shoulders, shrouded in the concealment imbuement's sapphire. A hint of an Army uniform solidified Filip's heat shimmer—some aftereffect of the storm-energy they'd dumped into him. Gerrit swept the workroom's walls aside. The alley stretched before him, an empty expanse of snow.

The snake lifted her head. «*Look harder.*»

Gerrit gaped. «Nina?»

The snake hissed, irritated. «*Look.*»

Struggling to think past the part of his brain panicking that he'd gone storm-mad and this was all some nuzhda-warped hallucination, Gerrit focused more deeply on sousednia. He'd sought an imbuement mage's solid sousedni-shape before; now, driving true-life from his awareness, he caught wisps of motion outside—mundanes. Lots of mundanes.

«Freezing sleet.» He focused back on the snake. «Tayemstvoy?»

She flicked her tongue at him. It felt oddly like a nod.

«And out front?» he asked.

«*Twenty-three more.*»

Gerrit dragged himself back to true-life, deciding to trust the snake's count. His stomach rebelled at the transition, and he pressed his head against the rough brick, panting while the world reeled. "We have company," he told Filip.

"I heard." He shifted under Celka's weight. "What now?"

Gerrit frowned. He wanted to quiz his strazh about how he'd been able to hear them in sousednia—but now wasn't the time. They were surrounded by Tayemstvoy.

CHAPTER FIFTY-FIVE

SOMETHING TAPPED CELKA'S forehead. *Tap. Tap-tap.* A ropy weight pressed against her back and something hard dug into her stomach. *Tap.*

She raised a hand weakly to bat it away.

Tap-tap. «*Wake up.*» The voice sounded strangely like Pa's.

She groaned.

"Celka?"

She blinked heavy eyelids. Lukska's workshop hung upside-down.

«*Glad you could join us,*» said the voice like Pa's.

Celka focused on sousednia. Nina tapped her forehead with her nose. Celka jerked in surprise.

The snake flicked her forked tongue. «*Calm yourself, little lightning rod.*»

Celka's chest went shuddery at the name, but she

forced down the loss. Pa wasn't here. The voice wasn't his. «What are you?»

«*A part of each,*» Nina said.

The world tipped sideways. "Celka?" Ctibor settled her on the ground and knelt before her.

Gerrit knelt, too, taking her hand. "Are you all right?"

"We imbued a talking snake?" She craned to look at Nina, who slithered to coil across Celka's lap.

"Apparently." Gerrit sounded worried.

"We're surrounded by Tayemstvoy," Ctibor said. "We need a plan."

She frowned. Her head felt muzzy. Everything sounded unnaturally quiet. They'd imbued, her and Gerrit. Together. She'd intended to kill...

Her gaze snapped to Ctibor.

Not Ctibor, Filip. He was Storm Guard. This was his fault.

«*You can trust him,*» Nina said.

"She's right." Filip wore the solemn intensity Celka had found so attractive in Ctibor. "I'm here to help." In sousednia, he smelled of steel and old books—just normal Ctibor—plus the springtime scent of turned earth and lilacs that he seemed to get when being especially earnest.

"You know he's telling the truth," Gerrit said.

She grimaced at Gerrit. "You knew all along."

"No," Gerrit said. "He hid from me. I never saw him before today."

"I had orders," Filip said. "I couldn't—"

«*They're setting up barricades outside,*» Nina said.

Panic drove Celka to her feet. The room wavered, red bricks darkening, her vision tunneling. Filip caught her waist, steadying her. At Gerrit's glower, he backed off.

"We have to fight." Celka wrapped Nina around her like a reptilian bandolier. Every motion felt like dragging herself through deep sand. She wanted desperately to lie back down.

"You can't hold a combat nuzhda," Gerrit said.

"I'll take an unimbued gun. Filip can use the imbuement."

Gerrit frowned, considering.

Filip met Celka's gaze, apologetic. Before she could ask what for, he shouted, "Hold your fire! We're Storm Guard."

"No!" Celka snarled. Blood and gun oil thickening the air, she lunged at Filip.

Gerrit caught her. "Celka, stop. He's right. There's three of us and at least thirty of them. We can't win this fight."

"We have to try."

A voice, distorted over a loudspeaker, called, "You have one minute to come out with your hands on your heads."

"Ten minutes," Filip bellowed back. "We need to recover from imbuing. We don't want more deaths."

The pause after his words gave Celka time to twist her sousednia back into a high wire.

"Ten minutes," the Tayemstvoy agreed, "or we gas the building."

"I'll go," Gerrit said. "Filip, give Celka the concealment

stone. Celka, activate it and walk out with us. Take Nina—maybe she's useful."

«Of course I'm useful.»

Celka shook her head. He couldn't do this. She wouldn't let him go back, not when they were so close to freedom.

"Make your rendezvous," Gerrit said. "I'll claim the pistol as my own imbuement, get them off your trail."

"There are two storm-marks. If I take Nina—"

"I'll say the other imbuement failed." He squeezed her hands. "Let me do this for you."

"You'll be trapped. Under your father's boot."

His jaw tightened. "I'll play the good soldier. Learn as much as I can. Once I gain the Stormhawk's trust, they won't watch me as closely. Get your friends to give me an opportunity. I'll get out." He gripped her hands so tightly that she had to return the pressure. "This isn't goodbye. I won't let it be goodbye."

Her throat choked, but no matter how she tried to invent another plan, everything else ended with them dead or storm-mad. "Promise me," she whispered.

"I promise." He studied her as though memorizing her face. As though he didn't believe it. "We'll see each other again."

After everything they'd been through, she couldn't believe she was about to lose him. They'd come so close to escaping. "Gerrit—" she whispered.

Before she could figure out what to say, he turned and started pulling off his disguise.

Filip placed the concealment stone in her hand, startling

her attention off Gerrit. "Be careful." His thumb swept her cheekbone. The caress recalled their kiss outside the bakery, and her breath quickened. His dark eyes begged her to come with them, to reconsider, but he only said, "I'll miss you." He touched her hip, gaze dropping to her mouth like he was going to kiss her again.

Celka stepped back.

"I told you as much truth as I could," Filip said.

She wondered if it was true. "When you lied to the Tayemstvoy about the lightning, that wasn't to protect me, was it. It was for Gerrit."

Filip's jaw muscles tensed. "I care about you, too."

She turned her back, unable to face his earnest concern.

Gripping the concealment stone, she focused on its river rock smoothness. Gerrit had given her the gift of freedom. She couldn't squander it.

She remembered Pa's strong hand gripping hers, laughter dancing in his eyes as tent canvas flapped behind them. But the scent of blood and shit in true-life made it hard to smell the cheap perfume and reach her old laughter.

Exhaustion pricked her eyes with tears, but she clung to the back lot's shouts and muttering clowns and, finally, the concealment stone hummed in her hand. She threw its blue lake glow around herself and Nina like a cloak.

Changing her sousednia so the big top's canvas separated the rest of her mind from the concealment nuzhda, Celka stepped along the high wire to join Gerrit and Filip. She was getting out, joining the resistance just like she wanted. It should have felt like victory. Instead, it felt like falling.

Gerrit will survive. She tried to believe it. Her pistol would impress his father, buying Gerrit space to imbue more weapons for the regime.

A cyclone seemed to sweep the circus, tearing away the big top's canvas. Celka slipped on the wire, fighting for balance as fear destroyed her concealment nuzhda. Lurching into true-life, she caught Gerrit's arm. "Wait."

"We have to go," Filip said. "The Tayemstvoy might—"

"You *can't*." Panic cracked Celka's voice. "Gerrit, you can't give the Stormhawk my pistol."

"You can imbue others," Gerrit said, not following. "The resistance won't—"

"*No*," she said. "You can't replicate the imbuement. They're *my* weaves. My crazy, non-Storm Guard weaves."

Understanding dawned, and he blanched.

Filip caught up. "When you fail to create more, the Stormhawk will realize you're lying." He swept the carnage around them. "He'll think you helped the resistance."

Silence settled over them, like the crowd's gasp as Grandfather wavered on the wire. But this time, the slip wasn't an act, and the fall would kill them all.

Gerrit swallowed hard. "Maybe I can. If I study it enough."

"No," Filip said. "It's suicide."

Celka tightened her grip on Gerrit's arm. Filip was

right. She'd made this mess, she couldn't leave Gerrit to pay its price. "I'm coming with you."

"But—" Gerrit started.

"He said his people would make us an opportunity." She darted a glance to Filip then focused back on Gerrit, hoping he'd understand not to mention Pa. Filip had heard Nina in sousednia; she couldn't risk that he might be able to hear her—or learn that her father was the Wolf. "*She* knows where he is." She had to trust that Gerrit would realize she meant Vrana. "I might be able to see him before..." Before he went completely storm-mad.

Gerrit nodded in grim understanding. "But—"

"You found hope before," she said. "You said your father wants you at his side."

Gerrit drew a deep breath, uncertainty vanishing beneath the soldierly mask that had once terrified her. "Right. Filip, once I've spoken to the Tayemstvoy, I'll send you to the circus to fetch my uniform from the snake trailer. They'll send red shoulders to accompany you, but you should still be able to warn Celka's family. The Tayemstvoy will arrest them and hold them until they're convinced of her loyalties."

Celka's chest tightened at the thought, but she forced herself to breathe. She was an imbuement mage, valuable to the regime. If she cooperated, the Tayemstvoy wouldn't hurt her family.

Gerrit asked Filip to grab their other imbuements, and Celka explained the secret compartment in her steamer trunk where she'd stored their imbued pistol and her knife, hoping Filip's warning would give her family time to get rid of everything treasonous. She passed Filip the concealment stone, too. He pocketed it with a solemn nod.

Celka turned her back to them while Gerrit sketched details of how they'd present themselves to the Tayemstvoy. She emptied her pockets of ammunition and dropped the unimbued pistol's empty holster from her hip. Remembering Pa's letter, she pulled it out. She wanted to read it again, but they didn't have time. Instead, she activated its combat trigger; the page burst into flames.

Panic clawed at her throat. She was the Wolf's daughter, Major Doubek's daughter, and she was going to hand herself to the State.

Focusing back on Gerrit, she tried to tell herself she'd be safe. Tried to convince herself that this was an opportunity. If Gerrit could deceive his father, they had a chance to learn valuable information for the resistance. And, no matter what, she and Gerrit would be together.

She darted a glance at Filip, her chest a mixed-up churn of emotions.

Then Gerrit caught her hands, and sousednia flared against her senses, true-life brightening. Steely calm had replaced his earlier desperation. "Thank you," he said.

Whatever she'd thought she shared with Ctibor, they'd never have this. Touching Gerrit brought the world into perfect alignment. It made her powerful. With Gerrit, she controlled the storms and beat a path out of a hopeless future. Gerrit understood loss, and he'd come so far from where he'd started. Filip wasn't storm-blessed; he could never understand Celka so deeply—could never build what Celka and Gerrit could build together.

CELKA PRESSED HER hand over Gerrit's heart, and he became suddenly, intensely aware of her. "Together," she whispered, "we're powerful." Her voice, at once so confident and so scared, made the walls he'd started to erect around himself shudder. He'd finally made his own his choice to join the resistance, and Celka had accepted him despite his father. But because of the sleeting Tayemstvoy, he had to return to the Storm Guard, to grim brutality and his murderous, hail-eating father.

Celka touched his cheek and, without thinking, Gerrit caught her hips and pulled her to him. She was so strong and smart and beautiful, and every time they touched, he wanted to touch more of her. She held his gaze, chin tilted as though to kiss him. But she didn't close the gap.

"How do we play this?" she asked him.

He'd finally started to dream of a future for them together, but she was right. One mistake, and the Stormhawk would use her to control him.

Except... just like before, he was thinking about everything wrong.

He wasn't a powerless cadet anymore. As an imbuement mage, Gerrit had power of his own. If he wanted the Stormhawk to bring him into his confidence instead of using him like a tool, Gerrit couldn't appear weak. Fear was weakness.

When he faced his father, he needed to control their conversation. His father would question his loyalty, and Gerrit couldn't afford a moment's doubt. He had to think like the loyal son his father wanted, had to step unflinchingly into the role his father had prepared.

The Stormhawk would not use Celka to control Gerrit because Gerrit refused to be controlled. He would serve the Stormhawk because he chose to. Because Bourshkanya was his birthright.

Slipping his fingers into Celka's hair, Gerrit pressed his lips to hers.

Storm energy exploded down his back, burning across his shoulders and down his arms, following the branching, bifurcating paths of his new storm-scar. Pain overwhelmed him for a fraction of a second before the world burst into vibrant clarity. His awareness expanded: dim light from the print shop's gas lamps revealed the minutest details of blood-spattered wood; icy wind whipped around him as sunlight cast knife-edged shadows across his mountain clearing.

Celka gasped then caught his face, holding him as she returned his kiss, trembling as power coursed between them. Her lips parted, and he touched her tongue with his.

She moaned softly, and fire arced through him.

The pain in his storm-scar simmered into an ecstatic buzz. The sensual pressure of her lips and the heat of her body against his filled his awareness—yet his senses expanded, and he saw and heard and felt the world more clearly than ever before.

"One minute!" echoed a voice over a loud speaker.

Suddenly, the heat of Celka's touch felt no longer delicious but dangerous. They weren't safe yet. He had a role to play, a mask to wear. Tensing, he pulled away.

Celka stepped back, fingers sliding down his arms to grip his hands a little too hard.

"We don't have time for this," Filip snapped.

Fear flitted across Celka's face, and she glanced at the door.

Gerrit drew a slow breath, settling his mask into place. He was Gerrit Kladivo. He answered only to the Stormhawk. Shoulders squared, he leveled a cool gaze on his strazh. "We have time if I say we have time."

Filip bristled, jaw working like he had something to say. Outside, the Tayemstvoy started counting down from thirty.

"Once we walk out there," Gerrit told Filip, "we're not cadets anymore. I'm the Stormhawk's son and you're my strazh." Filip undermining Gerrit's authority in front of the Stormhawk could get them all killed.

Filip looked away, just a brief flick of his eyes to the side, but enough. Gerrit hated it. Hated using his power against his friends. He crushed the emotion. For what came next, he couldn't flinch from power, no matter its cost.

Pulling out his identification folio, Gerrit shouted toward the door, "Hold your fire. We're coming out."

Gerrit strode through the shop's empty front room, Filip and Celka flanking him. Out on the street, sandbag barricades bristled with rifle barrels. The rain had stopped.

Hands up, holding only his identification folio, Gerrit stood in the middle of the street, giving the red shoulders space to surround them. The Tayemstvoy captain crawled out from behind the barricade, sneering triumph when they recognized Gerrit.

"All hail the Stormhawk," Gerrit said.

"Get on your knees," the captain ordered.

Gerrit ignored them. "I'm Gerrit Kladivo, son of the Stormhawk." He pitched the words to carry. Heads appeared over the sandbags, Tayemstvoy gaping between him and their captain. "I'm also an imbuement mage. What happened in the shop was a tragic... *misunderstanding*." He clipped the word to imply that any further mistake would land everyone a one-way ticket to a labor camp. He was his father's son now.

The captain straightened. "I have orders to—"

"You will wire my father." Gerrit paused long enough that the captain could speak—if they were fool enough to think they were still in command. The captain, wisely, stayed silent. "Tell the Stormhawk I'm ready to return."

ACKNOWLEDGEMENTS

I'M GRATEFUL TO so many people for helping bring this book to life. The seeds of this idea germinated for eight years, watered by hard work, revision after revision, panic that I'd torn out the book's heart in trying to make it better, and brilliant feedback from thoughtful readers. Thanks go to... My husband, Dr. Josh Boehm, for questioning assumptions I didn't even realize I was making, for brainstorming me out of dark corners, and for always believing in my work. My tireless, insightful agent, Lisa Rodgers, who loved this book from the beginning and helped me make it a thousand times better... and sell it. The No Name Writing Group—Rhiannon Held, Kate Alice Marshall, Erin M. Evans, Susan J. Morris, Shanna Germain, and Monte Cook—for seeing problems I couldn't see myself and helping me work out solutions; also for business advice and general wisdom. My editor, David Thomas Moore and all the wonderful folks at Rebellion for believing in this book and giving it a home and a beautiful package. Dr. Ian Tregillis for an early read that made me realize, amongst other things, that I wanted Bourshkanya to be fascist rather than just totalitarian.

Huge thanks also to people who helped me become the writer I am today. Especially… Jeanne Cavelos and her amazing Odyssey Writing Workshop, for teaching me to think critically about writing and giving me the tools to expand my craft. I don't think I've ever worked as hard as I did during those 6 weeks in 2009—I love you, strange toads! Mr. Nigro, my 5th grade teacher, who sparked my imagination both for science and speculative fiction. (Also, teachers everywhere; you rock.) My parents for encouraging my love of reading and science. Dr. Rachel Pepper and Dr. Moorea Brega for being amazing friends and early writing cheerleaders. My Ph.D. advisor, Prof. Masahiro Morii, for being okay with me sneaking off to Odyssey in the middle of my doctoral studies. My daughter, Alarice, who gives the best hugs and says things like "I believe in you, Mommy" when I'm stressed.

Special shout-outs also to… Gemma Sheldrake for designing fabulous circus ticket bookmarks and storm-scar temporary tattoos. Tim Powers and Nina Kiriki Hoffman for the Writers of the Future workshop and the attendant story prompt that grew into this book.

And to people who have fought and are fighting oppression, thank you. Your courage makes you powerful. I hope one day we'll all live in a kinder world.

ABOUT THE AUTHOR

Corry L. Lee is an author, PhD physicist, award-winning science teacher, data geek, and mom. In PhD research at Harvard, she shed light on the universe fractions of a second after the Big Bang. At Amazon, she connected science to technology, improving the customer experience through online experimentation. She's currently obsessed with nordic skiing, yoga, and delicious coffee. A transplant to Seattle, Washington from sunny Colorado, she is learning to embrace rainy days. Learn more at www.corrylee.com.

FIND US ONLINE!

www.rebellionpublishing.com

/rebellionpub   /rebellionpublishing   /rebellionpub

SIGN UP TO OUR NEWSLETTER!

rebellionpublishing.com/sign-up

YOUR REVIEWS MATTER!

Enjoy this book? Got something to say?

Leave a review on Amazon, GoodReads or with your
favourite bookseller and let the world know!